Also by Elly Griffiths

The Crossing Places
The Janus Stone
The House at Sea's End
A Room Full of Bones
Dying Fall
The Outcast Dead

The Zig Zag Girl

and coming soon
Somke and Mirrors

ELLY GRIFFITHS

THE GHOST FIELDS

Quercus

First published in Great Britain in 2015 by Quercus Publishing Ltd
This paperback edition published in Great Britain in 2015 by

Quercus Publishing Ltd
Carmelite House
50 Victoria Embankment
London
EC4Y 0DZ

An Hachette UK Company

A CIP catalogue record for this book is available
from the British Library

PB ISBN 978 1 84866 333 6
EBOOK ISBN 978 1 78429 364 2

10 9 8 7 6 5 4 3 2 1

Typeset by CC Book Production

Printed and bound in Great Britain by Clays Ltd, St Ives plc

For Sheila and Ian Lewington

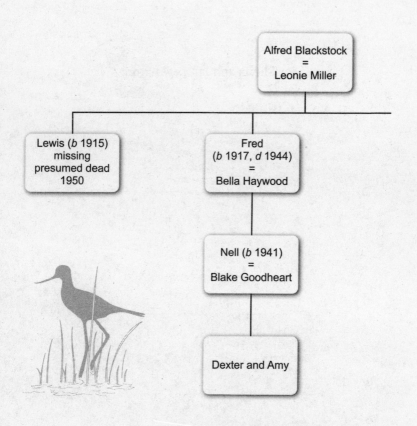

Alfred Blackstock
=
Leonie Miller

Lewis (*b* 1915)
missing
presumed dead
1950

Fred
(*b* 1917, *d* 1944)
=
Bella Haywood

Nell (*b* 1941)
=
Blake Goodheart

Dexter and Amy

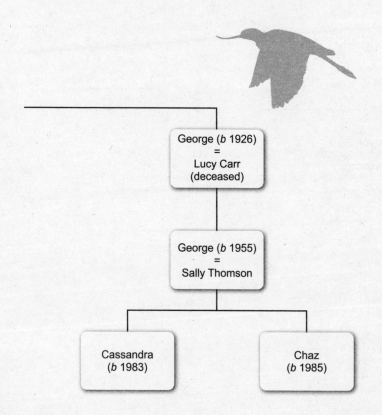

I hate the dreadful hollow behind the little wood,
Its lips in the field above are dabbled with blood-red heath,
The red-ribb'd ledges drip with a silent horror of blood,
And Echo there, whatever is ask'd her, answers 'Death.'

Alfred Tennyson, *Maud*

PROLOGUE

July 2013

It is the hottest summer for years. A proper heatwave, the papers say. But Barry West doesn't pay much attention to weather forecasts. He wears the same clothes winter and summer, jeans and an England t-shirt. It's sweaty in the cab of the digger, but he doesn't really mind. Being a man is all about sweat; anyone who washes too much is either foreign or worse. It doesn't occur to him that women don't exactly find his odour enticing. He's forty and he hasn't had a girlfriend for years.

But he's content, this July day. The Norfolk sky is a hot, hard blue and the earth, when exposed in the jaws of the digger, is pale, almost white. The yellow vehicle moves steadily to and fro, churning up the stones and coarse grass. Barry doesn't know, and he certainly doesn't care, that people have fought hard over this patch of land, now scheduled for development by Edward Spens and Co. In fact the Romans battled the Iceni on these same fields and, nearly two thousand years later,

Royalist forces engaged in bitter hand-to-hand combat with Cromwell's army. But today, Barry and his digger are alone under the blazing sun, their only companions the seagulls that follow their progress, swooping down on the freshly turned soil.

It's hard work. The land is uneven – which is why it has lain waste for so long – pitted with craters and gullies. In the winter, these fissures fill with water and the field becomes almost a lake interspersed with islands of grass. But now, after a month of good weather, it's a lunar landscape, dry and desolate. Barry manoeuvres the digger up and down, singing tunelessly.

It's at the bottom of one of these craters that the digger scrapes against metal. Barry swears and goes into reverse. The seagulls swirl above him. Their cries sound caustic, as if they are laughing. Barry gets out of the cab.

The sun is hotter than ever. It beats down on his baseball cap and he wipes the sweat from his eyes. An object is protruding from the ground, something grey and somehow threatening, like a shark's fin. Barry stares at the obstacle. It has a look of permanence, as if it has lain in the earth for a very long time. He bends down and scrapes some soil away with his hands. He sees that the fin is part of a larger object, far bigger than he imagined at first. The more earth he removes, the more metal is revealed. It gleams dully in the sun.

Barry stands back. Edward Spens wants this field cleared. Barry's foreman stressed that the work needs to be done as soon as possible, 'before the crazies get wind of it'. If he carries on, his digger will tear and crush the metal object. Or the unseen enemy will defeat him and the digger (property of Edward Spens and Co) will be damaged. Suddenly, unexpectedly, Barry remembers a book that was read to him at school about a vast man made of iron who is found in a junk yard. Just for a second he imagines that lying beneath the soil there is a sleeping metal giant who will rise up and crush him in its digger-like jaws. But wasn't the Iron Man in the story a goodie? He can't remember. Barry climbs into the cab and gets a spade. The ground is hard but the earth moves fairly easily. Barry labours away, his t-shirt sticking to his back, until he reaches something else, something even bigger. Breathing heavily, he puts the spade down and wipes away soil with his hands. Then he encounters something that isn't metal. It's glass, clogged with dirt and almost opaque. But Barry, driven by something which he doesn't quite understand, clears a space so that he can peer through.

A scream makes the seagulls rise into the air. It is a few seconds before Barry realises that he was the one who had screamed. And he almost does so again as he stumbles away from the buried giant.

Because, when he looked through the window, someone was looking back at him.

Not far away, across the fields where the Romans marched in orderly lines and the Royalist troops fled in disarray, Ruth Galloway is also digging. But this is altogether a more organised process. Teams of students labour over neatly dug trenches, marked out with string and measuring tape. Ruth moves from trench to trench, offering advice, dusting soil away from an object that might be a fragment of pottery or even a bone. She is happy. When she started this summer dig for her students, she was aware of the area's history, of course. She expected to find something, some Roman pottery maybe or even a coin or two. But, two days into the excavation, they made a really significant discovery. A body, which Ruth thinks might date from the Bronze Age, some two thousand years before the Romans.

The skeleton, buried in the chalky ground, isn't preserved as bodies found in peat are preserved. Five years ago, Ruth found the body of an Iron Age girl buried in the marshy soil near her house. That body had been almost perfect, suspended in time, hands bound with mistletoe rope, head partly shaved. Ruth had been able to look at that girl and know her story. This body is different and Ruth can't be sure of its age (she has sent samples for carbon-14 testing, though even that can be skewed by as many as a hundred years) but the skeleton is in the crouched position typical of Bronze Age burials and there are fragments of pottery nearby which look like examples of so-called Beaker ware. Beaker burials, which date back about four thousand years, are often distinguished by rounded barrows but there have been examples of flat grave sites too. Besides, the mound could easily have been destroyed by ploughing.

She excavated the bones yesterday, after photographing the skeleton, drawing it in plan and filling in a skeleton sheet for every bone. From the pelvic bones she thinks that the body is female but she hopes to be able to extract enough

DNA to make sure of this. Isotopic testing will indicate the woman's diet; her bones and teeth will tell the story of any disease or periods of malnutrition. Soon Ruth will know some of the answers, but she already feels a link with the woman who died so long ago. Standing in the field with the air shimmering in the heat, she allows herself a moment's satisfaction. It's a good job this and not a bad life, digging up the past under this high clear sky. It could be a lot worse. Her parents had wanted her to be an accountant.

'Ruth!' Ruth recognises the voice but she's in a good enough mood for it not to be dented by the appearance of her boss, Phil Trent. Even though he's wearing safari shorts.

'Hallo, Phil.'

'Found anything else?'

Honestly, isn't one Bronze Age body enough for him? It's one more than he has ever discovered. But, despite her irritation, Ruth secretly shares his hope that there might be more bodies buried under this soil. The position of the skeleton and the presence of beaker pottery indicate that this was a formal ritual burial. Could this be a barrow cemetery? If so, there will be others.

'Not yet,' says Ruth. She takes a swig from her water bottle. She can't remember a hotter day in Norfolk. Her cotton trousers are sticking to her legs and she is sure that her face is bright red.

'Anyway,' says Phil, 'I've had a thought.'

'Yes?' Ruth tries not to look too excited at this news.

'You know the English Heritage DNA project?'

'Yes.'

'Well, why not get them to include our body? We could test all the locals to see if they're any relation to him.'

'Her.'

'What?'

'Remember I said I thought it was a woman's skeleton?'

'Oh yes. Anyway, what do you think? It could really put UNN on the map.'

Putting UNN, the University of North Norfolk, on the map is an obsession with Phil. Privately, Ruth thinks that it would take more than a bit of Bronze Age DNA. But it's not a bad idea. The DNA project has been set up to discover if there are any links between prehistoric bodies and the local population. Norfolk, where the rural population is remarkably stable, would be an ideal testing ground.

'It's a thought,' says Ruth. 'Do you think they'd be interested?'

'Well, I spoke to someone from English Heritage this afternoon and they seemed keen.'

It is typical of Phil that, while ostensibly asking Ruth's advice, he has already set the plan in motion. Still, a hunger for publicity is not a bad attribute in a head of department.

'Do you want to have a look at today's finds?' asks Ruth. Although she excavated the skeleton yesterday and bagged up the bones herself, there are still a few interesting objects emerging from the trench.

Phil pulls a face. 'It's awfully hot,' he says, as if the weather is Ruth's fault.

'Is it?' says Ruth, pushing back her damp hair 'I hadn't noticed.'

Phil looks at her quizzically. He doesn't always get irony unless he's concentrating. Ruth is saved from elaborating by the buzz of her phone.

'Excuse me.'

When she sees 'Nelson' on the screen, her heart beats slightly faster. It's because I'm worried that it'll be about Kate, she tells herself. You can believe anything if you try hard enough. But, of course, it's a police matter. Ruth is seconded to North Norfolk's Serious Crimes Unit as a forensic archaeologist. It makes Phil very jealous.

'Ruth.' Typically Nelson does not waste time on the niceties. 'Where are you?'

'Near Hunstanton.'

'Oh good. You're in the area. That's handy.'

For whom? thinks Ruth but Nelson is still talking.

'Some builder has found a plane buried in a field near there.'

'A plane?'

'Yes. Probably from the Second World War. There are a few old RAF bases around here.'

'Well, you don't need me to dig out a plane.'

'The thing is, the pilot's still inside.'

A few minutes later Ruth is driving along the Hunstanton road with Phil at her side. She can't remember asking her head of department to join her but, somehow, there he is, wincing when Radio 4 blares out from the radio and asking her why she can't afford a new car. 'After all, your book was quite a success. Haven't you got a contract for another one?'

Ruth's book, about a dig in Lancashire, came out last year and has indeed attracted some praise in the scholarly journals. It was very far from being a best-seller though, and – after the advance has been earned out – her royalties will hardly contribute anything to her income. The book has made her mother proud, though, which is a miracle in itself.

'I like this car,' she says.

'It's a rust bucket,' says Phil. 'Why don't you buy one of those cool Fiat 500s? Shona's got one in ice blue.'

Ruth grinds her teeth. Fiat 500s are undoubtedly cool and Shona probably has one to match every one of her retro Boden frocks. Shona, Phil's partner and another university lecturer, is probably Ruth's best friend in Norfolk but that doesn't mean that Ruth wants to hear how cool and chic she is. She's quite happy with her old Renault, thank you very much. Who asked Phil to sit in it anyway?

She can see the field from a long way away. The digger perches precariously on a slope and next to it stand three men, one of whom is, unmistakably even from a distance, Nelson. Ruth parks the rust bucket by the gate and walks across the baked earth towards the group. Phil follows, complaining about the heat and people who are selfish enough to have cars without air conditioning.

Nelson sees her first. 'Here she is. Why have you brought Phil with you?'

Ruth loves the way he puts this. Phil would undoubtedly believe that he brought Ruth with him.

'He didn't want to miss the fun. Is this it?'

Her question is superfluous. Three-quarters of a wing

and half a cockpit lie exposed at the bottom of the shallow pit.

'American,' says Nelson. 'I can tell by the markings.'

Ruth shoots him a look. She thinks that Nelson would have been just the sort of boy to collect models of Second World War fighter planes.

'There was an American airbase near here,' says one of the other men. 'At Lockwell Heath.' Ruth recognises him as Edward Spens, a local property developer whom she encountered on an earlier case. Spens is tall and good-looking; his air of authority is only slightly dented by the fact that he's wearing tennis clothes. The third man, dressed in jeans and a filthy football top, stands slightly aside as if to imply that none of this is *his* fault. Ruth guesses that he must be the digger driver.

She looks at the exposed soil. It has a faintly blue tinge. She kneels down and scoops some earth in her hand, giving it a surreptitious sniff.

'What are you doing?' asks Phil. Clearly he's terrified that she's going to embarrass him.

'Fuel,' she says. 'Can't you smell it? And look at the blue marks on the soil. That's corroded aluminium. Did you have any idea that this plane was here?'

It is Edward Spens who answers. 'Some children found some engine parts in the field long ago, I believe. But no one had any idea that *this* was buried here, almost intact.'

Ruth looks at the cockpit. Although dented and corroded it looks remarkably undamaged, lying almost horizontally at the foot of the crater. She's no geometry expert but wouldn't you expect the prow of a crashed plane to be at a steeper angle?

'Where's the body?' she asks.

'Sitting in the cockpit,' says Edward Spens. 'It gave Barry here quite a turn, I can tell you.'

'Still got his bloody cap on,' Barry mutters.

Ruth kneels down and peers through the cockpit window. She can see exactly why Barry had such a shock. Sitting in the pilot's seat is a ghastly leathery figure, still dressed in the remnants of uniform, like some terrible joke about a delayed flight. Perched on the skull is a cap; the material has almost rotted away but the peak remains.

Ruth sits back on her heels.

'It's odd,' she says, almost to herself.

'What's odd?' asks Nelson. Alone of the men he doesn't seem to be suffering from the heat, though he is wearing his usual working clothes of blue open-neck shirt and dark trousers. Ruth, who hasn't seen him for a few weeks, thinks that he looks almost insultingly well, as if finding a body entombed in a plane is the ideal way to spend a summer day. She wonders if he's going away on holiday this year. That's the other part of his life; the part she can never really know.

'The soil is loose,' says Ruth. 'As if it's been disturbed recently.'

'Of course it's been disturbed,' says the driver. 'I drove a bloody digger through it, didn't I?' Spens makes a move as if to disassociate himself from the bad language but it takes more than that to offend Ruth when she's in her professional mode.

'The layers have been disturbed lower down,' she says. 'It's hot, not much rain; you'd expect the particles to be packed close together. And that's another thing. The topsoil is clay but there are chalk layers below. Chalk preserves bone but this body still has some skin on it. Look.'

Nelson leans forward. 'It's like that other body you found. The one on the Saltmarsh.'

Ruth looks at him. 'Yes. The skin preservation's typical of bodies found in bogs, not in chalky soil like this. The way the pilot's sitting too, hands on the joystick, it's almost as if he's been posed.'

Ruth leans in closer. She doesn't want to touch anything until they can do a proper excavation. Behind her, she can hear Nelson telling Spens that the field is now a crime scene.

'The thing is,' says Spens in his most confidential voice, 'we're rather up against it here. There's been a bit of ill-feeling about this location and I'd like to get the land cleared as quickly as possible.'

'I can't help that,' says Nelson. 'I have to get a SOCO team here and Doctor Galloway will need at least a day to excavate the body. Isn't that right, Ruth?'

'Scene of the Crime team?' says Spens. 'Isn't that going a bit far? I mean the poor chap obviously crashed his plane into this field during the war, seventy years ago. Must have landed in the chalk pit and been covered by a landslide or something. It's not as if there's been a crime or anything.'

'I'm afraid you're wrong,' says Ruth, standing up.

'What do you mean?' says Spens, sounding offended.

'I think a crime may have taken place.'

'What makes you think that, Ruth?' asks Phil implying, by his tone, that he is likely to side with the local captain of industry rather than his colleague.

'There's a bullet hole in the middle of his forehead,' says Ruth.

CHAPTER 1

September 2013

'Just one more picture.'

'For God's sake, Nelson, she'll be late for school on her first day.'

But Nelson is focusing the camera. Kate stands patiently by the fence, neatly dressed in her blue school sweatshirt and grey skirt. Her dark hair is already escaping from its plaits (Ruth isn't very good at hair). She holds her book bag in front of her like a weapon.

'First day at school,' says Nelson, clicking away. 'It doesn't seem possible.'

'Well, it is possible,' says Ruth, though she has lain awake half the night wondering how on earth she can entrust her precious darling to the terrors of education. This from a person with two degrees who works in a university.

'Come on, Kate,' says Ruth, holding out her hand. 'We don't want to keep Mrs Mannion waiting.'

'Is that your teacher?' asks Nelson.

No, she's the local axe-murderer, thinks Ruth. But she leaves it to Kate to tell Nelson that Mrs Mannion is very nice and that she gave her a sticker on the taster day and that she's got a teddy bear called Blue.

'We take it in turns to take Blue Bear home,' she informs him. 'But we've got to be good.' She says this doubtfully, as if it's an impossible condition.

'Of course you'll be good,' says Nelson. 'You'll be the best.'

'It's not a competition,' mutters Ruth as she opens the car door for Kate. But she has already had enough rows with Nelson about league tables and private schools and whether it's absolutely necessary for a four-year-old to learn Mandarin. In the end, Ruth had her way and Kate is going to the local state primary school, a cheerful place whose mission statement, spelt out in multicoloured handprints above the main entrance, reads simply: 'We have fun.'

'You're exactly the sort of person who's against competition,' says Nelson, putting away his camera.

'What sort of person's that?'

'The sort of person who does well in competitions.'

Ruth can't really deny that this is true. She has always loved learning and positively enjoyed exams. This is why she wants Kate to have fun and play with potato prints for a few years. Plenty of time for formal learning later. Nelson, who hated school and left as soon as possible, is anxious that his children should waste no time in scaling the slippery academic slope. He and Michelle sent their daughters to private schools and both went to university. Job done, though Laura is currently a holiday rep in Ibiza and Rebecca has no idea what she wants to do with her Media Studies degree beyond a vague desire to 'work in TV'.

'Say goodbye to Daddy,' says Ruth.

'Bye, Daddy.'

'Bye, sweetheart.' Nelson takes a last picture of Kate waving through the car window. Then he puts away his camera and goes back to have breakfast with his wife.

Ruth takes the familiar road with the sea on one side and the marshland on the other. Bob Woonunga, her neighbour, comes out to wave them goodbye and then there are no more houses until they reach the turn-off. It's a beautiful day, golden and blue, the long grass waving, the sandbanks a soft blur in the distance. Ruth wonders if she should say something momentous, tell Kate about her own first day at school or something, but Kate seems quite happy, singing a jingle from an advertisement for breakfast cereal. In the end, Ruth joins in. Crunchy nuts, crunchy nuts and raisins too. Yoo hoo hoo. Raisins too.

It still sounds funny to refer to Nelson as 'Daddy'. When Kate was three and asking questions, Ruth decided to tell her the truth, or at least a sanitised version of it. Nelson is her father; he loves her but he lives with his other family. Does he love them too? Of course he does. They all love each other in a messy twenty-first-century way. Nelson had been appalled when Ruth had told him what she was going to say. But he realised that Kate – a bright, enquiring child – needed to know something and, after all, what else could they say? Nelson's wife, Michelle, also took the agreed line, which

Ruth knows is more than she deserves. She's glad that Kate has Michelle in her life as Michelle is a proper homemaker, good at all the mother things. She would have done those plaits right, for a start (she's a hairdresser).

They drive past the field where the Bronze Age body was found in July. English Heritage have agreed to fund another dig and they will also include the project in their DNA study. There's even a chance that the dig might be filmed. Two years ago Ruth appeared in a TV programme called *Women Who Kill* and, while the experience was traumatic in all sorts of ways, she didn't altogether dislike the feeling of being a TV archaeology expert. She's not a natural, like Frank Barker, the American historian who fronted the programme, but the *Guardian* did describe her as 'likeable', which is a start.

'Mummy might be on TV again,' she says to Kate.

'I hope Blue Bear does come to our house,' says Kate.

She's right too. Blue Bear is more important just now.

Ruth had been scared that Kate would cry, that she would cry, that they would have to be prised apart by disapproving teaching assistants. But in the end, when Kate just waves happily and disappears into the sea of blue sweatshirts, that somehow feels worse than anything. Ruth turns away, blinking back foolish tears.

'Mrs Galloway?'

Ruth turns. This is an altogether new persona for her. She likes to be called Dr Galloway at work and she has never been Mrs anything. Mrs Galloway is her mother, a formidable born-again Christian living in South London, within sight of the promised land. Should she insist on Ms or would that blight Kate's prospects on the first day?

'Mrs Galloway?' The speaker is a woman. Teacher? Parent? Ruth doesn't know. Whoever she is, she looks scarily at home in the lower-case, primary-coloured environment of the infant classrooms.

'I'm Miss Coles, the classroom assistant. I just wondered if Kate was having school dinners or packed lunch.'

'Dinners,' says Ruth. She doesn't feel up to preparing sandwiches every day.

'Not a fussy eater then? That's good.'

Ruth says nothing. The truth is that Kate is a rather fussy eater but Ruth always gives her food that she likes. She dreads to think of Kate's reaction when presented with cottage pie or semolina. But surely school dinners are different now? There's probably a salad bar and a wine list.

Miss Coles seems to take Ruth's silence for extreme emotion (which isn't that far from the truth). She pats the air above Ruth's arm.

'Don't worry. She'll settle in really quickly. Why don't you go home and have a nice cup of tea?'

Actually I've got to give a lecture on palaeolithic burial practices, thinks Ruth. But she doesn't say this aloud. She thanks Miss Coles and walks quickly away.

Nelson, too, finds it hard to stop thinking about Kate. He wishes that he had been able to take her to school but it was generous enough of Michelle to agree to the early morning visit. The late breakfast together was meant to be Nelson's attempt to say thank you, but when he reaches the house, Michelle is on her way out of the door. There's a crisis at the salon, she says, she needs to get to work straight away. She kisses Nelson lightly and climbs into her car. Nelson watches as she performs a neat three-point-turn and drives off, her face set as if she's already thinking about work. Nelson sighs and gets back into his battered Mercedes.

But, when he gets to the station, there is some compensation. Amongst all the rubbish in his inbox, one email stands out: 'Dental records on skull found 17/7/13'. This is the American pilot, the one found in the summer in the cockpit of his buried plane. After Ruth had excavated the skeleton, an autopsy had found that death probably occurred as a result of the bullet wound in the temple. Here the investigation would probably have stalled without the generosity of the American Air Force, who had offered to fund DNA tests and extensive forensic investigations. Even so, the laboratories had taken their time. In August, Nelson had rather reluctantly accompanied Michelle on holiday to Spain (far too hot) and had returned to find that no progress had been made. Well, it looks as if they have a result at last. Nelson clicks open the email, still standing up.

'Cloughie!' he calls, a moment later.

DS Clough appears in the doorway, a half-eaten bagel in his hand.

'Look at this. We've got a positive match for our American pilot.'

Clough peers over his boss's shoulder. 'Frederick J. Blackstock. Who's he when he's at home?'

'Come on, Cloughie. You're from Hunstanton way. Don't you recognise the name?'

'Blackstock. Oh, *those* Blackstocks. Do you think he's related?'

'I don't know, but I'm going to find out.'

'Why would a Yank pilot be related to a posh Norfolk family?'

'Your guess is as good as mine, Cloughie.'

'Bit of a coincidence, isn't it?' says Clough, scrolling down the email. 'American pilot found dead right near his old ancestral home.'

'Exactly,' says Nelson, gathering up his car keys. 'And I don't believe in coincidence.'

It's impossible to ignore the Blackstock name in the Hunstanton area. There's the Blackstock Arms, the Blackstock Art Gallery, even the Blackstock Fishing Museum. The smug ubiquity of the name reminds Nelson of the Smiths in King's Lynn, a comparison that isn't exactly reassuring, given that a previous investigation involving the Smiths ended up combining Class-A drugs, an ancient curse and a poisonous snake. Unlike the Smiths, though, the Blackstocks still live in their ancestral home, a bleak manor house built on the edge of the Saltmarsh.

They drive (along Blackstock Way) past flat fields crisscrossed with tiny streams; mournful-looking sheep stand marooned on grassy islands and geese fly overhead, honking sadly. The house is visible from miles away, a ship rising from a grey-green sea.

'I wouldn't like to live here,' says Clough. 'It's as bad as Ruth's place.'

'It's a bit grander than Ruth's place.'

Blackstock Hall is indeed grand, a stern brick-built edifice with a tower at each corner, but there is no comforting stately home feeling about it: no National Trust sign pointing the way to the tea rooms, no manicured lawns or Italian gardens. Instead the grass comes right up to the front door and sheep peer into the downstairs rooms. If there was a path to the front door, it vanished years, maybe centuries, ago. Nelson parks by the side of the road and he and Clough approach the house through the fields.

'Bloody hell,' says Clough, 'the grass is full of sheep shit.'

'What do you expect?' says Nelson, hurdling a stream. The sheep stare at him with their strange onyx eyes.

'I expect a proper driveway, since you ask,' says Clough. 'Bunch of gyppos would do it for a grand.'

Nelson ignores this though he knows he should say something about the un-PC language. 'It's travellers, not gyppos, and we should respect different lifestyle choices, etc., etc.' Instead he says, 'Hope there's someone at home after all this.'

'There's smoke coming out of the chimneys,' says Clough. 'Probably burning a virgin for the harvest.'

'I should never have let you watch *The Wicker Man*,' says Nelson.

Despite the smoke, it seems at first that the house might be deserted after all. Finally, after almost five minutes, the heavy oak door opens slowly and a woman's face appears.

'Oh, there is someone here,' she says. 'We only really use the back door.'

'I wasn't aware of that,' says Nelson stiffly. 'I'm DCI Harry Nelson from the King's Lynn police. This is DS Clough. We'd like to speak to Mr or Mrs Blackstock.'

'You'd better come in then,' says the woman. 'I'm Sally Blackstock.'

The door opens with difficulty and Nelson sees that the hall is full of packing cases. Clearly Sally Blackstock was telling the truth about this entrance not being in use. She's an attractive woman in her mid-fifties, ash-blonde hair, blue eyes, no make-up. She reminds Nelson of an older version of Barbara in *The Good Life*.

'This is quite some house,' says Nelson.

Sally Blackstock laughs. 'It's a mish-mash really. Built in Tudor times, burnt down during the Civil War, rebuilt in the Georgian era. The Blackstocks have lived on this site for over five hundred years and it feels as if we've still got all their rubbish.' She gives one of the packing cases a feeble shove.

'Are you moving out then?' asks Clough.

Sally laughs. 'I should be so lucky! No, we're clearing up. I've got this mad idea about opening the house as a B & B. Now I wonder what I've started. Lunacy, the whole thing.'

As they follow Mrs Blackstock down a seemingly endless corridor, Nelson can't help but agree with her assessment. All the rooms in the house, though undoubtedly large and well-proportioned, are either empty or full of boxes. It's hard to imagine the place being transformed into a haven of breakfast tables and comfortable sofas. Eventually, though,

Sally turns a corner and admits them to a large kitchen complete with Aga, armchairs and an open fire.

'We practically live in this room, I'm afraid,' she says when Nelson comments on the fire. 'The rest of the house is just too bloody cold. Now, what's all this about?'

The sudden switch from Barbara Good to Margaret Thatcher takes Nelson by surprise, as does the gear change into an extremely patrician accent. He says, aware that he is sounding like a stage policeman, 'We've got some news regarding a gentleman whom we believe may be a family member. Frederick J. Blackstock.'

Sally Blackstock's mouth forms a small round 'o'. 'Fred?' she says. 'Freddy? But he died in the war. His plane went down over the sea.'

'Mrs Blackstock, do you remember reading in the local press about a Second World War plane being found near here? It would have been a couple of months back, in July.'

'Yes, I think I remember something.'

'Well, there was a body in the plane. Dental records have just identified the man as being Frederick Blackstock. I believe he would have been related to your husband?'

'Yes.' Sally Blackstock runs a hand through her hair, leaving it standing up in a crest. She waves a hand vaguely towards the armchairs. 'Do sit down, Detective er . . .'

'Nelson.'

'Yes. Nelson. Like the admiral. Frederick was my husband's uncle but he emigrated to America in the thirties. We knew he'd died in the war but we were told that his plane went down in the sea with no survivors. My husband will be amazed.'

'Where's your husband today?' asks Nelson, surreptitiously removing a dog's lead from the cushion of his chair.

'He's with Chaz. Our son. He's got a pig farm near here.' She pulls a face. 'I'll call him. Oh God, where's the phone? We don't get much of a mobile signal here,' she explains to the policemen, 'so I've got one of those cordless phones, but I can never find it.'

Clough finds it under a pile of *Horse & Hounds* and is rewarded by Sally putting the kettle on for tea. She goes into the pantry and they hear her leaving a message for her husband. 'Darling, something rather amazing's happened.' Nelson and Clough exchange glances.

Sally comes back into the room minus the phone. Nelson wonders where she's put it and whether she'll ever find it again. Mrs Blackstock, though, is suddenly all charm. She leans on the Aga and beams at the two policemen. 'The thing is,' she says cosily, 'there were three brothers. Shall I tell you the story?'

'Yes please,' says Nelson, trying not to sound as if he's in nursery school. He wonders what Katie's doing now. Perhaps she too is listening to a story. He sees Clough trying not to laugh.

'Lewis was the oldest. He fought in the war and was a prisoner in Japan. Had a terrible time by all accounts. Anyway, he was never the same again and, in 1950 or thereabouts, he simply vanished.'

'Vanished?' repeats Clough.

'Yes. They all thought he'd killed himself but no one ever said it aloud. George, my father-in-law, says it was an absolutely terrible time. His mother never could accept that Lewis was gone and she went a bit doolally herself. In the end, though, they had to admit that he wasn't coming back and Lewis was declared dead in the sixties.'

'And Frederick had already died in the war?'

'Yes. He was the second brother. He hated this place, that's what George always says. He said that the Blackstock land was cursed. He had a vivid imagination, like his mother. So Frederick emigrated to America and he fought with the US Air Force. He died in 1944, leaving George to inherit.'

'Your father-in-law?'

'Yes. He never expected to inherit, being the youngest son, but he tried to make a go of the place. My husband is his only child. He's called George too. Young George, even though he's pushing sixty.' She laughs and takes the hissing kettle from the Aga.

'So the family were told that Frederick's plane went down over the sea?' says Nelson, trying not to look as Sally sloshes hot water into the teapot. The police first aid course was a long time ago and he can't remember what you do about scalds.

'Yes.' Sally pours the tea and, after a few minutes' searching, puts a biscuit tin on the table. 'That's why I don't understand how he could have been found in that plane in the field.'

'We don't understand it either,' says Nelson slowly. The buried plane had been fairly easy to trace. The single-seater NAA P-51 Mustang D for Dog had gone down in a thunderstorm in September 1944. The pilot had bailed out and was found dead in an adjacent field. The plane had crashed into a disused quarry and was immediately buried by a landslide caused by the heavy rain. In the light of the fact that the pilot had been found, no attempt was made to recover the plane. Senior Airman Frederick Blackstock, on the other hand, was not meant to be anywhere near D for Dog. He was part of the ten-man crew of a B17 which had been shot down over the English Channel a week earlier.

'That's partly why we're here,' says Nelson, watching as Clough selects two biscuits conveniently stuck together. 'If your husband would agree to a DNA test, we could establish beyond any doubt that this Frederick Blackstock was a family member.'

'I'm sure he'll agree,' says Sally. She rolls her eyes upwards. 'I wish I could tell George, Old George, I mean.'

Her manner is now starting to seem slightly spooky. Why is she looking upwards? To indicate that Old George is watching them from heaven?

'When did George, Old George, die?'

She laughs again. The laugh, too, is starting to grate. 'Oh, he's not dead, Detective Nelson. He's upstairs having his mid-morning nap.'

CHAPTER 2

Ruth arrives at the school early but is surprised to see that she's not the only one. There's already a knot of mothers standing by the entrance to the infant school. What's more, they all seem to know each other, laughing and exchanging baker's bags full of after-school treats. Pre-school children are much in evidence, in prams and pushchairs and swinging on the school gates in defiance of signs telling them not to.

Come on, Ruth tells herself, you've got to try to be sociable. These are the people who'll invite Kate to parties and play dates. In time they might become your closest friends. She approaches the group, smiling ingratiatingly. Casually, unselfconsciously, the mothers turn their backs so that all she can see are ponytails and denim jackets. 'They're not as nice as the little custardy ones in Asda,' someone is saying. Ruth edges away, towards the gates. She is ashamed to note that, for the second time that day, she is nearly crying.

But then the door opens and Mrs Mannion stands smiling at the top of the steps. Little figures in blue sweatshirts can be seen jostling in the background. The teacher is careful to see that each child is delivered to the right parent but Ruth is surprised at how casual some of the mothers are. They head off for the gates pushing buggies and chatting to their friends with their five-year-olds trotting behind them. Don't they know how momentous this day is? thinks Ruth. But then some of the mothers have done this two or three times before. This is Ruth's only chance to get it right.

Kate is the fifth child to be handed over. She skips down the steps. 'Mum, we did music and I played the tangerine.' Mrs Mannion meets Ruth's eyes over Kate's (now very untidy) head. 'She had a great day. Really settled in well.'

'Thank you,' says Ruth, more grateful for the tone, which is both warm and professional, than the actual words.

'Come on, Kate. Let's go home. I've bought crumpets.'

Kate gives a little jump of delight. Crumpets are one of her favourite things.

'What did you have for lunch?' asks Ruth as they cut through the stream of parents now heading for the junior school.

'Meat,' says Kate briefly. 'I hated it. Can I have sandwiches tomorrow?'

Near the gates of another school, this one in King's Lynn, Nelson and Clough have been halted by the peremptory command of a lollipop man. They don't have the siren on the car and Nelson is quite happy to wait and watch the children straggling across the road carrying paintings and gym shoes and artwork made from crushed tissue paper. How have they accumulated so much stuff on the first day of term?

'It's Katie's first day at school today,' he tells Clough. The team all know about Kate but it's rare for Nelson to mention her directly.

Clough doesn't seem abashed. 'Bless her heart. She's growing up fast.' Clough likes kids. Nelson has noticed this before. He really should meet a nice girl and settle down. Nelson didn't care for Trace, Clough's ex, but since the break-up there has been nobody serious. Plenty of the light-hearted variety, if you listen to station gossip, which Nelson tries not to. Then he tells himself that he's Clough's boss, not some match-making crone from *Fiddler on the Roof* (he had been forced to watch this when Rebecca was in a school production).

'What do you think about our pilot?' he asks. 'The one who ended up in the wrong plane.'

'Fred?' says Clough. He always likes to be on first-name terms with the victim.

'Yes. Frederick Blackstock. One of the three Blackstock boys. Two dead, one slightly gaga.'

Old George had made his appearance towards the end of the interview at Blackstock Hall. And, though not exactly gaga, he had certainly seemed confused and even hostile.

'What's going on, Sally? I thought I heard voices.'

'It's the police, Dad. They've come to talk to us about the plane that was found in Devil's Hollow.'

Sally's tone had been soothing, conciliatory. Young George, who had arrived a few minutes earlier, said nothing. Nelson noticed that Sally called her father-in-law 'Dad'; he has never been able to call his mother-in-law 'Mum', maybe because he still has his own mother and she sometimes feels like one maternal figure too many. He also noted the ominous name of the field: Devil's Hollow. Jesus wept.

'What's that got to do with us?' Old George had said. 'Land doesn't belong to us any more. We sold it to that developer fella, didn't we? Chaz kicked up a fuss about it.'

'We sold it to Edward Spens,' says Sally. 'He's a nice chap.'

Old George had grunted but had seemed slightly mollified by the mention of Edward Spens. Probably glad that the land went to someone with the right sort of accent, thought Nelson, remembering his own encounters with the Spens family. Whatever you say about the upper classes, they certainly like to stick together.

Now he says, 'The question is, where has Fred's body been hiding all this time? And who thought that it would be a bright idea to put it in the plane?'

'I thought Ruth was onto that,' said Clough.

'She sent some samples off for analysis,' says Nelson. 'She said tests might be able to tell us if the bones had originally been buried elsewhere, what sort of soil and all that. Trouble is, it all takes so long.'

Nelson hates waiting for anything, particularly forensic tests. He remembers his early days as a policeman in Black-pool, when they would just hand a bloodstained bag to the in-house team: 'Forensicate that, will you?' Now they have to send away to some private forensics firm, and when the results come back they are hedged with so many 'mights' and 'maybes' that they are almost useless in court.

'What's the hurry?' says Clough. He might be talking

about his boss's driving. Free from the admonishing lollipop they are now speeding through the outskirts of King's Lynn. 'Chap's been dead for seventy years. Ruth was pretty sure of that.'

'But someone put him in that plane quite recently. Why?'

'To stop the development? Hasn't there been a bit of fuss about it?'

Nelson wonders if his sergeant is trying to be funny. 'A bit of fuss' hardly describes the bitter arguments played out in the local press over the summer. As far as Nelson can make out, the field (Devil's Hollow, God help us) is a site of both historical and natural interest. It's very near the place where Ruth found her Bronze Age skeleton and many people, Ruth included, think there may be a barrow cemetery nearby. It's also apparently the home of several rare plants and birds. There were also rumours – strenuously denied – that an energy company was going to start drilling on the land using the controversial fracking technique. Nelson remembers that the Blackstocks' son, Chaz, had been against the sale of the field.

'I think we should visit Chaz next,' he says.

'Doesn't he own a pig farm?' asks Clough, grimacing.

'Nothing wrong with a bit of pig muck,' says Nelson, swerving into the entrance to the police station. 'Aren't you a country boy?'

Clough says nothing. Nelson thinks that he might be offended by the description – Clough goes to great lengths to seem urban and edgy – but, not for the first time, he does his sergeant an injustice. Clough has been thinking.

'Where is this pig farm? Lockwell Heath? Out Brancaster way?'

'That's right.'

'Isn't that where the airfield was? The American airbase.'

'That's right,' says Nelson. 'The War Office said that the land had returned to agriculture.'

'What if it's a pig farm?'

'You've got something there, Cloughie. Let's go and see this Chaz tomorrow.'

When they enter the station, DS Judy Johnson is sitting in the desk sergeant's chair (with some difficulty, as she is heavily pregnant).

'Where have you been?'

'Blackstock Hall,' says Nelson. 'Then we drove over to Eye to follow up on those drugs leads. It's in the log book.' He says this rather defensively as he is often accused (by his boss, Superintendant Gerry Whitcliffe) of poor communication.

'You can't go out five minutes,' says Judy, 'without upsetting someone.'

'Who is it this time?' asks Clough, eying Judy warily as she gets to her feet. He is terrified that she will go into premature labour any day soon.

'One George Blackstock,' says Judy. 'He rang about an hour ago, accusing you of harassing his family.'

'Did he now?' says Nelson. 'Well, he hasn't seen anything yet.' Then he has a thought. 'Was it Old George or Young George?'

'Sounded pretty old to me,' says Judy, moving towards

the stairs.

'Shouldn't you be going home?' says Clough. 'Put your feet up?'

Judy smiles. 'Don't worry, Cloughie. Cathbad's done the birth chart and he says the baby's going to be late.'

Nelson and Clough exchange glances. 'Cathbad's a midwife now, is he?' says Nelson. Actually it wouldn't surprise him if Cathbad had done some lunatic course on DIY home births. Cathbad, Judy's partner, is a druid with an uncanny knack of turning up at the right, or at any rate the most tense, moment. He had been with Ruth when she had Katie, Nelson remembers.

'No,' says Judy with dignity, 'but Cathbad just knows things.'

And no one can really argue with that.

CHAPTER 3

Clough's hunch was correct. As Nelson drives across Lock-well Heath, he sees rows and rows of pigsties, endless lower-case letter 'm's silhouetted against the sky, but in the foreground there is what was unmistakably once a control tower, a square building topped with a hexagonal viewing tower. The doors and windows are boarded up but the steps to the tower remain in place, a rusting iron spiral. Sprayed on the wall are the words 'Bomb Group'. Nelson stops the car and he and Clough look at each other. There is something incredibly poignant about the building, so obviously deserted but equally obviously once vitally important. The wind, which is blowing strongly across the flat fields, rattles the wooden slats as if someone inside is trying to get out. The clouds above are brooding and grey.

'Bloody hell,' says Nelson. 'What a creepy place.'

'There are a lot of these abandoned airfields in Norfolk,' says Clough. 'They call them the ghost fields.'

The ghost fields. Nelson's not a fanciful man but, just

for a second, he imagines the sky full of lumbering Second World War planes, rising into the clouds and heading out to sea. He thinks of the men inside the control tower listening to their final briefing, not knowing whether they'll ever come back.

Clough's voice brings him back down to earth. 'I suppose this was the runway.' He points at the wide concrete path in front of them.

'I suppose so.' Nelson starts the car. As they get closer, they see two vast corrugated-iron sheds, big enough to house a plane.

'Hangars,' says Clough.

'Chaz is certainly making use of what was left behind.'

'Pigs on an airfield,' says Clough. 'It doesn't seem right somehow.'

'Pigs might fly,' says Nelson darkly.

Chaz Blackstock, who strides towards them from the direction of the largest shed, could easily have wandered in from a film about the First of the Few. He's even wearing a leather jacket. He's also tall and dark, with an effortless air of command. Only his shoulder-length hair strikes a twenty-first-century note. Nelson is prepared to dislike Chaz on sight but the voice disarms him. Instead of echoing his parents' upper-class accents, Chaz speaks in a low hesitant tone with more than a shade of Norfolk about the vowels.

'Detective Chief Inspector Nelson? Pleased to meet you.'

'Thank you for seeing us. This is Detective Sergeant Clough.'

The two men nod at each other. Nelson can see Clough

trying not to breathe through his nose. The smell of pig is all-pervasive.

'You know why we're here?'

'Yes. It's about Uncle Fred's body being found. What a turn-up for the books.'

'You could say that,' says Nelson, though it's not a term that he would ever use. 'Is there somewhere we can talk?'

'Yes. In the house. It's just a step away, across the next field.' He points to where a long, low building seems to be hunkering down in the grass, as if to escape the wind.

'Bit blowy today,' says Nelson as they set out.

'Yes,' says Chaz. 'I'd really like to put up a few wind turbines here. It's fabulously flat.'

It is certainly flat but Nelson finds it hard to see what's so fabulous about that. There's a desolate feel about the whole place, the boarded-up tower like a sentry at the gate, the wind blowing through the iron buildings with a high keening sound. The presence of the pigs, grunting and shuffling in their pens, doesn't help at all.

'What's in the old hangars?' asks Clough, stepping carefully at Nelson's side. From sheep shit to pig muck, thinks Nelson. Clough really shouldn't wear such expensive shoes. Even though they look like trainers.

'Farrowing sheds,' says Chaz, 'dry sow house, pig finishing house, weaning pens.'

The policemen are both silent. Nelson wonders if he's heard right. Pig finishing house?

'How big is the farm?' he asks after a pause.

'Thirteen acres,' says Chaz. 'Small but perfectly formed.'

He smiles rather charmingly, revealing a gap between his front teeth. 'You know, it's always been my dream to own a place like this.'

That was what his mother had said. 'Chaz was never interested in school work. Oh, he was bright enough but he just wasn't motivated. All he ever wanted to do was run his own farm.'

'Well, he's achieved his ambition,' Nelson had replied. 'Not many people do that.'

'Yes,' Sally had said. But Nelson thought that she sounded unconvinced. Chaz's sister, Cassandra, is apparently an actress, 'doing experimental plays in Lincoln'. Nelson thought that Sally didn't sound too delighted about that either.

But now Chaz shows an almost touching pride in his windswept collection of farm buildings. The house too, a sixties bungalow in urgent need of painting and repair, is presented as if it's a palace. As if it's Blackstock Hall, in fact.

'Here's the old homestead. Let's go into the kitchen. It's cosy in there.'

Cosy isn't quite the word Nelson would use to describe the sagging cabinets, rusting cooker and motley collection of chairs, but at least they are out of the wind. Chaz puts on the kettle and Clough tries surreptitiously to scrape mud (or worse) off his shoe.

'So . . . Chaz,' says Nelson. He has been invited to use this name but it still seems wrong somehow. 'You've heard that the body in the plane has been positively identified as your great-uncle Frederick Blackstock?'

'I thought you were going to do some DNA tests on Dad?'

'Yes. That's just to confirm the family link but the dental records were fairly conclusive.'

'None of us can understand how he got in that plane,' says Chaz, getting out a selection of mismatched mugs. 'We all thought that his plane went down over the sea.'

'Who told you that?'

Chaz frowns. 'Dad, I suppose. Or maybe Grandpa. He used to talk about the war sometimes.'

Nelson hasn't heard from Old George since the initial complaint about police harassment. In Nelson's view this was a pretty extreme reaction to some gentle questioning. He wonders why the old man feels so threatened.

'Your granddad mentioned to us that you were against the sale of the field where the plane was found.'

Chaz hesitates before replying, or maybe he is just occupied with pouring the tea. As he puts the mugs in front of them, he says, with no change in his hesitantly charming manner, 'I was against it, yes. I mean, I know the old dears needed the money, but it's breaking up the estate.'

'Breaking up the estate.' An old-school phrase if there ever was one. Of course Chaz will be in line to inherit the estate. Or is Cassandra older? In any case, there's probably some feudal principle that favours the son over the daughter.

'And that ghastly man, Edward Spens,' says Chaz, sitting down at the table. He has taken off his jacket and there are holes in both elbows of his jumper. 'He wants to build houses on the site. Hundreds of horrid little hen houses.'

Pig houses would presumably be perfectly acceptable, thinks Nelson.

'Would be better than fracking though, wouldn't it?' says Clough. Nelson is glad to see that he's been reading up on the issues.

'I don't know,' Chaz runs his hands through his hair. However much he rumples it, his thick dark hair always ends up falling across his face in a perfect Hugh Grant fringe. 'At least with fracking you wouldn't get hundreds of people living in what's practically our front garden.'

Nelson thinks that there are a couple of interesting things about this statement. Firstly, for all the holes in his sleeves, there's enough of the lord of the manor in Chaz to make him resent the arrival of hordes of plebeians at his gate. Secondly, although he is living away from home – living on his dream farm, in fact – Chaz still refers to 'our front garden'.

'When was the last time you went to Devil's Hollow?' asks Nelson. He still has trouble saying the name with a straight face. 'Have you been there since the land was sold?'

'I went once or twice,' says Chaz. 'Just to see what Spens was playing at. He says he isn't building lots of houses on the land but any fool can see that's what he's planning. I spoke to his oafish digger driver and he admitted that they'd been told to clear the land as quickly as possible.'

'You spoke to the driver? When? I thought work had only just started when the plane was found.'

'I can't remember.' Chaz turns away flicking back a lock of hair so that it falls perfectly. 'It might even have been on the morning of the day that they found Uncle Fred.'

'You were there that morning?'

'Yes, I think so.'

'And you didn't see the plane?'

'No. The bloke had just started work when I got there. It was a bloody hot day. I didn't hang around.'

'Will you go back again, when they start work again?'

Chaz looks up. 'But they can't go on with the work, not while the police investigation's going on. That's what I thought.'

Nelson shrugs. 'We've finished with the land. Doctor Galloway excavated the body and examined the context. We've got the plane out. As far as I can see, Edward Spens has the place to himself again.'

'What about the archaeology dig nearby?' says Chaz. 'Didn't they find something really significant?'

'I think so,' says Nelson. He remembers Ruth telling him about some Bronze Age body but he hadn't been listening properly, to be honest. He does remember that she said something about the television people being interested.

'The dig might be on TV,' he says. 'That's what I've heard.'

Chaz beams, suddenly expansive. 'If TV get involved, then all our problems are solved.'

What problems would they be? wonders Nelson.

Ruth is also thinking about TV. Specifically she is thinking about Frank Barker, the American academic who appeared with her on *Women Who Kill*. This is because she has just received an email from him.

Hi, Ruth (writes Frank, with no acknowledgement of the fact that he hasn't been in contact for over a year). I've been thinking a lot about you. I expect you heard about the WWII plane that was found near you? Well, an American TV company wants to do a programme about it. Turns out the pilot may have been in the US Air Force but he was really a Norfolk boy. Anyway, this company wants to do a documentary about American airmen in Norfolk, with a bit of human interest thrown in. They're going to contact the family to see if they want to be involved (apparently the daughter lives in Vermont).

So, Ruth, it looks like I might be back in Norfolk before Christmas. If so, it would be great to meet up. Do drop me a line.

All best,

Frank

Ruth stares at the email. She has a tutorial in ten minutes and should be preparing. Instead she lets herself think about Frank. She sees his tanned skin and greying hair, his loping athletic stride. But mostly she hears his voice, those warm Western tones that sounded reassuring even when he was talking about a long-dead Victorian murderess. 'She was unjustly accused and I care about injustice.' She hears Frank apologising for driving his car into hers; she remembers the look in his eyes when he said, 'I'd like to see you again. Before I go back to the States.' They had seen each other a few times and the relationship seemed on the verge of teetering into something else but, somehow, it hadn't happened. Frank had gone back to America and they had corresponded for a while. There was even some talk of Ruth going to visit Frank in Seattle. But, again, the talk had come to nothing. Something – Kate? her work? Nelson? – kept holding Ruth back. But now he was coming to see her. Well, strictly speaking, he was coming to see the airfields, but hadn't he said 'I've been thinking a lot about you' and 'it would be great to meet up'? Ruth continues to stare at the screen.

As she does so, another email pings up. This one says: 'Soil analysis: results'. Ruth reads quickly and reaches for her phone. Then she stops. She can hear her students scuffling outside. She hasn't got time for a proper conversation. She'll ring Nelson later. She closes her laptop and composes her face into a welcoming smile.

Nelson and Clough are in the middle of yet another field. This time the landscape is clearly in transition. The earth has been gouged and dissected. The grass has vanished under huge mounds of sand and cement. Work has definitely restarted at Devil's Hollow. In fact, thinks Nelson, it's no longer even a hollow. It's now a square of churned-up soil. A sign by the gate tells non-existent passers-by that a luxury development of beachfront apartments is being created by Spens and Co. There's no sign of the apartments yet but, if you look hard, you can just see the sea glimmering through the few remaining trees. Otherwise, it could be any building site anywhere in the country.

The digger stands, vibrating gently, in the middle of the field and next to it stands Barry West, looking unhelpful. He's clearly longing to get back to work (and to the sandwiches in his cab).

'This must be quite some job,' says Nelson.

Barry says nothing. He looks exactly as he did on the day that the body was discovered. In fact he seems to be wearing exactly the same clothes.

'When did work start up again?' asks Nelson.

'As soon as you lot finished messing around. A few weeks ago.'

Nelson decides to ignore the description of police forensic work as 'messing around'. 'Much more to do?' he asks.

'I'm nearly done. Building work starts next week.'

'I want to talk to you about the day the plane was discovered,' says Nelson. 'Do you remember that day?'

'Not going to forget it, am I? Bleeding dead body looking out at me.'

'I wanted to ask you about earlier in the day, before you found the plane. Did anyone come to the field asking about the building work?'

Barry looks at them under lowered brows. Ruth once told Nelson that most Europeans have four per cent Neanderthal DNA but clearly this is only an average.

'Yeah,' he says at last. 'Posh bloke. Long hair.'

Nelson and Clough look at each other. 'Do you remember what he said?'

'Was asking about the houses. How many there would be. That sort of thing. I told him that I only drove the digger.'

'Did he say anything else that you remember?'

'He said something about engine parts. I didn't know what he was going on about. I thought he was talking about the digger. A lot of these posh types like to pretend that they know about machinery. Mr Spens is the same.'

But what if Chaz wasn't just pretending to be Bob the Builder? thinks Nelson as he and Clough walk back to his car. What if Chaz knew the plane was there all along? After all, he must have played in these fields as a child. What if, in the course of some childish game, he had come across parts of the buried plane? And when he found out about the sale of the land, did he think that if the builders discovered the plane it would halt the development? What if he also calculated that the plane would make more of an effect if accessorised by a body?

Nelson looks back across the marshes. Blackstock Hall is clearly visible against the skyline, grey and forbidding. It's not exactly the front garden but the new development will certainly be in the eyeline of the Hall's occupants. What had Chaz said? That the sale of Devil's Hollow would be 'breaking up the estate'. An estate that would, presumably, belong to Chaz one day.

'What do you think?' he asks Clough as the car bumps along the unmade road.

'Bloke should wash more often.'

'About Chaz Blackstock. Why was he talking about engine parts? Do you think he knew the plane was here all along? After all, he was brought up here.'

Clough considers. 'It's possible. Grubbing about in the dirt, digging up buried planes, it's the sort of thing boys do.'

Nelson's elder daughter, Laura, had briefly been interested in engines. Her biggest treat had been when a local farmer allowed her to drive his tractor round the field. Nelson rather regretted it when this interest gave way to rather more stereotypically female concerns.

'Girls too,' he says. 'Cassandra may have known too.'

'But if they knew about the plane,' says Clough, wincing as Nelson narrowly avoids a gate, 'did they also know about Uncle Fred's body?'

Nelson is about to answer when his phone rings. It's on hands-free so he barks, 'Yes?'

'Nelson. It's Ruth.'

'Hi, Ruth. What is it? Has something happened to Katie?'

He hears Ruth sigh. Clough hears it too and grins.

'Kate is fine. Enjoying her second day at school. Remember, you rang three times to find out about the first day?'

'Has she done music again?'

'She wasn't "doing music".' He can hear the irritated quotation marks. 'She was banging a tambourine. I wouldn't book tickets for Carnegie Hall yet.'

Where? thinks Nelson. Aloud he says, 'So why are you ringing?'

'I've had the soil analysis results back on the body. The one found in the plane.'

'And what do they tell us?'

'The body was originally buried in anaerobic alkaline silt.'

'Tell me that in English.'

Another sigh. 'The plane was buried in chalky soil. Chalk's alkaline but it drains well so you don't get the skin preservation that you see in waterlogged anaerobic conditions.'

'The plane looked pretty well preserved to me.'

'Yes, metal's no problem. Bone too. You get very well-preserved skeletons found in chalk. It's just the way the skin was still attached.'

Nelson doesn't think he's ever going to forget the way the

skin was still attached. He remembers Barry's description of a 'bleeding dead body looking at me'.

'The way the skin was preserved was typical of marshy, boggy soil,' Ruth is saying. 'According to the soil analysis the body may have been buried fairly nearby – there are traces of marine life, for one thing – but in more marshy soil. Not the peat bogs, because they would have conserved it completely, but somewhere halfway between chalk soil and marshland. And it was wrapped in something. Remember I said that there were traces of something waxy on the bones?'

Nelson dimly remembers something of the sort. The trouble is, Ruth always gives him so much information that the important bits sometimes get filtered out.

'Well, the body may have been wrapped in oilcloth, tarpaulin, something like that.'

'Deliberately buried then? He didn't just lie where he fell?'

'It doesn't look like it. No.'

There is a silence. Nelson thinks of the house rising up out of the flat landscape. 'This marshy ground, could it be somewhere like the grounds of Blackstock Hall, for example?'

'It's possible.'

When Ruth has rung off, with promises to call later with news of Kate's second day at school, Nelson turns to Clough.

'I think it's time we had another word with Old George. He was the only one around at the time that Fred went missing.'

'Don't forget the other brother who mysteriously disappeared.'

'I won't,' says Nelson. 'Wonder if his body's buried in anaerobic whatsit too.'

'Better go gently, boss. Remember Granddad's already complained about us.'

'I'll take Johnson with me,' says Nelson. 'He can hardly get nasty with a pregnant woman.'

CHAPTER 4

Not far from Norwich (Norwich, Vermont, that is), Nell Blackstock Goodheart is reading a letter headed 'The History Men: Bringing the Past to Life!'. She reads impatiently, getting some of the breakfast preserves on the paper. When she has finished, she calls to her husband, Blake, who is watering the plants on the porch.

'Looks like they definitely want to make a film about Daddy.'

Blake Goodheart appears in the doorway, watering can in hand.

'Who are "they", honey?'

'The TV people. Remember, I told you about them?'

She doesn't show him the letter because she knows that the exclamation mark would cause him actual, physical pain.

Blake puts the watering can on the three-legged stool reserved for that purpose. Then he changes from his porch shoes (subtly different from his yard shoes) into leather slippers. Nell watches him. Forty years of marriage have made her supremely tolerant while never tempting her to join her husband in any of his foibles. She doesn't own a pair of slippers and regularly gardens in her bare feet.

Blake joins his wife at the breakfast table and pours himself coffee.

'Why would a television company want to make a film about Fred?' He has never met his father-in-law, who died when Nell was three, but, along with the rest of the family, he always refers to him with familiarity. Fred's shadow loomed large over Nell's childhood, just as his picture – sombrely handsome in his pilot's uniform – now looms over her night-stand. For over forty years Blake has gone to bed with that tense young face staring at him. It's no wonder that they're on first-name terms.

'Well, you know they found his body in the plane. They've positively identified him as being the pilot.' It will hardly be a body after all these years, she thinks. She doesn't say this aloud though; Blake is squeamish about all aspects of life – and death. 'It seems that they're planning a programme about American airmen in Norfolk.' She pronounces it 'Nor-fork'. 'And they want to include Daddy. Especially as he was born in those parts.'

'But you wouldn't want to get mixed up with something like that,' protests Blake. 'Television.' The couple possess one small set, which is kept in Nell's sewing room and reserved for the exclusive use of their grandchildren. But if Blake had his way, even this one concession to modern life would be banished. There's nothing wrong with playing cribbage in the evenings. Besides, reception is terrible in the Green Mountains.

'It'll be a proper academic programme,' says Nell. 'Frank Barker's presenting it. You know you liked his book about Victorian England.'

Blake grunts non-committally.

'And think how great it would be to see Norfolk and meet my Blackstock relatives. We always said we'd travel when we retired.'

'I haven't completely retired. There are my classes on the American Pastoral, for one thing.'

'I know, but they're evening classes. You could swap with one of the other tutors.'

Blake says nothing and so Nell presses her advantage.

'And we could have a proper funeral for Daddy. That would mean so much to me.'

Blake waves his hand out of the window, at the maple trees flaring against the mountains, at the white clapboard houses scattered at discreet intervals along the loggers' road.

'Why would you want to go to England and miss all this?'

'Oh, the fall.' Nell dismisses Vermont's pride and joy with a shrug. 'It's pretty while it lasts but soon it'll be winter. Snow and cold and not seeing anyone for weeks on end. I bet Norfolk's real temperate. They never have bad weather in England.'

'I don't know about that,' says Blake, but he knows that he's beaten all the same. 'I went to a conference in Cambridge once and there was ice on the inside of the windows.'

*

There's no ice on the roads but it's a grey foggy morning when Nelson and Judy drive out to Blackstock Hall. As they approach the house, the snipe rise out of the grass and zigzag drunkenly overhead. The sheep watch them morosely from their islands, smaller now after the night's rain.

'I wouldn't want to live out here,' says Judy as they park by the gates.

'Get along with you,' says Nelson. 'Cathbad would love it. Lots of sea and sky and miserable-looking sheep. He'd say that the place has good energies.'

Judy looks at him suspiciously. She hates people taking the mickey out of Cathbad but, on the other hand, she can't deny that Nelson is right. Cathbad would love this place.

Nelson, for his part, watches anxiously as Judy heaves herself out of the car and they begin the trek across the field. She's seven months pregnant but she looks more. He wishes she would go on maternity leave and take it easy, but Judy informs him that she wants to work 'right up to the last minute' so that she can make the most of her time after the baby is born. Judy's the wage-earner in the family, with Cathbad relishing the role of full-time father, though he is apparently much in demand as a 'spiritual counsellor' (Nelson doesn't like to think what that entails).

Nelson has rung ahead and courteously requested an interview with George the elder. 'Just a chat really. By all means have your son or daughter-in-law there too.' He can't complain about that, surely?

It seems that George has decided to make it a family affair. Sally meets them at the door and ushers them into the kitchen where both Georges, Old and Young, are sitting at the table by the Aga.

'Do sit down, Inspector Nelson and . . .' Sally looks enquiringly at Judy.

'This is Detective Sergeant Johnson,' says Nelson.

'Well, do sit down, Detective Sergeant Johnson. Goodness me, you look like you could do with a seat. When's the baby due?'

Nelson suppresses a smile. He has already heard Judy complaining about the way that her pregnancy has made her a public object ('Complete strangers patting my stomach. It's outrageous!') but she thanks Sally politely enough and volunteers that the baby is due early in December.

'Shouldn't still be working,' says Old George. 'Should be at home getting the nursery ready.'

'I need the money,' says Judy dourly.

Sally looks at Nelson rather accusingly ('making that poor girl work for a pittance') and offers Judy a cup of tea.

'Just water, please,' says Judy.

'Inspector?'

'Tea would be grand, thanks.' Nelson turns to Old George. He's still a tall man, face shrunken to emphasise a beaky nose and bushy white eyebrows. Nelson thinks that he must be in his late eighties.

'Mr Blackstock,' he says, 'I just wanted to ask you about your brother Frederick. We're trying to get a picture of him at the time of his death and you're really the only person who can help us.'

Old George glares at Nelson across the table. 'Got a letter

– no, not a letter, an *email* – from his daughter today. Eleanor her name is. Calls herself Nell. Nell Blackstock Goodheart. What kind of a name is that?'

'Americans always have lots of names,' says Sally vaguely, arranging cups on the table.

'She wants to come and meet us,' continues the old man. 'Says they're making a film about Fred or some such nonsense. She wants to come over with her husband for a family reunion. That's what she says, "a family reunion".'

'How nice,' says Sally. 'They can have the Blue Room, though it does leak a bit in winter.'

'Have you met Nell before?' asks Judy, managing to sound as if they're personal friends. This is why Nelson has brought her, of course.

'Once,' says Old George. 'She came over with her mother sometime in the sixties. Her mother, Bella her name was, wanted to see Fred's "resting place" as she called it. Look at the sea, I told her. He's under there somewhere. Fish food.'

I'm sure she found that very comforting, thinks Nelson. Young George speaks up suddenly. He looks very like his father, although his hair is grey rather than white and his nose doesn't quite dominate his face yet. It's not hard to see that he must once have been as handsome as Chaz.

'I remember Nelly,' he says now. 'She had lots of long dark hair. She took me for rides in her sports car. She was very glamorous.'

'She must be in her early seventies now,' says Sally.

'About fifteen years older than me,' says George. 'She was born in the war.'

'Tell me about Fred,' says Nelson. 'I understand he emigrated to America before the war.'

He's not sure who he expects to answer but it's Old George who speaks up, his harsh old voice softer now, reminiscent. 'Fred never liked the place,' he says. 'Said it was unhealthy, unlucky. He got that from our mother. She was American, you see. She married m' father when he went to the States before the First World War. She was an heiress, very wealthy, and she used to say that Pa had only married her so he could waste her money on this house. She might have liked Norfolk at first, I don't know, but by the time I was born she was always complaining about it. She was fanciful, you see. She said that nothing good would ever come of living on reclaimed land, land that should, by rights, be at the bottom of the sea. She said that the sea wanted the Blackstock lands back and one day it would come for us all. She used to say that she could hear the sea sprites singing at night. When Fred died, she said that was their revenge.'

Nelson and Judy don't look at each other. Nelson thinks that Old George's mother sounds not so much fanciful as plain mad. It's all bollocks, he tells himself. Besides, the sea sprites got it wrong, Fred hasn't spent all these years at the bottom of the sea. His bones have lain somewhere else entirely. But where?

'When did Fred leave for America?' asks Judy.

'1938,' says Old George with remarkable promptitude. 'I remember Pa saying that war with Germany was coming and he'd done it to get out of fighting. There was a bit of a row about that. But he did fight, didn't he?'

Judy and Nelson agree that he did.

'How old were you when he left?' asks Nelson.

'Twelve,' says George. 'I was born in 1926, the year of the General Strike.'

'Were you sad?' asks Judy. 'Did you miss him?'

For the first time Old George seems at a loss. He looks at his son and daughter-in-law as if expecting them to know the answer.

'Well, naturally,' he says at last, 'if you're used to having someone about, then you do, well, *notice* when they're gone.'

'Did you ever see him again,' asks Judy, 'after 1938?'

'No,' says Old George. 'We knew he'd got married because he told us in a letter but none of us ever saw him again. We didn't even know there was a child until after he was killed. Bella wrote and told my parents.'

'How did you find out that he was killed?' asks Nelson.

'Bella got the telegram,' says George. 'She was next of kin. Ma was upset about that. Bella telephoned to tell us. I remember being excited. People didn't make transatlantic calls in those days.'

Excited, thinks Nelson. Not exactly the usual reaction to news of your older brother's death. But, then again, he knows that the mind is a funny thing and maybe the teenage George's first reaction *was* excitement. Maybe he is just being honest.

'What about your other brother,' says Nelson. 'Lewis, wasn't it? I think you said he was a prisoner of war in Japan?'

'Yes. He was with the Royal Norfolk Regiment. He had a terrible war really. In France and then the Far East. We thought he was dead too for a while. Then we got the news that he was a prisoner of war. Ma was so happy. Later she said it might have been better if he had been killed.'

That's quite some statement, thinks Nelson. He wonders what it was like for the young George, spending the war years with his parents in this lonely house, both brothers presumed dead. Aloud he says, 'He suffered a great deal, you said.'

'He wasn't recognisable when he got home. For a while he didn't seem to recognise us either. Then he went away for treatment, and when he came back he seemed better. Quiet, kept to his room a lot, but basically OK. Then, years later, when I was working in London, he just disappeared.'

Old George blinks once or twice, almost as if, when he opens his eyes, he expects to see his older brother standing there, in front of him.

'Disappeared?' echoes Judy empathetically.

'Yes. He used to like walking across the fields very early with his dog. Then his dog died. Very sad but not unexpected. He was very old. Well, on the morning after Bingo died, Lewis set off for his walk on his own. He never came back.' His voice trails away. Sally leans over to pat the old man's arm. 'It's OK, Dad.' Young George seems lost in a world of his own.

'Do you have any pictures of your brothers?' asks Nelson. Judy shoots him a look, probably thinks he's being a bit insensitive, coming out with it like that, but Old George actually seems pleased by the change of subject.

'Yes, I sorted some out. Where are they, Sally?'

'Here.' Sally crosses over to the dresser and reaches for

a cookery book. 'I put them in here, just to be on the safe side.'

Of course, thinks Nelson, far safer in a Delia Smith book than in a photo album. Still, from what he's seen of the house, he supposes he should be grateful that the photographs have surfaced at all.

Three pictures emerge from Delia's Spanish Pork with Olives. The first shows two young men in cricket whites, arms across each other's shoulders. In front of them, holding a bat, is a boy in shorts and a school cap. George with his older brothers. The second shows one of the young men in khaki, a spaniel at his feet. Nelson assumes that this is Lewis, possibly with Bingo, the dog whose death caused such a violent reaction in its owner.

The third photograph shows a man in an American Air Force uniform. He has a thin moustache and Chaz's gap between his front teeth.

'Bella sent us that one after Fred was killed,' says George. 'Ma used to have it on her bedside table.'

'They were very handsome,' says Judy. 'You look just like them. You both do,' she adds to Young George.

'Thank you,' says the younger man. 'There is a pretty strong family resemblance. Chaz looks just like Dad did when he was younger.'

It is true that, in the pictures, the young men look strikingly alike but the camera was too far away to catch actual features and expressions. You are left with an impression of dark hair and wide grins, a certain swagger and confidence. Black shadows, white sun, no room for the subtleties of technicolour. Only the dog looks as if he has any presentiment of disaster. He squints anxiously at the camera, head on one side as if he alone can hear the sound of gunfire.

'So you never heard what had become of Lewis,' says Nelson, looking at the picture of the man and the dog.

'No,' says Old George. 'Someone saw him down by Devil's Hollow at sunrise but, after that, nothing. No body, nothing. Ma went on hoping for almost ten years but, in the end . . .'

'When did your mother pass away?' asks Nelson. He thinks he has asked it tactfully enough, he hasn't used the D-word at all events, but all three Blackstocks seem uncomfortable. They look at each other. Old George picks up the photographs and shuffles them like playing cards. Sally appears to be having a lengthy unspoken conversation with her husband. Eventually, she says, 'Leonie, George's mother, was very upset. She really . . . well, her mind was disturbed. That's what they said at the inquest.'

'She drowned herself,' says Young George, his voice unnaturally loud. 'At the beach just beyond Devil's Hollow. The sea got her in the end.'

CHAPTER 5

The presence of the TV cameras has ensured quite a crowd at Ruth's Bronze Age dig. As well as Phil and her students, there are also several other people from the university, including the Dean of Humanities and the Press Officer. She can also see Shona, her neighbour Bob Woonunga, and is that . . . ? But the gleam of purple cloak is unmistakable. Cathbad, in full druid's regalia, is making his way over to her, accompanied by another, similarly dressed, man.

'Hail,' says Cathbad, possibly thinking that the occasion calls for more than a simple 'hallo'.

'Yes, er . . . hail,' says Ruth. She actually saw Cathbad only the night before, when she dropped round some of Kate's old baby clothes for Judy, but Cathbad's manner seems to imply that they are meeting after a long and arduous journey.

'This is Hazel,' Cathbad indicates his companion. 'He lives in a yurt near Burnham Market.'

Of course he does. It's unthinkable that any of Cathbad's friends should live in an ordinary house, though he does himself these days.

'Hail,' says Hazel. He's a tall man, probably in his late thirties, with long dark hair in a ponytail.

'Hazel was involved in the campaign against fracking,' says Cathbad.

'I thought the energy company denied that they were ever considering fracking?'

'Of course,' said Cathbad. 'What do you expect them to say?'

There is no answer to this, as is often the case with Cathbad's pronouncements. Hazel smiles at Ruth as if he knows this too.

'I was at the henge dig too,' he says. 'I think I remember you.'

The henge dig. The years roll back in a dizzying swoop and Ruth sees the sea and the sky, hears Erik's voice exclaiming as the first oak post is uncovered. She sees Peter, her ex-boyfriend, Shona and Cathbad and, behind Cathbad, the other druids who had protested when the timbers were removed from the site. Hazel could easily be one of them. Is there something familiar about his face?

'You might remember me by my baptismal name, George Buggins,' Hazel is saying.

Jesus, thinks Ruth, no wonder he chooses to be called Hazel. But she is used to druids and their pseudonyms by now. After all, she has been close friends with Cathbad for a long time.

'I think I remember you,' she says, 'but it was a long time ago.'

'Fifteen years,' says Hazel. 'That's nothing.'

'All time is circular,' says Cathbad. It's another one of those unanswerable remarks, so Ruth doesn't answer it.

'Well, I hope you enjoy the dig today,' she says. 'Are you going to take part in the DNA project?'

'I am,' says Cathbad. 'I'm sure I have ancient druidical blood.'

'I'm not sure it will tell you that,' says Ruth. 'As far as I can tell, they can test your motherline DNA and your fatherline DNA. Then they put your data into a survey of known ancestry. That will show you the population you're closest to genetically. I'm not sure they have a section marked Mad Druid.'

Cathbad laughs but Hazel looks rather shocked. 'Druids are ancient shamans,' he says reprovingly. 'It's one of the oldest known religions.'

As far as Ruth's concerned that's nothing to be proud of. But she doesn't want to get into a row about religion and besides, she has a lot to do. She smiles apologetically, 'Well, do take the test. It's just a quick sample of saliva. If we get enough people, the results should be really interesting.'

'I don't believe in participating in scientific studies,' says Hazel.

'Oh, I don't mind,' says Cathbad, who was, after all, trained as a scientist.

'Well, I hope you do take part,' says Ruth. 'Now, if you'll excuse me, I'd better brief the volunteers.'

Ruth walks over towards the trenches that have been pegged out at intervals around the field. She is very hopeful of finding more burials. There are no obvious earthworks but the presence of Beaker pottery in the ploughed soil suggests that this could be an important Bronze Age site. If one body is buried with grave goods, the chances are that there'll be others. She could be onto something really big here. As she approaches the first trench, though, she sees Phil wearing a high-viz vest and holding forth. She grits her teeth. She must stop Phil taking over. 'Hi, Ruth,' says Phil, flashing his teeth at her. 'Just briefing the volunteers. Don't want anyone throwing away a piece of priceless pottery, do we?'

Ruth is pleased to see that the volunteers, mostly old hands from local archaeology groups, are staring at him stonily.

'I've got a plan here,' she says, addressing the volunteers directly. 'The original burial was found at these coordinates.' She points. 'We've done geophysics on the rest of the field and that seems to indicate the presence of circular features in this area. Dig slowly, log everything. Remember, the field has been heavily ploughed in the past; there could be plenty of material in the topsoil, so the smallest fragment could be significant.'

The diggers get to work deturfing, and Ruth is about to join them when a woman carrying a furry microphone bounds up to her. She's dressed in jeans and a jumper with pandas on it. She looks about twelve.

'Hi, Ruth. I'm Aimiee-Louise Laphan, the presenter of *Archaeology Matters*. We'd like to have an interview with you, if possible. I believe you discovered the body.'

Ruth is aware of a distracting presence at her left elbow, a sort of rustling, hopping motion. After a few moments, she takes pity on it.

'This is Phil Trent, Head of Archaeology at North Norfolk.'

'Phil!' Aimiee-Louise extends a hand and flashes a brilliant smile. 'Great to meet you. I'm just organising an interview with Ruth here. You must be very proud of her.'

'Oh, tremendously,' says Phil. 'Of course it's a team effort really.'

'Of course it is,' says Aimiee-Louise. 'Now if I could just get Ruth on her own. Over here by the trees.'

When the interview is over, Ruth escapes to a trench. She doesn't want to face Phil, who is sure that he should be the one in front of the cameras. Well, she agrees with him in a way. Phil is good-looking and charming; he should be a natural for TV. But, as with *Women Who Kill* two years ago, the director of *Archaeology Matters* seems to prefer Ruth. Maybe it's because she's *not* good-looking and charming. 'A natural,' one reviewer said, 'a straightforward academic.' For 'straightforward', Ruth had thought at the time, read 'not glamorous'. But she had been secretly pleased all the same.

Now she busies herself trowelling and sifting. This is proper archaeology, not the glamorous stuff. Digs can take weeks and there's never any guarantee that anything of significance will be found. These days TV shows want exciting finds in twenty-four hours, preferably accompanied by arc lights. She trowels in a pleasant trance.

'Well, here's the TV star herself hiding in a trench.'

A pair of expensive wellingtons has stopped in front of her. Looking up, she sees skinny jeans, a quilted jacket and a flash of Pre-Raphaelite red hair. Shona.

'Can I help?' Shona is saying.

Ruth's previous experience of Shona on digs tempts her to say no. She knows that Shona's initial keenness will soon wane and that she will gravitate, as if drawn by a siren call, towards the nearest cappuccino. Shona's coffee breaks have been known to take several weeks. Nevertheless she is fond of Shona, who has been her closest friend for many years, so she says, 'Of course,' and moves up.

But before Shona can lower her Hunters into the mud, a voice says, 'Excuse me?'

The voice is male so Shona twirls round on auto-charm.

'I'm from the DNA project,' says the voice. Ruth sees that it belongs to someone wearing trainers and faded jeans. Hunters and trainers move away but Ruth can hear Trainers saying, 'You see, red hair is a recessive gene and I noticed your lovely hair and I thought . . .'

Shona laughs and Ruth can imagine the lovely hair being tossed around. She climbs out of the trench.

'Are you going to do the DNA test?' she says. 'I'll come too. My back's aching.'

'Super,' says the man in trainers, though he doesn't mention Ruth's hair.

The DNA testing of the locals is taking place in a trailer which has been parked at the edge of the field. As they draw nearer, Ruth sees a second vehicle beside it, a dirty white Mercedes. Standing by the car, deep in conversation, are three men: Nelson, Clough and another member of the team, Tim Heathfield. Tim transferred from Blackpool CID two years ago, after working with Nelson on a case involving his old colleagues. He's handsome, intelligent and probably good-natured. All the same, Ruth is wary of him. There is something closed about Tim, something secretive. Ruth is secretive herself so she distrusts it in others.

Shona, on the other hand, seems positively excited. 'Oh, it's Nelson. Wonder why he's here. And who's that with him? The good-looking black guy? He's not your usual Norfolk policeman. Hi, Nelson!'

Nelson looks up and smiles briefly. He's not Shona's biggest fan. But he leaves his two sergeants and comes towards them.

'Hi, Ruth. Hallo, Shona. Ruth, I wanted to catch you.'

'Oh yes?' says Ruth, wishing Shona would leave them alone. She hates herself for wondering whether her hair is a mess. Knowing that she might be on television she had actually put on some make-up that morning but she is pretty sure that it has vanished now (how do women like Shona keep make-up on all day?). Surreptitiously she tries to comb out the worst tangles with her fingers.

Nelson hardly looks at her anyway. He has his police face on, frowning, impatient. 'I wondered if you'd look at some land for us,' he says. 'I want to know if it's possible that a body was buried there.'

'Are we talking about the pilot? I heard about it on *Look East*.'

'Yes,' says Nelson. He gives Shona an irritated look. 'I can't really talk about it here. Can you meet me at Blackstock Hall tomorrow? Ten o'clock.'

It's typical of Nelson that he assumes that Ruth has nothing better to do but it so happens that Ruth is free at that time. 'I may have to juggle things at work,' she says, 'but that should be OK.'

'Nelson,' cuts in Shona, 'are you going to have your DNA tested?'

Nelson looks across at the trailer. 'Is that what all this is about? No thanks.'

'What about you two?' Shona directs her question to Clough and Tim, who have come over to join them. She explains about the DNA project.

'You should do it,' says Clough to Tim. 'You're bound to be local. Just look at you.'

'We're all from Africa originally,' says Tim. 'Isn't that right, Ruth?'

'In essence, yes,' says Ruth.

'Come on then,' says Clough. 'I'm pretty sure I'll turn out to be a Viking warrior or something.'

The two men follow Shona towards the signs saying 'DNA Testing Here'. Ruth looks back at Nelson but he is on his phone, oblivious to everything. It has started to rain. Ruth puts up her hood and heads towards the trailer.

CHAPTER 6

Ruth has seen Blackstock Hall before. There's an oil painting of it in King's Lynn Library and it always features prominently on local postcards. But the painted and the photographic images have nothing on the reality: the grey towers rising up out of the mist, the fields merging into the sky, the eerie silence broken only by the geese calling plaintively from the marshes.

Nelson is already there, leaning against his car. He always manages to make Ruth feel as if she's late.

Ruth parks her Renault next to him, on the grass verge by the gate. After yesterday's rain the ground is waterlogged and boggy. She hopes that she'll be able to get the car out again.

'What do you think?' Nelson gestures towards the house. 'And I thought my place was isolated.'

Nelson laughs. 'That's what Cloughie and I said.'

Ruth is slightly disconcerted to think that she has been the subject of discussion between Nelson and Clough. She always wonders what Nelson's colleagues think of her. Well,

Judy's a friend, but the others – Clough, Tim and Tanya – they're a slightly unknown quantity. The one thing they have in common is a fierce loyalty to Nelson. Do they resent her role in his life? What *is* her role in his life?

If Nelson is indulging in such soul-searching, it doesn't show.

'We're looking for signs that a body's been buried and dug up fairly recently,' he says. 'What are we looking for apart from a bloody big hole?'

'A grave is a footprint of disturbance,' says Ruth. 'The soil will look different, even the colour of it. Sometimes there's a dip because, in time, soil compacts over a decomposing body and falls into the gap when the rib cage collapses. Even the vegetation will grow differently.'

'Decaying bodies are good for the flowers, are they?'

'Decomposition fluids can be toxic to some plants,' says Ruth. 'But some plants, like nettles, flourish.'

'But we're looking for a grave that has been disturbed.'

'We can still see the signs,' says Ruth. 'Places where the earth is looser, less compacted.'

'If we do find the original grave, 'says Nelson, 'will you be able to tell how long ago the body was dug up?'

'It's hard to be sure,' says Ruth. 'We might be able to do carbon dating on any objects found in the grave. The layers around the plane looked as if they'd been disturbed fairly recently. My guess is that the body would have been placed there a few weeks before the digger driver discovered it.'

'Fairly recently, a few weeks,' grumbles Nelson, holding

the gate open and leading the way across the field. 'It's all guesswork with you lot.'

Ruth ignores this. 'Have you told the family what we're doing today?' she asks.

'I've told them that I'm bringing a forensic archaeologist to have a look round,' says Nelson. 'I haven't said that we're looking for a grave site but they must know that's what I'm thinking. They haven't objected though.'

The way he says this makes Ruth think that the family have raised objections before.

'What do they think about the investigation?' she asks, trying to find a pathway between two giant puddles. She is wearing wellingtons but the water looks deep in some places. The last thing she wants is to disappear, like Dawn French in *The Vicar of Dibley*, into a bottomless pit.

'The old dad is a bit suspicious,' says Nelson, striding on ahead, regardless of the mud splattering his trousers. 'The dead pilot was his brother, so I suppose it's natural that he should be upset. The daughter-in-law is pretty vague about the whole thing and the son doesn't say much. The thing is, they all thought Fred died when his plane went down over the sea. It's a bit of a shock to find him in another plane altogether, just a few miles from the family home.'

'Do you really think someone killed him?'

'Come on, Ruth,' says Nelson. 'You told me yourself that he was shot in the head. Then someone wrapped him in a tarpaulin and buried him. Of course he was murdered. The question is, who killed him and where did they bury him?'

No, thinks Ruth, following Nelson as he takes the path to the side of the house. The question is, why did they dig him up again?

In the old aircraft hanger, now a farrowing shed, Chaz Black-stock is looking at his pigs. Usually this gives him great satisfaction, but today even the sight of a Gloucester Old Spot sow in full pig can't lighten his mood. He sighs heavily and his sister, Cassandra, who is standing next to him, asks him what he's thinking about.

'It's just all this business with Grandpa,' he says.

'What business?'

Cassandra has been away, touring in an experimental play about Sylvia Plath, but even so her lack of interest in the family is exasperating sometimes.

'Honestly, Cass. You must have heard about them finding Uncle Fred's body. It's all Mum and Dad can talk about. Did you know the Yanks are making a film about it?'

'Really?' From when she was a child, two words were always guaranteed to bring the stars to Cassandra's eyes – acting and film. See also: theatre, starring, premiere, centre-stage and Oscar.

'Yes. They want the whole drama, hero pilot returned to his family, dotty aristos wandering about, Norfolk in all its glory.'

'Handsome pig farmer grandson, gorgeous actress granddaughter.'

Chaz looks at his sister. She is one of the few people who can use the word 'gorgeous' about themselves and get away with it. Because, even in jeans and an old Barbour with her hair pulled back in a ponytail, she is effortlessly, film-star gorgeous.

'Are you imagining yourself in the starring role?' he asks.

Cassandra laughs but doesn't deny it. Chaz reflects, without rancour, that his sister usually takes the starring role in any given situation. He doesn't mind it; he's always preferred to stay in the background. Even today, in the bosky gloom of the shed, she looks like an actress ready to play the main part in some pastoral melodrama. There is something grand about Cass, something operatic that is quite out of tune with her surroundings.

'The thing is,' he says, with his eyes on the pig (she is operatic too, in her way), 'I'm worried about Grandpa. What if he has one of his turns?'

Cassandra turns to look at him. 'But he's been OK for years.'

'I know. But what if this sets him off again? Mum said that he was really bad after his oldest brother disappeared. This might bring it all back.'

'Mum doesn't know. She wasn't even around when Uncle Lewis went missing. She just makes these things up.'

Chaz knows that Cassandra is touchy when it comes to their mother but this strikes him as unfair. 'I don't think she makes things up. Grandpa must have told her. He talks to her more than he talks to Dad.'

Cassandra looks mutinous. 'There's no reason to think Grandpa will get sick again. He hasn't so far, has he?'

'Mum said he didn't like the policemen coming to the house.'

'Oh, that's just him doing his lord of the manor bit.'

'And he's furious about this American film. Says he doesn't even want to meet Fred's daughter.'

'He had a daughter? How old is she?'

'Older than Dad. He said she was really dishy when she was young. She came over in the sixties, with a miniskirt and an open-top car. I think Dad was quite smitten.'

Cassandra laughs. 'God, I hope she's not still wearing miniskirts. We want to come over well in the film, after all.'

'I'm sure *you* will,' says Chaz. And he means it.

At the back of Blackstock Hall, the land falls gently away towards the sea. The main entrance to the house is obviously here because a proper tarmacked drive leads up to the back door, which is the stable type with the top part open. There's a kitchen garden too, with raised beds and a small greenhouse. Everything looks pretty wild and gone to seed but, Ruth reflects, that probably because it's autumn. She's hardly an expert on gardening. As they walk past the rows of giant cabbages (who knew they grew so big?), Ruth casts an eye over the soil. It has been turned fairly recently, no doubt about that, but isn't that what you would expect in a garden? Then again, Ruth once found a body buried in a vegetable patch. She stops and looks at the earth. The topsoil seems to be mostly clay, clumpy and wet after the rain, but underneath there's some chalk – she can see white flakes in the compost heap. A skeleton might be well preserved in this environment, if it wasn't buried too deeply.

'What are you doing, Ruth?' calls Nelson from the gate. 'Planning on making cabbage soup?'

'I'm analysing the soil,' says Ruth with dignity. She spent several weeks on the cabbage soup diet. Never again.

Through the gate there are a few stunted apple trees, bent almost double by the wind. But to their right is something that makes Ruth and Nelson look at each other. It's a large stone cross, not visible from the house because it is situated in a slight dip. As they approach, they see that there are other crosses and headstones lower down the slope. The stone is almost the same colour as the grass, which makes the markers look as if they have grown there, strange hunched trees perhaps, or distorted rock formations.

Nelson has reached the biggest cross. Because of its position it seems to loom unnaturally large against the sky, like one of those optical illusion pictures beloved of tourists, where a person can hold up the Tower of Pisa. But here the effect is sinister, the massive crucifix seeming to overshadow Nelson, stretching its arms towards him. It's all Ruth can do not to call out.

'Admiral Nathaniel Blackstock, 1789–1850,' Nelson is reading. 'Safe in harbour. Looks like we've stumbled on the family graveyard.'

Ruth brushes lichen away from one of the smaller crosses. 'Ralph Blackstock, RIP. Also his beloved wife. I see she doesn't even get a namecheck.'

'There don't seem to be any new graves,' says Nelson. 'It's probably not consecrated any more.'

'And no signs of recent digging,' says Ruth, looking around

her. In fact the slope, with its grey shapes rising up out of the grass, looks like it hasn't been visited for centuries. She doesn't think she has ever seen a lonelier place.

Nelson is evidently thinking the same thing. 'I wouldn't like to be buried here,' he says. 'It's miles from anywhere.'

'What do you need near you when you're dead?' says Ruth. 'It's not as if you're going to be popping to the corner shop for milk.'

'You know what I mean,' says Nelson. 'It's bloody bleak.'

In fact the view is stunning. Beyond them lie the marshes, miles of flat grey grassland, interspersed with glimmering streams. In the distance is the sea, a line of darker grey against the sky. As they watch, a flock of geese fly overhead in a perfect v-shape.

'Of course, all this would have been under the sea once,' says Ruth. 'You can tell by the chalk.'

'What do you mean?' asks Nelson.

'Chalk is formed by marine deposits. All landscapes with chalky soil were under the sea once.' She stops because Nelson is looking at her oddly. 'What's the matter? I'm talking about millions of years ago.'

Nelson shakes his head. 'It's nothing. I'm just thinking about something Old George said. He's the granddad. He said that his mother hated this place because she thought nothing good would ever come of living on land that should really be at the bottom of the sea. She used to say that the sea wanted the land back.'

Ruth looks out over the grey-green landscape. It might just be her imagination but she thinks that she can hear the sea.

It has a roaring, urgent sound. She imagines the waves swallowing up the marshes and the grazing land, rising higher and higher until they cover the stone crosses and the garden wall and finally the house itself.

'She thought she could hear sea sprites singing at night,' says Nelson.

Ruth looks at him out of the corner of her eye. She is relieved to see that he's smiling.

'We must introduce her to Cathbad.'

'She died years ago,' says Nelson with an involuntary glance at the looming graves. 'Come on, let's go round the other side of the house.'

The inland side of the house boasts a barn, some outhouses – all derelict, a tree with a rope swing and an area fenced off by a low iron railing. Nelson hurdles this and, with rather more difficulty, Ruth follows. She sees immediately that they are in another graveyard, only this time the stones are small and regular in size.

She squats down to read the engraved letters. 'Blue, beloved friend. Rosie, never forgotten. Patch, faithful companion.'

She looks up at Nelson. 'It's a pet's burial ground.' She feels her eyes filling with tears. She can't bear to think what will happen when Flint dies.

'Jesus,' says Nelson. 'More money than sense, these people.'

Ruth turns away to avoid one of Nelson's lectures on profligate people (usually southerners) who spend money on their pets while there are children starving. As she does so, she notices something.

'Nelson. Look over there.'

One corner of the graveyard is undulating like a bedspread with a sleeping body underneath. The soil has been disturbed and the turf is bare in places.

'Something's been dug up here,' she says.

'Either that,' says Nelson, 'or they've just buried a bloody big dog.'

CHAPTER 7

'No,' says Sally Blackstock, 'we haven't buried any pets there since Rooster died. That was when the children were young.'

'Haven't you got a dog now?' asks Nelson. He has a vague memory of seeing a lead somewhere. Oh yes, it was on one of those scruffy armchairs in the kitchen. He had sat on it.

'No,' says Sally. 'Dear old Beau died in the summer.'

That figures. Nelson doesn't imagine Sally tidies up very often.

'What did you do with Beau's . . . er . . . remains?' he asks.

'Oh, the vet cremates them now,' says Sally. 'It's easier all round.'

They are standing in the kitchen garden. When Ruth and Nelson had walked back to the house, they had found Sally there, holding a large cabbage and looking thoughtful. Nelson had introduced Ruth and asked about the pets' burial ground, explaining that Dr Galloway thought there was evidence of recent 'digging activity'.

Now Sally points the cabbage's muddy roots at Ruth. 'I

know you, don't I? Weren't you on telly? Doing that show about Mother Hook.'

'Yes,' says Ruth, aware of Nelson's sardonic expression, 'I was on that programme.'

'It was with that dishy American, Frank Barker. George and I are big fans of his. Is he nice in real life?'

'Yes,' says Ruth. 'Very nice.'

'Leaving the dishy Frank Barker aside,' says Nelson, 'do you know of any reason why anyone may have been digging in the pets' burial ground?'

'No,' says Sally. 'It's a mystery, isn't it?'

'It's a mystery all right,' says Nelson as they make their way back over the field. 'The mystery is how that family keeps going. They're all living on a different planet.'

'What about Sally's children?' asks Ruth, stepping sideways to avoid a sheep. 'What are they like?'

'Son's a pig farmer. His farm's on the site of the old airfield. He seems OK. Bit of an upper-class boy playing at working, but OK.'

'Like Marie Antoinette.'

'If you say so. I haven't met the daughter. Apparently she's an actress.'

'Do you really think someone from the family dug up Fred's body? What was it doing in the pets' burial ground in the first place?'

'We've got to find out if it was Fred's body that was buried there. Will your excavation do that?'

'Maybe,' says Ruth cautiously. 'We can take soil samples.

Find out if there's any human matter there. And there may well be something in the context. Scraps of uniform, hair, that sort of thing.'

'You really think there'll be something left behind?'

'There's always something left behind,' says Ruth.

They have reached the cars. The rain has started again, a thin drizzle that you don't notice until your hair is completely wet. Ruth looks at Nelson and sees that he has raindrops on his eyelashes. She looks away again.

'Sally didn't seem to mind the idea of an excavation on her land, did she?' says Nelson.

'No, she seemed quite excited about it.'

'That's because she thought your American friend might turn up.'

'He's not . . .' begins Ruth. But Nelson has already got into his car and is backing out with a squeal of tyres and a fine spray of mud. He winds down his window.

'I'll wait until you've got your car out.'

'I'll be OK,' says Ruth. 'Don't worry.'

She half expects him to argue or to make some comment about the car's decrepitude. But instead he raises his hand in mock salute and he's gone, driving far too fast in the middle of the road. He has always been terrible at saying goodbye.

Nelson's car is nowhere in sight by the time that Ruth reaches the roundabout and the turn-off to the university. He is probably halfway back to the station, getting ready to hassle the team about drug dealers from the Far East and teenage hooligans in the marketplace. She is aware that the case of long-dead Frederick Blackstock is not exactly top of his agenda. But something happened on the lonely marshland where the sea comes whispering in over the flat fields. Someone has been digging there fairly recently and someone undoubtedly placed Frederick's skeleton in the cockpit of the abandoned plane, ready to grin up at Ruth as she brushed the soil away.

Nelson obviously thinks that the Blackstocks are hiding something. He once told Ruth that he could smell murder and, though she had laughed at the time, she thinks that she knows what he means. Even when she is excavating the remains of people who died thousands of years ago, she thinks that she can tell when death had been from unnatural causes. A grave is a footprint of disturbance, that's what she told Nelson, and she thinks that the disturbance stays in the air – and in the land – for a very long time.

Why did Nelson drive off so suddenly? Was it the mention of Frank Barker? She doesn't flatter herself that Nelson is jealous of Frank. Why should he be jealous when he's married to the beautiful Michelle? Any jealousy in their relationship, she thinks wryly, is all one-way. It's probably more that Frank represents everything Nelson despises. He's an academic who's on television. A good-looking American academic who presents history programmes on television. Ruth can't think of anybody more likely to ignite Nelson's famous short fuse.

Well, Nelson needn't worry. She hasn't heard from Frank since the email ten days ago. As she parks in her slot outside the Natural Sciences building, she thinks that she will bury herself in her work and forget about dead pilots, American TV – and Frank. It's a busy term and she has plenty to occupy herself. As well as the coursework, there's the Bronze Age dig and the DNA project. As Phil would say, UNN is finally making its mark in the world.

When she gets to her office and types in her password, she sees that an email has been sent to her university address. It's from someone called Earl Kennedy, who turns out to be the executive producer of *The History Men: Bringing the Past to Life!*. Earl will be in Norfolk next week for a preliminary meeting to discuss the programme about American airmen. He would be honoured if Ruth could join them with a view to contributing her ideas and possibly appearing on the programme. It'll be a small meeting, he says. Just himself, the director and the presenter, Frank Barker. Has Ruth possibly come across Frank before?

Ruth sits at her desk staring at her poster of Indiana Jones. Harrison Ford stares back as if he understands.

Nelson drives back to the police station in a bad mood, though he couldn't have said why. He'd enjoyed the time with Ruth; he likes watching her work and admires her expertise. It had been – what's the word? – companionable, standing with her looking out over the marshes. There's never any subtext with Ruth, none of the flirting and game-playing that Michelle and even his daughters go in for. She just talks to you and he likes that. So why is he now storming through the briefing room looking for someone to argue with? Maybe it's the Blackstocks. They annoy him – the charming Sally and the ineffectual George, not to mention the dotty granddad. Why wasn't Sally more worried about the discovery in the pets' burial ground? It's as if the whole thing is a game to her. Where's Uncle Fred? Is he in the sea, in the garden or in a plane in Devil's Hollow? Well, this isn't *Where's Wally?*, he tells her in his head, it's a murder investigation.

Except it isn't, not really. He's aware that Whitcliffe doesn't want him to spend any more money on a cold case. If it weren't for the American Government, they would never have identified the body in the first place. Unless Ruth uncovers some really compelling forensic evidence, the investigation will stay where it is, stalled, stuck – as Cathbad sometimes says about the marshes – between life and death.

He's thwarted in his attempt to find someone to bully. Judy and Clough are out on a case and everybody else seems to be at lunch. Tara, his PA, is eating sandwiches at her desk and the desk sergeant is having a long telephone conversation about a missing dog. In the incident room, though, he finds Tim packing his gym bag.

'Going out?'

Tim looks defensive. 'No, I'm going to the gym after work. I've just bought some shampoo.' He waves the bottle in front of Nelson.

Tim's always at the gym. It's good for a policeman to be fit but there's something obsessive about Tim's exercising. He eats healthily too, salads instead of sandwiches and bottled water instead of coke. And the shampoo is one of those poncy brands that includes conditioner. It all makes Nelson a bit suspicious of his sergeant. Maybe he should try to get to know him better.

'Are you settling in OK in Norfolk?' he says. 'Bit different from dear old Blackpool.'

Tim looks surprised. 'I've been here two years.'

'Got yourself a girlfriend yet?'

Tim turns back to his gym bag. 'No.'

This is obviously a touchy subject. Better stick to work. 'I've just been to Blackstock Hall,' he says. 'Ruth Galloway was looking to see if our pilot could have been buried there.'

'Really? Did she find anything?'

'She thinks there's a distinct possibility that he was buried in the pets' graveyard.'

'They've got a special graveyard for pets?'

'It's the sort of thing the upper classes do. They like their pets more than their children.'

'Can Ruth be sure?'

'She's going to do an excavation, run some more tests.'

'What do the family say?'

'The old man's a bit hostile but his daughter-in-law treats it like one big garden party. She was almost hanging out the bunting for the excavation.'

'Sounds like fun.'

'I might send you along,' says Nelson. 'See what you get out of them. Sally, the daughter, might take to you.'

'Why?'

'You're young,' says Nelson gloomily. 'Mind you, she was drooling over that history bloke, Frank Barker, and he's ancient.'

'I haven't met Frank Barker.'

'You haven't missed much.'

'I'd like to work with Ruth though,' says Tim. 'You and she go back a long way, don't you?'

Now it's Nelson's turn to look away. 'She's all right. Or she was until she became a TV star. Now let's get back to work.'

CHAPTER 8

The meeting is at the Le Strange Arms in Hunstanton. It's a large comfortable hotel, popular for parties and wedding receptions. At the end of the car park there's a wooden fence and a grassy dune and then you're on the beach, miles of sand and sea and cloud. Ruth parks her car as near to the edge as she can and breathes in the salty air. It's a calm, still day but there's a feeling of expectancy in the air. According to the weather forecast, storms are due at the end of the month. Ruth remembers the strange sensation she had, standing by the family graves at Blackstock Hall, the feeling that the sea was just waiting for its chance to reclaim the land. The tide is out today, the sands are shimmering with secret pools, but Ruth knows that it is out there, a great, surging mass of water, ready to roll in and swallow anything in its path. The tide comes in faster than a galloping horse, Erik used to say, and look at all the myths linking horses and the sea. Kelpies and hippocamps and white manes in the waves. Ruth shakes herself and turns towards the comforting bulk of the hotel. Now is not the time to be thinking of Erik.

The receptionist tells her that the meeting is in the Oak Room but, before he can direct her there, Ruth dives into the ladies to repair her hair and face. She still hasn't heard from Frank but Earl did say that he'd be at the meeting. She has put on some make-up but when she looks in the mirror, she sees that the lipstick has completely worn off and there's a streak of mascara on her cheek. She wipes this off with a paper towel and applies more lipstick, a shade called Morning Coffee, given to her by Shona. Is it a good thing to have lips that look like coffee? At least it's not too bright. Her face looks very pale, almost green, but maybe that's the lighting. She pulls a comb through her hair and smiles at herself encouragingly. Frank once said that he preferred women to look natural but, in Ruth's experience, that's what they say before they run off with an exquisitely made-up bottle blonde.

Ruth steps back into the lobby. The polite receptionist tells her the way to the Oak Room and there's no more excuse to delay. Should she knock? No, she's an invited guest, the archaeology expert. Ruth squares her shoulders and pushes open the door.

He's there. He stands up when she enters and she remembers that this was one of the things she liked about him, an old-school courtesy that seems very American somehow.

'Ruth,' he says with a smile. He comes round the table and kisses her on the cheek. She can smell his aftershave. Is it worn in her honour? She knows that she is blushing.

There are two other men in the room, and one comes forward with his hand outstretched.

'Earl Kennedy,' he says. 'Happy to meet you.'

Earl Kennedy is a small man, brown and shiny like a nut. Ruth finds herself slightly bending her knees in an attempt to appear smaller.

'Let me introduce our director, Paul Brindisi.'

'Yes,' says Ruth. She holds out her hand to Paul Brindisi, who is dark and intense-looking. 'Hi, I'm Ruth Galloway.'

'Ruth was terrific in *Women Who Kill*,' says Earl. 'Really natural and down-to-earth.' Earl gestures for Ruth to sit on his right, opposite Frank. 'We've got coffee, tea, juice. What will you have?'

'Coffee would be great, thanks.'

Paul pours coffee from the jug on the table, from which Ruth deduces that director ranks lower than producer.

'We're really excited about this programme, Ruth,' says Earl, fixing Ruth with his bright black eyes. 'Shall I fill you in?'

'Yes please.'

'Essentially *The History Men* is about presenting the human side of recent historical events. We've done the *Titanic*, the story of Italian immigrants – focusing on Paul's actual ancestors – the Depression and the Gold Rush. Now we want to focus on World War Two and it seems to me that this dead pilot, Fred Blackstock, is our ideal way in. He was a Brit who chose a new life in the US and then died a few miles from his ancestral home here in Norfolk. How's that for irony? We've contacted Fred's family in the US. His daughter, Nell, is a real sweetheart. She's keen to come over here and trace her dad's past. Kind of a family reunion with some history thrown in. Whaddya think?'

Ruth feels rather dazed by this account. Her first thought is that the discovery of Fred's body was not only ironical but mysterious, sinister even. But she realises that Earl doesn't understand all the implications of Fred's body turning up in the wrong plane.

'Have you spoken to the British side of the family?' she asks.

Earl's eager expression doesn't falter but Paul and Frank exchange glances.

'Sure, sure,' says Earl. 'Seems that Fred's brother is still alive. Old George his name is. How about that?'

'And are they prepared to take part in the programme?'

'We're in negotiations,' says Earl. 'The old guy is a bit uneasy but the daughter-in-law thinks she can talk him round. After all, it's an emotional time for the family. But you know what? Often these programmes can be real cathartic. They can bring healing. We've got therapists on hand if anyone wants to talk. Sometimes things come to the surface that have been buried for years.'

'The thing is,' says Ruth, 'there may be a bit more to it than that.'

'Whaddya mean?'

'I excavated the body from the plane found in the field and I think it had been put there fairly recently.'

'How can that be, Ruth?' says Earl. 'I understood the plane was buried in a chalk pit.'

'It was,' says Ruth, 'and chalk preserves bone but it destroys flesh. The body in the plane still had flesh on it, leathery brown flesh typical of bodies found in marshy soil. That's why I was pretty sure that it hadn't been sitting in the plane for seventy years. Besides, records show that the pilot's body was thrown clear and found in a nearby field. Fred Blackstock was meant to be in another plane altogether. A plane that had been shot down over the North Sea a week earlier.'

Earl and Paul exchange glances again.

'So you're saying that Fred Blackstock was in another plane?'

'Yes.'

'A plane we haven't got?'

'Yes.'

Earl spreads out his hands. 'The thing is, Ruth, this is a story about a family. A family who have been through the horrors of war. A family reunited, a family reconnected, a family . . .'

Regurgitated? thinks Ruth. Aloud she says, 'So you don't want me to say that the body was in the wrong plane?'

'On balance,' says Earl, 'no.'

'What do you want me to say?'

'You excavated the body,' says Earl. 'You can tell us exactly how it felt. And you can talk us through the DNA tests, stuff like that. Frank here will do the war background but you can be the white coat. Besides, it'll be good to have a British voice. Hasn't she got a cool accent, guys?'

Frank and Paul agree that Ruth's accent is very cool. Ruth, who has never thought of her voice (basic South London overlaid with university lecturer) as anything other than boring, says, 'Have you talked to the police? It's an ongoing investigation.'

She thinks that Frank is looking at her. She has never discussed Nelson with Frank but she's pretty sure that he's got some questions about their relationship.

'Sure,' says Earl. 'I've talked to a guy named Gerry Whitcliffe. He's happy that the programme happens as long as we don't step on any toes. I mean, it's a cold case, right? It's not likely that the police will find anything. Our programme will centre on the human interest. What does Nell feel, seeing her dad's childhood home and the planes he flew? How does she feel meeting her British family after all these years? We'll look at some of the old airfields. Frank says there are dozens round here. What are they called again, Frank?'

'The ghost fields,' says Frank. 'In 1942, a new airfield was built every three days.'

'Isn't that great?' says Earl. 'The ghost fields. That might even be the title of this episode. And there are still watch towers and mess houses standing in the fields, some of them with really cool graffiti – American flags and love hearts and dancing girls. That's our story. These boys, far away from home in the middle of the English countryside, ready to go out and die for our freedom. That's the real story here.'

'There were decoy sites too,' says Frank. 'Fake aerodromes built to confuse the Germans and divert attention from the real thing. They're called the shadow fields.'

'The shadow fields,' repeats Earl happily. 'Isn't that priceless?'

Ruth looks at Frank, who smiles back rather ruefully. She doesn't know about him but she felt a shiver run down her back at the name. Ghosts and shadows. She doesn't think that Earl's programme will be quite the heart-warming love-fest he envisages.

'And Frank says that the land where the plane was found has a real interesting history,' Earl continues. 'Something about the Bronze Age?'

'Ruth's the expert on all that,' says Frank quickly.

'There's some evidence that there may have been a Bronze Age burial site nearby,' says Ruth. 'So far one body has been found but I'm supervising a dig to see if we can find any others.'

Earl leans back in his chair. 'How about that? A Bronze Age body? Can this picture get any better?'

'The field's known locally as Devil's Hollow,' offers Ruth.

She thinks that Earl might be about to explode with happiness.

'A television programme? Are you mad?'

'Really, Harry.' Whitcliffe shifts irritably in his chair. 'There's no need for that sort of reaction.'

'Sorry,' says Nelson, not sounding it. 'But this is an ongoing police investigation. We can't have a film crew flat-footing around, getting in the way.'

At the words 'film crew', Whitcliffe raises a hand to flick his hair into place. Nelson watches him dourly. His boss is younger than him, but not by much. But where Nelson's dark hair is greying at the temples, Whitcliffe's is a uniform rich brown. Rumour has it that it's dyed but Nelson's hardly an expert on these things. 'He's had Botox too,' says Tanya, a DC on Nelson's team. 'You can tell when he smiles.' But

Whitcliffe rarely smiles at Nelson, so this too he has to take on trust.

'They're hardly going to get in your way, Harry,' says Whitcliffe. 'As I understand it, the programme will be concentrating on the family of the dead pilot, not on DNA tests and suchlike.'

There are many things Nelson could say to this. He could say that the family of the dead pilot are the main suspects for his murder. He could say that DNA tests and suchlike are a staple of modern police work. He could say that while Whitcliffe will doubtless be prancing around in front of the cameras talking about his 'mission to protect', he, Nelson, will be hard at work behind the scenes solving crimes.

What he actually says is: 'Will Ruth Galloway be involved?'

'Ruth who? Oh, the forensic archaeology girl. I don't know. Apparently the programme's going to be fronted by some American historian.'

'Frank Barker,' says Nelson.

'Yes. I think that was the name. Are you getting interested in history in your old age, Harry?'

'No,' says Nelson.

'Well,' Whitcliffe smoothes his hair again, 'I don't think you need to worry too much about the TV people. Apparently they do want to film the funeral service though. Do you know when that is?'

'At the end of the month, according to Sally Blackstock.' Rather to Nelson's surprise, Sally had rung him with this information. She also told him that she is planning a little party after the event 'to showcase our new B & B facilities as much as anything'. Nelson seriously doubts that Blackstock Hall will ever be in a state to be showcased as anything other than a crumbling ruin but he had kept his counsel. Wisely, as it turns out. 'We hope you'll be able to come, Detective Chief Inspector,' Sally had said. 'And your charming archaeologist friend. Ruth, wasn't it?'

He contemplates mentioning the party now to watch Whitcliffe angle for an invitation, but that pleasure will have to wait.

'I'm planning an excavation at Blackstock Hall next week,' he says. 'Do you think your TV friends will want to film it?'

'I wouldn't think so,' says Whitcliffe. 'Excavations are always so muddy, aren't they?'

By the time that Earl has outlined his plans for the programme he now definitely calls 'The Ghost Fields' Ruth feels that she has lost the will to live. It's not that Earl's synopsis is bad; she can imagine that people would be interested in the story of Nell Blackstock's homecoming, her reunion with her British family and her voyage of discovery into her father's war years. 'Lots of shots of the empty airfields,' enthuses Earl, 'the wind blowing and maybe some ghostly effects, planes taking off on deserted runways, that sort of thing.' It's more that Ruth can't quite see where she comes in. Earl doesn't seem remotely interested in how Fred's body came to be in the wrong plane or in Ruth's explanations about chalk versus clay burials. He is vaguely interested in the forensic analysis but only in so far as it proves that the dead man was a member of the Blackstock family. 'Genuine British aristocrats,' says Earl happily. 'Pity they haven't got a title though.'

What does Frank think about it all? It's hard to tell, even though Ruth keeps sneaking glances at him. He listens politely to Earl's story outlines, occasionally offering a word or two of historical context. Sometimes Ruth thinks that he's smiling to himself rather sardonically and once he looks directly at her and grins, a 'can you believe this bunch?' grin, but then his face is blank once more and he nods solemnly as Earl tells him that he wants to create a 'real Battle of Britain vibe'.

Where is Frank staying? Ruth knows that he has a flat in Cambridge, where he once studied, but she thinks he mentioned that it was let out to tenants. Maybe he's staying in Norwich, or even King's Lynn? She hopes that they will get a chance to talk after this interminable meeting. Maybe they can go and have a cup of tea somewhere, or even an early lunch. She remembers the first time she met Frank – after he crashed his car into hers – having lunch at a lopsided pub in the centre of Norwich, feeling as if they had known each other for ever. She realises that Frank is standing up.

'So sorry,' he says to the room at large, 'but I've got an appointment. I'll catch up with you all later.'

He walks round the table and stops by Ruth's chair. 'Good to see you again, Ruth,' he says softly.

Ruth doesn't know what she replies. Inside she is screaming, 'Where are you going?' She had been so sure that, after the formal meeting was over, she and Frank could go somewhere and . . . well, take up where they left off two years ago.

Earl too is looking after Frank with a slightly disgruntled expression.

'Where's he off to in such a hurry?' he says.

'Who knows with Frank?' They are almost the first words Ruth has heard Paul say. He has an accent that she recognises from films as old-school New York.

'Of course,' says Earl. 'You know him pretty well.'

'Should do,' says Paul. 'Seeing as he's dating my kid sister.'

CHAPTER 9

Ruth drives away feeling angry with Frank, Earl, Paul, Paul's kid sister and, most of all, herself. How could she have assumed that he was still interested in her? After all, she hasn't heard from him in more than a year. Surely that should have told her something. What's the usual reason for a man not being in contact? Because they've met someone else, of course. Paul's 'kid sister'. Just how young is this woman anyway? Twenty-five? Twenty? Eighteen? Frank is over fifty and has three grown-up children. If he's going out with an eighteen-year-old, then Ruth really is better off without him.

She'd wanted to ask more (Gloria her name is. Gloria!) but she'd also wanted to get away from the Le Strange Arms as fast as humanly possible. So she'd thanked Earl for a very interesting meeting, promised to stay in touch and headed off to the car park, where the sea had almost reached the sand dunes. Frank was nowhere in sight. Where did he have to go in such a hurry? To meet Gloria and go for a romantic walk on the beach? To head back to their hotel and enjoy the crisp white sheets and room-service lunch? It's not as if Ruth was planning to go to bed with Frank herself but – grinding gears – it would have been nice to have the option.

With this in mind, Ruth has cleared the whole day. Sandra, Ruth's childminder, will collect Kate from school and Ruth has arranged to pick her up at Sandra's at five. She could go back to the university and catch up on some marking but, instead, she takes the turning for the Saltmarsh. The thought of a rare few hours alone in her house is enough to make her momentarily forget Frank, Gloria, room service, everything.

She's angry because this is unlike her. It's not in Ruth's nature to imagine that men are interested in her. She's more likely to make the opposite mistake, and there are a few missed opportunities that still torment her (Dan on the number 68 bus, Erik during the henge dig). But Frank really did seem to like her, especially in the beginning. She remembers the way he had looked at her, his blue eyes crinkling at the corners, smiling in that special way that seemed to imply that he, alone of all the company, really understood her. Well, maybe he smiles that way at all the girls. More gear grinding as Ruth turns onto the raised road that leads to her cottage.

The tide is in and Ruth never ceases to be surprised at the way that land suddenly becomes sea, dry patches of sand and grass becoming cool blue lagoons, the desert transformed into the ocean. In fact tides are particularly high this autumn and Ruth is sure that the water is nearer her front door than ever. Perhaps she ought to get some sandbags in, just in case.

There is something else at her front door, a man leaning on the fence looking out over the sand dunes and the incoming tide. For one crazy moment Ruth thinks it's Frank (so *that's* why he left early), but then she sees that the man is darker than Frank and slimmer. When he turns, a characteristic sweeping motion even without his cloak, she recognises him as Cathbad.

Ruth parks her car and gets out. She's pleased to see Cathbad, even if this means that she'll miss her precious hours of solitude. Hang on, though. Does this visit mean . . .

'Judy . . . ?' she asks.

'It's OK.' Cathbad grins. 'She hasn't had the baby yet. I just came round for a chat. I haven't seen you since the dig.'

Ruth doesn't ask how he knew she'd be home early. Cathbad just knows these things. She gets her bag out of the car and fumbles for her key. 'When's the due date again?' she asks.

'Early December but I think she's going to be late.'

'She?'

'I'm pretty sure this one's a girl. Anyway, I don't like the impersonal pronoun.'

'Did the scan show anything?' Ruth has never forgotten the moment when she learnt that she was expecting a girl. That sudden rush of recognition. The feeling of carrying a real person inside you.

'No,' says Cathbad. 'But if you combine Judy's age with

the number of the month when the baby was conceived, the resulting number is even.'

Ruth knows better than to challenge the absolute scientific veracity of this. She opens the door, thinking that a cup of tea with Cathbad is always good value – even if it isn't an intimate rendezvous with Frank.

Flint, Ruth's cat, is standing at the top of the stairs looking accusing. He wasn't expecting her back until six (Ruth always tells him the exact time) but he manages to convey the impression that she is late and he is starving.

'Hallo, Flint,' says Cathbad, who believes that he has a psychic connection with the cat. 'How are you?'

'What would you do if he answered you?' says Ruth.

'He is answering me,' says Cathbad. Flint is certainly communicating something, rubbing himself around Cathbad's legs and purring loudly. Ruth tries not to think that they're talking about her.

'Where's Thing?' she asks. Cathbad is the owner of a mad but extremely friendly bull terrier. Not that he would put it like that, of course. 'We can't own our fellow creatures,' he once said as Thing dragged him along the beach, 'we're just permitted to share their space.'

'With Judy. She's off work today.'

'How's she feeling? You get so tired in the last few months. And she's got Michael to look after.' Michael, Judy's son, is three. He has two fathers: Cathbad, his biological father, and Darren, Judy's ex-husband.

'She is tired, of course,' says Cathbad. 'I make her infusions every night and I burn ginger roots to prevent sickness. Michael's no trouble. He's an old soul.'

Ruth smiles. She is very fond of Michael. 'Is he excited about the new baby? I'm envious. Kate would love a brother or sister.'

'She can share this baby,' says Cathbad. 'Families are just modern constructs, after all. We're all children of the Great Creator.'

Ruth, who knows just how far Cathbad has gone to secure his own bourgeois family unit, says thank you very much. Then she goes into the kitchen to make the tea. Flint follows anxiously.

When Ruth comes back into the sitting room, Cathbad is standing by the bookcase examining a paperback copy of Ruth's book, *The Tomb of the Raven King*.

'I enjoyed this,' he says. 'Is there going to be a sequel?'

'I've got a contract for another one,' says Ruth, 'but I haven't started it yet.' This is one of her favourite worries when she wakes in the middle of the night. Her editor, Javier, has requested a synopsis by the end of October. The problem is that Ruth can't think what to write about. *The Tomb of the Raven King* had a real story and – rare for archaeology – a proper ending. Where can she find another buried king? If only she'd been one of the team who discovered Richard III's body under a car park in Leicester.

'Why not write about the dead pilot?' says Cathbad, when she confides this dilemma.

'I don't know,' said Ruth, thinking of Blackstock Hall and

the family graves, the mist floating in from the sea. 'It's all a bit complicated.'

'Hazel says that the land is cursed,' says Cathbad as if he is relaying the weather forecast. 'Devil's Hollow and the land around Blackstock Hall.'

'Did he say why?' asks Ruth, offering Cathbad a biscuit and taking one herself.

'Legend has it that the Devil was building a dam at Old Hunstanton,' says Cathbad. 'He took the soil from Devil's Hollow, hence the name.'

'Why does the Devil always do that?' says Ruth. 'He's a shockingly bad digger. I wouldn't have him on one of my excavations.'

Cathbad smiles. 'There's a bad history about the place. Bloodshed, evil deeds. There was a massacre there in the Civil War. You said yourself that there may be a Bronze Age burial ground.'

'Burial grounds aren't necessarily bad places,' says Ruth. 'I would have thought that a druid would like them – life and death, portals to the afterlife and all that.'

Cathbad acknowledges this with another smile. 'All the same,' he says, 'Devil's Hollow didn't bring your pilot much luck, did it?'

'It's stranger than you think,' says Ruth. She tells him about the body, how she doesn't believe it can have lain in the chalky ground all that time, how she suspects that Frederick Blackstock was buried somewhere else, maybe in the grounds of his ancestral home. She doesn't stop to question why she is willing to confide in Cathbad when she withheld this information from the TV people. After all, even Nelson confides in Cathbad. One way or another, he has been part of several police investigations. Nelson always says that Cathbad would have made a good detective.

His eyes gleam at the story. Cathbad loves a good conspiracy. 'Hazel was right,' he says. 'He always says that the Blackstock family are bad news.'

'How does he know them?'

'He used to have his yurt on their land.'

'Well, I suppose it was quite nice of them to let him stay there,' says Ruth. 'I rather liked Sally Blackstock.'

'Oh, the younger generation are all right,' says Cathbad. 'It was the older lot that were the problem.'

'Old George?' says Ruth. 'Nelson mentioned him. He was Fred's brother.'

'Further back than that,' says Cathbad. 'Old George's parents. You know his mother killed herself? Drowned herself on the beach by Devil's Hollow.'

'Nelson mentioned something about her,' says Ruth slowly. 'She thought that the land was cursed because it ought to be at the bottom of the sea.'

'There's something in that,' says Cathbad. 'The boundaries between land and sea are blurred in Norfolk. That's what makes it such a special place, of course. And look at places where the sea has taken the land back. Dunwich, for example.'

'Dunwich is in Suffolk,' says Ruth, but she takes the point. Dunwich, an important town in Anglo Saxon times, is now really just a small village. Most of the old town, including – it is said – eight churches, is underwater. Coastal erosion and a series of disastrous floods have eaten away at the landscape. During one particularly violent storm in the fourteenth century, the entire village of Newton, a few miles up the coast, was swept away. Legend has it that you can still hear the church bells ringing under the sea.

'Anyway,' says Cathbad, 'Hazel says that the mother – Leonie her name was – put a curse on the whole family. They can never escape the Blackstock lands.'

This was certainly true of Fred, thinks Ruth. He probably thought he had escaped when he emigrated to America but the war came and there he was, soon to be dead and buried under that same Norfolk soil.

'How does Hazel know all this?' she says. 'Old George's parents must have died long before he was born.'

'Oh, he's heard stories,' says Cathbad vaguely. 'All druids love a good story.'

Devil's Hollow is a churning pit. The digger moves to and fro, its movements seemingly random and jerky. Yet in the far corner of the field a line of bricks shows that progress is being made and Edward Spens's beachfront apartments are one step closer to being completed.

Chaz Blackstock and his father stand glumly at the gate, watching.

'I used to come here as a boy,' says George. 'Wonderful place for rabbits.'

'Why did you sell it then?' says Chaz. He says it without any real heat though. This argument has been rehearsed so many times over the last year that both of them know how it goes.

'We needed the money,' says George. 'The Hall costs a bomb to keep up and you don't honestly think we'll ever turn it into a profitable B & B, do you?'

'Mum thinks we will.'

George watches as the digger piles earth into a crater. Despite everything, there's something hypotonic about it, the uneven space becoming transformed into a smooth square, a blank canvas for the developers.

'Your mother's a wonderful woman,' he says. 'She's always got a plan. Now she thinks we can let rooms to the film people.'

'I don't know why you agreed to the film,' says Chaz. He too is watching the digger as if transfixed.

'Mum thought it would be good publicity for the Hall,' says George. 'Besides, it'll be good to see Nell again.'

'Sounds as if you fancied her a bit.'

George laughs. 'I was madly in love but she was fourteen years older than me, all smoky eyes and shimmering limbs. She was very sweet to me though. Used to take me out in her sports car. Even took me up to London to see a show. *Hello, Dolly!* I've never forgotten it.'

'Have you spoken to her recently?'

'She rang the other day to talk about the funeral service. She sounded just the same but she must be over seventy now.'

'Is she married?'

'Yes, with children and grandchildren. She's bringing her

husband with her. He's called Blake and he's a university lecturer.'

Chaz groans. 'Sounds like fun.'

'Oh, Cassie can talk to him. She's good at that sort of thing.'

'Yes, she's the clever one,' agrees Chaz.

They watch the digger for a few more minutes. It reminds Chaz of days when they used to go fishing together. The hours of companionable silence which stretch so far that talking becomes almost a physical effort.

This time George breaks the surface. 'It's madness really,' he says. 'Building on a flood plain like this. The tide used to come up this high when I was a boy.'

'Let's hope that a really high tide comes and washes away Edward Spens's horrid little hen houses,' says Chaz.

'Don't wish for that,' says George. 'It's a frightening thing, the sea in an angry mood.'

'Is Mum still keen on having a party after the funeral?' says Chaz.

'A wake, she calls it,' says George. 'I just wish she hadn't invited that policeman.'

'What policeman?'

'The one who came asking questions about Fred. Mum's invited him to the service and to the party afterwards. He's bringing an archaeologist with him.'

'An archaeologist?'

'Yes. I told you. They were looking in the grounds of the Hall to see if Fred could have been buried there. They don't think he was in the plane all that time, you see.'

'You didn't tell me that archaeologists were involved.'

'Didn't I? Well, this woman seems fairly pleasant. Ruth Something, she's called. But we don't really want her sniffing round the place, asking lots of questions. It might upset Dad.'

'He's been fine recently though, hasn't he? Hasn't had one of his funny turns in years.'

'I know. But we don't want to rock the boat, do we?'

Chaz looks at his father. 'No, we don't want to do that.'

Behind them, the digger plunges its teeth into the earth.

CHAPTER 10

Nelson drives home feeling frustrated with Whitcliffe and the Norfolk police in general. Why couldn't he be in Blackpool, investigating real crimes with his old mate Sandy Macleod? There are too many bloody bodies buried in Norfolk, that's what. 'It's what I love about Norfolk,' Ruth had said once. 'The layers and layers of history under your feet.' But, just at this moment, Nelson longs for a straightforward smash-and-grab, a mugging (no one badly hurt, of course), a drugs kingpin hunted down to his lair. Something that doesn't involve all this pussyfooting about, all this *diplomacy*. Even the word had a slippery *Guardian*-reader sound that he distrusts. Why should he have to share his crime scene with Whitcliffe and a bunch of Yanks blathering on about the war? A war which, Nelson thinks savagely, they didn't enter until bloody half-time.

He knows that his hostility to the TV crew has something to do with Ruth. He may not be prone to self-reflection but he does acknowledge that much. He had been surprised when Ruth proved a TV success in *Women Who Kill*. It's not that he doesn't know how good she is. Sometimes, when he's watching her work, he feels an admiration and a pride that take him by surprise. It's more that he thinks of Ruth as a very private person, living in her isolated house, always alone or with Katie, totally absorbed in her work. It was a shock to see her on the screen, to share her with so many other people. And, most of all, it was a shock to find himself sharing her with Frank Barker.

Nelson takes the turning for home. He knows that he has no excuse for resenting Frank or anyone else in Ruth's life. He made his decision; he elected to stay with Michelle and their daughters. It's none of his business if Ruth has another relationship. In fact, if he were a nice person, he should be pleased for her. Frank is single (he checked) and is clearly eligible in every way. But Nelson has often examined his conscience (it comes of being brought up as a Catholic) and has come to the gloomy conclusion that he's not a very nice person. He feels jealous. He wants Ruth and Katie for himself, waiting for him in that little house on the edge of the marshes. But he does at least acknowledge that he has no right to think this way.

He cheers himself up by imagining the supper that Michelle will be preparing. His mother, Maureen, often refers to Michelle as a 'proper old-fashioned wife' and, while this description never ceases to irritate him (coming, as it does, from a woman who squashed her own husband as flat as a piece of lasagne), he has to admit that there is some truth in it. Michelle has a full-time job as the manager of a hair-dressing salon but she does almost invariably produce a hot meal at the end of the day. She also favours high heels and make-up and has never once changed a plug. Nelson smiles as he negotiates the familiar streets, remembering that time when, in his absence, Michelle asked a neighbour if he could mend the fuse on her hair straighteners. The neighbour had, of course, been only too pleased. Men are usually happy to help Michelle.

But Michelle's car isn't in the drive. And when Nelson opens the front door, he isn't greeted by the homely smell of shepherd's pie but by a slightly musty silence. He still can't get used to this. His daughters have both left home now but he expects them to be here, watching American crap on the TV and making themselves complicated snacks involving tacos and grated cheese. As he stands in the hallway, curiously unwilling to go further into the house, his phone pings. A text from his wife.

Mtg at work. Will be bit late. Sorry!

The message ends with three kisses and a sad face.

'We have to stop this,' says Michelle.

'Stop what?' says Tim, rather sulkily. 'We haven't done anything yet.'

'You know what I mean.'

They are sitting in Tim's car, which is parked by the beach at Cley next the Sea. The recent rain has flooded parts of the car park and this, combined with the incoming tide, makes Tim feel as if he is surrounded by water. It makes him feel uneasy. And now Michelle is doing the whole hair-twisting, I'm-a-terrible-person thing.

'We can't keep seeing each other,' she says.

'We can't stop seeing each other,' says Tim. 'You're my boss's wife. We're going to see each other sometimes.'

His voice is harsh and Michelle's eyes fill with tears. He moves to comfort her, despite knowing that this is the most dangerous thing he can do. She leans against him, burying her face in his shirt. He kisses her ear, her cheek, her neck and then the whole thing is starting again.

'I love you,' he says. She doesn't say it back but then he doesn't expect her to. Instead she twists her head so that her lips meet his.

CHAPTER 11

Ruth is rather surprised to receive a warm welcome from Sally Blackstock when she arrives at the Hall for the excavation. Families are not normally delighted to have their gardens dug up by a forensic archaeologist on the hunt for signs of illicit burial. But Sally is all smiles and invites Ruth in for a coffee 'before the hard work starts'. It's a cold day with the wind bowling merrily over the flat fields, so Ruth says yes.

In the kitchen, she finds Judy and Tim also drinking coffee.

'The boss'll be here soon,' says Tim as soon as he sees Ruth. 'He got tied up on another case.'

Ruth doesn't like to think that 'where's Nelson?' is written all over her face. Even if this is, in fact, what she was thinking.

'I'm sure we can get on without him,' she says. 'How are you, Judy?'

'Fine,' says Judy, adjusting her position in the rocking chair. 'Uncomfortable.'

'Shouldn't still be working,' says a voice in the background.

It's an elderly man in a green cardigan. Ruth guesses that this must be the grandfather, the one who raised objections about Nelson's questioning.

Sally says, without turning round from her coffee-making, 'Ruth, this is my father-in-law, George Blackstock. Dad, this is Ruth, the archaeologist I was telling you about.'

'Another girl,' says George. 'Why are all the jobs going to girls these days?' He slaps Tim – suddenly and unexpectedly – on the back. 'What are you doing about it, lad?'

Tim chokes and tries to mutter something about all being equal now.

'Bet it's not like that where you come from,' says George.

'I was born in Essex,' says Tim. Ruth has noticed before that he always meets racist comments with absolute calm. She thinks it must be a way of hiding anger.

'So was I,' says Sally. 'I'm an Essex girl at heart. I was a nurse in London when I met George. All this was a real culture shock for me.'

She laughs gaily but Ruth imagines that, whichever part of Essex Sally calls home, it won't feature in the TV programme *The Only Way Is Essex*. Sally's pink-and-white face has clearly never seen a spray-tan in its life.

George sits opposite Ruth at the table. She is beginning to find his intense stare rather intimidating. Maybe it's his eyebrows, which are alarmingly long and shaggy.

'So you're digging up our pets' burial ground, are you?' he says.

'I'm going to be working in that area, yes,' says Ruth.

'Absolute sacrilege,' says George. 'Buried a lot of faithful friends there: Kipper, Max, Nero, Trumpeter, Bingo, Charlie, Jethro. They deserve to lie in peace, don't you think?'

'I'll be very careful,' says Ruth, slightly dazed by the string of names. Is it normal for a family to go through so many dogs? 'I'll try not to disturb existing graves. It's pretty clear where there's been recent activity.'

'Recent activity,' George mimics her voice. 'What does that mean?'

'Dad.' Sally puts her hand on his shoulder. 'We've talked about this. It'll be fine.'

Ruth expects the old man to turn on his daughter-in-law but instead he lapses into a rather sulky silence, glaring at Ruth from under the jutting hedgerow of hair. Ruth has had enough.

'We should make a start,' she says. 'I need to photograph the site and mark up a grid before we do any digging. And it gets dark early these days.'

Nelson turns up just as Ruth, at her sweatiest and most mud-stained, is getting down to the first layer of chalk. A young policeman has been sent to help with the spadework but Ruth can never resist getting her hands dirty. She is sifting through the topsoil when she becomes aware of a brusque voice asking Tim if she (Ruth) has found anything yet. She can't hear Tim's reply but his tone sounds soothing. She grits her teeth. Nelson always expects archaeologists to turn up vital evidence after digging for two minutes. It takes time, she always tells him. Just like police work takes time.

As a matter of fact, she is already certain that digging has taken place in this area. The soil is looser, for one thing, less compact, as if it has been disturbed fairly recently. The layers are also confused, chalk and soil mixed together. There's a flattened area of vegetation nearby which looks as if it could have been the place where earth from the grave was piled up before being replaced. The soil in the trench is also richer, darker and more organic-looking than the earth in the surrounding area (exposed in the vegetable patch, for example). This could point to something organic having been buried here. Often, with burials in open ground, scavenging animals will take away body parts or even move the corpse altogether, but Ruth believes that this body was protected in some way, covered by a shroud or tarpaulin. There are some animal bones but these are only to be expected. She puts them aside as respectfully as possible. Luckily Old George isn't watching. Presumably he has stayed in the house.

There are a few interesting finds though. Ruth arranges these on her tarpaulin.

'Found something?' asks Nelson.

Ruth looks up. Nelson looms over her, blocking out the light. It reminds her of the first time she saw him, in the corridor of the university, looking altogether too large and solid for the flimsy academic surroundings.

'Some glass,' she says. 'And a few coins.'

'Glass? How can that be important?'

'It can help us establish the date the soil was disturbed,' says Ruth, putting the glass into a paper evidence bag.

Nelson grunts and backs away. She hears him talking to

Tim and then Sally's voice, those effortlessly carrying upper-class tones.

'Why don't we all break for lunch? I've made leek and potato soup.'

It feels strange, eating lunch in the cosy kitchen with Old George at the head of the table and Sally bustling around them, offering crusty bread and homemade lemonade. It's as if they're at some jolly social occasion – a harvest supper per-haps – instead of investigating a crime. Ruth is now almost certain that Fred's body was once buried in the pets' burial ground but here she is, smiling at his family and accepting another helping of soup as if she hasn't a care in the world.

'Marvellous soup, Mrs Blackstock,' says Tim. Ruth noticed that Sally had given him by far the largest portion and now she shoots him a positively flirtatious look.

'Would you like some more, Sergeant?'

'I shouldn't,' says Tim, smiling at her.

'Oh, get along with you. You're as slim as anything. Have some more.'

'Thank you,' says Tim. Ruth and Nelson exchange glances. Judy has already left and Tim is only having lunch with them because Sally pressed him to stay. Ruth thinks that Nelson will send him back to the station as soon as they've finished eating. She hopes so. She finds Tim's presence slightly dis-concerting and, though she doesn't want to admit it, even to herself, she would like some time alone with Nelson.

'I hope you'll stay with us for the filming, Dr Galloway,' Sally is saying. 'I'm hoping that all the TV people will stay here. Including that lovely Frank Barker.' She gives another of her slightly manic laughs. Old George watches her glumly from under his eyebrows.

'Thanks,' says Ruth, 'but I'll probably go home every night. I live quite near here and I've got a young daughter.'

'Let her father look after her,' says Sally. 'That's what they're for. George was wonderful with the little ones. Young George, that is. I don't think Old George has ever changed a nappy in his life.'

Her father-in-law agrees fervently that he hasn't. Ruth wonders where Young George is today. He may be a new man but it seems he's not above leaving his wife to look after his dad.

'I don't live with Kate's father,' says Ruth. 'It's complicated.' She doesn't look at Nelson.

'Everything's complicated these days,' says Sally. 'It's the same with my children. Neither of them are married. Chaz lives on his own on that dreadful pig farm and Cassandra hangs round with these awful arty types. Mind you, she's very excited about the TV programme. I think she's hoping a casting director will discover her.'

'Television's for stupid people,' says Old George.

'Get along with you, Dad,' says Sally. 'You love *Hollyoaks*.'

The old man brightens immediately. 'Is it on now?'

'Soon,' says Sally soothingly. 'More bread anyone? Cheese? Coffee?'

'We'd better crack on,' says Nelson. 'And Sergeant Heath-field needs to get back to the station.'

*

Young George is at the pig farm. He has been helping Chaz get a rather recalcitrant boar into the finishing shed. Now they are sitting down to lunch, not such a civilised affair as Sally's, but companionable none the less. Hazel has just returned from the market, where he was delivering a truck-load of porkers. He works for Chaz sometimes in return for bread and board, and these are being provided now. They eat together at the kitchen table, bread, cheese and pickles. Chaz has opened a bottle of his home-made cider.

'When will it be safe to go back to the Hall?' asks Chaz, cutting himself a hunk of bread.

'I don't know,' says George gloomily. 'She can't keep digging all day, can she?'

'Who's digging?' asks Hazel.

'The archaeologist, Ruth Whatshername. She's digging in the pets' burial ground because she thinks Uncle Fred was buried there.'

'Whatever gave her that idea?'

Chaz shrugs. 'Search me? But they know things, these forensic archaeologists, don't they? They know where bodies have been buried.'

'What does Old George think about it?' asks Hazel.

Young George raises his eyes to the ceiling. 'You can imagine. He's going on about all the faithful friends buried there. Then he gets onto the seas rising and the end of the world. Sally had to give him a tranquilliser yesterday.'

'What does he think about the TV programme?' asks Chaz.

'I was a bit worried that it would upset him,' says George.

'But he hasn't really mentioned the TV people at all. It was the pets' burial ground that really got to him. But he's quite excited about Nell and Blake coming. Looking forward to telling them all his tales of doom and gloom.'

'Bet he's not as excited as you,' says Chaz, with a sidelong glance at Hazel.

George laughs. 'I'm an old man now and Nell's an old woman. I don't think there's anything to get excited about.'

'You're not old,' says Chaz, 'You're only fifty-eight. Look how you wrestled that pig to the ground this morning. You were like a machine.'

George laughs, wryly this time. 'A very old and creaky machine. No, I feel a bit sad about seeing Nell actually. She was so young and beautiful. I'd rather just remember her like that.'

'You're a bundle of laughs,' says Chaz. 'You must get it from Grandpa.'

There's a pause while they all think about Grandpa. Then Hazel says, 'What exactly is this TV programme about?'

'As I understand it,' says George, 'it's part of an American series called *The History Men*. The idea is to tell the human story behind historical events. They want to use Fred to tell the story of American airmen in Norfolk.'

'Are you all going to be in it?' asks Hazel.

'I hope not,' says George. 'They want to film Nell, but I hope the rest of us can stay in the background. They'll want to come here, of course, because this is where the base was.'

Chaz groans, pouring himself another mug of cider.

'You could charge them a location fee,' says Hazel. 'Might as well make some money out of it.'

'You're very practical for a druid,' says Chaz.

At the Hall, as the afternoon progresses, the atmosphere becomes sombre, almost tense. Maybe it's because of the darkening sky, the wind gaining strength and humming across the marshes. By three o'clock it is almost dark. Maybe it's because Ruth has suddenly gained an audience. As well as Nelson, Sally is watching her closely and even Old George makes an appearance, wrapped up in a greatcoat and muffler.

The young policeman is sent home as soon as the hard digging is completed and Ruth works alone. She is analysing the soil, taking samples, looking at anything that may give her clues about what happened on this little plot of land. She's not surprised to find no skeletal matter – the body was wrapped up after all – but the soil might contain traces of blood, hair, even DNA. She works in silence, aware of the watchers above and of the animal graves all around her, darkening now against the stormy sky. *Blue, beloved friend. Rosie, never forgotten. Patch, faithful companion.*

She is just about to suggest that they bring the excavation to a close – she has all the samples that she needs and the wind is bitterly cold now – when the last rays of the setting sun pick out something in the churned-up topsoil. It's a tiny gleam of silver. Ruth looks but the sun has already sunk out of sight behind the outhouses and the trench is almost in darkness. She digs in the spot where she thought she saw it and, after a few minutes, her gloved hand closes on something small and metallic. She lifts it out.

'What's that, Ruth?' asks Nelson.

Her first thought is that it's a dog-tag, a soldier's identity disc. But then she sees that, although she is literally correct, her find is rather more prosaic. It is a dog-tag but it's a tag belonging to a dog, a metal disc from a collar. 'Bingo', it says and there's an old fashioned telephone number underneath. 'Flaxman 9618'.

Silently she hands it to Nelson. Sally and Old George come forward to look.

'Bingo,' says Nelson. He turns to Old George. 'Wasn't that the name of your brother's dog? The one that died just before he went missing?'

Old George lets out a sound that is somewhere between a howl and a sob.

CHAPTER 12

'Why was he so upset?' says Ruth. She and Nelson are talking in hushed voices, despite the fact that they're sitting in Nelson's car, a good fifty yards from the house.

'I don't know,' says Nelson. 'But he certainly went into meltdown, didn't he?'

The moments after the disc had been found had certainly been uncomfortable. Old George had sunk to his knees on the muddy ground, sobbing and clutching at his woolly cardigan. Sally knelt next to him.

'Dad? Dad. It's all right.'

Ruth, feeling oddly guilty, had climbed out of the trench with Nelson's help. She was just in time to hear Old George saying tearfully, 'He was a good dog. Bingo was such a *good* dog.'

Sally had led the old man into the house, leaving Ruth and Nelson to bag up the few finds and put the soil back in the ditch. It was dark by the time they had finished, and when Nelson mentioned that he had a flask of coffee in his car, it seemed natural for them to repair there, discussing the case. The wind, stronger now, batters against the sides of the car.

'I'd better get home,' says Ruth, not moving.

'Do you think today's dig will tell us anything?' asks Nelson.

'I'm pretty sure there was a body buried there,' says Ruth, 'but beyond that . . .'

'But how did Fred's body, if it was Fred's body, end up back here when it should have been at the bottom of the sea?'

'I don't know,' says Ruth. 'But I'm going to see if I can find out some more.'

'Are you going to talk to the US Air Force then?' says Nelson. 'Good luck, if so.'

'I thought you said they'd been very helpful.'

'To the police, yes. But you're a civilian.'

Nelson seems to be deliberately trying to wind her up. Ruth says, as evenly as possible, 'I've contacted the Air Force Research Agency in Alabama but, actually, there's a small RAF museum at Blickling Hall, near here. I'm going to pay them a visit.'

But Nelson seems not to have heard.

'Have fun,' he says. 'I know you like Americans.'

A particularly rough gust of wind rocks the car and Ruth thinks that it's time to go.

Tim is on the way to the gym. 'Leaving early?' asks Clough when he sees the sports bag coming out. Tim doesn't rise; he's not leaving early and Clough knows it. Clough tries a new tack.

'A man can do too much exercise.'

'How would you know?'

'Bet you I could still do more push-ups than you.'

'OK,' says Tim, facing him across the briefing room, half-serious, half-joking. 'Let's do it.'

'My money's on Tim,' says Judy from across the room.

'Not in front of a pregnant woman,' says Clough.

Tim laughs and heads for the door. He can hear Judy and Clough arguing as he heads for the stairs. They're like quarrelsome siblings sometimes.

Tim is used to families. He has two brothers and two sisters. Tim is in the middle, the clever one who escaped to university. His brothers both ended up in trouble with the police, his sister Alesha had three children before she was twenty. The youngest sister, Blessing (guess who's the favourite?), also shows signs of being able to keep her head down. She's at sixth-form college. Tim doesn't talk about them much at work, though he sometimes shows pictures of his nieces and nephews. There are ten altogether, his brothers both being rather reckless progenitors.

Maybe this is why Tim has never married. Maybe this is why he's now in love with a married woman who shows no signs of leaving her husband. Tim left a message for Michelle (he uses a different phone for her, a subterfuge that always makes him feel faintly sick) asking her to meet him at the gym. She hasn't answered yet.

Tim met Michelle when Nelson invited him for Sunday lunch soon after he first came down from Lancashire. Then he had thought her the perfect wife, beautiful, supportive, also a cracking cook. But she had been Nelson's, inseparable from him. Then he began to see her at the gym, started to hear rumours about the perfect marriage. The story at the station was that the boss had had an affair with Ruth Galloway and that her child was his. Judy and Clough were annoyingly tight-lipped about the whole thing, even when Tim asked them directly. Still, the idea that there might be cracks in the golden edifice gave Tim the courage to ask Michelle to join him for a coffee in the cafe at the sports club. Over the next few months coffee became lunch and then, daringly, dinner. By the time that Tim first kissed her, by the old quay at night, he felt as if he had been in love with her for ever.

She hadn't kissed him back. She'd given a gasp and pushed him away. Then she'd run back to her car. He'd heard her high heels skittering over the bridge and wondered if she'd ever speak to him again. But the next day, at the gym (neither of them would ever consider missing a day, whatever the circumstances), she'd explained that she hadn't responded because she was scared.

'Of what?'

'Of myself. I don't want to have an affair with you, Tim.'

He'd been surprised – almost shocked – that she'd come out with it like that.

'Harry hasn't always been faithful,' she'd said, her pale face luminously beautiful in the harsh light of the cafe. 'But my marriage is important to me.'

'I understand,' said Tim. He did. His dad had run off when Blessing was a baby and Tim hasn't seen him for more than ten years. When he gets married, he wants it to last, to be perfect. Which is probably why he's still single at thirty-two.

'I love Harry,' she said. 'But it's difficult.'

'What's difficult?'

'Because I think I love you too.'

That had been the beginning of it. The beginning of kisses in the car park, of meetings at the gym (the exquisite agony of sharing a jacuzzi or watching her take a pool-side shower), of lunches where they talked endlessly about 'the situation' without ever getting nearer to a solution. They have been seeing each other for over a year and still haven't slept together.

Now, though, when Tim sees her car parked outside the gym he feels a rush of almost pure pleasure. His life has become infinitely more complicated since meeting Michelle and he really can't imagine the whole thing ending well but there's no doubt that he loves her. Sometimes he finds himself jogging through The Walks in King's Lynn first thing in the morning shouting her name to the rough sleepers and astonished pigeons.

CHAPTER 13

Blickling Hall is a beautiful redbrick mansion, rather like Blackstock Hall in appearance, but without its general air of decay. And while the Blackstocks are surrounded by depressed-looking sheep, Blickling Hall is set within manicured lawns surrounded by dark yew hedges and bordered by exquisite flowers. There's also a moat (now empty), a walled garden and a ghost. A portrait in the gallery bears the inscription *Anna Bolena hic nata 1507* (Anne Boleyn born here 1507), though historians tend to be sniffy about the date, and a carriage containing the headless queen is meant to draw up to the gates when the moon is full. But there's no carriage bowling along the gravel drive when Ruth pays her visit. In any case, she is concerned with the Hall's more recent history. During the Second World War, Blickling Hall was requisitioned by the officers from RAF Oulton and there's a small museum on site dedicated to Air Force history.

Ruth had intended to be at the Hall by mid afternoon but she was held up by a seemingly endless syllabus meeting, chaired (of course) by Phil. She had rung the historian, Dr Raymond Alder, and he had been most understanding. 'Just come when you can.' Sandra, too, had been quite happy to keep Kate for a few more hours. Even so, Ruth can't suppress a feeling of unease as she drives between the yew hedges at four o'clock. It's already almost dark and, somewhere in the house, a clock is telling the hour in sonorous tones.

'Dr Galloway.' A tall man in jeans and a black jumper comes striding towards her.

'Dr Alder?'

'Ray, please.'

'It's very good of you to see me,' says Ruth, trying to smooth her crumpled cardigan at the back. She feels sweaty and untidy after a day's teaching. But it's cold in the courtyard and she's already wishing that she'd got her coat out of the boot. Ray seems impervious to the temperature.

'I'm delighted that someone from the university is taking an interest,' he says. 'I contacted Phil Trent recently but he never got back to me.'

That figures. Phil once told Ruth that the trouble with the Second World War is that it 'isn't sexy'.

Rather to Ruth's disappointment, Ray leads her away from the Hall towards an outhouse. It's an impressive building in its way, with gable ends and fluted stonework, but Anne Boleyn's ghost is certainly not going to walk here. Inside, it's a barn-like space, white-painted, with a gallery running around three sides. They climb the open staircase and at the top there's an exhibition of patchwork – jewelled colours against the white – and a trestle table.

'I've sorted out some photographs for you,' says Ray, pointing towards the table.

Ruth leans over to look. The faded pictures show huge aeroplanes with men standing on stepladders to reach the propellers, sprawled on the wings doing repair work or just grinning beside the monstrous creatures, dwarfed by the great khaki wings.

'They were B24s and B17s,' says Ray. 'The B17s were the famous Flying Fortresses.'

Ruth is looking at the men. They are wearing overalls and leather jackets, flying goggles still perched on their heads. They are laughing and gesticulating, as if the killing machines behind them are nothing more than a backdrop. Two men are holding up a sign saying 'Lucky Bastards Club'.

'If you completed thirty missions, you were part of the Lucky Bastards Club,' says Ray. 'Not many did.'

'The man I'm interested in, Fred Blackstock, flew in a B17,' says Ruth. 'He was a tail gunner.'

Ray pushes a diagram towards her. 'The B17s had a ten-man crew. Pilot, co-pilot, bombardier, navigator, flight engineer, radio operator, two waist gunners, a ball turret gunner and a tail gunner. The tail gunner was most important defensively because they had to guard against attacks coming from behind them. It was incredibly dangerous. They were reckoned to have a one in four chance of completing a tour of duty.'

'Fred's plane went down over the sea,' says Ruth. 'Is there any way he could have survived?'

'I've looked it up,' says Ray, reaching for a ledger. 'B17 *Shamrock*, shot down on the sixth of September, 1944, no survivors. The tail gunner did have an emergency exit below the horizontal stabiliser but very few of them managed to use it.'

'Where was it shot down?' asks Ruth. 'Is there any way he could have got out through the emergency exit and swum ashore?'

Ray looks at her curiously. 'Well, according to records, the *Shamrock* was only about twenty minutes from home when it came down. Lockwell Heath is unusual because it's on the north coast. Most US bases were further south. I suppose someone could have reached the shore. Why?'

Ruth doesn't know if she should but, in the end, she tells Ray the whole story, how Fred Blackstock's body came to be found in a single-seater plane which crashed during a thunderstorm a week after the B17's demise.

Ray shakes his head. 'It's impossible. If Fred was trained as a tail gunner, he wouldn't have been able to fly one of those light reconnaissance crafts.'

'I know,' says Ruth. 'The body must have been put there later.'

'But why?'

'I don't know,' says Ruth.

Ray still looks curious but refrains from asking any more questions. Instead he takes another photograph from a manila envelope.

'I thought the family might like to have this,' he said. 'I had a copy made. That's *Shamrock*.'

In the picture, the plane's massive wings seem almost benign, sheltering the crew that stands in their shadow. On the cockpit is a crudely drawn shamrock and the words 'The Luck of the Irish'.

'The pilot was called Sean Fitzgerald,' says Ray. 'That's probably where the Irish bit came in. I think this one must be Fred. The tail gunner normally stands at the end.'

Ruth peers at the picture. It's hard to tell for sure but the tall dark figure looks very like the man in the picture Sally showed her a few days ago. She looks at the men standing confidently in the Norfolk field, miles away from home with death staring them in the face. Their luck ran out, she thinks, and feels the tears prickling behind her eyelids.

'Thank you,' she says. 'I think the family would love to have this.'

Driving home, she thinks that Fred's daughter must have arrived from America by now. The funeral is on Sunday. What if she drops in at Blackstock Hall and shows her the photograph? It's on the way to Sandra's house; it would only take a few minutes. She's aware that she's doing what Nelson calls 'amateur sleuthing', that she wants to see the family's reaction to the picture, but she tells herself that she's just doing a good deed, something to make up for the distress she caused Old George over the pets' burial ground.

She starts to have doubts as soon as she knocks on the front door. It's nearly six now. What if they're all having a jolly family meal? The sound of her knock echoes through the house but no one appears. Ruth starts to back away.

'Yes?' A woman is standing at the door. Not Sally but an elderly woman dressed in a black uniform and a white apron.

'I just dropped in to see Mrs Blackstock,' says Ruth.

'This way,' says the woman. Is she actually a maid?

'If I've come at an inconvenient time . . .'

'This way.'

Ruth follows the woman along the panelled corridor. Then, to her horror, the woman flings open a door and announces, 'A visitor for Mrs Blackstock.'

She is in a dining room.

It's a vast space, more suited to a state banquet than a cosy family supper. The room is lit by candles and Ruth sees a long polished table and, most disconcerting of all, a full house of Blackstocks. They are all standing with their glasses raised, apparently frozen in the middle of making a toast. Through the gloom, Ruth sees Sally and her husband, Old George at the end of the table, two younger people and an older man and woman. The woman looks straight at Ruth with an expression of polite interest.

'Ruth!' exclaims Sally.

'I'm terribly sorry,' Ruth backs towards the door. 'I had no idea that you were in the middle of eating.'

Old George ignores her. His eyes are glittering. Is it madness or the candlelight? He raises his glass.

'To Fred,' he says.

The Blackstocks raise their glasses. The flickering light glitters on silver and cut glass.

'To Fred,' they reply.

CHAPTER 14

Ruth is surprised at how moving she finds the funeral service. Fred's coffin, covered with the Stars and Stripes, is carried into the church by six RAF men in dress uniform, their gold braid and polished boots somehow shocking in the dim light of the church. Father Tom preaches about peace and reconciliation and the choir sings 'Dear Lord and Father of Mankind'. Outside, as the wind blows the poplars into a frenzy, a lone piper plays at the graveside.

One of the soldiers takes the flag and folds it in a complicated way, ending with a neat triangle of cloth, which he hands to Nell. Ruth, who met Nell briefly last night, thinks that she looks very moved. Nell's husband, Blake, who Ruth recalls as one of the figures around the dining table, takes her arm reassuringly. Blake is wrapped in an immense black coat with a red scarf tied tightly round his throat. Ruth remembers him complaining last night about how cold England is. Next to the American couple, Ruth sees Old George scowling underneath a wide-brimmed trilby. Sally and Young George are on either side of the old man, and behind them are Chaz and Cassandra. Ruth met Sally's children last night too and once again is struck by their glamour. Cassandra is pure Anna Karenina in a short black coat and fur hat, Chaz darkly handsome, his black hair falling onto his velvet collar.

Ruth still feels embarrassed when she remembers bursting in on the Blackstock family dinner, the old retainer at the door, the candlelight, the table, the formally dressed figures with their glasses raised. It was as if she had staggered into a Tolstoy novel. She had made her excuses and left but Sally had come after her, followed by Nell. Ruth had produced the photograph and Nell had been delighted.

'It's so dear to see Daddy with his comrades.'

Neither of them mentioned the fact that Fred was clearly a member of a ten-man team and not a lone pilot.

'I'll treasure it for ever,' said Nell.

Now Ruth watches as Fred's coffin is lowered into the grave. It's a moment that never ceases to shock, no matter how long ago the death. The crowd begins to disperse and, conspicuous amongst the sea of black, she sees Cathbad and Hazel, both wearing purple cloaks, standing to one side of the grave. The TV cameraman is filming them surreptitiously. And there's Nelson, accompanied by Tim Heathfield and Clough, moving forward to talk to Sally Blackstock. The cameraman, who has, up until now, been the soul of discretion, allows himself a few shots of the grave and of Nell Blackstock walking away, clutching the folded flag to her chest.

Ruth stays back. She doesn't much want to talk to the TV people or to the family. She is still wondering whether to attend the 'celebration' at Blackstock Hall. Clara, her regular babysitter, is looking after Kate and she never minds staying late but, all the same, Ruth doesn't like the thought of being stuck at the Hall for hours, especially with this storm brewing. When she thinks of the scene last night, she is struck by a slight but real jolt of fear. She remembers Old George howling in the pets' burial ground and standing at the head of the table proposing a toast. She thinks she has seen enough of the Blackstocks for the time being. On the other hand, she would get to see Nelson. And Frank.

She saw Frank as soon as she entered the church. He was hard to miss, with his height and breadth. He was sitting between Paul and Earl and, as far as Ruth could see, there was no sign of the elusive Gloria. Frank looked round the church at one point but Ruth had cleverly concealed herself behind a pillar and, in any case, she knows that Frank's long sight is not good. He claims that he can never find his glasses but Ruth has always suspected that it's only vanity that stops him wearing them all the time. He does have very piercing blue eyes.

Now Ruth can see the three TV people walking through the graveyard. In their black suits they look oddly intimidating, like something from a gangster film. Ruth looks round for a handy tombstone to hide behind but she's obviously in the newer part of the cemetery, all neat white stones and, of course, the pile of flowers and freshly dug earth around Senior Airman Blackstock's grave. She sets off down the path, head down.

In the car park, the official cars are just leaving. From the look of the other cars, parked in all directions like a complicated Tetris puzzle, it will be some time before Ruth can get her Renault out. The TV van is also parked across one of the exits, making a bottleneck of the winding country road. Ruth retraces her steps. She'll wait in the graveyard for a while and then escape when everyone else has left and go straight home. It's not as if anyone will miss her, she thinks savagely. Apart from a smile and a half-wave, Nelson has ignored her completely. Frank hasn't even noticed her. Cathbad is busy being a druid with Hazel. She can see them talking earnestly to one of the TV crew.

The wind is getting up now. It is riffling through the flowers around the new grave, making the cellophane flap like the wings of a great wounded bird. The temperature has dropped and it's suddenly bitterly cold. Ruth decides to wait in the church porch. There's a little stone seat in there and at least she'll be out of the wind.

But as she rounds the corner to the church, she has a shock. A man is already standing in the porch. A tramp, she thinks at first. He has long grey hair and a beard that reaches almost to his waist. There's something eerie about him, as if a stone wizard has suddenly come to life and is observing the mortal world with a view to doing something nasty to it.

Ruth backs away. 'Sorry,' she says.

'Don't be sorry,' says the man. 'The church belongs to us all.'

His voice takes her aback. It's deep and cultured, slightly amused. There's also a trace of an accent. Scottish? Irish? Something soft and rather romantic. Ruth sees now that the man's clothes aren't exactly shabby either. He's wearing a waxed Barbour, a bit battered but no more so than any coat belonging to the hunting, shooting, fishing set. He has boots on too, proper walking boots splashed with mud, and there's a staff leaning against the wall. Perhaps it's the staff, but the man has the look of having come a long way. There's an infinite weariness about him.

'Have you come for the funeral?' she asks.

He looks at her. He has very pale-blue eyes that look as if they're used to scanning far horizons. She thinks of a sailor and of someone else, a memory that's disturbing as well as heart-warming.

'Yes,' he says. 'I've come for the funeral. To pay my respects to Fred. What about you?'

'Yes,' says Ruth. 'That is, I never knew Fred but I've come to . . . pay my respects.'

He looks at her again. That penetrating look, half-amused, half-cynical. Ruth finds herself blundering on, 'I'm an archae-ologist. I was involved with finding the body. Fred's body . . .' Her voice trails away.

Now it's the man's turn to state his connection to Fred, but he says nothing. He looks away from her, towards the graveyard, where the rowan tree stands black against the gathering clouds. What did Cathbad tell her about rowan trees? Something about them being planted in graveyards because they're meant to guard against evil spirits.

Through the trees she can see cars moving along the path.

'I'd better go,' she says.

The man says nothing but, when she turns back, he raises his hand in a gesture reminiscent of Cathbad's hail and farewell.

But it's not Cathbad he reminds her of. It's Erik.

*

The car park is empty apart from Ruth's Renault and a long black car with tinted windows. Frank, Earl and Paul are standing by the limo, deep in conversation.

Ruth has nowhere to hide. She tries to head straight for her car but Frank sees her and calls, 'Ruth!'

'Hi!' she shouts back, not coming closer. She scrabbles in her bag for her keys. Why can she never find anything in her organiser handbag?

'Ruth.' Oh dear, now he's next to her, looking down from his six-foot-something height.

'Hallo, Frank. Just looking for my car keys.'

'I was hoping to have the chance to chat to you. Are you going to Blackstock Hall now?'

'I wasn't going to,' says Ruth. 'It's getting late and there's meant to be a storm coming.'

'Oh, the famous St Jude's Storm. Cathbad was talking about that. The weather seems OK at the moment though.'

The weather might seem OK to an American – used to tornadoes and snowstorms – but it seems pretty wild to Ruth. She can hear the wind rattling the lych gate.

'Do come,' says Frank. 'Just for a bit. I haven't seen anything of you since I've been in England.'

Ruth makes the mistake of looking up at him, at those bright blue eyes crinkling at the corners.

'Oh, all right,' she says. 'Just for a little bit.'

A field opposite the house has been cordoned off for use as a car park. It's pretty full by the time that Ruth arrives so she parks on the verge, hoping for a quick getaway. The black car, with Paul at the wheel, purrs to a halt behind her. She feels a bit embarrassed to be making an entrance as part of the TV contingent but it can't be helped. They trek across the field to the front door, Frank striding ahead and Earl complaining about the sheep.

'Are you sure they're friendly, Frank? That one over there looks real evil.'

'Sheep aren't evil, Earl. They're sacred animals in England.'

'Jesus,' says Paul, 'listen to that wind.'

Ruth has been thinking the same thing. The wind, which seemed wild in the graveyard, sounds positively savage roaring across the open fields. The few trees are bent almost double and even the house, with its towers and buttresses, seems insubstantial all of a sudden, as if the storm might blow the whole edifice away.

'It's atmospheric,' says Earl. 'We must get Steve and his boys to take some footage.'

Ruth knows that Steve is the director of photography, a powerful presence on the set. She saw his van in the car park. Presumably he and his team are already filming the house and its inhabitants.

They are met at the door by Cassandra bearing a tray of champagne glasses.

'Hi. I'm Cassandra Blackstock.' She flashes them a megawatt smile.

'I'm Frank Barker,' says Frank. 'Do you know Dr Ruth Galloway from the university?'

'We met briefly last night,' says Cassandra. Ruth thinks she sounds rather wary.

Frank is continuing with the introductions. 'And this is Earl Kennedy and Paul Brindisi from *The History Men*.'

'Hi.' Is it Ruth's imagination or does Cassandra's smile stretch even wider? Of course, she's an actress. Clearly she's hoping to make an impression on the TV men. Ruth is now ignored completely.

That suits Ruth. She edges away, finds a glass of orange juice and tracks down Cathbad and Hazel, who are drinking champagne in the library.

'At least they call it a library,' says Cathbad, 'but there aren't any books here.'

It's true that the handsome shelves spanning floor to ceiling are empty apart from a few encyclopaedias and a jumble of electrical equipment.

'They're not big readers, the Blackstocks,' says Hazel. Ruth remembers Cathbad saying that Hazel knew the family well.

'Have you met Fred's daughter?' she says. 'I thought she looked close to tears during the service.'

'Nell,' says Hazel. 'I met her just now. Seems like a nice lady.'

'Must be hard for her,' says Ruth. 'I don't suppose she ever really knew her father.'

'Nobody here really knew him,' says Cathbad. For some reason, Ruth thinks of the man at the church. Did he know Fred? But he's not old enough, despite the grey beard. But if he didn't know Fred, why was he at the service?

'Old George knew him,' says Ruth. 'He was his brother.' She had spotted Old George on her way through the house.

He was holding court in the drawing room, surrounded by younger members of the family.

'Old George is a deep one,' says Hazel. 'He'll be feeling it today but he won't let it show.'

'They're a cold bunch, the English aristocracy,' agrees Cathbad.

'Cold?' says a voice. 'Everything's cold in this goddamn house.'

Ruth looks up and sees Nell's husband, Blake, the man with the red scarf. Now he has ditched the scarf, though he's still wearing his coat.

'You're the girl who made such a dramatic appearance at the dinner party,' he says. 'Banquo's ghost.'

'I'm Ruth Galloway,' says Ruth. 'I'm really embarrassed about the other night.'

'Don't be,' says Blake. 'It fitted right in with the general atmosphere. Old George going on about storms and omens, everyone else seething with suppressed emotion. Or they would be if this house wasn't cold enough to freeze the heart. I'm just looking for a room with a temperature sufficient to support human life.'

'Well, it's not very warm in here,' says Ruth. 'But there is a radiator. I'm sitting on it.' She gets up.

Blake comes forward eagerly to put his hands on the radiator, which is the sort found in old school buildings, waist-high rounded metal, lukewarm to the touch.

You're the archaeologist, aren't you?' says Blake. 'You seem to have caused quite a stir in the Blackstock household.'

'Have I?'

'Well, all that stuff about Fred's body being buried somewhere around here. Chaz and Cassandra were talking about it earlier. I see you've been digging in the grounds.'

'Yes.' Ruth feels a little wary of Blake, who has a manner reminiscent of her old history tutor at university, detached and interested at the same time. But she also likes him for the same reason and it's rather cosy, the four of them huddled round the radiator in the old library. She starts to relax.

'I've been digging,' she says. 'But I haven't found anything conclusive.'

'What about the Bronze Age site?' asks Hazel. 'Have you found anything there?'

'No,' says Ruth. 'It's a puzzle. We were so sure it was a large burial site but so far we've only found one body.'

Cathbad and Hazel start talking about the site – about burial rituals and druidical practices and the perils of disturbing the dead. Ruth goes to the window. She wants to check on the weather. She gets out her phone. No signal. She remembers this from the day of the excavation. It adds to her growing sense of panic. If the wind gets much worse, she'll head home, even if she hasn't had the chance of that chat with Frank.

She pulls aside the rather mildewed velvet curtains. The library faces east, towards the marshes. Ruth expects to see windswept grass and a stormy sky. Instead she sees a figure standing stock-still in front of the house, staring up at the windows. It's the man from the church. How the hell did he get here? There were no other cars in the car park. Did he walk? But it's at least five miles from the church. The man doesn't look as if he has just arrived either. In fact he looks as if he's been standing there for ever, leaning on his staff, the wind blowing his hair and beard.

Ruth is suddenly aware that Blake Goodheart is standing beside her.

'It is an ancient Mariner,' he quotes. 'And he stoppeth one of three. "By thy long grey beard and glittering eye, Now wherefore stopp'st thou me?"'

CHAPTER 15

Ruth heads for the drawing room, intending to find Sally, say goodbye and thank you, and beat a hasty retreat. But before she can get there, a figure drifts out of one of the downstairs rooms. Nell.

'Doctor Galloway?' she says. 'Have you got a few minutes?'

Ruth has time for anyone who uses her proper title. 'Yes,' she says.

Nell leads her to a seat in the hall, a sort of church pew with wooden back and tapestry cushions. It feels like an oddly clandestine place to meet.

'It was so sweet of you to bring me Daddy's photograph, Doctor Galloway. I'm very grateful.'

Ruth makes self-deprecating noises. Nell leans forward. She has blue eyes, as blue as Frank's.

'I believe you were the one who actually found my father's body.'

'Well, it was the digger driver who found the plane,' says Ruth. 'I was just called in when they saw that there was a body inside.'

'From something Cassie said, though, I gather that you think Daddy wasn't the pilot of the plane. That his body was put there on purpose, some years later.'

Chaz and Cassandra have been talking, thinks Ruth. Didn't Blake say that earlier? She wonders how much she should tell Nell. Should she voice her suspicions about the pets' burial ground? But it will take weeks to get the samples back from the lab and even then they might be inconclusive. On the other hand, doesn't Nell deserve to know the truth about her father, whatever that truth is?

'I'm pretty sure that your father's body hadn't been in the plane all those years,' she says at last. 'The preservation of the body . . .' She pauses, not wanting to go into too much detail. 'The preservation was more consistent with bodies found in marshy soil, not in chalk.'

Nell's blue eyes are wide. 'So you think his body was buried somewhere else and then put in the plane?'

Ruth admires Nell's succinct summing-up. 'Yes,' she says. 'Though I can't be sure where the body was buried originally.'

'But you've been digging in the grounds of Blackstock Hall?'

'Yes.' There's no point in denying it. Presumably everyone in the family knows by now.

Nell looks out towards the front door, a massive oak affair slatted with metal. She says, almost to herself, 'But why would someone bury him here and then dig him up, years later?'

'I don't know,' says Ruth. 'That's the problem with archaeology. It always raises more questions than it answers.'

Nell is about to speak when someone calls her name. Blake is hurrying down the corridor towards them.

'I have literally lost all feeling in my extremities,' he tells Nell.

Ruth excuses herself and goes into the drawing room in search of Sally. Rather to her discomfort, she finds her hostess deep in conversation with Nelson, her hand on his arm. There's no sign of Cassandra or the TV crew. Old George sits by the fire surrounded by people who could be described as 'awful arty types', who are hanging on his every gloomy pronouncement. Chaz and his father, Young George, stand by the window, looking like stags at bay.

'Ruth!' Sally sounds delighted to see her. 'I was just talking about you.'

Ruth looks at Nelson, who gives her a rather sardonic smile.

'I was saying that we should do a proper dig in the grounds,' says Sally. 'There must be all sorts buried there. After all, this house has been here since Tudor times. We could see if we could get *Time Team* interested.'

Sally's involvement with the American TV company seems to have gone to her head. Ruth does agree, though, that there might be some interesting finds in the grounds. 'There might even be prehistory,' she says. 'After all, the house is quite near the Bronze Age burial site.'

Cathbad and Hazel have also found their way to the drawing room and are in the process of topping up their glasses. Ruth has noticed before that Cathbad, while claiming to embrace only the simple things of life, has quite a taste for champagne. At this last remark of Ruth's, they both head towards her.

'Do you really think there might be a burial site here, Ruth?' asks Cathbad.

'Well, it's possible,' says Ruth, rather flustered to discover that she has an audience. Chaz and his father have also now joined the circle.

'If we find something, it might stop the development on Devil's Hollow,' says Chaz excitedly.

'It's a nightmare,' says Hazel. 'I was there yesterday and three houses are almost up.'

'I know,' says Chaz. 'It's going really fast.'

'Edward Spens is power mad,' says Cathbad.

'He's a property developer,' says Nelson. 'He develops property. What do you expect him to do? After all, you sold him the land, didn't you?'

He addresses this last question to Young George, who looks down and mutters something about needing the money.

'We wouldn't have sold it if we didn't have to,' says Sally with spirit. 'George is passionate about keeping the estate intact for future generations.'

'Does that mean you?' Nelson asks Chaz.

There is a pause before Sally says, 'Actually, Cassie is heir to the estate. It seemed fairer, as she's the eldest. It involved quite a lot of faff, though, getting the entail changed so she could inherit. But George is all for equality.' She looks fondly at her husband.

'Of course,' says Blake, who has also joined the group, 'if

that had been done years ago, Nell would have inherited the place, not George.'

There's a silence. Nell appears at her husband's side. 'Talking about me? Hope it's something nice.'

'I should go,' says Ruth.

In the hallway, she extricates her anorak from the curly coat stand, thinking that a whole lot of family skeletons are coming to the surface this evening. All in all, she's happy to be leaving. Frank is obviously having a lovely time with the beautiful Cassandra and hasn't given her a second glance. She wonders briefly what has happened to the bearded man, the Ancient Mariner. Is he still out there, staring up at the house? She shivers and puts on her coat. At least it's only a short drive home.

But as she approaches the front door, it opens, bringing a blast of wind strong enough to make her step backwards. Frank stands on the threshold, coatless, his hair wild.

'Ruth! Are you going?'

'Yes, I've got to get back to Kate.'

'It's only five o'clock.'

'But it's already dark,' says Ruth, 'and there's a storm coming.'

'Cathbad says the storm won't break until midnight,' says Frank.

Ruth doesn't ask why Frank has suddenly started believing (and quoting) Cathbad's weather forecasts. 'I've got to go,' she says.

'Just stay for a few minutes,' says Frank. 'I've hardly spoken to you.' He draws her towards the church pew in the hallway. They sit side by side; it feels a lot cosier than it did with Nell.

'Where's Cassandra?' asks Ruth.

Frank grins. 'In the grounds. She's showing Earl and Paul the best places to shoot tomorrow. It was a bit cold for me so I came back. Plus I've got a low tolerance for acting talk.'

'Cassandra's an actress, I understand.'

'She is indeed. I think I've had the whole of her résumé tonight.'

Ruth wonders why Frank is complaining. After all, he's the one who likes the company of young women. Then she jumps because Frank puts his hand on hers, 'Ruth. Why didn't you come and see me in Seattle?'

Ruth tries to move her hand away. 'It was difficult,' she says. 'With Kate and everything.'

'I would have been delighted to see Kate too,' says Frank. 'You know I would.'

'Why do you care?' says Ruth, trying to make her voice sound light. 'Paul tells me you're dating his kid sister.' She tries and fails not to put ironical quotation marks around the words.

Frank leans back. 'Ruth . . .' he says.

But Ruth is never to learn what Frank was going to say because, at that moment, Clough bursts in through the front door, carrying Cassandra in his arms.

'She's been attacked,' he says.

CHAPTER 16

Nelson is furious with Clough. Why did he have to come barging in like that, making the whole thing into such a drama? On the other hand, it was lucky that he'd been on hand to come to Cassandra's rescue. Nelson had sent Tim home (he was keen to get to the gym and there didn't seem any point in having the three of them hanging around) but he was pleased that he and Clough had stayed. Even though he had no reason to suspect that anything would happen at the party, he has still been on the alert. That was why he had sent Clough out to patrol the grounds, in the face of his sergeant's extreme reluctance. He hadn't expected Clough to have to fight off a violent attacker. If that was indeed what he had done.

Nelson had come to the door of the drawing room just in time to see Clough striding through the hall with the girl in his arms. For some reason, Ruth was there too, squashed up on a little seat with her American friend. The sight did not do much to soothe Nelson's feelings.

'What the hell's going on?' he said.

'It's Cassandra, boss,' said Clough. 'Somebody leapt on her in the graveyard.'

'Bring her in here,' said Nelson.

Clough had brought Cassandra into the drawing room and laid her on the sofa. Nelson saw that her hair was matted at the temples and that there was blood on Clough's jacket and on the pale-lemon sofa. He called an ambulance as Sally came running to her daughter's side.

'Darling! What's happened?'

'I was walking across the field,' said Cassandra, her voice high and shaky, 'where the old gravestones are. I stopped because I had a text on my phone. You can't get a signal up at the house and I wanted to answer. The next thing I knew, someone had hit me over the head. He . . .' she pointed at Clough, 'he saved my life.'

Clough coughed modestly. 'Just doing my job.'

Sally sent someone (her son, Nelson thought) running to get water and bandages. The father was there now too, standing around rather ineffectually and patting his daughter's hand.

Nelson turned to Clough. 'Did you see the assailant?'

'No. I was just walking the perimeter of the grounds when I heard a shout. I came running and Cassandra was on the ground. She said that someone had leapt on her from behind. I had a quick look around but couldn't see the attacker. Then I thought my priority was to get Cassandra to safety.'

'He picked me up like I weighed nothing,' said Cassandra.

Chaz brought a bowl and some bandages, Sally tenderly wiped her daughter's forehead as Nelson became aware that the room was suddenly full of people. Old George was there and the American couple. Looking round he saw Ruth and the TV bloke, Frank, standing by the door, both looking very shaken.

Nelson leant over to talk to Cassandra. 'Miss Blackstock, did you get a chance to look at your attacker?'

'No.' Cassandra's eyes filled with tears. 'Like I said, he jumped on me from behind.'

'He knocked you to the ground. Is that right?'

'Detective Inspector!' exploded Young George. 'She's in no condition to answer your questions.'

'Just trying to get a picture of events,' said Nelson. 'The first few minutes are vital in any investigation. My sergeant and I will go out and check the grounds now.'

Cassandra reached out a trembling hand to Clough. 'Don't send him away. I feel much safer when he's here.'

So that was how Nelson had ended up searching the grounds on his own. The wind was even stronger now and he found himself bending almost double as he stepped out from the shelter of the kitchen garden. It was pitch black away from the lights of the house but, out towards the sea, there was a faint light, a sort of phosphorescence that glimmered and flickered. He could hear the waves too, a roaring, angry sound. Nelson shone his torch on the gravestones and on the stone cross. It was too dark to see anything else. As he made his way back towards the house, he saw two of the American film people standing in the pets' graveyard rhapsodising about the scenery, oblivious to the gathering storm.

Nelson shone his torch at them.

'There's been a serious assault,' he said. 'No one's to leave the house.'

Now Nelson is trying to maintain some sort of order at the house. Cassandra has been taken away by ambulance and Sally has gone with her. 'Goodbye,' she said to Clough, raising her eyes to his face. 'And thank you.' 'It was nothing,' said Clough. 'Take care of yourself, darling.' Darling! That was hardly the way for a police officer to talk to a member of the public but Nelson hadn't felt up to rebuking the hero of the hour.

Nelson gathers everyone together in the drawing room. Cathbad and his druid friend are there, both looking intrigued. Nelson is relieved that they refrain from mentioning bad energies or ancient curses or any of that new-age crap. They had been out in the grounds too; Hazel communing with the storm (his words) and Cathbad, rather more prosaically, ringing Judy. Mobile phones have a lot to answer for, thinks Nelson. Because of the weak signal up at the house, everyone seemed to be in the grounds ringing or texting. Cassandra had just received a text when she was attacked. Who knows how many other calls and texts were made in the course of the evening? He himself had made two calls while he was outside, one to Michelle to tell her that he might be late and one to his daughter Rebecca to remind her to get her MOT booked. Both calls had gone straight to answerphone.

Sally and her husband, together with the American woman, Nell, had been talking to Nelson when the alleged attack took place. Blake Goodheart claimed to have popped upstairs 'to fetch a warmer sweater'. He's certainly wearing a heavy-looking jumper but Nelson can't remember what he had on earlier. He'll have to check. The grandfather hadn't stirred from his chair by the fire where he had been chatting to two of Cassandra's actor friends – Syd and Eddy (both women). Ruth and Frank had, of course, been having their cosy chat in the hall. What had they been talking about, he wonders. They hadn't sat together in church (he had checked) and afterwards, at the graveside, Ruth seemed to be deliberately keeping apart from all the other mourners. She had been wearing her impartial professional face. Nelson recognised it immediately.

Nelson questions the two Americans, Earl and Paul. They are both very polite and call him 'sir' a lot but Nelson can't rid himself of the impression that they view the afternoon's events as a cute English ritual, like croquet or high tea. Earl says that they had walked around the house with Cassandra and that she had then shown them the marshes and the old graves. She had then excused herself to make a telephone call (another one!) and the two men had wandered into the pets' burial ground, where they had become embroiled in a passionate argument about shooting schedules. Had they heard a scream? No, but the wind was so goddamned loud it was hard to hear anything. In that case, why stand out in it chatting about timetables, thinks Nelson, but he doesn't say this aloud. It is hard to think of the TV men as suspects, although (as he often says to his team) everyone is a suspect until proved otherwise. Assume nothing.

He goes into the hallway to make a call to the hospital. Of course he can't get a signal. This bloody house, it's conspiring against him. He steps outside the front door and is rewarded by two wavery bars, enough to get through to A and E. Cassandra has been examined. She has a head wound and slight concussion. She's having some stitches and then she'll be discharged. He goes back into the house to pass on this news.

'Shall I go to the hospital and bring her back?' asks Clough.

'I'm sure the Blackstocks can stretch to a taxi,' says Nelson.

'Nelson,' says a voice behind them. It's Ruth. Clough melts away tactfully.

Ruth looks tired, thinks Nelson. She's wearing a black dress which makes her look slimmer than usual. He wonders if she wore it for the funeral or for her American friend's benefit. At least there's no sign of him.

'I need to talk to you,' says Ruth. 'But quickly because I have to get back to Kate.'

'Of course.' Nelson is galvanised instantly. They sit on the wooden bench recently occupied by Ruth and Frank.

'When you searched the grounds,' says Ruth, 'did you see anyone hanging around?'

'Nobody except for your TV pals,' says Nelson.

'They're not my pals,' says Ruth. 'But did you see someone else, a man with a long grey beard, leaning on a staff?'

'Who's this?' says Nelson. 'Old Father Time?'

Ruth ignores this. 'I saw this man at the church,' she says. 'And a bit later, I saw him in the grounds. Then I heard that Cassandra had been hit over the head and I thought maybe it was the kind of blow you'd get from a wooden staff.'

Nelson is interested now. 'Can you give me a full description of the man?' he says. 'Did anyone else see him?'

'I don't know,' says Ruth, 'but Blake Goodheart definitely saw him. You know, Nell's husband. He said he was like the Ancient Mariner.'

'Wasn't he the bloke who killed a seagull?'

'An albatross, yes. It brought him a lot of bad luck.'

'This family doesn't exactly need more bad luck,' says Nelson. 'You'd better be getting home now. I'll take a statement tomorrow. Is Clara looking after Katie?'

'No,' says Ruth in what he recognises as her patient voice, 'I've left her home alone with an Indian takeaway. Of course she's with Clara. But I want to get back before it gets too late.'

'Well, drive carefully,' says Nelson. 'The wind's getting up.'

The wind is certainly fierce now. Ruth's little car wobbles to and fro as she turns onto the exposed A149, driving past the golf links and the beginning of the marshes. Ruth clenches her hands on the wheel, trying to keep the car steady. The rain has started too, huge drenching waves of it that seem to be flung against the car by some malevolent hand. Ruth switches on Radio 4 for comfort but it's a dramatisation of *Wuthering Heights*, and after a few minutes of desolate moorland and doomed love, Ruth turns it off again. I cannot live without my life. I cannot live without my soul. That's all very well, Ruth tells Cathy, but sometimes you just have to.

She's so happy to see the signpost for New Road. Nearly home, back to Kate and safety. But, as she turns onto the road over the marshes, she is hit by a wind so strong that she struggles to keep the car on the road. She mustn't go over the edge, there are ditches on both sides of the road; if she goes over, she'll be killed or, at best, stranded until morning. The rain is so heavy now that the windscreen wipers can't cope and Ruth is driving almost blind. There's a dull roaring in the distance. Is that the wind or the sea? She thinks of sea sprites and nixes and the ghosts of dead children singing under the sea. She thinks of old Mrs Blackstock saying that the sea would get her in the end. Presumably she's out there too, wailing in the darkness, whitened bones and hair like green seaweed. Ruth realises that she's almost crying as she wrenches the steering wheel back. Oh God, just let her get home safely.

And then – oh, thank you, God – there's the light from her cottage. The bushes opposite are bent almost flat and, as she parks her car, she sees a slate come crashing down from the roof.

Clara opens the door before she has a chance to knock.

'Thank God you're back,' she says. 'I was starting to get worried.'

'How's Kate?'

'She's fine. She's had her bath and we're just watching *A Hundred and One Dalmatians* before bedtime.'

Of course, it's only seven o'clock. Ruth feels as if she's been out all night. She sits on the sofa next to Kate, pink and glowing in her Dora the Explorer pyjamas.

'Hallo, sweetheart.'

Kate points at the screen. 'They get home in time,' she says. Recently Kate has developed a worry about being in time for things. Ruth doesn't know where this fear has come from. Sandra always collects Kate from school punctually and, if

Ruth has been late at the childminder's a few times, Kate can hardly remember that, can she? She's particularly worried about getting home in time for Christmas and the sight of the puppies running along in the snow always sparks a few anxious queries.

'Yes,' says Ruth. 'They get home in time for Christmas. Everyone's happy at the end.'

'Would you like a cup of tea?' says Clara. 'You must have had an awful drive.'

'I'll make it,' says Ruth. 'And you'd better stay the night here. Honestly, the wind's so bad I thought it would blow me off the road.'

'Thanks,' says Clara. 'I must say, I was dreading the drive back.' She sits on the other side of Kate. 'It'll be fun,' she says. 'We can have a sleepover.'

'Sleepover,' repeats Kate. It's one of her favourite words.

CHAPTER 17

Nelson wakes to find that three of his fence panels have fallen down in the night. A quick glance around the cul-de-sac shows that many fences have met the same fate. There's a trampoline upside down on someone's lawn and a couple of recycling bins are bowling along the road. It's still pretty windy out there. As he watches, a tarpaulin becomes detached from a car and flies into his next-door neighbour's cherry tree. Nelson shuts the door.

He goes back into the kitchen and turns on the TV (there's a tiny set by the microwave because Michelle likes to catch up on *Coronation Street* while she's cooking). He puts on the kettle and slots a slice of bread into the toaster. It's part of their morning ritual; he always wakes first and he always makes the tea. He has a piece of toast while he's waiting and Michelle has her healthy breakfast of yoghurt and fruit when she comes downstairs. Nelson usually has another piece of toast then, just to keep her company.

The TV news is full of last night's storm. St Jude's Storm, they're calling it. Nelson remembers Cathbad using the name but had dismissed it as typical Cathbad nonsense. As usual, though, it looks as if Cathbad's cosmic weather forecast was accurate. The screen is full of fallen trees and crashing waves. Flights have been cancelled and trains derailed. A teenage boy has been swept out to sea in Newhaven. The sea is a dangerous enemy.

Nelson thinks about last night as he pours boiling water into the teapot (he always makes a proper pot). Was Cassandra really attacked in the grounds of her parents' house? She certainly had a bash on the head, whatever happened. Could she have fallen, hit her head on a gravestone and made up the attacker later? She might even have been hit by a branch or something and just assumed it was an assailant. She looks like a girl who enjoys the limelight. Nelson remembers Clough staggering in with the wounded victim in his arms. That was quite some entrance. Well, he'll go round today and check Cassandra's story. He'll take Clough with him as the girl seems to like him so much. *I feel much safer when he's here.* That's not how most people think about Cloughie.

And what about Ruth's bearded man, the stranger who suddenly materialised in the grounds of Blackstock Hall? If it had been anyone else but Ruth, Nelson would have taken this story with a pinch of salt. But Ruth's not the type to make up mysterious strangers. So if the man exists, who is he and why was he hanging about outside during the worst storm for years? Could the bearded man – Ruth's Ancient Mariner – have attacked Cassandra? But why? Nelson eats his toast, watching as a weather forecaster points gleefully at the whirlpool of arrows covering south-east Britain. 'We haven't seen the last of the bad weather yet,' she's saying happily.

'Harry.'

Michelle is standing in the doorway, wrapped in her white dressing gown. As she crosses the room, he thinks that she's lost some weight recently. She's always been slim but now she looks almost wiry and the arm that points to the garden has definite muscle tone. Too many visits to the gym and not enough meals out, he thinks. But before he can suggest a romantic dinner for two, Michelle says, 'Our fence is down.'

She sounds irritated and unreasonable. Nelson feels himself getting aggrieved in turn. Surely it's not his fault that the fence is broken? It's not as if he blew it down like the big bad wolf.

'Fences are down everywhere,' he says.

'It's so annoying,' says Michelle. 'Our patio heater's blown over too.'

'Good job I put the garden furniture in the garage last night,' says Nelson.

'When's it all going to end?' says Michelle, sounding as if she's asking an altogether bigger question.

Nelson hands her a cup of tea. 'Wind's going to die down later today. That's what the weather forecast says.'

'What do they know?' says Michelle. She sips her tea moodily.

'Be careful driving in to work,' says Nelson. 'There might be trees down.' He hopes Ruth got home all right. He'll ring her when he gets to the station. He sees Michelle looking at him and immediately feels guilty. He should not be thinking about Ruth, not while he's in the kitchen with his wife.

'Maybe you should take the day off,' he says. It's meant to be a peace offering but Michelle immediately takes offence.

'I know you don't think my job's important but I still have to go to work. I'm the manager, you know. I bet you don't take the day off just because a few trees are down.'

That's different, thinks Nelson, but he knows better than to say this aloud.

'I'm off to have a shower,' he says. 'There's no peace for the wicked.'

He doesn't know where this last remark came from. It sounds like one of his mother's sayings and, like a lot of her statements, it's pretty unanswerable. At any rate, Michelle, still looking out at the windswept garden, doesn't attempt to answer it.

When Nelson finally arrives at the station, after a tortuous route avoiding fallen trees and flooded ditches, he finds that his day has been overtaken by storm-related problems. The emergency services are busy all over Norfolk and Nelson spends the morning allocating officers to the worst-hit areas. Judy isn't in. Tim looks less than delighted to be put in charge of an operation to rescue seals at Blakeney Point. 'I'm not a great one for marine wildlife, boss,' he says. 'Then you've relocated to the wrong county,' Nelson tells him. Like-wise, Tanya is not thrilled to find herself redirecting traffic in King's Lynn town centre to avoid an overturned tanker.

Clough, on the other hand, clearly enjoys rescuing an old lady from her storm-damaged cottage in Holt. Heroism is getting to be a habit with him.

It's afternoon by the time Clough and Nelson set out for Blackstock Hall. The wind has died down and the weather is sunny and cold, the waterlogged fields reflecting a bright-blue sky. Nelson doesn't attempt to park in the muddy lane by the Hall. He leaves his car on the road and he and Clough begin the trek over the fields.

'It's very open round here,' says Nelson. 'Not many places for a secret assassin to hide.'

Clough recognises the mockery in the words and says, with dignity, 'It was dark, boss, and blowing a gale. I reckon Jack the Ripper himself could have hidden amongst those gravestones. Bloody spooky, it was.'

'Is that who you think it was, Jack the Ripper?'

'You're not taking this very seriously,' says Clough, making a detour to avoid a particularly muddy puddle. 'The girl was terrified. And you saw her head. Someone had whacked her pretty hard.'

'She was certainly injured,' says Nelson. 'But it's possible that she could have fallen and hit her head on something. But I am taking it seriously. There was quite a lot of publicity around the funeral, not to mention the TV interest. If someone had it in for Cassandra, it wouldn't have been difficult to work out where she was.'

'Or it could have been one of the family,' says Clough. 'Check the family first, that's what you always say.'

'You're right,' says Nelson. 'But there's another possible

option.' He tells Clough about Ruth's mysterious bearded man.

'Blimey, boss,' says Clough. 'He sounds like something out of *Harry Potter*. Are you sure Ruth didn't just imagine that she saw him?'

'It's not like Ruth to imagine things,' says Nelson. 'And she says she talked to this man. Blake Goodheart saw him too, apparently.'

They have almost reached the house. The low ditch meant to keep the sheep away from the lawn is swollen with water, presenting a more formidable obstacle than usual. Two sheep stranded on the wrong side look at them suspiciously.

'How are we going to get over this?' asks Clough. 'Long jump?'

'There's a bridge,' says Nelson, pointing.

'Correction,' mutters Clough. 'There's a plank.'

The two men negotiate the slippery plank without mishap. The water below is clogged with leaves and fallen branches. It's probably not that deep but, nevertheless, falling in would be unpleasant. Nelson is relieved when they get to the house. He feels that he's had enough of the countryside for a while.

Sally opens the door at the first knock. This time there's no mention of their having come to the wrong door. They are clearly welcome guests, especially Clough.

'Come in. Come in. Cassie was just saying that she was hoping you'd call round.'

Was she indeed? Nelson doesn't approve of getting too friendly with witnesses (or suspects) but he smiles and accepts Sally's offer of tea. There's no point in antagonising people, after all. Besides, if the family are well disposed towards the police, it might prove useful later on.

'How is Miss Blackstock today?' he asks as he follows Sally into the kitchen.

'Much better,' says Sally, 'but she's still allowing her mum to give her some TLC. Here she is.'

Cassandra is sitting at the kitchen table, her hands wrapped around a mug of tea. It's an attitude that Nelson recognises from his own daughters: body hunched forward, jumper pulled down over the hands, hair hanging forward over the face. It's a stance designed to say 'treat me gently, I'm very sensitive'. Rebecca employed it every time he tried to have a serious chat with her about homework. Sally, though, seems to take it at face value.

'She's still feeling a bit fragile, aren't you, darling?'

'I'm OK,' says Cassandra bravely. 'It's lovely to see you again, Sergeant Clough. And you too, Detective . . .'

'Detective Chief Inspector Nelson,' says Nelson. 'We just wanted to ask you a few questions about yesterday, Miss Blackstock. Is that all right with you?'

'Call me Cassie. Yes, of course. I'm not sure what I can remember though. It's all a bit fuzzy.'

'Let's see if we can help you,' says Nelson. 'You went for a walk in the grounds with Earl Kennedy and Paul Brindisi. Is that right?'

'Yes. They wanted to see some possible locations for shooting. For the TV programme. And I thought, as I'm in the business . . .' She looks at them from under her eyelashes.

As far as Nelson can make out, Cassandra Blackstock's

acting career is limited to playing odd roles with an avant-garde theatre company in Lincoln. But he just smiles and asks her to continue. Sally places tea and fresh scones in front of them. There are definitely some advantages to paying afternoon calls with Clough.

'We went round the house but it was a bit too dark to see anything. I showed them the old family graves because they're so spooky and atmospheric. Then, just as we were going back to the house, I got a text. I needed to call back immediately so I asked the others to go back to the house without me.'

'Do you mind me asking who the text was from?' says Nelson.

'My agent,' says Cassandra, blushing. 'I thought it might be about a part I'd auditioned for. So Earl and Paul went on ahead and I stayed to make a call.'

'In the graveyard?' asks Nelson. 'Can't have been very cosy.'

'I wasn't thinking,' says Cassandra. 'I was just so excited about the part. So I called Tobias but he was engaged. Then I saw I had a text from a friend so I was looking at that when . . .'

Nelson waits patiently. Clough tries to demolish a scone and look sympathetic at the same time.

'When?' prompts Nelson at last.

'When someone hit me over the head really hard. I screamed. I think I fell over. I'm sorry . . .' She puts a hand to her head. 'It's all a blur.'

'Are you OK, darling?' asks Sally.

'I'm fine,' says Cassie. 'It's just . . .'

'You're being very brave,' says Clough.

Nelson gives him a look but Cassandra flashes him a brilliant smile.

'I'm trying,' she says. 'I just can't remember anything after falling over. The next thing I remember is you carrying me into the house.'

Nelson thinks he'd better interrupt before things get too nauseating.

'You say someone hit you over the head, Cassie. How did they hit you? From behind?'

'Yes. I didn't see their face.'

'Did you hear them? Did you hear them creeping up on you?'

'No.' She shivers. 'But the wind was very loud and I was so preoccupied with my phone.'

Famous last words, thinks Nelson. He dreads to think how many people step out into traffic or into the paths of attackers just because they're 'preoccupied with their phone'.

'Is it possible,' he asks gently, 'that you just fell and hit your head? After all, it was very dark out there.'

'No!' For the first time, Cassandra drops her sensitive pose and sits upright. 'I definitely felt someone hit me. It felt like he hit me with an iron bar or something.'

'He?'

'It must have been a man. There was so much force behind the blow.'

But women can use force when they have to, thinks Nelson. And it doesn't take much strength or daring to hit a defenceless woman in the dark.

'Mrs Blackstock.' He turns to Sally, who is now holding her daughter's hand. 'Can you get me a list of everyone who was here yesterday?'

'I'm sure I can,' says Sally. 'It was invitation only.'

'Did you know everyone by sight?'

'I think so. Except for the TV people.'

'You don't remember seeing an old man with a long grey beard? He was spotted in the grounds just before Cassie was attacked.'

'No.' Sally and Cassandra both look at him wonderingly. Nelson braces himself for more Harry Potter jokes but Sally says suddenly, 'Oh, was that the man that Blake saw?'

'Possibly.'

Sally turns to Cassandra. 'Blake said that he saw this weird old man in the grounds. Said he reminded him of the Ancient Mariner. Well, everything reminds Blake of something from a book.'

'Did anyone else see this man?'

'Your archaeologist friend, I think. Blake said they were together in the library when they saw him. Hazel was there too. And his friend, Cathbad.'

'But you didn't see him?'

'No.'

'Did you notice him at the church?'

'No, but it was all so emotional, I don't think I took anything in. Wasn't it lovely when they played the last post?'

Nelson agrees that it was. 'You didn't see this man in the grounds?' he asks Cassandra.

'No. Do you think he was the one who attacked me?'

'Let's not jump to conclusions,' says Nelson. 'But I'll circulate a description, just to be on the safe side. Where are Blake and his wife today?'

'Oh, they went to Lynn to see the museum,' says Sally. 'Madness going out in this weather. But apparently they're interested in history.'

Nelson is just about to draw the interview to a close when, somewhere in the room, a phone rings. There's the usual hassle while Sally struggles to locate the cordless phone (this time it's in the spice rack).

'Hallo, Chaz. How nice of you to call . . . Oh. Yes, he is here. All right. Just a moment.' She turns to Nelson. 'It's Chaz. He wants to talk to you.'

Nelson has a brief conversation and then turns to Sally. 'Thank you for your time. We'll be in touch. Hope you continue to feel better, Cassie.' To Clough: 'Let's go.'

'Where?'

'I'll tell you on the way.'

He explains as they walk back over the darkening fields. 'We're off to the pig farm. Chaz thinks that he's found something in one of his pens.'

'What?' Clough grimaces.

'Human teeth.'

CHAPTER 18

It's dark by the time they reach the pig farm. The old control tower is a ghostly white shape in the middle of the first field but the other buildings have disappeared completely. One feeble light shines from the bungalow. Even the pigs are silent. Do they go to sleep at night? wonders Nelson. He knows nothing about pigs but he has an uneasy feeling that he's about to learn more.

Chaz meets them at the door. He has a large torch in his hand.

'Good of you to come,' he says. 'I hope this isn't a wild goose chase.'

I hope so too, thinks Nelson. Aloud he says, 'Perhaps you can tell us what you found.'

'I'll show you,' says Chaz. He leads the way across the black fields, the torch illuminating a narrow pathway ahead. They walk in single file, Nelson trying to not hear Clough's muffled groans and expletives. They reach one of the old hangers and Chaz fumbles to open what appears to be a huge door. Inside, there's a smell of hay and animals and a sense of being in a massive space.

'There's a light,' says Chaz. 'Hang on a moment.'

The next minute the hanger is filled with cold white light. The building is divided into pens and, judging by the shuffling and grunting sounds, it seems that the pigs are waking up.

'This is where I keep the growers and the finishers,' says Chaz. 'Young pigs,' he says, probably noting the incomprehension on the faces of the two policemen. 'Growers are pigs that have been weaned and are about to be sold.'

'Sold for slaughter?' asks Nelson, feeling rather insensitive saying these words in the presence of the animals. He hopes they aren't listening.

'Yes,' says Chaz. 'We're a pretty small operation really. Free range. The pigs can wander about during the day but we keep them inside at night. They're very happy.'

Until they're slaughtered, thinks Nelson.

'What are finishers?' asks Clough.

'Growers that have finished growing,' says Chaz with a laugh. 'They can be quite feisty so we keep them here away from the sows and the piglets.'

Nelson dreads to think what a feisty pig looks like.

'Can you tell us where you found the teeth?' he asks.

'Here.' Chaz gestures at the nearest pen, which is empty. 'I had four or five growers in here. I fed them this morning but didn't let them out because the weather was so foul. When I came to feed them this evening, I saw that they were snuffling in the corner of the pen as if they were feeding on something. I went to have a look and I saw some . . . well, some remains. I got the pigs out of the pen – took some doing, actually – and telephoned the police station. I was told you were at Blackstock Hall so I called there.'

Nelson steps into the pen. One look is enough. In the corner of the pen are some bones that look distinctly human.

'Here are the teeth,' says Chaz. 'I put them in a bucket.' He rattles the pail cheerfully. Again, one look is enough.

'We need to seal off the site,' says Nelson. 'I'll get the Scene of the Crime boys here in the morning.'

Clough, who has been maintaining a stunned silence, says, 'Are you telling me that these pigs could have eaten someone?'

'It's possible,' says Chaz, sounding apologetic on the animals' behalf. 'Pigs are omnivorous, you see. They would eat a human body if there was one to hand. And the growers are always hungry.'

'Jesus.' Clough sounds like he's about to be sick.

'But you checked them in the morning,' says Nelson. 'Could they eat a body that fast?'

'Oh yes,' says Chaz. 'They could strip a body to the bone in minutes.'

'I think I'll wait outside,' says Clough.

Michelle and Tim are sitting side by side in the jacuzzi. They are, basically, having a bath together but nobody – not even Nelson, should he make an unprecedented visit to the leisure centre – could accuse them of impropriety. Sometimes these sessions are agony for Tim but tonight, feeling Michelle's leg against his, he wishes that they could stay there for ever. There is something cosy about being in this brightly lit space at night. The pool is almost empty but they can hear salsa music filtering through from a dancercise class. The glass roof shows the night sky and the stars.

'Are you happy?' he asks. As soon as he says it, he knows that he's asked the wrong question. The thought of being happy with him invariably makes Michelle feel guilty about Nelson.

'I can't be happy,' she says. 'Not while all this is going on.'

'But nothing is going on,' says Tim.

Michelle sighs and leans back, her long blonde hair floating out in the foamy water.

'Please don't start that conversation again.'

'Why not?' Tim feels his good mood ebbing away as the bubbles seep from the jacuzzi, leaving the surface flat. They should get out now but they both stay where they are.

'Nothing is going on,' he continues. 'We're having an affair but we're not having an affair.'

'If we're not having an affair,' says Michelle, 'then why do I feel so guilty?'

'Maybe you'd feel less guilty if we actually slept together,' says Tim. Well, it's worth a try.

He half thinks that she's going to walk out. He imagines her storming away to the ladies' changing rooms, the water dripping off her hair and swimming costume. In a way, he wants it to happen. Michelle has never really been angry with him though she sometimes mentions arguing with Nelson. If she really loved him, surely they'd fight sometimes?

But instead Michelle looks at him seriously, smoothing back her hair with one hand. Her unadorned face is heart-stoppingly beautiful.

'Harry has to go on a training course in December,' she says. 'If he does, maybe we can spend the night together.'

CHAPTER 19

Ruth gets the telephone call just after she has dropped Kate off at school. When she sees the name on the screen, she stops in a lay-by and presses call return.

'Hi, Nelson. What is it?'

'Hallo, Ruth. Fancy coming to look at some human remains?'

'Tempting,' says Ruth. 'Where are they?'

'At a pig farm on Lockwell Heath. But here's the twist. The pig farm is owned by Chaz Blackstock.'

'Have you got SOCO there? You won't need me.'

'Always good to have a second opinion. Besides, I thought you might be interested.'

Ruth considers. She doesn't have any lectures until the afternoon but she had planned to get into the office early and make a start on her end-of-term marking. All the same, Lockwell Heath is very near. It's practically on the way to the university.

'I'll be there in fifteen minutes,' she says.

When she gets to the pig farm, the SOCO team have

already got to work. There's an awning over the entrance to one of the huge barns and white-coated figures are moving purposefully to and fro. Nelson and Clough are standing by Nelson's car. When she gets closer, she realises that Clough is eating a bacon sandwich.

'Not very tactful,' she says.

'You should have seen him last night,' says Nelson. 'He was almost sick when Chaz was telling us about the piggies' eating habits.'

'They eat us,' says Clough thickly, 'I eat them. It's only justice.'

'Is that was this is about?' says Ruth. 'Pigs eating a human body? I've read about that. A farmer in America was eaten by his own boars.'

'We're not sure what's happened yet,' says Nelson. He's always very careful about not jumping to conclusions. It's one of the things that Ruth admires about him.

'Chaz called us in yesterday,' Nelson continues. 'He found his pigs eating something. When he looked more closely, he thought it could be human remains. There's not much left.' He glances at Clough. 'Just some bones and a few teeth.'

'We should be able to tell if they're human or not,' says Ruth. 'And we should be able to get some DNA too. This is a bit of a weird place, isn't it?'

'It used to be an American airbase,' says Nelson. He gestures towards the barns. 'These were the hangars. Didn't you see the control tower on your way in?'

'I saw something,' says Ruth. In truth, she had been so concerned with not missing the turn-off for the farm that she'd hardly noticed her surroundings. She vaguely remembers a building with its windows boarded up. And, come to think of it, the driveway had been unusually long and straight. Was that the runway? She thinks for a moment. Lockwell Heath . . . American airbase . . .

'Hang on,' she says, 'was this the base where –'

'Where Fred Blackstock was stationed?' says Nelson. 'Got it in one.'

Ruth looks around her with new eyes. Behind the hangars, the flat fields stretch away as far as the eye can see. She tries to imagine the sky filled with planes, heading out across the sea. To what? To certain death in many cases, Fred Blackstock's included. The ghost fields. She shivers.

'Are you cold?' says Nelson. Although the wind is not as strong as it was yesterday, there's still a chill in the air.

'I'm OK,' says Ruth. 'I'd better get going. I suppose I should get some coveralls.'

Ruth detests wearing coveralls but she knows that the SOCO team will insist. She introduces herself to the senior officer and climbs into the paper jumpsuit. Great. Now they can fly her above the field as a windsock.

Inside the barn, the remains have been carefully numbered and bagged. Usually Ruth prefers to see bones in situ, but in this case she imagines that there was very little to learn from the context. Anyway, there isn't much left: a few pieces of what look like skull and leg bones and a handful of teeth.

'They're human, aren't they?' says the senior officer, a pleasant man called Mike Halloran.

Ruth nods. 'Yes, one tooth has even been filled. An old fash-ioned aluminium filling too, which may help with dating.'

'We can send them for DNA testing,' says Mike. 'Might help us identify the poor sod.'

'Was there anything else?' asks Ruth. 'Fragments of clothing? Anything that might have fallen out of a pocket?'

'No, nothing,' says Mike cheerfully. 'Pigs did a pretty thor-ough job.'

'Blood?'

'A bit on the floor of the pen and some blood-stained straw. We've bagged it up.'

'Might help with the DNA.'

'Yes, but that only helps with identification if the deceased was on a register somewhere. My guess is that it was some poor down-and-out who crept in here to get out of the storm.'

Nelson shares this opinion. 'We'll search the missing per-sons database,' he says, as Ruth divests herself of the hated coveralls, 'but nobody's been reported missing recently. I think we're looking at a vagrant, someone who's not on any list anywhere. Poor bastard. He certainly picked the wrong place for a kip.'

Ruth thinks this sounds all too likely but Clough says, 'I don't like it, boss.'

'Don't worry, Cloughie,' says Nelson. 'I won't let the nasty piggies get you.'

Clough ignores this but stands his ground. 'I don't like the Blackstock connection. First Cassandra Blackstock gets attacked and then a body's found on her brother's farm.

It's a coincidence and you always say you don't believe in coincidence.'

Nelson can hardly deny this. Even Ruth has heard him make this statement. He says, in a more serious tone, 'We're investigating the attack on Cassandra but it's hard to see a link to this death. I agree though. We should watch the Blackstocks.'

'Taking my name in vain?' Chaz Blackstock has made an almost noiseless appearance, looming up from the shadow of the barn wearing a long black raincoat. Ruth is struck again by how dramatic he looks, with his dark hair and intensely blue eyes. He also reminds her of someone.

'Just finishing off here,' says Nelson breezily.

'Do you think you'll be able to identify the . . . the remains?'

'We'll try to extract some DNA,' says Nelson, 'but that doesn't help much unless we've got something to match it against.'

'The police investigation won't affect the filming, will it?' says Chaz.

'What filming?' says Nelson.

'*The History Men* are filming here tomorrow,' says Chaz. 'Doctor Galloway's involved, aren't you?'

All three men stare at Ruth. She mutters something incomprehensible.

'Well, far be it for the police to stand in the way of a television programme,' says Nelson. 'After all, what's really important here?'

Clough grins appreciatively but Chaz elects to take this at face value. Perhaps he's just not very bright, thinks Ruth.

'Oh, good show. I'll see you tomorrow then, Doctor Galloway.'

'Yes,' says Ruth. 'No. Maybe. I'd better get off to work now.'

She drives away feeling the conflicting emotions that usually accompany an encounter with Nelson. Pleasure in his company, irritation at his police persona, jealousy of his other life, confusion at the mention of *her* other life – it all combines to make working together rather an uneasy affair. She wonders if Nelson sometimes finds it awkward too. Probably not. He's very focused when he's working on a case. Probably just sees Ruth as another expert witness to be bullied or cajoled. Mind you, he was rather caustic about the TV company. Is it possible that he resents Ruth's involvement with them?

She hadn't known quite what to say to Chaz when he mentioned *The History Men*. She hadn't heard anything about a shoot at Lockwell Heath. In fact, she hadn't even twigged at first that the pig farm was the same place as Fred Blackstock's airbase and Earl Kennedy's ghost field. Now that she does know this, she agrees with Clough. It's all rather sinister somehow. First the plane in Devil's Hollow, the plane that had the wrong pilot inside. Then the pets' graveyard at Blackstock Hall, where something, or someone, has obviously been exhumed fairly recently. Then the funeral and the strange man at the church. Then the attack on Cassandra, and now the discovery of human bones at Chaz Blackstock's farm. Too many discoveries involving the Blackstock family, too many mysteries and too many bones. Bones that turn up at the wrong time and in the wrong place. It could be coincidence but she thinks again of the marshland stretching to the sea, the grey man standing there as if carved of stone. *Nothing good will ever come of living on land that should really be at the bottom of the sea.* Fred Blackstock should be lying at the bottom of the sea, but Ruth is almost convinced that he has spent the last seventy years buried amongst the Blackstocks' faithful canine friends. Why? And whose bones are now scattered over the floor of the pig shed? Living close to your animals is all very well but this is getting ridiculous.

The campus is quiet as she parks outside the Natural Sciences block. The grounds took rather a battering in yesterday's storm – there's a bench in the ornamental lake and a fallen tree has narrowly missed the statue of Elizabeth Fry – and today many of the students seem to have elected to stay away. Well, that suits Ruth. If no one turns up to her tutorial at two, she'll have more time to get on with her marking.

But as she nears her office, she sees an ominous shape lurking in the corridor. Phil. He is pretending to pin something on the noticeboard but he's obviously lying in wait for her. Can she back away silently? No, it's too late. He's seen her.

'Ruth! I wondered when you were getting in.'

Like many of Phil's remarks, this is guaranteed to set Ruth's teeth on edge. As long as she turns up for tutorials and lectures, her time is her own. But Phil always manages to make her feel as if she's skiving.

'I was involved in a police investigation,' she says. She knows that this will drive him crazy. He envies Ruth's association with the police and the access it gives her to inside information (not to mention TV coverage).

'Oh?' he says, putting his head on one side in a way that is obviously meant to be charming. Ruth opens her door with her key card, 'Did you want something, Phil?'

'Oh, yes.' He fiddles with the drawing pin in his hand for a moment. 'I was wondering . . . they're filming at Lockwell Heath tomorrow, aren't they? The old airbase?'

'I think so.' She doesn't say that she has only just found this out herself.

'Are you going?'

'I don't know. I'm pretty busy with marking.'

'I thought I might,' says Phil. 'Just to see what's going on. After all, they may want an archaeologist's perspective.'

You hope, thinks Ruth. Rumour has it that Phil has memorised one or two TV-friendly sound bites, just in case.

'Will Frank Barker be there?' asks Phil.

'I'm not sure,' says Ruth. 'Now, if you'll excuse me . . .'

But when she sits at her computer, she sees that she has two interesting emails. One is from Paul Brindisi and it's an invitation to attend tomorrow's shoot at Lockwell Heath. The other is from the DNA Project. It is headed 'Fascinating Discovery'.

We analysed the DNA from the Bronze Age body against samples supplied by local residents (writes Dr Helga Henson) and we have found common ancestry with a local family – the Blackstocks. We then cross-referenced the volunteers and came up with another close match, one which would indicate a common ancestor.

Ruth looks at the name of the volunteer found to share the Blackstock DNA.

David Clough.

CHAPTER 20

'So I could be a lord or something. Lord Dave of Norfolk.'

'I don't think that's quite how it works, Cloughie,' says Nelson. 'Apparently you're related to the Blackstocks somewhere along the line, that's all. It hasn't made you the heir to the throne.'

When Ruth told him about Clough's DNA match, Nelson decided to give him the news in private. After all, it's potentially rather a sensitive subject. Clough has lived in the area all his life. If someone in his family has been over-friendly with the local landed gentry, then that could be embarrassing for him. Nelson knows very little about Clough's family. His mother lives in Hunstanton; Clough is a surprisingly dutiful son and often visits her on a Sunday. There's never been any mention of a father. Clough has a younger brother who has had a couple of near-misses with the law. Clough, by his own account, was no angel in his youth. This doesn't bother Nelson. Teenage delinquents often make rather good policemen. He might have been a delinquent himself if he hadn't been so scared of his mother.

But Clough doesn't seem embarrassed in the least. In fact he seems rather taken with the idea that he might have aristocratic blood.

'Fancy being related to the Blackstocks. No wonder I get on so well with Cassie.'

It's Cassie now, is it? thinks Nelson. He wonders whether Clough has given any serious thought to the implications of the results. Nelson has George Blackstock the Younger's DNA on file (he supplied a sample to establish the link with the dead pilot). He thinks it might just be worth running a Familial DNA Analysis, comparing this specimen to Clough's. This will establish if there's a close family connection. Clough is about the same age as George Blackstock's children. What if George Blackstock is his father too? It's not impossible. Clough's mother lives in the area and (by her son's own account) 'she's still quite fit-looking'. Did George Blackstock imagine that he had some kind of right to seduce local girls? There's a foreign phrase for it, *droit de* something or other. Nelson looks at his colleague, who is still rambling on about his aristocratic connections. Like the Blackstocks, Clough is tall and dark-haired. It's hard to see a connection between the thickset Clough and the effete Chaz Blackstock but isn't there something that echoes the older George about Clough's prominent nose and heavy eyebrows? Nelson doesn't know. He's terrible at spotting resemblances. Michelle's always saying things like 'isn't Laura like my mum about the ear lobes?'. Nelson doesn't feel qualified to adjudicate in such esoteric matters. Likewise, he doesn't feel able to voice his concerns to Clough, especially when the possibility of a closer family relationship obviously hasn't occurred to him. He'll get Clough's DNA analysed, and in the meantime, he'll just have to do his best to keep his sergeant away from 'Cassie'.

'I might drop in on the Lockwell Heath farm today,' Clough is saying. 'See whether anything else has turned up in the pigswill.'

'No,' says Nelson. 'They'll be busy with the filming today. Let's wait until we get the DNA results on the remains. Shouldn't be long now.'

'DNA, eh?' Clough is still chuckling. 'Fantastic stuff.'

'From this lonely airfield, situated on the far eastern edge of Britain, the 444th Bombardment Group began their perilous mission. This building was once the control tower, where the young pilots were given their last-minute instructions before heading out to their planes. These brave men knew heavy losses. In December 1944, just a few days after arriving in Norfolk, they lost three aircraft during a raid on Kiel. Four months later, exhausted crewmen returning to their base were bombed as they climbed out of their aircraft. They died right here on the runway.'

Frank pauses, looking out into the middle distance. The camera, which has been following his slow progress from the control tower, stops too, and revolves slowly to take in the level fields, very green after the recent rain, the hangers black against the horizon and the wide, white sky. Ruth hopes that the soundman picks up the skylark singing, a sweet spiralling sound high above them.

Ruth is standing nearby because it's her turn next. Frank

is going to ask her about finding Fred's body. They're going to film at Devil's Hollow next week. Now Frank takes a swig of water and a make-up girl wipes his face. He smiles his thanks but seems to accept these attentions as his due.

'That's great, Frank,' shouts Paul, who has been looking at the monitor. 'Real moving stuff.' He looks around. 'Ruth!'

'Yes,' says Ruth. To her knowledge this is the fourth time that Paul has checked that's she's there. He's either got a very bad short-term memory or advanced OCD.

'Ruth,' Paul smiles at her with auto-charm. 'Frank's going to tell us a bit about Fred and then he's going to ask you about finding the body. I thought we could shoot the two of you walking along the runway. Might as well make use of the good weather.'

'OK,' says Ruth, her heart sinking. In her (admittedly limited) experience of filming, it's surprisingly difficult to walk and talk at the same time. But Paul's right, it is a beautiful day, not a breath of wind after the storms of two days ago. The pig farm is looking its best, bleak and scenic at the same time. The TV cameras have, so far, managed to avoid the pigs altogether, concentrating on the control tower (the camera zeroing in on the faint words 'Bomb Group') and the runway. There's no lack of family interest, either. Nell, Blake and Cassie are all in attendance, though none of them are due to be filmed today. Early next week, Paul will film a long segment with Nell at Blackstock Hall, 'looking at some of your dad's favourite places.' 'I've no idea what they were,' Nell had said, suddenly sounding panicked. 'No problem,' said Paul. 'We'll make it up.'

Now the cameras are rolling again and Frank is standing on the runway, his eyes crinkling against the autumn sun.

'Senior Airman Frederick Blackstock was twenty-seven years old when he was posted to Lockwell Heath Airbase. In some ways it was a homecoming. Fred had been born and brought up just a few miles from here. But in 1938, he emigrated to America in search of a better life. He married a New England girl, Bella Haywood, and they had a daughter, Nell. Fred was not to know then that when the country of his birth needed help, he would be one of the thousands of Americans who answered that call.'

Ruth notes that, according to *The History Men*, Fred has definitely become an American by 1938. She also questions whether Fred really did go to the States 'in search of a better life'. He was hardly on the breadline in England after all. All she does know is that Fred shared his mother's view that Blackstock Hall and the surrounding land were somehow unlucky. She wonders if the TV programme will mention this.

'On September thirteenth, 1944, the single-seater Curtiss P-36 Mohawk D for Dog set out from Lockwell Heath on a reconnaissance mission. The plane never returned. It was believed to have crashed in a violent thunderstorm but no trace was ever found of the aircraft. Then, in July this year, a truck driver clearing land just a few miles south of here made a startling discovery. I'm joined by Doctor Ruth Galloway, Professor of Forensic Archaeology at the University of North Norfolk.'

Ruth barely has time to notice that Frank has skated over the fact that Fred was not, in fact, the pilot of D for Dog and that the real pilot's body was found a few hundred yards away. She thinks of the ten men standing beside the Flying Fortress. The *Shamrock* and her crew are clearly not going to feature in Paul's version of events. Instead she tells Frank about the plane unearthed by Edward Spens's driver in Devil's Hollow.

'How did you know you had found the remains of a World War Two aircraft?' asks Frank, turning towards her with his easy, on-screen intimacy. But what if it's not just for the camera? Despite herself, Ruth feels her heart beating faster. God, she hopes she isn't going red.

'The soil had a bluish tinge,' she says, 'which comes from corroded aluminium. It's sometimes called Daz because it's meant to look like blue washing powder and it's typical of this sort of wreckage. Then we saw the cockpit, which was still intact. There was a body inside.'

'That must have been quite some moment.'

'Yes. It gave the digger driver an awful shock.' Will Americans understand the word 'digger'? Well, she can't worry about that now. She thinks of the moment when she looked through the glass and saw the figure sitting in the pilot's seat. Paul has told her not to mention her doubts about how long the body had been in the ground or about the bullet hole in the skull ('This is meant to be a heart-warming story, not *Murder She Wrote*'), but she can't help injecting a note of caution when Frank asks her about the body.

'I thought the skin was remarkably well preserved for

human remains buried in chalky ground,' she says. 'The plane had actually landed in an old chalk pit.'

'But DNA analysis proved that the remains were those of Frederick Blackstock?'

'Yes,' Ruth admits. 'It did.'

'Cut,' says Paul. 'Well done, Ruth. It's cute that you're so British and unemotional.'

'Is it?' says Ruth.

But Paul has moved away to film the wild geese flying low over the marshes. Ruth doesn't doubt that this will come complete with some analogy about flight and freedom and the green fields of England. A runner offers her a lift up to the house ('There's tea and coffee and a selection of muffins') and she accepts gratefully. It may be a perfect autumn day but it's still very cold, especially when you've been hanging around for ages in a light jacket because your anorak makes you look like a barrage balloon. Besides, she's always wanted to go in a golf cart.

In Chaz Blackstock's surprisingly spartan kitchen she finds the rest of the Blackstocks, together with Cathbad's friend Hazel. He seems to be on very good terms with Chaz.

'Have you done your bit?' asks Nell. 'I'm terrified about next week.'

'It's not too bad,' says Ruth, accepting a cup of tea from Chaz. 'You'll be fine.'

'TV reduces everything to the lowest common denominator,' complains Blake. 'I heard that presenter fellow giving the dates of World War Two. Surely everyone knows that?'

Ruth has heard it said that Americans think that the war dates from 1941 to1945 but she decides not to say this.

'I liked Paul,' says Cassie, who is sitting on the kitchen table, fetchingly attired in jeans and a Swedish crime girl jumper. 'He wants to interview me about my memories of Uncle Fred.'

'It would be remarkable if you had any, my dear,' says Blake, 'considering that he died about forty years before you were born.'

'I mean family memories,' says Cassie, batting her eyelashes at him. 'I'm sure Grandpa has some.'

'He's even asked me to be in his film,' laughs Hazel. 'I think I fulfil the role of harmless English eccentric.'

It would be easy to write Hazel off as an eccentric, thinks Ruth, but, as with Cathbad, this would be a mistake. She remembers that Hazel had been one of the druids who had protested against the henge dig. They had been passionately committed to their cause and actually rather frightening.

She addresses Hazel now. 'Are you going to mention the Bronze Age burials?'

Hazel smiles at her. He's really rather attractive in a grungy way. 'I certainly am. I'm going to say that all the land around Blackstock Hall is a sacred landscape and that Edward Spens builds his ghastly housing estate at his own risk.'

'Good luck with that,' says Chaz gloomily. 'I went down there yesterday and the building work's pretty advanced.'

Interesting that Chaz keeps such a close watch on the site, thinks Ruth. He's the one who really knows this land best and loves it the most. And his sister, of course. Ruth looks at Cassandra and is surprised to see her face brighten as if lit from within.

'Dave!' she says in delight.

'Hallo, all,' says a familiar voice. 'Guess who turns out to be related to the Blackstocks?'

Clough has joined the party.

Somehow Paul produces pizzas for lunch. Ruth has no idea how he has found a company that delivers out to the wilds of North Norfolk but the pizzas arrive in bona fide cardboard boxes, still hot and surprisingly good. They eat in the kitchen, Nell, Blake, Chaz and Paul at the table and the rest of the family and crew perched on work surfaces or sitting on the floor. Phil turns up in time for lunch and is busy suggesting to Paul that he might be able to fill in 'some of the general archaeological background'. Paul seems unconvinced.

Ruth finds herself wedged between Frank and the fridge.

'This is cosy,' he says with a grin.

Ruth agrees that it is. She had intended to play it cool today, to be the mysterious, aloof professional. But it's impossible to be a woman of mystery while eating a slice of pepperoni pizza. Besides, she's worried about falling off the kitchen cabinet. It's all right for Frank; his legs are so long that they're practically touching the floor.

'It's nice to see the family so involved,' says Frank, looking over to where Nell and Blake are showing the crew photographs of their grandchildren.

'Yes,' says Ruth. 'I think it means a lot to Nell, seeing the place where her father was stationed.'

'Do you know if the family had any idea that he was here at the time?'

'I don't think so,' says Ruth. 'From something Old George – Fred's brother – said, I don't think they knew he was based here until they got the news of his death. Odd that he didn't get in touch.'

'There was probably some kind of family rift,' says Frank. 'I guess we'll never really know.' There's a pause and then he says, 'It's hard to imagine, isn't it? Living here, at Lockwell Heath. Having a drink in the officer's mess, playing some sport – apparently there were squash courts here too – all the time knowing that you might die any day, that you probably would die before you got much older. Their courage must have been extraordinary.'

'Yes,' says Ruth, thinking of the pictures she had seen of the men and their planes. 'It's hard to get much sense of what this place would have been like . . . then.'

'There's a mural in one of the farm buildings,' says Frank. 'Chaz says it was painted by one of the crew of the 444th.' He calls over to Chaz, 'Is it OK if I show Ruth the mural?'

'Be my guest,' says Chaz. 'I think Paul's going to film it later. Isn't that right?'

'I sure am,' says Paul. 'The viewers will love it.'

In the hall, they pass Clough and Cassie sitting on the stairs. They look extraordinarily comfortable together, thinks Ruth. Clough is leaning back on his elbows and Cassie is whispering something in his ear, her long dark hair falling forward. They don't appear to notice Ruth and Frank leaving. Ruth is relieved; she doesn't want Clough reporting back to

Nelson. What is Clough doing here anyway? Isn't he meant to be working?

Outside, the runway seems to be full of cars. Ruth recognises the camera van and Clough's sporty Saab. The vehicles give the farm an oddly purposeful air and make it easier to imagine it as it would have been during the war, a hive of activity and enterprise, lights shining all night and the fields full of winged monsters. Earlier, on camera, Frank had demonstrated the wingspan of one of the bombers, 'as wide as ten men standing abreast'. They must have looked awe-inspiring, thinks Ruth, like the *Angel of the North*. Terrifying too.

Frank leads the way past the hangars to a brick-built building standing on its own at the edge of a field. 'Chaz thinks this was part of the operations block,' he says. 'There were barracks here too and a cafeteria and the squash court. You can see some of the walls.' Ruth looks at the field, where several large pigs are snuffling happily. She sees that they are snuffling past squares of concrete that still have a few bricks standing here and there. It's hard to imagine a whole complex of buildings here. This part of the airbase has thoroughly gone back to nature; the pigs are in control now. It's like a scene from *Animal Farm*. The last remaining building looks lopsided and incomplete, almost apologetic.

'Chaz stores hay in here,' says Frank. 'It's quite damp, unfortunately, which has affected the paint.'

When Frank opens the door, Ruth almost cries out in surprise. The mural is mildewed and faded but still the effect is startling – an entire wall has been painted to show a blue sky upon which yellow planes dive and turn. Near the foot of the wall a series of squares represents the airbase. The biggest square is proudly flying the Stars and Stripes.

'They think it shows US Liberators in a dogfight with German Dorniers,' says Frank. 'See, that plane is on its way down.' Ruth sees that a plane emblazoned with a swastika is heading vertically downwards, towards a sticky confrontation with a rather stylised tree. She thinks of the plane in Devil's Hollow, its surprisingly gentle trajectory, its shocking cargo.

'Do we know who painted it?' she asks.

'It's not signed,' says Frank, 'but there's something that may be a clue.' He points to the top right-hand corner where, almost hidden by encroaching mildew, a small dog sits on a cloud.

'It may be a reference to the artist's name or nickname,' says Frank. 'I'm going to look through the list of personnel at the airbase to see if I can uncover anything. What do you think of the painting?'

'It's very . . . evocative,' says Ruth. This is true. The brush-work may be crude, the planes out of perspective and the figures barely more than stick men but there's something about the work of the unknown airman that brings back the past more effectively than any documentary or reconstruction. For a moment Ruth feels that if she were to pull open the rusty iron door she would find a bustling airbase, full of grim-faced men in olive green uniforms, and not a sleepy Norfolk farm with pigs grunting amongst the fallen leaves.

'Ruth,' says Frank, bringing her crashing back to the present, 'we need to talk. Are you free for supper tonight?'

'I've got to pick Kate up from the childminder.' It's half-term, a holiday which previously had gone unnoticed in Ruth's calendar but now presents all sorts of logistical challenges.

'I could come with you. We could all go out together.'

'No.' Ruth can just imagine how that would look to Sandra. 'I don't think so. I've got a lot of marking to do.'

'What about Friday?'

'It's Kate's birthday.' She'll be five, something that doesn't seem quite possible to Ruth. They are planning to celebrate it with Judy and Michael, swimming followed by pizza.

'Tomorrow then. Thursday. Please. I'd really like to spend some time with you.'

What can Ruth say except, 'All right then'?

CHAPTER 21

Ruth had forgotten that Thursday is Halloween. Kate's birthday is the next day, All Saints' Day, and over the years this brighter festival has come to eclipse its dark forerunner. Ruth only remembers the date when Cathbad opens the door wearing a skeleton mask.

'Woo!' he says, waving his arms wildly. This is for Kate's benefit and she squeals with delighted fright. Thing hides behind Ruth. He's very timid for a bull terrier.

'Hi, Kate,' Judy appears in the background. 'Come in. Michael's waiting for you. Happy Halloween,' she says to Ruth, 'I've come as the Incredible Hulk, as you can see.'

'You look great,' says Ruth but, in truth, Judy does suddenly look a lot bigger. Ruth remembers this from her own pregnancy. After the first queasy months, you get quite used to being pregnant and feel you could carry on indefinitely. Then, just at the end, Nature weighs in to remind you why you have to give birth – you suddenly become huge and uncomfortable and you can't sleep because a tiny foot is kicking you from the inside. Judy looks like she has reached that stage, though by Ruth's calculations she still has a month to go.

Kate has come for a sleepover. When Clara couldn't babysit, Ruth considered cancelling her date with Frank. But when she casually mentioned this to Judy over the phone, Judy came up with this alternative. Ruth was reluctant at first. She didn't want Kate to wake up on her birthday morning in someone else's house. But Kate was all for the idea and, in the end, Ruth had given in. She will go round to Judy and Cathbad's for a birthday breakfast and then they'll all go swimming (Judy has the day off). In fact Ruth feels that she will agree to almost anything to avoid throwing a birthday party and inviting all the children in Kate's reception class. She had been amazed to learn, from other mothers, that this is the accepted protocol these days. 'So none of the kiddies feel left out, you see,' explained Chelsea, one of the friendlier of the teenage mums in the playground. At the thought of thirty children in her cottage, Ruth feels quite sick. And the idea of having the party in a public space – McDonald's, say, or a soft-play area – sounds, quite frankly, like a Disney-themed version of hell.

Now Kate skips off happily into the sitting room, where Michael has constructed a den in her honour by draping sheets over most of the furniture. Ruth and Judy perch on the uncovered edge of the sofa.

'Are you sure it's not too much trouble, having Kate?' says Ruth.

'It'll be no trouble,' says Judy, easing herself backwards. 'Cathbad will do all the heavy-duty playing.'

As if to corroborate this, Cathbad bursts into the room, still wearing his mask, and proceeds to lay siege to the den. Thing barks wildly from the hall.

'Does he ever play quietly?' asks Ruth.

'Hardly ever,' says Judy. 'Though he does read a good bedtime story.'

This conjures up such a cosy image that Ruth suddenly feels reluctant to go out into the cold and spend an uncomfortable evening exchanging small talk and trying not to mention nubile kid sisters. She'd rather watch *The Secret Garden* with Kate, Michael, Judy and Cathbad, eat organic chicken nuggets and have an early night. But she has squeezed herself into her best trousers and a sparkly top so she has to get on with it.

'Have a lovely time,' says Judy at the door.

'I'll try,' says Ruth.

She is meeting Frank at the restaurant. She thought it would be easier if she had her car with her; she can escape at any time and she won't be tempted to drink too much. Frank has chosen a restaurant on Blakeney Quay because 'apparently the views are spectacular', but it's pitch black by the time that Ruth arrives and all she can see of the water is a dark void where boats clink gently against each other.

Frank is waiting for her in the bar. When he stands up, she is struck again by how tall he is. Like Nelson, he gives the impression of dwarfing all the other men in the vicinity. But, unlike Nelson, Frank doesn't seem threatening. He's more like a large, gentle animal, an Old English sheepdog perhaps, or a grizzly bear. But, then again, bears aren't particularly gentle in real life, as opposed to children's stories. Maybe Frank, too, is steelier than he looks.

He's certainly all charm tonight, ordering her a drink and complimenting her on the sparkly top.

'I should have come dressed as a witch,' says Ruth. Compliments always make her feel nervous. 'Seeing as it's Halloween.'

'It's funny,' says Frank. 'Back home, kids dress up for Halloween. I mean, trick or treating's a big deal. But they dress as all kinds of things, not just witches and monsters. I remember one year Sean was determined to be a dinosaur. Took Ali months to sew on the spikes.'

Frank hardly ever mentions his kids, Ruth realises. They're grown-up now, of course. The mention of his dead wife is unusual too. She notes that Frank – for all he claims to be a new man – didn't do the sewing himself.

'I don't like all the dark stuff,' says Ruth, 'though Cathbad would say that it's in the tradition. The Day of the Dead and All Saints' Day.'

'How's Cathbad celebrating tonight?'

'He's babysitting,' says Ruth. 'What are you going to eat?'

While they wait for the food, they talk about Lockwell Heath and the American airbase, about history on TV and Hilary Mantel's books. It's not until they have finished their main course that Frank says, 'I want to explain about Gloria.'

'There's nothing to explain,' says Ruth.

'We're not . . .' For once, the ever-articulate Frank seems lost for words. He runs his hands through his hair and fiddles with his wine glass. 'I'm not . . .'

'For God's sake,' says Ruth, 'don't say "it's nothing serious". Honestly, it's nothing to do with me.'

Frank sighs. 'We've been seeing each other for about three months. Gloria's a researcher on one of my regular programmes. We've got a lot in common.'

'How old is she?' asks Ruth.

Frank looks surprised. 'How old is she? Thirtyish, I suppose.'

Ruth looks sceptical. Gloria may not be the teenybopper she had imagined but 'thirtyish' is still quite young for a man in his fifties.

'I didn't think you were interested in me,' says Frank suddenly. 'When I invited you to Seattle, you suddenly went silent. I didn't hear from you again. I thought I'd come on too strong.'

Ruth considers. Is that what happened? She remembers getting the invitation and feeling gratified and worried in equal measure. America suddenly seemed an awfully long way away. Could she really bear to be apart from Kate? But if she took Kate with her, would she be able to cope with a querulous child on a transatlantic journey? Was it fair on Kate? Was it fair on Frank? She certainly remembers lying awake at night with these thoughts chasing around in her head. But had she really never contacted Frank again? It's possible, she supposes. It's just not the way she remembers it.

'I'm sorry,' she says at last. 'I did want to come. It's just, it suddenly seemed . . . too much.'

'I thought it might be because of Nelson,' says Frank.

Ruth stares at him. She has never told Frank that Nelson is Kate's father. Can he possibly suspect?

'What do you mean?' she says at last.

'I don't know,' says Frank. 'It just that he sometimes seemed rather possessive of you and Kate.'

'There's nothing between me and Nelson,' says Ruth. 'We're just friends. Besides, he's married.'

'I'm sorry,' says Frank. It seems that they have been saying nothing else to each other all evening. 'Looks like I got it all wrong.'

'Well, it's OK now,' says Ruth with bracing cheerfulness. 'You're with Gloria and you've got loads in common and everything.'

'Yes,' says Frank. 'It's just . . . well, *we* had loads in common, Ruth. I really thought we might be able to make a go of it.'

Ruth notes the past tense. 'You can't look back,' she says. 'That way madness lies.'

Frank laughs. 'I'm a historian and you're an archaeologist; that's what we do – look back.'

'Well, it's time we stopped,' says Ruth. 'Are you having coffee?'

Clough and Cassandra are also out on a date. At least that's what Clough is calling it in his head. He has taken some trouble choosing the venue, a Mexican restaurant that was well reviewed in the *Eastern Daily Press* (Clough reads it at the barber's). He thought it would be the kind of trendy place that Cassie would like (cocktails were mentioned) but he had reckoned without the Dia de los Muertos, the Hispanic version of Halloween. They are met at the door by capering ghouls in devil masks and, when they eventually find their table amongst the drapes and floaty cobwebs, they are offered drinks in tiny glass skulls.

'What is it?' asks Clough.

'Traditional Guatemalan' is the not altogether reassuring answer.

Clough drinks. It's horrible, managing to be sweet and acidic at the same time, but it's probably not actually on the list of poisons.

'I wouldn't bother if I was you,' he tells Cassie.

'Oh, I'll try anything once,' she says, draining the liquid.

This is distinctly hopeful.

The food, which comes on wooden blocks, is your average Old El Paso stuff. Clough tries to talk to Cassie about her job and her family and her ambitions and all that women's magazine stuff. But it's hard when the band are playing loud enough to wake the dead. But then again, maybe that's the idea.

'So, why did you become a policeman?' asks Cassie, doing some of the *Woman's Own* stuff herself. Unfortunately, just at that moment, Clough swallows a chilli by mistake. He chokes and splutters while Cassie pats him on the back. His eyes stream. The devil masks of the waiters blur and pulsate. The music seems to be beating into his skull.

'Dave?' She leans over. He can smell her perfume, something lemony and slightly spicy. 'Shall we go to a pub?'

Clough wonders if it's too soon to ask her to marry him.

Frank insists on walking Ruth to her car. Outside the restaurant, the water slaps against the harbour wall and the boats are still jangling gently, as if they are having a whispered conversation. The sea is out there, thinks Ruth. You can't see it but it's there. Miles and miles of dark water, just waiting. She feels oddly light-headed, even though she has only been drinking mineral water.

The lower part of the car park is still waterlogged. At the top end, Ruth's Renault sits beside Frank's hired car, a Golf this time.

'Do you remember when I crashed into you?' says Frank. 'Talk about an explosive start to a relationship.'

But do they have a relationship? thinks Ruth. It seemed possible once, but now she thinks that they were just cars that passed in the night.

'Kate still talks about that day,' says Ruth. 'Turns out to be her favourite car journey ever.'

'She's a great kid,' says Frank.

'She is,' agrees Ruth. She searches in her organiser handbag for her car keys. Why can't she ever find anything in any of its endless pockets?

'Ruth,' says Frank. And then he steps closer and kisses her. A proper kiss – a film star kiss, the last swooning moments before the credits roll. It's not a friend's kiss or a colleague's kiss. Surrendering to it, Ruth thinks that she no longer understands anything any more.

'Have you arrested hundreds of people?' asks Cassie.

'Hundreds,' says Clough. 'I've probably arrested half the people in this pub.'

Cassie laughs, though it's nearer to the truth than she thinks. Clough has found a real drinker's pub, one frequented by Irish Ted and the field archaeology crew and miraculously free from music, cocktails or waiters in devil masks. The clientele is almost entirely male, dour pint-swillers gathered around the television or the pool table. Cassie, in her black lace dress, has already caused quite a stir, especially when she played – and beat – Clough at pool.

Now they are on their third pints (Clough has never met a girl who drinks pints before; his head is swimming), sitting in a dark corner by the fruit machines.

'Why did you become a policeman?' Clough has a feeling that she has asked this before. He tries to answer the question honestly.

'I wasn't much good at school,' he says. 'My mum thought I was bright but I didn't do any work. I was only interested in playing football. I thought about joining the army but the idea of being stuck in some desert waiting to be shot, it didn't appeal somehow. That left the police. My kid brother had been in trouble a few times and the local police had been really good about it, really tried to help. I suppose that gave me the idea.'

'Were you ever in trouble?'

'Just fighting. The usual stuff. Nothing serious.' Clough hopes she won't ask him about Mark. He doesn't want to spend the evening talking about his brother's life of crime.

'What's your boss like?' she asks. 'He seems a bit serious.'

Clough smiles. 'He's all right. It makes you serious, this job. We've had some tough cases over the past few years. But the boss . . . he's seen us through it. He looks out for us and we look out for him. We're a team.'

'It sounds as if you like him.'

Clough considers. He's not given to questioning whether he likes people or not, especially other men.

'I'd trust him with my life,' he says at last.

'That's quite some reference,' says Cassie. 'Do you still play football?'

'Sunday mornings,' says Clough, relieved at the change of subject. 'You can come and watch if you want.'

'I'd love to. What shall we do between now and Sunday?'

'I've got a few ideas,' says Clough.

'So have I.' And she's the one who leans over to kiss him, to the envious amusement of the men by the pool table.

Ruth lies awake watching the clouds scudding across the moon. She hasn't pulled the curtains and can't be bothered to get up now. She should be asleep, she should be taking advantage of Kate's absence and having an uninterrupted night. But, right now, she feels that she will never sleep again. Her nerves are tingling, she feels painfully conscious of the sheet against her skin, of the breeze that's moving her open curtains. After *that* kiss, Frank had simply said goodnight, they'd got into their separate cars and driven away. But the kiss has changed everything. *Can* a kiss change everything, when you're a forty-five-year-old single mother? It's different when you're sixteen and the whole evening rests on whether he'll kiss you at the end of the slow dance. Maybe Frank kisses all his female friends like that. He's the one in a relationship, after all. Maybe it didn't mean anything to him. But remembering Frank's expression – half rueful, half something else Ruth doesn't even want to name – she knows that it did mean something. But what? She looks at the alarm. One a.m. Perhaps she should read for a bit, listen to the World Service, make herself a milky drink. But she does none of these things. She just lies, completely still, watching the sky.

Later still, Clough is leaving Cassie's flat in Spalding. It's not that he wants to leave – in fact, the way he feels now, he'd like to stay in Cassie's bed for the rest of his life – but he's working tomorrow (today now) and needs to get home to shower, change and generally sober up. Cassie has called him a minicab. 'Don't get up,' he'd said but, when he looks back, she is standing in the window, wrapped in a sheet, waving. Clough waves back, wondering why he suddenly feels like crying.

Cassie's flat is in a mews, a tiny space carved out behind the High Street. She has told him that the cab will wait on the main road and he can see its yellow light now. He takes the short cut that he remembers from last night, between two tall old houses. As he does so, someone steps into his path. The first thing he sees is a devil mask and he wonders why the waiters from last night have followed him. Did he forget to leave a tip or is it some weird Day of the Dead thing?

Then. Blackness. Nothing.

CHAPTER 22

Nelson is making toast when he gets the call. He wants to get into work early and hassle the lab about the DNA analysis on the pig farm remains. He's also hoping to see Katie, as it's her birthday, but he knows he will have to tread carefully on this one. He and Michelle have bought her a present though. It sits, wrapped in pink paper, on the hall table, reminding Nelson what an amazing wife he has.

The call is from the hospital. He listens intently, rings off and tries Judy's phone. No answer. He tries Tim, who answers on the third ring.

'Hi, boss.'

'Tim. Cloughie's been stabbed. He's in the Queen Elizabeth. I'm on my way. Can you meet me there?'

'Stabbed. Jesus. How bad is it?'

'I don't know. He's in theatre now. One of the ambulance men recognised him and called me. He was picked up in Spalding.'

'Spalding? What was he doing there?'

'I don't know,' says Nelson, making a mental note to check Cassandra Blackstock's address.

'I'll get going now,' says Tim. 'I'm at the gym.'

Even in his agitated state, Nelson has time to question the sanity of someone who goes to the gym before seven o'clock.

'I'll see you there,' says Nelson. 'I've got to call his mum first.'

Nelson rings Mrs Clough and arranges for a police car to pick her up and take her to the hospital. While he's doing this, Michelle comes into the kitchen. By the time he's off the phone she has made him a cup of tea.

'Drink this. You've had a shock.'

'I haven't got time.'

'Just a sip. What's happened to Dave?'

'He's been stabbed. I don't know anything else.'

He takes a gulp of tea and Michelle doesn't press him to have more. 'Will you ring me as soon as you know how he is?' she says. She's known Clough a long time. The girls call him Uncle Dave.

'If I can,' he says, gathering up his keys.

Michelle hugs him. 'He'll be fine, Harry. Cloughie's tough. That's what you always say.'

'I hope so,' says Nelson. 'I really hope so.'

Nelson arrives at the hospital at the same time as Tim. They are shown to a visitors' room, where a woman and a man are sitting side by side on a low sofa, not talking.

'Mrs Clough?' says Nelson.

'Yes. Lindsay Clough. Are you DCI Nelson?'

'Yes.' They shake hands. Clough's mother is a good-looking

woman, maybe in her mid fifties, with carefully streaked hair and a rather improbable suntan. She has obviously dressed in a hurry – her cardigan is done up on the wrong buttons and she's wearing battered pumps that could double as slippers – but you can tell that this is a woman who normally takes pride in her appearance. The man is a younger version of Clough with the addition of a few tattoos and piercings. Clearly this is the delinquent little brother. What was his name?

'This is my son Mark,' says Lindsay Clough. 'He came as soon as he heard. He and Dave are very close.'

Mark glowers at the floor.

'Have you had any news?' asks Nelson.

'Not really. They're still operating. Apparently he was stabbed in the chest.' She dabs her eyes.

'Bishoy, the paramedic, said that he was conscious when they picked him up,' says Nelson. 'That's a good sign.'

Lindsay Clough is looking at Nelson with a mixture of trust and resentment. 'How did it happen?' she asks.

'I don't know,' says Nelson. 'Clough . . . David . . . was off duty last night.'

'Off duty?' she says in surprise. 'But they said he'd been found in Spalding. I thought he must be on a case. He seems to work all the hours that God sends.' Again, that note of resentment.

'He was with a bird if I know Dave,' says Mark.

Nelson and Tim exchange glances. They know that they are both thinking the same thing.

'But why would he be attacked if he was off duty?' says Lindsay.

'I don't know,' says Nelson again. 'But I've got officers on the scene now. I'll find out who did this. I'm sending Detective Sergeant Heathfield to take charge of the search.' He looks at Tim, who nods.

'Are you Tim?' says Lindsay Clough suddenly. 'You're the one who's always at the gym. Dave likes you but he says you're a bit too good at football.'

'Dave's better than me,' says Tim. 'He could have been a professional.'

'He's too lazy,' says Mark. 'He likes a pint and a pie.'

This simple truth strikes them all to the heart. Lindsay Clough's eyes fill with tears. 'I wish they'd give us some news,' she says.

There's a particularly hellish feeling about a public swimming pool in half-term: the amplified shouts of the children, the smell of chorine, the soupy water, the cracked tiles in the changing rooms. Ruth and Cathbad are in the shallow pool with the children. Judy sits on the side holding the towels ('If I got in, the water would get out'). Kate, resplendent in her new Hello Kitty costume, is thoroughly over-excited. She has only recently learnt to swim without armbands but that doesn't stop her diving headfirst down slides and launching herself onto the inflatable octopus in the centre of the pool. Michael is far more cautious. He follows Kate at a distance but always checks before running, jumping or otherwise compromising his safety. When Cathbad starts a game of tag, Kate shrieks delightedly when she's caught; Michael accepts it solemnly, as if being 'it' is a burden he has to bear.

Watching him, Ruth feels her heart contract. Sweet Michael, will life be difficult for him? Kate (like her father) has courage enough for anything, hurdles will disappear before her single-minded determination to succeed. But Michael, who has already been through so much in his three years of life, will always see both sides of a question. And that, Ruth knows, can make things very complicated.

Ruth likes swimming but wading waist-deep in warm water is not really her idea of fun. At least if you're swimming properly, your body is hidden underwater. Now she feels that far too much flesh is on display. Mind you, she's not the fattest mother in the children's pool, though she's almost the only one without a tattoo. She's just about to suggest that they break for lunch when Judy stands up suddenly. The towels fall to the floor.

'Hallo?' Judy is on her mobile. A lifeguard comes over to tell her that this is not allowed but backs away at the expression on her face.

'When?' she is saying. 'Where is he now?'

Ruth checks to see that Cathbad is with both children and climbs out of the pool.

'What is it?' she asks. Judy's face is as white as the diving board.

'It's Clough,' she says. 'He's been stabbed. They think he might die.'

Judy drives to the hospital, trying to keep her breathing steady. Going into premature labour will not help anyone. She still can't quite compute the message she has just received from Tim. Clough is in hospital. He was stabbed in the chest. Doctors have operated but his condition is still critical. 'The doctor came in just as I was leaving,' said Tim. 'Frankly, it didn't look good. Clough's mum was in pieces. The boss was trying to comfort her but you know he's not good at that stuff. Besides, he was pretty cut up himself. I think he could do with some support.' 'I'm on my way,' Judy had said.

She had only turned her phone on because she wanted to play a surreptitious game of online Sudoku. She had immediately seen the three missed calls from Nelson and was about to ring back when Tim's name had appeared on the screen. She is grateful now that it was Tim who told her. Hearing the news from Nelson would have been too much for her self-control. They have been through too much together, the three of them. Tim is still on the outside, for all that they like and trust him. It was easier hearing the news from him.

Only a few years ago, thinks Judy as she negotiates the roundabout outside the hospital, she would almost have stabbed Clough in the chest herself. When they met on the sergeant's training course, there had been instant hostility between them. Clough, who had worked his way up from a cadet, insisted on treating Judy as a flighty female for whom policing was a charming hobby to be enjoyed for a few years before settling down to marriage and children. Judy, who had wanted to join the force since an encounter with a mounted policeman aged five, deeply resented this. Judy and Clough had both ended up working for Nelson and became locked in a rather adolescent battle for his favour. When Clough earned his stripes first, Judy had been almost eaten up with jealousy. Now, five years and several demanding cases later, there is a deep respect between them. But it was during that terrible time when Michael went missing that Clough really became a friend. Clough is Michael's godfather. He can't die. Judy just won't let him.

Nelson is in the car park, talking on his phone. Judy sees his face and, for a moment, she thinks she is too late. She had never seen the boss looking so bleak. But he sees her, ends his conversation and says immediately, 'He's still with us.'

'Thank God,' says Judy. 'What happened? Tim didn't give any details.'

'We don't know much,' says Nelson. 'I'm on my way to the station now. He was found at about five this morning in Spalding. He was in a little alleyway just off the main road and he'd been stabbed. A passer-by raised the alarm but the paramedics thought he may have been there a while. Any longer and it would have been too late. He's lost a lot of blood.'

'Why was Clough in Spalding?'

'I don't know but I could make a guess.'

'Involving a woman?'

Nelson smiles. 'Exactly. Did you ever meet Cassandra Blackstock?'

'No. Is she the daughter of the Blackstocks at the Hall? The one who was attacked the other day?'

'Yes. She and Cloughie hit it off immediately, helped by the fact that she thinks he saved her life. I got a check on her address and she lives in Spalding.'

'So you think they were together last night?'

'That's my guess. Tim's been round to her house but there's no answer as yet.'

'Gosh.' Judy absorbs the implications of this. 'Do you think this attack was linked to the Blackstocks?'

'That's exactly what I think,' says Nelson. 'Clough himself said he didn't like all the coincidences around the Blackstocks. I think he was right. I've been a bit slow on this case but now it's going to get serious.'

He looks so grim that, for a second, Judy wants to tell him to go easy, not to do anything dangerous. Then she thinks: someone has tried to kill one of the team; that's as serious as it gets.

'How is he?' she asks.

Nelson rubs his eyes. 'The knife penetrated the chest wall and there was a build-up of blood in the lung cavity. That's why they had to operate so quickly, get tubes in and so forth. He's stable now but still critical apparently. He's lost a hell of a lot of blood. But it could have been worse. The knife didn't penetrate the heart or the lungs.'

If it had been worse, Clough would have died, thinks Judy.

'Have they found a weapon?' she asks.

'No. We're still looking. Tim's coordinating the search, doing door-to-door, all that.'

'He'll do a good job,' says Judy.

'Yes,' says Nelson. 'He will.' There's a pause and then he says, 'Whoever did this, they meant business.'

'You think it was a deliberate murder attempt?'

'Yes, I do. They left him for dead. Single stab wound straight to the chest. He wouldn't have had a chance to fight back. And he would have fought. You know Cloughie.'

'Yes, he would,' says Judy.

Nelson seems to pull himself together with an effort. 'His mum's still in there,' he says. 'Can you talk to her? Look after her? She's got her son with her – Cloughie's brother – but he's not much help, to be honest.'

There was a time when Judy would have resented this, would have fought against being the one who always has to do the touchy-feely stuff. 'It's just because I'm a woman,' she used to say. 'No,' Nelson would reply. 'It's because you're good at it.' But now she only feels relief that she can, at least, do something. After all, she's not exactly going to be chasing villains in her current condition.

'Don't worry, boss,' she says. 'I'll look after her.'

And she squares her shoulders and heads into the hospital.

CHAPTER 23

It's mid afternoon by the time Tim gets to speak to Cassandra Blackstock. He went to her house as soon as he arrived in Spalding (the address had been texted from the station). He rang the bell marked 'Cassie' accompanied by a drawing of a flower. No answer. Tim scribbled a few words on his card and pushed it through the letterbox. Then, at three, he gets a call on his mobile.

'Is that Tim Heathfield?'

'Speaking.'

'This is Cassandra Blackstock. You put your card through my door.'

'Yes,' said Tim. 'Can I come round? It's easier to explain in person. I'm in Spalding.'

A pause, then, 'OK. I'll see you in a minute.'

Tim is impressed both by Cassandra and her apartment. The former, casually dressed in jeans and a grey jumper, is simply stunningly beautiful. The latter, furnished with an eclectic style that favours ethnic throws and polished floorboards, would not be out of place in an interiors magazine.

It's hard to imagine Clough in these surroundings. Or is it? Tim has always admired Clough's ability to stay exactly the same whatever the company or the circumstances. He knows that he himself is a chameleon, his accent going up- or down-market depending on his audience. Cloughie, though, is always Cloughie. He probably threw himself down on Cassandra's cream satin chaise longue, drank a can of beer and ate a pork pie.

'What's this about?' Cassandra looks pale and rather frightened.

'It's about my colleague David Clough. I understand you may have been together last night.'

Cassandra gives an involuntary glance towards what is probably the bedroom. 'Yes,' she says, 'we were. Why?'

'Please sit down, Miss Blackstock. This may be a shock for you.'

Cassandra remains standing. 'What is it?'

'Sergeant Clough was attacked last night. We think it happened as he left your house. He's in the Queen Elizabeth Hospital.'

Now Cassandra does sit down. Her hand goes to her mouth. 'Oh my God. I saw policemen in the mews this morning. Is that what that was about?'

'Yes,' says Tim. 'Do you feel up to answering some questions?'

'Is Dave OK? What happened?'

'He was stabbed in the chest,' says Tim. 'Doctors have operated and his condition is critical but stable.'

'Stabbed?' Cassandra's eyes are huge. Tim is prepared to

be cynical but her shock and concern do seem to be real. 'Can I see him?'

'I'll have someone drive you there. But if I could just ask a few questions first. Can I get you some water?' This last because Cassandra really does look deathly white.

'Yes please.' Tim finds his way into an immaculate galley kitchen. The tap is so highly designed that it takes him a few minutes to turn it on. He carries the glass of water back to Cassandra, who is still huddled on the sofa.

'Thanks.'

Tim sits opposite. 'So, you and Sergeant Clough . . . Dave . . . went out last night.'

'Yes, we went to La Choza in King's Lynn.'

Now that does surprise Tim. He's seen La Choza advertised and it seems the type of place that Clough would avoid like the plague.

'We had a meal there and then we went to a pub.'

That's more like it. 'Do you remember the name of the pub?'

'The Wheatsheaf, I think.' Tim, who doesn't have Clough's encyclopaedic knowledge of Norfolk pubs, makes a note to look this up.

'We left the pub at about midnight and we . . .' Cassandra colours, 'we came back here.'

'Did you get a cab?'

'Yes. I've got an account with a minicab firm. I can give you their number.'

'Thank you. And when did Dave leave your apartment?'

'At about three. He said he had to work today.'

Despite everything, Tim can't help feeling slightly envious of Clough. It hadn't taken him long to get his girl into bed. Unlike Tim, who is still restricted to shared jacuzzis.

'Did he call a cab? Was it the same firm?'

'Yes. I called it for him. I told him the cab would be waiting on the High Street. He must have taken the short cut through the alley.'

'Did you see anything? Hear anything?'

'No. I waved and then I went back to bed. I got up at nine and I had a rehearsal in Lincoln at ten. I've just got back.'

Tim makes a note to check this. 'Did you see anything untoward last night?' he asks. 'Anyone hanging around? Anything that seems odd to you in retrospect?'

Cassandra shakes her head. 'No.'

'Did Dave seem worried about anything?'

Now Cassandra actually laughs. 'I don't know him very well but I don't think he's much of a worrier.'

'He's not,' says Tim. 'I'll get someone to drive you to the hospital now.'

Ruth hopes that Kate will not expect a five-star birthday tea when they get home. She thinks that her daughter has had a good birthday. Kate enjoyed the pool and, though lunch was a subdued affair for both adults, Kate and Michael had a wonderful time helping to roll the pizza dough and sprinkling it with olives and salami. Kate is still wearing her paper chef's hat when Ruth stops outside the cottage.

'Have you had a nice day, darling?' she asks.

'Yes,' says Kate. 'Have I got birthday cake?'

Ruth has taken the precaution of buying a cake (making one seemed a step too far) and she presents it now with five candles. Kate blows them out, makes a wish, takes a huge slice, then forgets about it. She seems quite satisfied with her day and rather sleepy. Ruth hopes she'll go to bed early. She wants to have a glass of wine, collapse in front of the TV, and worry about Clough.

While they were eating pizza, Judy called from the hospital to say that Clough was still in intensive care. There's been no more news and Ruth doesn't expect any. She knows that she's a long way down the list of people who need to be kept informed. Nevertheless, she can't stop thinking about Clough. He's always been there, as long as she's known Nelson. Clough, the loyal sergeant, efficient, slightly wayward but always to be relied on in a crisis. He was there the first day she met Nelson, when she was called in to examine bones found buried on the Saltmarsh. She still remembers Clough laughing when she declared that the bones were probably two thousand years old. She hadn't liked him then, had thought him a typical boorish policeman. She knows better now. Clough might have missed the training course on political correctness but he was definitely there for the sessions on loyalty, courage and bloody-minded tenacity. He saved Nelson's life once. He has battled a wild horse and followed a series of mystic instructions that led him to a missing child. You underestimate Clough at your peril. Yet, even as she thinks this, he could be dead and she wouldn't know. All that force of character, all that unsubtle kindness, wiped out in a second.

'He'll be all right,' Cathbad had said. 'Clough's a Taurus and they're practically indestructible. Especially with his moon in Leo.' He had meant it kindly but Ruth hadn't felt reassured. She has never been able to share Cathbad's belief in star signs. She's Cancer, kind-hearted and domesticated according to the books, which just goes to show you that it's all rubbish.

Ruth and Kate sit on the sofa watching *Dora the Explorer*. Flint sits between them, purring loudly. Ruth doesn't know about Kate but she can feel her own eyelids beginning to droop.

'*Hola*, Mother Duck.'

'*Hola*, Dora.'

Dora helps Mother Duck carry her eight babies over the river and Ruth lets her mind drift towards Clough and Judy and Nelson, towards the sea and the secret path across the marshes, towards Blackstock Hall and the gravestones disappearing into the fog, towards a blue sky upon which yellow aeroplanes play a deadly game of tag.

'Mum,' says Kate, her face very close to Ruth's, 'there's someone at the door.'

For a moment, Ruth – still in the liminal zone between sleeping and waking – feels frightened. Who could be knocking on the door at five o'clock in the afternoon?

'Who is it?' she shouts.

'It's me, Nelson.'

As soon as Ruth opens the door, Kate catapults herself into her father's arms.

'Daddy! Have you brought me a present?'

'Kate!' Ruth is shocked at such naked consumerism but Nelson doesn't seem to mind. He puts a pink-wrapped parcel on the floor. 'Happy birthday, sweetheart.'

As Kate tears off the paper, Ruth says, 'Is there any news?'

Nelson shakes his head. 'Johnson's just left there. No change. It's because of the shock and the blood loss, apparently. We should know some more tomorrow.'

Nelson words are almost drowned out by Kate's cry of delight. She has uncovered a Sylvanian windmill and is in raptures. She adores Sylvanians – the woodland creatures in Victorian dresses, the tiny furniture, the eclectic range of dwelling places (windmill, mansion, riverboat). She hugs Nelson fiercely and plants a kiss on his cheek. Ruth turns away. She always finds it distressing to see Kate and Nelson together. Poor Kate. She should really have a stable paternal figure like Daddy Mouse in his plus fours. There are no single-parent Sylvanian families.

'Do you want a cup of tea?' she asks.

'Just a quick one,' says Nelson. 'Then I ought to get home. I just came to drop off the present really.'

Ruth wonders what Michelle thought about the present. Or did she even chose it? Ruth would put nothing past her. She makes the tea and pours juice for Kate. She can hear Nelson and his daughter playing with the windmill.

'Who lives in this room?' Nelson is asking.

'The Mummy Rabbit and the Daddy Rabbit,' says Kate. 'They sleep in the same bed.'

Where did she get that idea?

Ruth and Nelson drink their tea and watch Kate playing.

Ruth always finds these moments unsettling. It's as if they are playing at being a family, but when his allotted time is up, Nelson leaves and goes back to his real home. Kate seems to accept these partings with equanimity but Ruth finds it hard sometimes.

'Are Clough's family with him?' she asks. 'They live in Norfolk, don't they?'

'His mum does. She's at the hospital now. Johnson was trying to persuade her to go home to get some rest. I've never heard Clough mention his father.'

'There's a brother isn't there?'

'Yes. He's there too. Looks a right layabout but at least he's there to support his mum.'

Ruth thinks Nelson looks sad. She knows how close he is to his team. He feels responsible for them. It's part of his apparently endless paternal streak. 'He'll be OK,' she says. 'He's tough. Cathbad says so.'

Nelson smiles faintly. 'If Cathbad says so, it must be right.'

'Who do you think did it?' asks Ruth. 'Is it linked to the attack on Cassandra?'

'You'd better watch it, Ruth,' says Nelson. 'You're starting to think like a policeman.'

'So you think they are linked?'

Nelson sighs. 'Clough was with Cassandra last night.'

'Really? Were they on a date then?'

'That's one word for it. Clough left Cassandra's flat early this morning. Someone was lying in wait, jumped out and stabbed him. Were they trying to get Cassandra? I don't know, but it must be a possibility.'

'Pretty hard to mistake Clough for a woman.'

'You'd think so, wouldn't you?'

'Have you spoken to Cassandra?'

'Tim has, and Judy said she turned up at the hospital this afternoon. Said she seemed pretty upset, but it could all be an act.'

'Why would it be an act? She can't be involved. I mean, she was attacked herself.'

'She *said* she was attacked,' says Nelson.

'But she couldn't have hit herself on the head.'

'Stranger things have happened.'

'Seems a bit far-fetched to me. Don't you always say that the obvious solution is usually the correct one?'

'I say a lot of things,' says Nelson. 'But it hasn't got me very far in this case. I think it all comes back to the Blackstocks. Remember, Clough just found out that he was related to them.'

Ruth stares. 'Do you think someone attacked him because of that?'

'I don't know. Cloughie turned up at the shoot on Wednesday, didn't he? Was he going on about having a DNA link to the Blackstocks?'

'He did mention it, yes.'

'Who was there?'

'Me, Chaz, Cassandra, Nell and Blake. Cathbad's friend Hazel was there too.'

'And all the film crew.'

'Yes.' Ruth watches Kate turning the windmill sails. 'But you can't think any of these people were involved.'

'I don't know what to think but two people have been attacked. Not to mention the poor sod at the pig farm.'

'Any luck with the DNA from the bones?'

'No. We should get the results soon but that might not get us much further.'

'Remember my Bronze Age body was a Blackstock too.'

'There are too many bloody Blackstocks,' says Nelson. And they sit in silence for a while, watching Kate arrange her Sylvanians in size order.

CHAPTER 24

Nelson is at his desk early on Saturday morning. Michelle doesn't complain, even though Nelson had promised her a trip to the garden centre. She knows that Nelson has to feel that he's doing something. It would drive him mad just to sit at home waiting for news.

The first thing Nelson does is to ring the hospital. No change. Clough is still stable but critical. 'That's good news,' says the nurse. Nelson puts the phone down, musing on this paradox. How can it be good news to continue being critically ill? But at least Clough is still hanging on in there and, if he knows his sergeant, he will be fighting to stay alive. He loves life, does Cloughie: playing football, drinking pints, eating takeaways, chasing women. It's a lifestyle that causes Clough much envious ribbing from his colleagues but, when Nelson thinks about it now, it seems a pretty good way to spend your time. Exercise, food, romance. Only the second of these is a constant in his own life. He too was a keen footballer in his youth but he hasn't played for years. And as for romance . . . He shakes his head, not wanting to discuss this, even with himself. Instead he says a prayer to the God he only half believes in. Dear God, Our Lady and all the saints, please save Clough. Nelson's mother will probably be arranging the flowers in her parish church, ready for mass tomorrow. Nelson makes a mental note to ring her later and ask her to pray too. Maureen Nelson has a hotline to God and her prayers are almost always answered.

Nelson looks over the evidence from yesterday. Tim has done a good job. All the witness statements are already on the computer, filed and cross-referenced. Clough was found at approximately five a.m. by a local newsagent, Tomasz Karadzas, who was on his way to open his shop. Mr Karadzas didn't attempt to move Clough but he covered him with his coat and called an ambulance. For this alone, thinks Nelson, he deserves a citizenship medal. In fact he'll nominate him for one. There's no doubt that Clough would have died if he'd been left there much longer. There don't seem to be any witnesses to the actual attack. Everyone in the vicinity in Spalding claimed to be tucked up safely in their beds at three o'clock in the morning. None of the residents of the mews had heard anything. Tim has tracked down the minicab driver, who said that he'd waited on the High Street for five minutes and, when no one appeared, simply drove on to his next job. No, he didn't hear anything or see anyone running away. This must mean that the assailant went the other way, back through the mews, which may suggest some local knowledge. Tim asked the driver why he didn't go looking for his missing passenger. 'Get outta my cab at night?' had been the answer. 'You must be kidding, mate.'

Officers have carried out a fingertip search of the area. There's only one item that looks potentially interesting. It's a Halloween mask, a crude red devil's face, found in the alleyway near Clough's body. Nelson decides to send the mask off for DNA analysis. It's possible that it contains traces of sweat or even hair. Again, the DNA won't be useful unless it matches someone currently on the register, but you never know. At any rate, it's the only lead they have.

As he fills in the DNA request, Nelson also makes a note to chase on the pig farm remains. Testing can take months but, in emergencies, it's possible to get results in twenty-four hours. Nelson believes in treating every case as if it's an emergency.

Nelson reads through the transcript of Tim's interview with Cassandra. There's no reason to doubt the girl but there's something about her that Nelson doesn't quite trust. It's not her beauty. Nelson likes beautiful women; after all, he married one. It's more a certain theatricality, a suspicion that she enjoyed her moment in the limelight the other day. Then again, she is an actress. It's not a crime to enjoy being the centre of attention. But if Clough had been lured to the alleyway where his attacker was hiding, there was only one person who could have done the luring. Either that or someone is out to get both Cassandra and her new boyfriend. A jealous lover? Again, that's possible. Women who look like Cassandra always attract jealous lovers. Nelson decides to look into her background and generally keep an eye on Miss Blackstock. His fears about her possible blood relationship to Clough he keeps to himself. If Cassandra is secretly Clough's half-sister, there's nothing he can do about it now. He just hopes that they used contraception last night.

Tim comes in at nine. His hair is wet, as if he's just come from the gym. Nelson compliments him on his work yesterday.

'Did you input all the data yourself?'

'Yes. Came in last night and did it. I didn't think any Intel people would be around. Any news on Cloughie?'

'No change. I'll pop into the hospital later.'

'No change is good news though, isn't it? It means he isn't any worse.'

It means he isn't any better either, thinks Nelson. Tim's optimistic outlook irritates him slightly but then, Tim hasn't known Clough for long and he did do a good job at the crime scene yesterday. He means well.

'The hospital said it was good news,' he concedes.

'Are you going to ring Judy and tell her?'

'Later.' Nelson looks at the clock. 'I'll let her have a lie-in first.'

'She did look knackered yesterday,' says Tim.

'I wish she'd just bloody go on maternity leave,' says Nelson. 'But she's insisting on working right up to the last minute.'

'My sister was the same,' says Tim. 'Said she wanted to use all her maternity leave after the baby was born.'

Tim doesn't talk about his family much, thinks Nelson, and when he does, it's always like this. Inoffensive little snippets that don't really tell you anything. Well, he's a private person. Nelson respects that. It makes him hard to get to know though.

'I'm going to pop into Costa for coffee and a Danish,' says Tim now. 'Do you want anything?'

It is always Clough who does the food run. He seems to feel the need to eat almost constantly although, annoyingly, never appears to put on any weight. Nelson feels that he ought to eat something in Clough's honour but he's just not hungry.

'Just get me a black coffee,' he says. 'That's a good lad.'

Jesus, he thinks, as Tim's footsteps die away. I'm starting to call the young officers 'lad'. I really am getting old.

Ruth often finds Saturday evenings hard. The day is pure joy – a lie-in (if Kate allows it), the chance to spend some proper time with her daughter, a glass of wine or two after Kate has gone to bed – but the evening still feels like a time when you should be going out or settling down with your partner for a slobby evening of takeaway and crap TV. Ruth works hard to make the weekends fun, to do things with Kate, not just sit around imagining the rest of the world enjoying a Waltons-style family life. Today they have been to the park, to a cafe for lunch and to an afternoon showing of a Disney film.

Back at the cottage, Ruth struggles to stave off that Saturday-evening feeling by making an elaborate meal of mushroom risotto. Unfortunately Kate picks out all the mushrooms because they taste slimy. After supper, Ruth turns on the television to hear, on local news, that 'the man found stabbed in Spalding has been identified as off-duty police officer David Clough from Hunstanton'. Off-duty police officer. How dull it sounds, how run of the mill. Nothing like the reality as Ruth imagines it: Nelson pacing his office in King's Lynn, Clough's mother by his bedside, Judy and Cathbad attempting to carry on as normal. Judy had texted Ruth earlier, saying that Clough was 'stable'. She has heard nothing else and, it appears, there is nothing else to say.

Ruth turns off the television and she and Kate play a rather fractious game with the Sylvanian windmill, which, to Ruth's dismay, has become a prison.

'Who told you about prisons?' she asks. If it was Nelson, she'll kill him.

'They're in *The Wind in the Willows*,' says Kate. 'We had it at school.'

That's OK then. You can't argue with classic children's literature. Or can you? It's all rather nasty as far as Ruth can remember. And didn't Kenneth Grahame's son kill himself?

After another half-hour of Daddy Mouse escaping from prison dressed as Mummy Mouse, Ruth announces that she is going to run Kate's bath.

'I don't want a bath,' says Kate.

'Of course you do,' says Ruth. 'The Sylvanians are always having baths. Look at their lovely bathroom in the windmill.'

'Flint never has a bath.'

Flint, who is sitting on the sofa, closes his eyes in silent agreement. Before Ruth can get into an argument about the pros and cons of bathing, the phone rings.

'Is this a bad time?' It's Frank.

'No,' says Ruth. 'It's fine.'

'I suddenly thought that you might be in the middle of bedtime. I'm a bit out of touch with the schedule.'

'It's OK. I was just trying to persuade Kate to have a bath.'

'I remember when Jane hated having her hair washed. Used to scream the place down. Now she seems to spend half her life having her hair done.'

Ruth stores away this titbit about Frank's only daughter.

'It was great to see you on Thursday,' Frank is saying.

'Great to see you too,' says Ruth. She knows that, even at this distance, she is going red.

'I was wondering if you were coming to the shoot on Monday. At Blackstock Hall.'

No, Ruth wasn't planning to go to the shoot. As far as she knows, she isn't needed and she has plenty of work to do at the university. Besides, she feels as if she has had enough of the Blackstocks for a while, especially after Nelson's comments yesterday. She realises that Frank doesn't know about Clough but feels curiously reluctant to tell him.

'It would be lovely to see you,' says Frank. 'Maybe we could even get away for lunch.'

'I don't know,' says Ruth. 'I'm pretty busy at work. I'll see what I can do.'

Nelson is back at the hospital. Lindsay Clough is still there in the waiting room as if she hasn't moved in the last twenty-four hours. The only difference is that Mark isn't there. 'He works on Saturdays,' says Lindsay. 'If you can call it work.' Nelson decides not to enquire further.

Clough has been taken back into the theatre. The consultant thinks that there may be further damage to the pulmonary artery. 'That's lungs, isn't it?' says Lindsay. 'I didn't like to ask too many questions.' 'I think so,' says Nelson, wishing he'd paid more attention in biology lessons at school. He'd only really been interested in sexual reproduction, but that's a Catholic boys' grammar school for you.

Nelson tries to find a doctor to give Lindsay more information but it's Saturday evening and the place feels like a ghost ship. There's one harassed nurse on duty on the ward and she just says brusquely that she'll let them know when she has any news. The only comfort he gets is from a cleaner slowly pushing a mop up and down the corridor. 'He'll be fine,' she says. 'I'm praying for him.' Nelson thanks her and resolves again to ring his mother. He buys Lindsay a cup of tea and a KitKat from the vending machine and goes back to the waiting room.

At seven o'clock, the surgeon himself makes an appearance, still wearing his surgical scrubs. 'Good thing we operated because there was a bleeding wound on the anterior wall of the left pulmonary artery.'

Lindsay doesn't seem to take this in and Nelson can't say he blames her. 'Will he be OK now?' she says.

'The operation was a success,' says the doctor, 'but we're not out of the woods yet.'

What the bloody hell does that mean? thinks Nelson. He'd be crucified if he said something like that in a press conference.

'Can we see him?' asks Lindsay.

'When he comes round,' says the doctor, backing towards the door. 'I can't see why not.' Meanwhile Nelson is thinking: *we?*

There are so many tubes sticking out of him that Clough is almost unrecognisable. His eyes are closed and he looks pale and unshaven.

Lindsay takes his hand. 'Oh Davey,' she says.

'He might not be able to hear you,' says the nurse. But Clough opens one eye.

'Hallo, Mum.'

Lindsay Clough starts to cry. Nelson pats her awkwardly on the shoulder.

'Hallo, boss,' says Clough.

'Evening, Cloughie. Have you been getting into trouble again?'

Clough smiles faintly. His lips move and Nelson just catches the words 'red devil'.

CHAPTER 25

'Red devil,' says Tim. 'That's Man U. isn't it?'

'Cloughie doesn't support Man U,' says Nelson. 'He's a Chelsea man through and through.'

'At least it's a proper team,' says Judy. 'Not like Blackpool.'

'Watch it, Judy,' says Tim. 'Blackpool were in the Premiership for ten minutes back in 2010.'

'And we'll be there again,' says Nelson. He doesn't mind the teasing. It's part of the general relief that Clough seems to be out of danger. Football chat is the team's preferred way of letting off steam. With Nelson, Tim, Clough and Judy all supporting different clubs, there's plenty of scope for discussion. Judy, loyal to her local roots, supports Norwich City and Tim is an Arsenal fan. That figures, thought Nelson, as soon as he discovered this fact. There is something smooth and metrosexual about Tim that Nelson equates with the North London club.

'Red devil,' he says. 'That must mean the mask.'

Nelson is even happier now that he sent the devil mask away for DNA and fingerprint tests. If the attacker has form, which is a real possibility, they're a step closer to an arrest.

'Pretty stupid of the assailant to throw away the mask,' says Tim. 'He must have known that we'd get something from it.'

'Maybe he just panicked,' says Nelson. 'It's hard to think clearly in the heat of the moment.'

'Or maybe it meant something else,' says Judy. 'A sign or something.'

'What do you mean?' asks Nelson.

'Well, it was Halloween,' says Judy. 'Maybe the devil mask was a kind of occult touch.'

Judy sounds slightly defensive but of course the only person likely to laugh at such a theory is currently in Intensive Care.

'Cloughie was in La Choza on Thursday night,' says Tim. 'They do all sorts of things for Halloween. The Day of the Dead and all that Mexican stuff.'

Judy laughs. 'I'd pay good money to see Cloughie in La Choza.'

'Seems to have impressed Cassandra Blackstock though,' says Tim. 'After all, they ended up in bed together.'

'That's as maybe,' says Nelson, a shade disapprovingly. 'But it might be worth going back to La Choza. It's not impossible that someone followed them from the restaurant. People will remember them. Cassandra's a very striking woman.'

'You can say that again,' says Tim.

'No thanks,' says Nelson. 'Now let's get on. We've got a lot to do. Tim, you work your charm at the restaurant and the pub. Which one was it?'

'The Wheatsheaf.'

Nelson laughs. 'That's more Cloughie's taste. A real drinkers' pub. They'll remember them all right. We'll do some more door-to-door in Spalding and I've organised a leaflet drop too. Free-phone number if anyone's got any information. We need to talk to Clough as well, get a proper statement from him. Judy, will you do that?'

'Of course,' says Judy. 'I'm going to see him after work.'

'Well, he may not be up to giving a statement today,' says Nelson. 'He was pretty groggy when I saw him.' On Saturday night, after his brief burst of speech, Clough had fallen into an uneasy sleep. Nelson had left Lindsay at his bedside. He had called on Sunday to hear that Clough was 'progressing well' and due to be moved to a normal ward on Monday. Even so, Nelson doubts that Clough will be up to providing a coherent witness statement. It's good of Judy to visit him though. The two are closer than you'd think.

'Give him our love,' says Tim.

That seems a rather metrosexual way of putting it but Nelson can't think of a better phrase offhand. 'Let's get to work,' he says.

Ruth doesn't know how it happened but, on her way home, she finds herself taking the turning for Hunstanton and Blackstock Hall. She very much hadn't planned to attend the day's shoot. She has plenty of work to do; the sensible thing would be to drive home after her tutorials and put in a few hours' marking before collecting Kate from the childminder. Instead, here she is, driving across the flat fields towards the house on the edge of the marshes.

As she parks on the verge, she can see the camera crew busy in the grounds. The camera van is parked in the sheep field and, as Ruth gets closer, she can see a man with a furry microphone following Nell as she walks slowly around the house towards the pets' burial ground. Sally Blackstock is watching from the front door.

'Hallo, Ruth,' she greets her warmly. 'Are you going to do another interview?'

'No.' Ruth suddenly feels rather embarrassed. 'I just came to see what was going on.'

'Oh, I'm the same,' says Sally. 'I'm absolutely fascinated by all this film stuff. Mind you, I wouldn't like to be in front of the camera. They were filming Cassie this morning and she was an absolute natural. I don't know how she does it.'

'Is she OK?' asks Ruth. 'After what happened to Clough . . . David?'

'Oh, she was very upset about that,' says Sally, shepherding Ruth into the house and towards the welcoming Aga. 'She seems terribly keen on this chap. But she spoke to the hospital this morning and they say he's out of danger.'

Ruth has had the same message from Judy. All the same, it doesn't answer the question of why Clough was attacked in the first place. If she were Cassandra, she'd be feeling nervous to say the least.

'In a way,' says Sally confidingly, 'I'm enjoying being able to look after Cassie a bit. We haven't always had the easiest of relationships, especially when she was a teenager. Mothers and daughters, you know.'

Ruth does know. The closest relationship in her life is with her daughter. What will she do when Kate gets to the scary teenage years? At least Nelson has some experience of adolescent girls; Ruth will be on her own.

In the kitchen, she finds Old George grumpily reading *The Times* and – oh God – Frank drinking tea and discussing books with Blake.

Frank stands up when he sees her. 'Ruth!'

'Oh,' says Sally in her vague way, 'I forgot you knew each other. Would you like a cup of tea, Ruth? I've just made a fresh pot.'

'Thank you,' says Ruth.

'Hallo, Ruth,' says Blake. 'We were just discussing Thoreau.'

'Oh,' says Ruth, trying to remember who Thoreau is. Didn't he write something about a pond?

Blake puts on what she already recognises as his quoting voice, '"If the day and the night are such that you greet them with joy . . . that is your success. All nature is your congratulation . . ."'

There's no answer to this, though Ruth wishes Cathbad were there to attempt one.

'This is a fascinating place,' says Blake in his normal voice. 'When you stand on the beach here, it's as if you're standing at the very end of the earth.'

Old George looks up from his newspaper where he is ringing the Deaths with a red pen. 'You live on the edge of the Saltmarsh, don't you, Ruth?'

'Yes,' says Ruth, wondering how on earth he knows this.

'Then the sea's coming for you,' he says. 'That's what my mother used to say. The seas are rising. Soon your little house will be swept away.'

'Isn't it time for your nap?' says Sally.

'Did you hear about the Bronze Age body found near here having a genetic link to your family?' asks Ruth, hoping to steer the conversation away from the apocalypse.

'No,' says George suspiciously. 'What body?'

Ruth elaborates, feeling that she isn't doing a very good job of explaining about Bronze Age settlements and burial practices.

'So this woman died, what, four thousand years ago and you say she's related to my family?' says George. 'Preposterous.'

It isn't going well. 'That's what makes it so interesting,' says Ruth. 'The Bronze Age is the time when people stopped moving around, stopped being nomadic hunter-gathers basically, and formed settled communities. The DNA link shows that there must have been a settled population here for thousands of years.'

'The landscape must have been very different four thousand years ago,' says Blake.

'It was similar in some ways,' says Ruth. 'This would still have been marshy, tidal land. Lynn, as in King's Lynn, is the Celtic word for tidal lake. Of course, if you go further back, things were very different. Only ten thousand years ago Britain was still linked to mainland Europe. You could walk to Scandinavia from Norfolk.'

'Ridiculous,' says Old George.

'Nell thought it was really interesting about the Bronze Age body,' offers Blake. 'I know she feels a real link to this part of the country. If there were Blackstocks living here four thousand years ago, that kind of explains it.'

'Fred didn't feel much of a link to Norfolk,' says Old George. 'He went halfway round the world to get away from the place.'

But he came back, thinks Ruth. He came back and he died here, not far from the place where his Bronze Age ancestor was buried. She wonders what Fred would have made of this coincidence.

'Nell was great in her interview with me earlier,' says Frank. 'Talking about how her dad would have wandered these fields with his dog.'

'He was Lewis's dog really,' says Old George. 'Fred took him for walks sometimes but Lewis was the one he loved.'

Ruth thinks of the disc that she found buried in the pets' graveyard. *Bingo. Flaxman 9618.* She remembers Old George saying 'he was such a *good* dog'. She doesn't think that she should mention it now.

'It was tough,' says Blake, 'your eldest brother disappearing like that. What do you think happened to him?'

'I think the sea got him,' says George. 'I think he drowned.'

There's a silence and then the stable door bangs open. Nell stands on the doorstep. She's wearing a long grey coat and, for a moment, looks utterly unworldly, like a spectre, the lady from the sea. She raises one hand as if about to confer a blessing – or a curse. George cowers away from her.

The vision speaks. 'I'm freezing,' she says. 'Do you know where my mittens are, honey?'

Blake hurries to help his wife. George goes back to his paper.

Ruth watches a little more of the filming. The camera crew are down by the family graveyard. Ruth sees Ben, one of the cameramen, lying on his stomach in the long grass to get a suitably impressive shot of Admiral Blackstock's cross. Later, Frank strolls amongst the graves, providing a breezy summary of the relevant British history. 'Admiral Nathaniel Blackstock would have fought in the Napoleonic Wars, that series of skirmishes between Napoleon's French Empire and Britain and her allies. As a young man, he might even have been involved in the naval battle of Diamond Rock, where the British attempted to defend a strategic position in the West Indies. After the surrender of the rock, the naval commander was court-martialled, which would have had a lasting effect on the young Nathaniel.'

Ruth has to admire his style. As far as she is aware, no one knows whether Admiral Blackstock went anywhere near the Napoleonic Wars, much less Diamond Rock. She also thinks it's a bit rich of Frank to describe the wars as 'skirmishes'.

Frank continues, looking out over the luminous silver marshes. '"Safe in harbour" reads his tombstone, and it certainly would have been a welcome rest after a lifetime spent at sea. Conditions were harsh, even for an admiral. How often must he have dreamt of this quiet hillside and peace at last?'

It's hardly a hill, thinks Ruth, more of a gentle slope. It's only the relentless flatness of the rest of the landscape that makes the stones loom so large against the sky. The shadows are getting longer though. She looks at her watch. Half past four. Sandra will have collected Kate from school but Ruth needs to pick her up at the childminder's at five. She raises her hand to Frank, trying not to distract him, and heads back to the house to say goodbye to Sally.

She finds the lady of the house in the kitchen with Nell. They have their heads together over a cookbook.

'So if we multiply the flour by three . . .' Sally is saying.

They both look up as Ruth comes in.

'Just trying to sort supper out,' says Sally. 'It's a bit of a strain feeding ten people every night.'

'Are all the TV people staying here?'

'Just Paul, Frank, Steve and Jill, one of the researchers. Apparently the producer's staying at the Le Strange Arms. And we've got Cassie staying for a few nights. And Nell and Blake, of course, though Nell's a great help.' She smiles affectionately at the American woman.

'I suppose it's good practice for the B & B,' says Ruth.

Sally groans. 'I've gone right off that idea. It's changing the sheets that I can't stand.'

Ruth says goodbye, adding that she can see herself out. Goodness knows she's had enough practice by now. Outside, it seems to be getting dark very quickly. Her car looks lonely sitting by the side of the road. As she gets in, a voice calls, 'Ruth!'

It's Frank. He's hurrying across the field towards her.

'Are you rushing off?' he asks.

'I've got to pick Kate up from the childminder.'

'Would you like to have dinner again one night?'

There are lots of things Ruth would like to say to this. She would love to have dinner with Frank again but what about Gloria and what about that kiss? How would such an evening end up? She has her suspicions (or fantasies) but they are best kept to herself.

'That would be nice,' she says. 'I'm sorry. I've got to go now. I can't be late.'

Ruth always worries about being late for her daughter ('Don't be late for Kate' runs in her head all day, like a particularly annoying nursery rhyme) but, in fact, Sandra is very laid-back about times. She keeps Ruth talking so long on the doorstep that she's worried that Kate will fall asleep in the car and so be wide awake at her theoretical bedtime of seven-thirty. To avoid this, she keeps up a flow of sound all the way home, a mix of merry chit-chat, Bruce Springsteen songs and the occasional half-remembered hymn.

'I know about Jesus,' says Kate. 'We did him at school.'

They are driving along New Road now and it's properly dark. Ruth is used to it, this journey into nothingness, but it always makes her nervous, especially when she has Kate in the car. There are no lights ahead, only the sickly beam of her own headlights. She can hear the sea and the wind and the sudden call of a night bird. Kate is silent but she isn't asleep. Ruth checks in the mirror. Kate is gazing out of the window with a very solemn expression on her face. What is she thinking about? Kate has never lived anywhere else so maybe this is just home to her, a cosy place of refuge. Ruth certainly hopes so.

'Car,' says Kate suddenly.

As she says this, Ruth's car is suddenly flooded with light. There's another car behind them. It must have been travelling fast because it appears out of nowhere but, having caught up with them, it appears to be content to stay behind, keeping an exact two-second distance like you're taught in driving lessons. Where can the car be heading? The only houses on this road belong to Ruth, Bob Woonunga, and a London couple who use their cottage as a holiday home. She knows that Bob is away on one of his seemingly endless poetry tours. Could Sammy and Ed be arriving for one of their rare visits? The car behind seems big and purposeful, the sort of jeep-like vehicle that Ed would drive.

Ruth indicates that she is stopping (something she doesn't bother with when the road is empty) and comes to halt outside her house. The car carries on, past the weekenders' cottage, until its brake lights are out of sight. Now Ruth is really puzzled. The road leads only to a car park by one of the birdwatching hides. Is that what this is about? A group of birdwatchers on a night-time excursion? It's possible, she supposes. Nevertheless something about the car and its sudden appearance makes Ruth feel uneasy.

The security light comes on as she gets Kate out of her car seat. Ignoring her protests, Ruth carries her daughter to the front door. For once she finds her keys quickly and then they are inside. Ruth puts the chain on the door and turns on all the available lights. Kate runs upstairs in search of Flint but Ruth stays by the window, looking out.

She watches for a long time but the car doesn't come back along the road.

CHAPTER 26

Nelson's bullying works. He gets the DNA analysis on the pig farm bones early on Tuesday morning. As he suspected, though, it doesn't tell him very much. Only a very small amount of DNA can be recovered from bones and, although this can be enhanced by a process called PCR, which can determine sex, that's still not much use unless the DNA profile matches a sample already on the register. In this case, all the results show is that the victim was a man. Nevertheless, Nelson looks very carefully at the report from the forensics laboratory. Then, with a fine disregard for a memo from Whitcliffe entitled 'Saving Resources Where We Can', he telephones the lab and asks them for an interpretation of the results, one comparing the pig farm DNA profile to the sample given by George Blackstock and another comparing George Blackstock to David Clough.

'I'd like the results in twenty-four hours, please,' he says, chancing it.

'That's what they all say,' says the receptionist.

As he's putting the phone down, the superintendent him-self enters, without knocking of course.

'Ah, hallo, Harry!' Why is he sounding surprised? Who does he expect to see in Nelson's office? 'Just popped in to ask about David.'

'He's a lot better,' says Nelson. 'Still quite weak because he lost a lot of blood but the doctors say he's doing well. Johnson's with him now, getting a statement.'

'That's good news,' says Whitcliffe. 'I'll have Jenny send him flowers.'

'I'm sure he'd like that.' Nelson can just imagine Clough's face when he receives Whitcliffe's bouquet.

'Are you any further on with finding his assailant?'

'Not really. We've done door-to-door and a leaflet drop but no witnesses have come forward. We have got a potential DNA specimen though.' He explains about the mask.

'Red devils, eh?' says Whitcliffe. 'Sounds like something that warlock friend of yours would come up with.'

'Cathbad's a druid,' says Nelson. 'And he's DS Johnson's partner now.'

'I'll never understand that,' says Whitcliffe, shaking his head. 'To leave her husband for that long-haired lunatic.'

No, Nelson tells his boss silently, you'll never understand it. Not in a million years. Aloud he says, 'I'm running DNA tests on the mask.'

'Well, don't spend too much of our forensics budget,' says Whitcliffe. 'There's a good chap.'

*

Judy is sitting by Clough's bed, eating grapes.

'Why does everyone send sick people fruit?' says Clough. 'I don't want fruit. What I really want is an Indian takeaway.'

'You must be feeling better,' says Judy. When she had visited Clough yesterday, he had looked pale and hollow-eyed, lying flat on his back and still hooked up to countless tubes. He had rallied a bit when he saw her, asking if she had got lost on the way to the maternity wing, but he was still a ghost of his former self and Judy had left feeling rather worried. But when she called in this morning, he had been sitting up in bed watching *Antiques Roadshow* and complaining about the lack of Sky Sports. It is true what Cathbad says: Clough really is indestructible.

Clough is in a small room off the main ward. This is because Nelson impressed on the nurses the need to interview Clough in private. Judy thinks that Clough will soon be bored with this splendid solitude. He's not really one for enjoying his own company. She's the opposite. She's dreading being on a ward with other new mothers. With any luck, they'll let her go home as soon as she's had the baby.

Judy gets out her witness statement pad.

'Name?' she says.

'David Elvis Clough.'

'You're joking! Is your middle name really Elvis?'

'My mum's a big fan.'

Judy stares at him but Clough meets her eyes innocently. She writes down all three names in block capitals.

'Age?'

'Thirty-five.'

'You're a year younger than me.'

'You're getting on, Johnson.'

'Tell me about it.'

Judy sits with her pen poised.

'Well, what are you waiting for?' asks Clough. 'Aren't you going to ask me to tell you, in my own words, exactly what happened on the night of October the thirty-first?'

'OK,' says Judy. 'David Elvis Clough, can you tell me, in your own words, exactly what happened on the night of October the thirty-first?'

Clough sighs. 'The problem is, I don't really remember much. I left Cassie's flat at about three . . .'

'Cassie being Cassandra Blackstock?'

'Yes. Cassandra Blackstock. Have you met her?'

'Once. When she came in to see you on that first night.'

Judy looks up in time to catch Clough's expression of delight. 'She came in to see me? I didn't know that. Was she upset?'

'She seemed very upset,' says Judy. 'And she's been on the phone to the hospital every day. Is that what you wanted to hear?'

Clough grins. 'Well, it's nice to be appreciated.'

'So . . . back to the thirty-first. Actually, we're talking about the morning of the first, aren't we?'

'I left the flat at about three. Cassie had called a minicab and she said it would be waiting on the main road. She lives in a mews, she's got a really smart apartment. I could see the taxi's lights so I took a short cut between two buildings. Then this man in a devil mask just stepped in front of me.'

'How did you know it was a man?'

'Good point,' says Clough. 'I just assumed. There had been waiters in devil masks at the restaurant earlier and I suppose I thought of them. I was taken aback. Not scared, you understand. Just surprised. I think I said something. Then he, she, whatever, lunged forward and I don't remember anything else until I came to in the ambulance.'

'Do you remember what you said?'

'Something like, "What are you doing here?" I wasn't thinking that clearly, to be honest. I'd had a fair amount to drink and . . . well, my mind was on other things.'

'Did you cry out?' asks Judy. She remembers Tim saying that no one in the mews had heard anything.

'I don't think so. I can't be sure.'

'Can you remember anything else about the assailant?'

Clough frowns up at the ceiling. 'I think he was tall. That's why I thought of a man. Dark clothes.' He looks at Judy. 'Sorry, I'm being a typical crap witness. I always thought that if I was involved in a crime I'd give a perfect description, right down to shoe size.'

'It's the shock,' says Judy. 'When Michael was taken, I couldn't remember anything. It was a struggle to remember my own name.'

'You'll never find the knifeman though, will you? No witnesses, pathetic description.'

'We've got the mask,' says Judy. 'We're getting it tested for DNA and fingerprints.'

Clough brightens. 'That's fantastic. Can't be a professional then, leaving behind evidence like that.'

'Did you think it was professional?'

Clough shrugs. 'It was so clean. Just one lunge forward. No noise, no unnecessary movement. Single wound, straight to the chest. That sounds like someone with form, doesn't it?'

'It does,' Judy agrees. 'I even wondered if they left the mask behind on purpose.'

Clough doesn't laugh. He looks at Judy with narrowed eyes. 'As a sort of message, you mean? Why?'

'I don't know,' says Judy. 'But the whole thing's a bit weird, isn't it? Why would anyone want to attack you?'

'I would have thought you could come up with a list a mile long,' says Clough. 'Any copper has enemies.'

'But coming straight after the attack on Cassandra,' says Judy, 'we've got to look at a link between the two. It was even a similar attack, a quick blow and then a hasty retreat.'

'Except that Cassie was hit with a blunt object, not a knife. Thank God,' he adds.

'Maybe that was all there was to hand.'

'That's just it,' says Clough. 'It was opportunistic. This was planned. At least, I assume so. Don't suppose there are many knife-wielding maniacs on the streets of Spalding.'

'I don't know. But we're working full-out on it, I can tell you that.'

'What's the investigation called?' asks Clough. He's usually the one who comes up with the names, inevitably based on Mafia films.

'Operation Red Devil.'

Clough lies back on his pillows. 'Red Devil,' he says. 'I like it.'

Cassandra Blackstock is, at this moment, standing in a windswept field talking about the devil. *The History Men* are filming at Devil's Hollow and, although the original plan was to shoot Hazel discussing ley lines and prehistoric burials, it was soon decided that Cassie would be a more photogenic subject. Hazel does not seem at all offended. He and Chaz are leaning on the gate, watching Cassie's performance.

'Local people believe that the devil haunts this site,' Cassie is saying, her hair flying out in a witchy halo. 'There was an ancient graveyard right here, beneath my feet, and on stormy nights strange lights are seen as the dead try to find their way home.'

'She's talking crap,' says Chaz. 'Local people believe nothing of the sort.'

'I think she's merging together the legend of the will o' the wisps with the Bronze Age burials and a dollop of the story about the devil building a dam,' says Hazel. 'It's fascinating really.'

'People have also seen a headless horseman riding through the fields,' puts in Cassie for good measure. 'It's believed to be that of a Cavalier soldier killed in the Civil War. The battle took place *on this very spot*.' She stares dramatically into the camera.

'It that right?' Chaz looks at Hazel.

'Who knows?' Hazel sounds amused. 'She looks fantastic.'

Chaz says, 'They should have filmed you. You really know all this stuff.'

'It doesn't matter,' says Hazel. 'The point is that English Heritage might see this and decide that Edward Spens can't build here after all.'

The cameras have cleverly avoided filming the building work but it's there all the same, half the field churned up, lines of bricks rising from the sea of mud. Chaz stares at Hazel.

'Do you really think that'll happen?'

'It could do. It's a great publicity opportunity. That's why we should be glad they're using Cassie, even if she is a bit free and easy with the facts.'

'You heard what happened to that policeman?' says Chaz. 'The one Cassie's dating.'

'Is Cassie dating a policeman?' says Hazel. It's not the question you'd expect and confirms Chaz's suspicion that Hazel has a slight crush on Cassie. Although there's nothing odd in that; most of his friends have a crush on her.

'They've seen each other once or twice,' says Chaz. 'Well, this chap, Clough his name is, was attacked right outside Cassie's flat.'

'Do you think it's linked to the attack on Cassie at Blackstock Hall?'

'I don't know,' says Chaz. 'But these are very odd times.'

They both watch as Cassandra runs up the hill, looking over her shoulder as if pursued by the Headless Horseman. The camera follows her adoringly.

CHAPTER 27

Ruth drives home, trying to ignore the explosions all around her. It's fireworks, she tells herself, nothing to be afraid of. But the sudden crashes and flashes are disconcerting, to say the least.

'What is it?' asks Kate as a particularly loud bang seems to rock the little car.

'It's Bonfire Night,' says Ruth. 'Nothing to worry about. It's fun. Look at those pretty stars.'

The fountain of yellow and white stars on the horizon is, indeed, pretty. Kate watches for a second and then says, 'Why is Bonfire Night?' She has been like this ever since she learnt to speak. She will keep asking questions around a subject until she gets an answer she likes. Ruth is afraid that Kate has inherited tenacity from both parents.

'Well, it's a night when people light fireworks to remember a man who tried to blow up Parliament. The people who run the country.'

Another silence. More explosions.

'And did he?'

'Did he what?'

'Blow up the people?'

'No. They caught him in time and then they . . . er . . . killed him.'

'That's bad,' says Kate. 'If he was sorry.'

'Well, it was a long time ago,' says Ruth, feeling that she's not doing a very good job of explaining crime and punishment through the ages. 'They did things like that then.' She doesn't think she'll go into hanging, drawing and quartering just now. What would Frank make of her historical analysis? Frank is on her mind because she's going to see him in a few hours. She's cooking him dinner.

Once they leave King's Lynn, there are fewer fireworks. The night is dark and silent although the occasional sulphuric flare lights up the horizon. It'll be Nelson's birthday in two days' time. He's a Scorpio, like Kate. Ruth wonders how he'll celebrate. Perhaps Michelle will throw a surprise party for a few hundred of their closest friends. Even so, she doubts she'll be invited. Stop thinking about Nelson, she tells herself, for what seems to be the thousandth time in her life.

The blackness of the road across the marshes is almost comforting. The little car trundles on in its own circle of light. Ruth thinks about the mysterious car that followed them yesterday. Or did it follow them? 'It's not all about you,' her mother used to say. Probably the car was full of innocent birdwatchers off for a midnight ramble. But she's involved in a case where two people have been attacked. Could someone be trying to stop her finding the truth about Fred Blackstock? It's happened before, but Fred has been dead so long that

Ruth doubts that they'll ever know what happened that night in 1944. The truth will probably become the romantic legend expounded in the *History Men* TV special 'The Ghost Fields'. Of course, there are the bones found at the pig farm too but Ruth inclines to the theory that they belonged to some poor unfortunate who hid in the barn to shelter from the storm. There's death, all right. Murder too, Ruth is sure of that, but it all happened so far in the past that it's hard to see who would care enough to kill to keep the secret. But Clough was attacked and left for dead so someone somewhere is still feeling murderous. Thank God Clough seems to be on the mend, Judy says.

At the cottage, Ruth makes Kate's supper and sets about preparing a more sophisticated repast for Frank. She's making boeuf bourguignon, which, in Ruth's version, involves braising some beef, bunging in some wine and hoping for the best. Kate watches with interest as she eats her pasta. 'It's burning,' she says helpfully. 'It's meant to be like that,' says Ruth with more confidence than she feels.

She wants to get Kate into bed early so that she has time to change and put on some make-up before Frank arrives. But, as usual, things don't go to plan and Kate is still in the bath when the fateful knock sounds on the door. Ruth runs downstairs with her hair wild and a wet towel round her neck.

Frank, sleek and handsome in a pink shirt, kisses her on the cheek and presents her with flowers and a bottle of wine.

'Oh . . . er . . . thank you. Come in.' Ruth ushers him into the sitting room, kicking Sylvanians aside as she does so.

'I'm just putting Kate to bed. I'll get you a glass of wine.' Should she open his wine or not? What's the right thing to do? In the end she gives him a glass of white that is at least cold and saves his bottle of red for dinner.

When she returns with the wine, Frank is on the sofa reading *Green Eggs and Ham*.

'I used to love this when I was a kid.'

'Oh yes. Dr Seuss. Kate likes it too. She chants it all the time.'

'I do not like green eggs and ham. I do not like them Sam I Am.'

'Bit of a cheat to call a character "Sam I Am",' says Ruth. 'So easy to rhyme.'

Upstairs, she gets Kate out of the bath, hoping to tuck her up in bed with the nightlight and a soothing story tape. But of course Kate is filled with manic energy and frantic curiosity about the visitor downstairs.

'Can I see him? Can I show him my reading book?'

'It's Frank,' says Ruth. 'Do you remember, he took us to see that ruined church that time?'

'I love Frank,' beams Kate. 'Can he come up to say goodnight to me?'

So Ruth has to invite Frank upstairs. Something she wasn't intending to do except under very different circumstances.

'Hi, Kate,' he says. 'I like your bedroom.'

'Mum painted it,' says Kate. 'I wanted red but she did green.'

'Green is cool for a bedroom though. Red might keep you awake.'

'Will you read me a story?' asks Kate, spinning it out for as long as she can.

Ruth is about to protest but Frank produces *Green Eggs and Ham*, which he has brought upstairs with him. A riotous retelling ensues.

'I like your voice,' says Kate.

So do I, thinks Ruth.

Kate is finally persuaded to lie down and think about sleep and Ruth and Frank go downstairs.

'She's a great kid,' says Frank. 'It only seems a few minutes since my three were that age.'

Ruth knows that Frank's wife died when his children were still teenagers. She wonders if he's thinking back to a happier time when they were one big happy family in the Seattle house that she's never seen.

Filling Frank's glass, she goes into the kitchen to check the food and surreptitiously apply some make-up. Looking at herself in the oven door, she wishes that her face wasn't so pink, a combination of cooking and embarrassment. Surely at forty-five she's too old to blush? At this rate she'll go straight from adolescence to menopause without ever having experienced the joy of perfectly tinted skin. She puts on some mascara and hopes that it won't run. With any luck she won't be crying much this evening.

The food isn't bad. At least there's plenty of it and Frank's good red wine helps. He has a second helping, which Ruth feels is a good sign. She can never really cope with making puddings but there's cheese and some grapes.

'It looks like a Roman banquet,' says Frank, gesturing

towards the grapes and the half-full glass of wine in front of him.

From Ruth's point of view this is an unfortunate remark as it reminds her of Max, the only man in recent years with whom she has had anything like a serious relationship. Except Nelson, that is. Max is an expert on the Romans, though Ruth has always found them rather cold and militaristic. She prefers the Ancient Britons with their henges and causeways and appealingly chaotic beliefs.

'They used to recline after banquets,' she says. Oh God, she's blushing again. 'If you let a slave recline, it meant you were giving them their freedom.'

'Shall we?' Frank gestures towards the sofa.

Flint is reclining on the sofa but, to Ruth's surprise, he doesn't flounce away when Frank sits next to him. Instead he rubs himself against Frank's leg and shuts his eyes. Frank strokes him and the cat rolls onto his back.

'I'm afraid he's getting fur on you,' says Ruth. She's horrified to find herself feeling jealous of Flint.

'I don't mind,' says Frank. 'I love cats. We had dogs and cats when the kids were growing up. I miss them. Jane had stick insects too. I don't miss them so much.'

'Jane's at university, isn't she?'

'She's just graduated. Natural Sciences. So I suppose the stick insects had their uses.'

'What about your other children?'

'Fred's still in Africa. It was meant to be a gap year after university but he loves it so much that I don't think he'll ever come back. He's doing relief work in Malawi. Sean's at Brown, majoring in drinking and baseball.'

'Sounds like my university years. Apart from the baseball, that is. I can never get the point of baseball. Is it like rounders?'

She is aware that she is talking wildly. This is because Frank's arm has stretched along the back of the sofa and is stroking her neck.

'I never liked sport,' she goes on. 'Except swimming and . . .'

Frank's lips touch her neck. She turns towards him and finds that they are kissing, lying full-length on the sofa like a couple of freed slaves. Flint departs in high dudgeon.

'No. Wait.' Ruth struggles to sit upright.

'What do you want to wait for, honey?' asks Frank.

'Gloria,' says Ruth. Though she could think of other reasons too. 'What about Gloria?'

'I've ended it with Gloria,' says Frank. 'She's a fine person but there just wasn't this connection.'

'Do we have a connection?' asks Ruth.

'What do you think?' asks Frank, leaning forward to kiss her again.

I think we have a connection, thinks Ruth. We're both middle-aged and lonely and miss the pleasure of lying in someone's arms. But there's more to it than that. It's about the past and the present and the ghost fields and the fear that time is running out as it ran out for the pilots of 444th Bomb Group.

'Is this OK?' asks Frank, more seriously.

In answer, Ruth pulls him towards her. One day the sea will rise and flood the marshes and drown every living soul that lives there. But not yet. Not yet.

CHAPTER 28

When Nelson gets into work on Wednesday morning, the latest DNA analysis is waiting for him. He sits for a long time, looking at the lines of the graphs and the typed explanations underneath. It seems that Clough's love life is safe. He does not share a close familial connection with George Blackstock.

The same cannot be said of the man whose bones were found at the pig farm.

'So the man at the pig farm could be George Blackstock's son?' says Judy.

'Or his father,' says Nelson. 'As I understand it, Y-chromosome results are identical in the paternal line, so a grandfather, father and son would have the same sequence reoccurring.'

'Short tandem repeats,' cuts in Tanya Fuller. 'I've been reading up on it.'

Judy and Tim exchange glances. Tanya is a DC who, because of Judy's impending maternity leave and Clough's sickness, is now an Acting Detective Sergeant. As Tim said to Judy when this was announced, it's only a matter of time before she gets this title tattooed on her forehead.

'You think George Blackstock the younger had an illegitimate son?' says Tim.

'I'm not ruling it out,' says Nelson. He doesn't add that, until a few hours ago, he had thought that Clough might be that son.

'So George's son turns up,' says Tim, 'and is found dead at the home of his legitimate son, Chaz. Motive for murder, wouldn't you think? And who would know better about the pigs' omnivorous tendencies?'

'But Chaz called the police,' says Judy. 'Why would he do that? We'd never have found the bones otherwise.'

'Our first job is to put a name to this mysterious Blackstock,' says Nelson. 'Ask around at hotels and B & Bs near Hunstanton. Look for someone who booked in and never checked out.'

'We've got no name though and no description,' says Judy.

'I never said that it was going to be easy,' says Nelson.

But, in the end, it is easy. Judy, setting out on a tour of seaside hotels, finds a B & B in Burnham Market where a Mr Patrick Blackstock checked in on Saturday 26th October, went out on Sunday 27th, supposedly to attend a family funeral, and never returned.

'What did he look like?' asks Judy.

'A bit weird actually,' says the landlady. 'He had long grey hair and a beard. He looked a bit like a wizard. But he was very pleasant,' she adds, as if this was not to be expected. 'Nicely spoken too.'

'Bit of an Irish accent,' adds her husband.

'Weren't you worried when he didn't come back to his room?'

'Annoyed more than worried, dear,' says the landlady. 'But it happens a lot. More than you'd think.'

'Did he leave any possessions behind?'

'Nothing important,' says the landlady, sounding slightly defensive. 'He must have had his wallet and phone with him. Mind you, he didn't look the type to have a mobile phone.'

If he did have a phone, it was eaten by the pigs, thinks Judy.

'What about a passport?' she asks. 'Did you take a copy for your files?' She remembers this happening on her honeymoon and how mortified she'd felt to see her married name in print for the first time. Well, she has changed back to her maiden name now.

'I didn't ask to see a passport,' says the landlady. 'You don't need a passport to travel to Norfolk.'

Judy asks if she can see the possessions Patrick Blackstock left behind in his room. The landlady goes to a cupboard and gets out a plastic bag.

'Not much, I'm afraid.'

Judy looks. The landlady's right. A plaid shirt, blue striped pyjamas, thermal underpants and a tourist guide to North Norfolk. Judy opens this last. The page on Hunstanton is turned back, showing a snowy winter view of Blackstock

Hall. 'This beautiful stately home,' reads the caption, 'is still the home of the Blackstock family today.'

'Why didn't you call the police?' asks Judy.

The landlady shrugs. 'If we called the police every time a guest ran off without paying . . .' She looks at Judy as if registering the significance of her visit for the first time. 'Why? What's happened to him?'

'Nothing good,' says Judy grimly.

At Head Office, the Intel Unit searches electoral rolls and censuses for Patrick Blackstock. Remembering the accent, Judy asks for the search to be widened to include Ireland. Eventually they find him: Patrick William Blackstock from Belfast, born 1953, son of Lewis Blackstock and Mary O'Donnell.

'Lewis Blackstock,' Judy looks round at Nelson, who is reading over her shoulder. 'Isn't he . . . ?'

'The son who was missing believed dead,' says Nelson. 'Yes. But instead of killing himself, he apparently made his way to Ireland, got married and had a son.'

'Born 1953,' says Judy. 'That would make him sixty. How old is George Blackstock, Young George?'

'About the same age,' says Nelson. 'I think Sally described him as "pushing sixty".'

'Do you think they had any idea about this Patrick's existence?'

'Well, if they did,' says Nelson, 'they kept pretty quiet about it. I think we need to have a chat with them.'

'Patrick would be the heir, wouldn't he? After all, he was the son of the eldest son.'

'Yes,' says Nelson. 'Sally said something about changing the entail so that Cassandra could inherit before Chaz, but Patrick would supersede them both.'

'Except he's dead.'

'Except for that,' says Nelson, gathering up his car keys. 'Come on, let's pay the Blackstocks a visit.'

It's late afternoon and already dark by the time that Nelson and Judy arrive at Blackstock Hall. The lights are on in the house, visible for miles across the dark fields. It should be a welcoming sight, thinks Nelson as he and Judy start the trek to the front door, but somehow the illuminated windows have an almost sinister effect. Nelson thinks again of an ocean liner, the *Titanic* sailing to its doom with all lights blazing.

They should have gone round to the kitchen door, thinks Nelson as the sound of his knock echoes through the house. But this visit seems to demand the formality of the main entrance. Besides, if Sally wants to open the house to guests, surely she should get used to opening the door?

It's some minutes though before they hear the bolts going back. Judy is shivering and Nelson is pawing the ground with impatience. He's also wondering just when Sally started locking the door at five o'clock in the afternoon.

'DCI Nelson!' says Sally in apparent delight. She is wearing an apron and has flour in her hair. 'What a nice surprise.'

'Can we come in?' asks Nelson. 'We've got some news that might interest you.'

'Of course,' says Sally. 'Come into the drawing room.'

The drawing room seems to be full of people. Like a play, thinks Nelson (although he doesn't go to the theatre much). He had half expected the film people still to be there but, when he looks round, he sees that the room is, in fact, full of the Blackstock family. Old George is sitting by the fire and Nell sits opposite him, sewing something that glows in the firelight. Cassie and her father, Young George, are at a table by the window playing chess. Blake is reading at a nearby desk. Chaz is on the sofa, apparently asleep.

Judy moves closer to the fire. Nell springs up and offers her a chair.

'I'm fine,' says Judy. 'Honestly.'

Nelson wishes she would sit down. Heavily pregnant women make him nervous. Once he has got over his shock at finding the whole family assembled, he's rather pleased. He might as well tell them all at the same time. That way he can watch their reactions, both to the news and to each other.

'I'm glad to catch you all together,' he says, 'because I've had some interesting news today.'

They are all looking at him now. Judy is sitting in the fire-side chair and Nell is next to Chaz, who's rubbing his eyes, on the sofa. Sally hovers by the door.

'We've had the DNA results on the bones found at the pig farm,' Nelson goes on. He takes a printout from his pocket. He doesn't need it really but he feels that the moment deserves a bit of drama. 'Analysis of the Y-DNA,' he reads, 'shows that the dead man had a direct paternal link to George Blackstock junior.'

All eyes turn towards Young George, who blinks rapidly.

'What does that mean?' asks Cassie.

'It means that the man whose bones were found at the farm shares a direct male ancestor with Mr Blackstock, either a father, grandfather or great-grandfather.'

'How can that be?' asks Chaz slowly. 'If he shared a father with Dad, he'd be his brother. It's like one of those ghastly riddles.'

'A brother or a cousin,' says Nelson. 'We've made enquiries in the local area and we believe the remains to be that of Patrick Blackstock, son of Lewis Blackstock.'

Old George stirs in his chair. 'Son of Lewis?' he says. 'But I don't understand. Lewis is dead. Sally, what's he saying?'

His daughter-in-law comes over to hold the old man's hand. 'I don't understand either, Dad,' she says. 'I think DCI Nelson is saying that Lewis isn't dead.'

'He's dead now,' says Nelson, 'but he didn't die in 1950. He emigrated to Ireland, married and had a son – Patrick. We believe that Patrick attended Fred's funeral and may have been seen by some of you.'

'The Ancient Mariner,' says Blake suddenly. 'Was he the Ancient Mariner?'

'The old man that you saw,' says Nell. 'The old man with a beard. Was that him?'

'We believe so,' says Nelson. 'His description matches that of a man called Patrick Blackstock who checked into a Bed and Breakfast in Burnham Market on the day before the funeral. He never checked out.'

'What are you saying?' says Chaz. 'That this Patrick chap was killed and one of us did it?'

Interesting, thinks Nelson. Very interesting. 'Well, he's certainly dead,' he says. 'The rest is still under investigation.'

'He needn't have been killed,' says Cassie. 'He could have gone to sleep in the barn and been eaten by the pigs. You always say that they could eat a man, Chaz.'

Another interesting insight into Chaz Blackstock's mind, thinks Nelson.

'It's hard to imagine why someone who had a comfortable B & B room waiting for him would go to sleep in a pig pen,' he says.

'Maybe he was drunk,' says Cassie, who seems to be thinking very quickly. 'And wasn't that the night of the storm? He could have crept into the barn for shelter.'

'It's possible,' concedes Nelson.

'But we'll never know, will we?' says Chaz, who is becoming louder and more confident. 'The man's dead and we've only got a few of his bones left. We'll never know what happened to him.'

'We've got several other lines of enquiry,' says Nelson. But, in his heart, he knows that Chaz is right. He is sure that Patrick Blackstock was murdered and that the murderer was probably one of his long-lost relatives. But, with no evidence but a few dry bones, it's going to be impossible to prove. As long as the family stick to their stories, he'll never find out what happened at Blackstock Hall on the night of the storm. He looks around the room. Apart from Sally and Blake, they are all blood relatives. Old George by the fire, Cassie and Young George with the chessboard between them, Chaz leaning forward pugnaciously, Nell looking troubled.

Suddenly they all look very alike. I'll never be able to break them, he thinks. It's one of the worst things that can happen on a case, to be sure of what happened but not be able to prove it. He remembers being involved, as a young policeman, in the case of a child who appeared to have been shaken to death. The parents had denied it, had backed each other up, had protested their innocence and, in the end, they had got away with it. Nelson's friend Sandy Macleod had offered the idea that a bit of carefully directed violence might force a confession. Nelson didn't go along with the suggestion, though he has sometimes regretted this.

'The case is ongoing,' he says now. 'I'm travelling to Ireland in a few days to meet Patrick Blackstock's relatives.'

A silence greets this statement. The fire crackles and Old George can be heard saying, 'Lewis? What happened to Lewis?'

Clough is in a much better mood than his boss. He is enjoying an Indian takeaway brought in by Tim. The smell is so all-pervasive that four nurses have already been into his room, two to complain and two to beg for onion bhajis.

'This is more like it,' he says. 'It's been years since I had proper food.'

It's only been six days since your Mexican meal at La Choza, thinks Tim. But he's glad that his gesture has been appreciated. It was Judy who suggested that a takeaway might be more acceptable than fruit or chocolates and, as usual, she was right.

'Have some,' says Clough, pushing a foil container towards Tim.

'No thanks,' says Tim. 'You're OK. I'm going to the gym after this.'

'You're always at that gym,' says Clough. 'It's an obsession.'

'What about you and football?'

'You know what they say,' says Clough. 'Football's not a matter of life and death, it's more important than that.'

There's a brief pause and then Tim says, 'You seem to be a lot better. When do they say you can go home?'

'Tomorrow or the next day,' says Clough, spearing a cube of chicken tikka with a plastic fork. 'I'm a medical miracle.'

'When will you be back at work?' asks Tim. 'Not that we miss you or anything. Tanya hasn't enjoyed herself so much in years. She'll be after the boss's job next.'

'Oh, I'll be back in a few days,' says Clough. 'It'd take more than a stab wound in the chest to keep me away.'

CHAPTER 29

Nelson travels to Ireland the next day. Although his mother, Maureen, is a proud Irishwoman, this is the first time that he has visited the land of his ancestors. Patrick lived in Belfast, which Maureen would have considered suspicious for a start, but Nelson is surprised to find himself in a vibrant and attractive city; his taxi takes him past a mix of old and new buildings, a bustling waterfront and enough shopping centres to satisfy even Michelle. The taxi driver keeps up an apparently endless flow of talk, informing Nelson, in a pleasantly dry brogue, that the *Titanic* was built in Belfast (not a good omen) and that there's a Bronze Age henge called The Giant's Ring just outside the city. This connection to North Norfolk makes Nelson feel nervous, as does the driver's road sense, which is even worse than his.

The taxi drops Nelson at Belfast School of Art, where Patrick was a teacher. It's a glassy modern campus in the middle of the oldest part of town. He has to concede that his image of Belfast, constructed almost entirely from his memories of the Troubles in the seventies and eighties, is nothing like the reality. This is a proper city and he feels his urban spirits rise.

He is meeting a woman called Alice O'Brien, described as Patrick's closest friend amongst the faculty.

'It's good of you to see me,' he says. 'I know you must be very busy.' He says this because Ruth is always telling him how hard university lecturers work.

'I wanted to help,' says Alice. 'I was very fond of Patrick. It's hard to believe that he's gone.'

People have a problem saying 'dead', thinks Nelson. He understands this but the euphemisms make him nervous sometimes. If someone has just fallen asleep, why the hell are they burying them?

Alice is an attractive woman in her fifties. She has long hair, black streaked with grey, and it suits her. Michelle always says that she's going to cut her hair short when she reaches fifty. Nelson hopes this isn't true.

'How long had you known Patrick?' asks Nelson.

'Almost fifteen years. Ever since he came to work here. We got on from the first. He was an artist, I'm a writer.' She waves vaguely at the books on the shelf behind her. Nelson remembers that Alice O'Brien teaches creative writing. So you can get degrees in that now. Jesus wept.

He wants to ask about the nature of the relationship between Alice and Patrick but before he can frame the question, Alice volunteers that their friendship was 'purely platonic'.

'I don't think Patrick was that way inclined.'

'You mean he was gay?'

'No,' says Alice. 'He was an aesthete, a loner. I don't think he had relationships with men or women.'

'What do you know about his family?'

'He was an only child. His mother died when he was in his twenties. Patrick was very close to his father, though; he cared for him until he died.'

'Did you ever meet his father?'

'A couple of times. He was very old when I knew him and in the early stages of dementia, but he was always very sweet to me.'

These sweet, gentle Blackstocks are a different breed from the family Nelson knows. He wonders if Lewis Blackstock was suffering from dementia or whether he'd been unhinged by the sights he saw in the war. Either way, it was clear that his son was a devoted carer.

'Lewis died in 2003,' says Nelson. 'Is that right?'

'I think so. It would have been about ten years ago.'

'Did he ever talk to you about his wider family?' asks Nelson. 'About the Blackstocks?'

'No,' says Alice. 'I knew they were from Norfolk but that was all. I didn't even realise that he had relatives left there. But you say he attended a family funeral?'

'Yes. It was the funeral of Patrick's uncle – Lewis's brother – who died in the war. He was in the air force and his plane crashed. His body was only found recently.' He realises that this summary leaves out rather a lot of the story.

'It's possible that Patrick read about the find in the papers,' Nelson goes on. 'There was quite a lot of publicity at the time. We found a guidebook to Norfolk amongst his belongings.

He'd marked the page about Blackstock Hall, the family house.'

'Blackstock Hall? Is it a proper stately home then?'

'It's a large house,' says Nelson. 'I wouldn't say it was stately exactly.'

'And there are Blackstocks still living there?'

'Oh yes,' says Nelson. 'Including Lewis's younger brother George, who's in his late eighties. Did the old man never mention them?'

'He did say something once,' says Alice. 'But I dismissed it at the time because, as I say, he was apt to get a bit confused.'

'What did he say?' asks Nelson. 'Can you remember?'

Alice is silent for a moment, looking into the distance. There's a poster over her desk showing a girl floating in water, flowers all around her. The walls of Nelson's office are full of flow charts and performance targets but if he had space for a picture, he would pick something a bit jollier.

'We were talking about the place where the two rivers meet,' says Alice at last. 'That's where the name Belfast comes from, Beal Feirste, it means river mouth. Anyway, I was saying that there's all sorts buried in the silt there – going back to prehistoric times – and Lewis said, "Where I come from, the land is red with blood."'

'Is that all?' says Nelson. '"Where I come from, the land is red with blood"?'

'Yes. I had no idea what he meant but it stuck in my mind. It's such an arresting phrase.'

But I'm not making any arrests, thinks Nelson, as the taxi takes him back to the airport. The visit hasn't taught him much, except that Patrick Blackstock was a kind, gentle man who looked after his father. The father who had walked out on his family fifty years ago and never once looked back. The man who said that he came from a land 'red with blood'. Did this refer to Norfolk's history – all that prehistoric stuff that Ruth's always coming out with – or did he mean something more specific? Was he referring to his mother's belief that the land was cursed? Lewis's mother, Nelson remembers, killed herself some years after her son's disappearance. Did Lewis ever know this? Would it have made a difference?

Nelson has contacted Patrick's solicitor, who told him that his client's will left his pictures to Alice and everything else to Alzheimer's research. So maybe Lewis really did have dementia. It occurs to him that Patrick won't ever get old enough to have Alzheimer's.

Nelson asks the taxi driver to go past Patrick's house. It's off the Sydenham Bypass, a pleasant Victorian villa with a monkey puzzle tree in the garden. According to Alice, it's where Patrick had lived with his parents. What made a man who still lived in his childhood home suddenly decide to travel to another country to attend the funeral of an uncle he had never met? Nelson has to concede that he will never know.

'Grand little property,' says the driver. 'Thinking of moving to Belfast?'

'No,' says Nelson. 'I'm not moving anywhere.'

Tim and Judy are doing research of their own. Nelson told them to investigate Cassandra Blackstock and that's just what they are doing. This is made easier by the fact that she's on Facebook, where she is apparently 'in a relationship with Dave Clough'.

'That was quick,' says Tim, looking over Judy's shoulder. 'Does his profile say he's in a relationship?'

'No, but he doesn't go on Facebook much. It's mostly pictures of his Sunday football team.'

From Facebook, though, they learn that Cassandra studied English and Drama at Bristol University, that she has an impressive number of friends (over three hundred) and a propensity for going to parties dressed as Marlene Dietrich. A Google search yields an Equity profile and even a Wikipedia entry, which sounds as if it was written by Cassandra herself: 'This talented actress . . .'

Tim stares at a picture of Cassandra dressed as a badger in a community-theatre production of *The Wind in the Willows*. She even looks sexy with a black-and-white striped face.

'You should go and see her,' he tells Judy. 'Find out if she's got anything to hide.'

'Do you think she has then?'

'I don't know, but I think she'd have more trouble hiding it from another woman.'

Cassandra is still staying at Blackstock Hall. She takes Judy up to her room 'so they can talk in peace'.

'It's great being back at home,' she says, arranging herself elegantly on the single bed. 'But it's impossible to have any time to yourself. Mum keeps asking me if I'm all right, if I want a cup of tea. It's driving me mad.'

It doesn't seem too bad to Judy, having someone fussing over you and offering you tea. Cathbad adores her but he's more likely to build her a ceremonial fire than put the kettle on. Her own mother is a school secretary with a busy social life and Judy hasn't lived at home since she was eighteen. She eases herself into the only available chair, a flimsy white affair with a gingham cushion, and looks around.

This is clearly Cassandra's childhood room. The bed has a pink duvet and countless fluffy cushions. On the walls, ponies fight for space with heavy metal bands and Tolkien illustrations. Judy wonders why the room hasn't been redecorated. After all, Cassandra must be nearly thirty. She also thinks that if Cassandra likes fantasy and heavy metal, she really is Clough's ideal woman.

'This room was too small to get the B & B treatment,' says Cassandra, correctly interpreting Judy's glance. 'Unlike Chaz's, which has had a total makeover.'

She laughs but Judy thinks that Cassandra likes the idea of having this room to escape to, a place where she can be a child again. And wouldn't we all like that, given the chance?

'I was just wondering if you'd remembered anything else about the evening of October twenty-seventh, when you were attacked in the grounds here,' says Judy. 'Sometimes people do remember things some time after the event, when the shock has worn off.'

Cassandra flicks back her hair and assumes a remembering pose. Or maybe she is remembering. The trouble with Cassandra is that she always looks so theatrical. Even now, curled up on the bed in her grey jumper and black leggings, she looks like a prima ballerina on her day off.

'I remember looking at my text messages,' says Cassandra. 'And then someone hitting me over the head. That's all really.'

'Did you hear them coming up behind you?' asks Judy. 'Footsteps? Breathing?'

'No,' says Cassandra. 'I didn't hear anything. I was so absorbed in my message.'

'Who was it from?' asks Judy. She wonders if anyone has asked this before.

'A friend,' says Cassandra. Judy waits. Cassandra twists her hair. 'I'd had a message from my agent, Tobias, earlier,' she says, 'and I thought it was him again. But it was from a friend. Georgie.'

'Boy Georgie or girl Georgie?'

'Boy.'

'Boyfriend?'

'No.' More hair-twisting. 'I've sometimes thought he wanted to be more but, no, he's just a friend.'

'And what was the message about?'

'Just asking where I was, that sort of thing. Wondering when he was going to see me.'

Judy thinks that Cassandra is lying but what can she do? She's not a suspect or even a person of interest in the enquiry. She's wondering what she can ask next when Cassandra says, 'I've heard a lot about you.'

'Excuse me?'

'Dave talks about you a lot.'

'He does?'

'Yes. You're very close, aren't you? I was quite jealous at first but Dave told me that there would never be anything like that between you. You're just mates, he says.'

'That's nice of him.'

'Yes, isn't it? He says that you're really close because you've been through so much together. You, Dave and Nelson.'

'That's true, I suppose.'

'It's almost like you're a family. Nelson's the father and you and Dave are brother and sister.'

Much as Judy hates to admit it, there is some truth in this. Why else have she and Clough fought for Nelson's attention all these years? Why else does she feel so close to Clough? She has nothing in common with him, sometimes she doesn't even like him, but there are times when she feels closer to him than to anyone in the world.

Aloud she says, 'We're colleagues, that's all.'

'I envy you.' Cassandra's eyes have a misty look. Is she imagining herself as a policeman's wife? 'Dave can't wait to get back to work. I bet he'll be back as soon as the doctors give him the go-ahead.'

CHAPTER 30

But the doctors don't give Clough the go-ahead for another three weeks. He is due to resume work on Monday the ninth of December. Judy is going on maternity leave on the sixth, which is also the date of the Blackstocks' 'wrap party' celebrating the end of the filming. Judy seems increasingly twitchy as this date approaches. Maybe it's because Clough is coming back just when she's leaving, maybe it's because Tanya is showing signs of enjoying her Acting DS status too much ('Don't worry Judy,' she told her colleague, 'I'll look after the boys when you're away'). Either way, Judy is so bad-tempered during her last few days at work that Nelson and Tim often hide in the gents when they hear her coming.

Nelson is fed up too. He's almost certain that Patrick Blackstock was killed by a member of his estranged family, but with no evidence, there is no way he can prove it. Similarly, it seems that the death of Senior Airman Frederick Blackstock will for ever remain a mystery. But Nelson is sure that the answer has something to do with Blackstock Hall, that it lies buried deep in the family grave, or at least in the pets' burial ground. But, again, with limited resources and no new evidence, there is nothing he can do.

Even the investigation into the attack on Clough is moving slowly. There don't seem to be any witnesses. The DNA found on the mask doesn't match any held on the register and, although he's asked for further tests, the results haven't come back yet. The attack on Cassandra is even less likely to be solved. Once again there are no witnesses and there is a general feeling that Cassandra might even have imagined the assault. As Whitcliffe put it to Nelson in one of their weekly meetings: 'A highly strung girl, an actress, probably in an extremely emotional state, just come from a funeral, been drinking, a howling gale. Put those together and what have you got?' Nelson doesn't bother answering the question. For his own part, he believes that someone did creep up behind Cassie while she stood amongst the family tombstones, someone who was willing to take any chance to do away with the Blackstock heir. But what are his policeman's instincts against Whitcliffe's all-too-rational version of events? Again, it's not worth answering.

To add to Nelson's woes, he is booked to go on a training course from the sixth to the eighth of December. The course, 'Community Engagement in Twenty-first-century Policing', is, of course, Whitcliffe's idea. 'You'll enjoy it, Harry,' he said, passing him the application form which he had already counter-signed. 'You never know, you might even join the twenty-first century.' Then, seeing Nelson's face, 'It's in York, a lovely city. Why don't you take Michelle and make a mini-break of it?' It's a measure of Nelson's desperation that he did suggest this idea to Michelle. She hadn't been keen. 'I'm really busy at work in December, and what'll I do in York all day when you're on the course?' 'There's a cathedral,' said Nelson but he hadn't pressed the point. Michelle isn't really one for old buildings.

Now, as Nelson packs his overnight bag, he reflects that Michelle hasn't been herself recently. She normally loves the build-up to Christmas: buying presents, ordering the turkey, getting the tree down from the loft, forcing him to go to parties. But this year she has seemed lethargic and uninterested. Maybe it's the weather, which is still stormy and grey with an unrelenting icy wind. Maybe it's because Laura is staying in Ibiza for Christmas with her new boyfriend. He'll have to do something to cheer Michelle up. Go to a show in London, perhaps. She'd like that. As long as it's not a musical. There are limits to being a good husband.

At least the course means that he'll avoid the party at Blackstock Hall. The Blackstocks are the very last people he wants to see, except perhaps the American film crew. He has heard rumours that Ruth is now very friendly with Frank Barker. Well, that's OK (he supposes) as long as he doesn't have to see them together. He has ordered Judy to go to the party though. Someone has to keep their eye on the Blackstocks and, as Judy is off on maternity leave next week, it'll be a nice treat for her.

You're all heart, he tells himself.

*

Ruth is not looking forward to the party either. It'll be the first time that she and Frank will be seen together as a couple. They have seen each other most nights since the boeuf bourguignon evening. Ruth doesn't stop to think about the wisdom of this. She doesn't ask herself what will happen when Frank goes back to America. She just lets herself be carried along by the tide.

But the tide is one thing, the party is another. She wants to look her best, glamorous even. She has to buy something nice to wear and, if possible, lose about two stone. So Ruth is at the gym. She has actually been a member there for ten years. When the receptionist made her a new card (everything has been automated since Ruth's last visit), she commented that Ruth was one of their oldest members. She didn't add that Ruth has visited the gym only twice in those ten years, which averages out, Ruth calculates, at about a thousand pounds a swim.

But now she's determined to do it properly. She has had an induction with a charming young man called Dean and, for the last month, has been to the sports club three times a week. She spends half an hour in the gym, following the programme designed for her by Dean, and then she swims for half an hour. She hates it. She hates the other members in their designer sportswear, running marathons on the treadmill, then stopping to do complicated stretches, carrying their little bottles of water everywhere. She hates the changing rooms where the women strip off and then wander around naked chatting about their Pilates sessions. She even hates the pool, which is too warm and emits a stinging smell of chlorine. It'll be worth it if she gets fit but, so far, she has only lost one pound. It doesn't help that the only place in the club that she likes is the cafe, which sells delicious Danish pastries.

But today Ruth is determined. The party is tomorrow. Surely it's not too late to change her body shape completely? She slogs away on the cross-trainer, ignoring the flashing lights informing her that she has so far burnt one hundred calories, approximately a third of a Mars bar. It is so boring, that's the problem. Everyone else has iPods to plug in but Ruth is stubbornly old fashioned and prefers her transistor radio. There's a television but it's too far away and, besides, at this hour it always shows a breakfast TV programme of breath-taking vacuousness. Ruth is reduced to looking out of the window, but the view is pretty boring too. Just the car park, a few trees and a recycling station. She watches as a man and a woman walk out to their car. The woman has long blonde hair and, even from the back, has the sort of figure that makes Ruth feel envious. The man is tall and athletic, carrying his sports bag high on his shoulder. At the car, they stop and kiss. Maybe they aren't a couple then. Maybe they are illicit lovers who just meet at the gym. There's certainly something going on, judging by the length and passion of the kiss. Then the woman puts her bag in the boot and turns to say something to the man. He reaches out and touches her cheek. Ruth stops. The cross-trainer bleeps at her angrily but she ignores it. The man turns and heads off towards his own car. For a moment he is staring directly at Ruth but can't see her because of the tinted glass. She recognises him though. It's Tim.

And the woman is Michelle.

Ruth drives to the university in a daze. She can't stop thinking about Michelle and Tim, replaying their embrace in the car park like a dreary X-rated film on a loop. Are they having an affair? Something must be going on. No two adults kiss like that unless they're having an affair. It's a strange thing but Ruth's first emotion was disappointment. She has got so used to thinking of Michelle as perfect – the beautiful loyal wife who loves her husband so much that she can even forgive him for fathering a child with another woman – it's a shock to realise that she is human after all. Not just human but cheating on her husband with one of his own team, a young man who is supposed to like and respect Nelson. When she thinks of this double betrayal, Ruth finds herself feeling physically sick.

What should she do? She can't imagine herself telling tales to Nelson. The tale-teller never comes off well in these situations and, besides, she doesn't really know what's happening between Michelle and Tim, if anything. Should she speak to Michelle, tell her what she saw? Her entire body shrinks from the thought of such a confrontation. What would Michelle say if she was accused of infidelity by the woman who slept with her husband and had his child? What about Tim? Could she talk to him? No, that's even more impossible. She hardly knows him. Besides, that might mean telling Tim the truth about her own relationship with Nelson. Thinking this makes

Ruth feel ashamed, for herself, for all of them. But then, her predominant emotion is one of shame. Because, when she saw Michelle and Tim, almost her first thought was: if Nelson finds out about Michelle, perhaps he'll leave her. Perhaps he'll marry me.

Why should she think this when she's having what is, frankly, a rather passionate affair with Frank? Why should she fantasise about being married to Nelson when she doesn't want to marry anyone? She and Nelson would kill each other in a week, arguing about whether Kate should be allowed to play on the wet grass or watch unsuitable Disney films. Even after a night of great sex with Frank, she's quite keen to get him out of the house so she can be alone with the view and her daughter and her cat. She doesn't want to live with a man. So why, while she was still standing on the cross-trainer, did a shamefully regressive picture of a white wedding flash into her mind? 'Do you, Ruth Alexandra, take this man . . .' She takes the turn for the university, glad that no one else is privy to this image.

The campus is like a ghost ship. Term is nearly over and a lot of the overseas students have already left. She walks up the stairs to her office, hoping to spend a couple of hours getting to grips with her marking. But no sooner has she opened the first of the mid-sessional booklets, 'Field Techniques in Archaeology', when there's a knock on her door.

For one mad moment she thinks it's Michelle, come to confess about Tim and throw herself on Ruth's mercy. But that's crazy. Michelle didn't see Ruth at the gym and she's not exactly the confessing sort (unlike her husband, she's not a Catholic).

'Come in,' says Ruth, still in her angel of mercy voice.

It's Phil. Ruth's voice changes very quickly.

'Hi, Phil. What do you want?'

'Just wondering if you were going to the party at Blackstock Hall tomorrow? Shona and I are thinking of putting in an appearance.'

Putting in an appearance. That's exactly how he (and Shona) would see it. Even so, Ruth feels guilty about Shona. She hasn't seen her for weeks. It's partly because she knows that Shona would wheedle the truth about Frank out of her in seconds. Not that her relationship with Frank is exactly a secret. It's just that's she's not quite ready for it to be common knowledge, discussed at university dinner parties by Phil and Shona and their friends, picked over by Clough and the police team, known to Nelson.

'I'm going to the party,' says Ruth. 'I might not stay long though. Horrendous rain is forecast.'

'Oh, forecasters always get it wrong,' says Phil. 'I'd like to go. After all, we were there when the plane was first discovered. We've been involved in this story from the beginning.'

I was there, thinks Ruth. You just tagged along for the ride. Aloud she says, 'Are you looking forward to seeing the finished film? I think they're going to show it tomorrow.'

'I'm not that bothered about the film,' says Phil. That's because you're not in it, thinks Ruth. 'I'm sure it's very American and sensationalised. No, I'm just interested in the archaeological investigation.'

Phil has shown so little interest in the archaeological investigation that he has never even asked about Ruth's dig at Blackstock Hall or about how Fred's body came to be in the plane in the first place. This is just as well, really, because Ruth's dig was inconclusive. She is pretty sure that the soil in the pets' graveyard showed traces of decaying human body matter but the samples she took proved difficult to analyse because too much animal matter was mixed in. The context didn't yield much either, besides the dog-tag and the Victorian glass. But Ruth is sure that the earth had been moved fairly recently and that a human body had once been buried amongst the dogs and cats.

'There's not much to say about the archaeological investigation,' she says now. 'It's a bit frustrating really.'

'What about the body that was found in the pig farm? You were involved with that too, weren't you?'

Nelson told Ruth about the body turning out to be that of Patrick Blackstock but the information hasn't been released to the general public and, in this instance, Ruth regards Phil as very much one of the public.

'The police are still awaiting DNA results, I think.'

'And they say universities are slow.' Phil turns to leave, pausing at the door to ask Ruth if her American friend will be at the party.

'If you mean Frank,' says Ruth evenly, 'yes.'

Phil heads off down the corridor whistling 'I Like to Be in America'.

*

Ruth's American friend is waiting for her when she gets back to the cottage. She had said that she'd be home at five but she was held up by traffic and by collecting Kate from her childminder. This has happened a few times but something stops Ruth from giving Frank a key to the cottage. He's going back to America in a few weeks, says the voice in her head, you don't want things to get too serious. A key, now that's serious. Besides, Frank always says that it's no hardship to wait outside.

'The view's different every day. I could never get tired of looking at it.'

She loves the fact that Frank loves the view. And further than that, she's not prepared to go.

'Sorry I'm late,' she says now. 'Traffic. Camper vans. Horse trailers. All the usual stuff.'

'I've never known such a place for camper vans and horse trailers,' says Frank, swinging Kate up into the air. 'Maybe they could get the horses to pull the vans and halve the traffic.'

'Cathbad used to live in a horse-drawn caravan,' says Ruth, opening the door. 'When he lived in Ireland.'

'Figures,' says Frank, who has come to know Cathbad well over the last few weeks.

Kate drags Frank off to look at her Sylvanians. Kate's enthusiasm for Frank has become rather worrying for Ruth. It's all very well for her to decide that she won't think about her feelings for Frank until he's on his way back to America, but what will Kate make of this romantic fatalism? She's not going to accept the explanation that Frank's not coming round for tea any more because Mummy's afraid of commitment. She'll miss Frank and she'll keep asking questions about him until Ruth either explodes or gives her a proper answer. Kate has already chatted about Frank on days out with Nelson, prompting several sarcastic asides: 'Your American friend is quite the Mary Poppins'. Even if he goes away, she'll keep talking about him. And why shouldn't she? As far as Kate is concerned, Frank is her friend.

Ruth makes tea and puts the crumpets under the grill. Frank has said that he'll make supper tonight so she doesn't have to worry about that. Frank is a good, if limited, cook, specialising in the meals he taught himself to make after his wife's death: spaghetti bolognaise, chilli con carne, steak and roast chicken. Ruth doesn't mind; these meals suit her fine. It's bliss to have someone else cooking for her and to eat the meals together, drinking wine and talking about their various days. This is how Ruth has always imagined Nelson's home life, Nelson and Michelle sitting down to cosy meals together, laughing softly and talking about delicious trivialities. But it turns out that, instead of cooking Nelson's supper, Michelle has been busy kissing Tim at the gym. Does Nelson know? Does he care that his marriage might be about to collapse?

Frank comes into the kitchen just in time to save the crumpets from burning. They eat them in the sitting room while Kate watches *Dora the Explorer* and Flint, probably jealous, claws steadily at the sofa.

'Stop it, Flint,' says Ruth. He blinks at her and carries on.

'Are you looking forward to the party tomorrow?' asks Frank.

'Not really,' says Ruth. 'I don't like parties and the weather's meant to be horrible.'

It's raining now, it sounds as if someone is throwing little stones against the window. High tides and heavy rain mean a serious risk of flooding, as the news is always reminding Ruth. She is sure that this morning the sea was nearer than ever, swallowing the water meadows, edging closer to the road.

'It'll be OK,' says Frank. Ruth has noticed that he likes parties, that he's rather social in fact. Another thing they don't have in common. 'We're hoping to show the film. The dailies have been looking really good. We're having a post-production meeting tomorrow and then hoping to have a version to show over at the Hall. I'd really like Nell to see it before she goes back to the States.'

'I like Nell,' says Ruth. 'She's very sweet.'

'I like Sally too,' says Frank. 'The women in that family are worth ten of the men.'

'You might have something there,' she says.

'Ruth,' says Frank. There is something in his voice that makes Kate look round from the screen. Even Flint stops clawing momentarily.

'Ruth,' he says, 'Paul and Earl are going back to the States a couple of days after the party. There's a lot of editing to be done.'

'I suppose there must be,' says Ruth. She knows absolutely nothing about film editing.

'But I was thinking of staying on for a couple of weeks.'

'That would be nice,' says Ruth, her throat dry.

'Would it?' Frank takes her hand. 'Would it, Ruth?'

'Yes,' says Ruth. 'Term's over in a week. If the weather gets better, we could go on some trips, we could . . .'

'The thing is,' says Frank, 'I might even be able to stay for good. That is, if you wanted me to.'

CHAPTER 31

Ruth and Judy are planning to travel to the party together. It makes sense; Cathbad is looking after both children and Judy is finding it uncomfortable to drive. She is very near her due date now, although she keeps insisting that the baby will be late because Cathbad says so. Ruth, remembering how she went into labour at one of Cathbad's Halloween parties, looks at Judy dubiously as she squeezes into the passenger seat.

'Are you quite sure you want to go to this party?'

'Yes,' says Judy. 'Besides, the boss told me to.'

'You don't have to do everything Nelson says,' says Ruth.

Judy looks at her. 'That's kind of the point of him being the boss.'

'Clough could go instead,' says Ruth. 'He'd love to. Cassandra will be there.'

Ruth hasn't seen Clough since she visited him in hospital a few weeks ago but, if the rumours are to be believed, he and Cassandra are now inseparable.

'Clough'll probably be there anyway,' says Judy. 'But the boss told me to go.' Her face takes on a mulish look. Ruth wonders whether she is slightly put out by Clough's return to work. Anyway, there's clearly no changing her mind.

'Let's get going then,' says Ruth. 'We don't want to be too late back. Not if this rain keeps on.'

It has been raining all day. As they drive through the fields, the sky and the land seem to meet in a dreary grey no-man's-land. Ruth swerves to avoid the puddles at the side of the road, ever-expanding pools reflecting more sky turning from grey to black. It's only four o'clock (the party is billed as 'early evening drinks') but it's already nearly dark. Ruth puts on her headlights and grips the wheel tightly. It would be easy to drive off the road in these conditions and she doesn't fancy her chances out there in the watery landscape. Her little Renault is a trusty steed but she's pretty sure it can't swim.

Neither of them speaks much on the drive. Judy has her eyes shut and appears to be asleep. Ruth is thinking about her conversation with Frank last night. *I might even be able to stay for good . . . if you wanted me to.* Does she want Frank to stay for good and what did his offer actually mean? He explained that he was taking a break from TV and planning to write a book. The tenants would be leaving his flat in Cambridge and he could easily come to England and write 'for six months or so'. The fens, he thought, would prove a great inspiration. And Ruth? Would she inspire him? Maybe she could even make a start on her own book, the sequel to *The Tomb of the Raven King*. Maybe they could work together, exchanging proofs and reading their work in progress to each other. 'There would be no point in me staying,' he'd said, 'if you didn't think that there was some future for the two of us.'

Did she think they had a future? She had been so used to thinking of their affair – if it is an affair – as a time-limited thing, a holiday romance if you like. And now it has become something altogether more serious. At least Frank isn't suggesting that they move in together but, even so, he is certainly implying that their futures are in some ways interlinked. Are they? And what has this to do with her embarrassing fantasy of marrying Nelson? 'Do you, Ruth Alexandra, take this man . . .' She brakes fiercely to avoid a puddle and Judy wakes up.

As they park on the grass verge by Blackstock Hall, geese swim serenely on a lake beneath the trees. But surely there wasn't a lake there before? Wasn't that the field where cars were parked on the day of the funeral?

'Blimey,' says Judy, rubbing her eyes. 'Did the house always have a moat?'

Ruth looks across at the Hall. The streams that used to criss-cross the fields have merged to form a sea of water, black and sinister in the evening light. The house now stands on an island, like a lighthouse or a ruined castle. Although there are lights at the windows, the whole place has suddenly taken on an uninhabited aspect. It feels like the last place in the world to attend a party.

'Shall we go round to the back door?' says Ruth.

The south side of the house is dryer and the driveway is clear, although they have to skirt several large puddles. It's now too dark to see much but there's a feeling that the water is very near, lapping at the edges of the kitchen garden. It's still raining hard.

Ruth knocks on the stable door and Sally answers almost immediately. She is smartly dressed in black with pearls round her neck.

'Thank goodness you've come,' she says. 'Nell and Blake are stuck in London. Apparently the trains are all up the spout. And the film people are having a meeting at the Le Strange Arms, though they should be along later. I hope so. There's enough food and drink to sink a ship.'

Under the circumstances, it's not the best of metaphors.

The drawing room has obviously been tidied up for the party. The firelight glitters on the rows of glasses and cool jazz ripples from Chaz's iPod. Old George is wearing an actual dinner jacket and bow tie. He beams at them with the most warmth he's ever shown.

'Welcome, ladies. What would you like to drink?'

Ruth and Judy are a disappointment in this respect. They both opt for orange juice but Chaz, who brings the drinks, compensates by adding ice, lemon and a cocktail stirrer.

'Where's Cassandra?' asks Ruth.

'Oh, she's coming with Dave,' says Chaz. It takes Ruth and Judy a few beats before they realise he means Clough. Young George, also in black tie, hovers around with trays of canapés.

'Where's Frank?' he asks Ruth. 'Is he coming later?'

Ruth doesn't like to think that she and Frank come as a package. 'I don't know,' she says. 'I presume he's coming with the TV crew.'

'I hope they get here,' says Chaz. 'Cassie texted to say that the A17 was already pretty bad.'

Ruth looks at Judy. Neither of them wants to get trapped

at Blackstock Hall. In the silence that follows Chaz's remark they can hear the rain falling outside.

'Don't worry,' says Young George. 'If it gets too bad, you can always stay the night here. We've got plenty of room.'

That's what I'm afraid of, thinks Ruth.

Michelle and Tim are also listening to the rain. They are lying on a four-poster bed in a luxurious country house hotel, an open bottle of champagne on the bedside table. There's a free-standing copper bath at the end of the bed. 'I can run it for you if you like,' the porter had said, rather lasciviously. 'Rose petals and everything.' 'That's OK,' said Tim, giving the man an over-large tip just to get rid of him. 'We can manage.'

But, having gone to extraordinary lengths to plan this night away, the lovers seem slightly at a loss as to what to do next. Tim thinks that they should have sex, get the moral hurdle over with, then go out for a meal. It's only five o'clock after all. Michelle is staring up at the draped canopy. It's hard to know what she's thinking.

Tim raises himself on one elbow and strokes her hair.

'I can't believe we're really here,' he says.

'Nor can I,' says Michelle. There is nothing in her tone to indicate whether the realisation is a dream or a nightmare.

'And we've got the whole night,' says Tim.

Michelle looks at him, saying nothing. There's a smattering of freckles over the bridge of her nose that he's never noticed before.

'You're so beautiful,' says Tim, kissing her neck and sliding his hand downwards.

He hears her breath quicken and, for a few minutes, it seems as if he will get his reward for all the months of patient waiting in car parks and jacuzzis. Then Michelle sits up, doing up her silk blouse.

'No,' she says. 'I'm not ready.'

Tim counts to ten under his breath. 'What do you want to do then?' he says, trying to sound understanding and not resentful. 'We can hardly go out for a walk in all this rain.'

'We could have tea in the garden room,' says Michelle. 'It looked really nice on the way in.'

Tim had hardly noticed his surroundings. He had been so eager to get into the bedroom and consummate their non-relationship. He feels that he has drunk more tea over the last year than ever in his life. He honestly thinks that if he doesn't have sex with Michelle soon he will die of frustration.

'OK,' he says, breathing hard. 'Let's go and have some tea.'

At Blackstock Hall, the rain continues to fall. Ruth has discussed the Bronze Age with Young George and the *Antiques Roadshow* with Old George. Judy and Chaz have shared memories of growing up in the King's Lynn area. Now an uneasy silence reigns in the drawing room. Sally enters, wearing an apron over her smart black dress.

'There's food in the dining room. Why don't you have some before the others arrive?'

Ruth doesn't think she can be the only one to doubt whether the others will ever arrive. Nevertheless she likes the idea of some food. She and Judy follow their hostess into the dining room.

This room faces east and the curtains are open. Ruth goes to the window and gives a gasp. The kitchen garden, the orchard wall and the family graveyard have vanished and rolling towards the house is a long silent wave of water.

Old George is looking over her shoulder. When he speaks, his voice has a kind of fatalistic hysteria.

'The sea's rising,' he says. 'It's my mother's curse. We're all going to be drowned.'

Frank, Paul and Earl stand in the porchway of the Le Strange Arms, contemplating the flooded car park.

'There's no way you can drive the limo in this,' says Earl. 'It's a goddamn deluge.'

'What about the party?' says Frank. 'They're expecting us.'

'I'm sure Ruth can cope without you,' says Paul. 'If she's got any sense, she'll have stayed home anyway.'

Frank doesn't answer. Although Paul hasn't said anything, Frank knows that he's angry with him for ending the relationship with Gloria. For his part he hopes that Ruth has stayed at home. He doesn't like to think of her stranded at the Hall, surrounded by mad Blackstocks, worrying about Kate.

'I'm sure you guys can stay at the hotel tonight,' says Earl. 'They've had a few cancellations, what with the weather and everything.'

Paul turns to accompany the producer inside but Frank stays under the porch trying to get a mobile phone signal. It suddenly seems vital to contact Ruth.

*

'I'm sorry,' says Ruth. 'I think we should leave.'

'But you've only just come,' says Sally.

'Look at all that rain though,' says Ruth. 'And I'm sure it'll be worse on the coast road.'

Given that Old George is still going on about drowning and floods and Sodom and Gomorrah, Sally can hardly argue. She fetches their coats and accompanies them to the back door.

'Drive carefully,' she says.

'I will,' says Ruth. She is relieved to see that the driveway is still above water. Will her car be all right? They must hurry. As she steps outside, her phone pings. It's a text from Frank.

Are you at blkstk hall? floods here. pls take care. ring me.

I'll ring when I get home, she thinks. Back to Kate and safety. She and Kate might even stay at Cathbad and Judy's for the night. If they really are flooded, it would be cosier to be with other people. Bob is back from his travels and he'll feed Flint.

'Are you ready?' she asks Judy.

Judy is standing in the kitchen doorway, clutching Sally's arm.

'I'm really sorry, Ruth,' she says. 'I think my waters have broken.'

CHAPTER 32

Ruth stares at Judy in horror. 'They can't have,' she says. 'Cathbad said the baby was going to be late.'

Judy gives her a twisted smile. 'Cathbad was wrong.'

He can't be, is Ruth's first incoherent thought. He's never wrong. She stands rooted to the spot as the rain runs down her face.

Luckily, Sally takes charge. 'Come and sit down,' she says, leading Judy back into the kitchen. And, although re-entering the house feels like the very last thing in the world that she wants to do, Ruth follows.

Judy is sitting on a chair by the Aga, breathing hard.

'Are you having contractions?' asks Sally briskly. 'How far apart?' She turns to Ruth. 'Don't worry. Remember, I told you I used to be a nurse?'

Of course. A wave of relief rushes over Ruth. Sally used to be a nurse; she can take charge. Oh, how could she ever have thought Sally vague and ineffectual? The woman is an angel.

'I've been having twinges all day,' says Judy, 'but I thought they were just Braxton Hicks.'

Having twinges all day! Ruth can hardly believe her ears. How could Judy have let them come here, to this house in the middle of the flood plains, knowing that she was having labour pains? Not for the first time, Ruth wonders if all police officers are certifiably mad.

'How far apart are they now?' asks Sally, draping a towel over Judy's lap.

'I don't know,' says Judy. 'Maybe five or ten minutes.'

'Are they getting stronger?'

'Yes,' says Judy, her eyes wide. She looks at Ruth. 'I'm sorry. I should have said.'

'It's OK,' says Ruth. She comes forward to hold Judy's hand.

'Time the next contraction,' says Sally. 'I think we should get you to hospital. We've got time if we go now.'

'But what about the floods?' asks Judy, squeezing Ruth's hand tightly.

'Chaz has got a four-by-four,' says Sally. 'That'll get through. But you need to go now. I'll fetch him.' She hurries out of the room.

The pressure on Ruth's hand becomes unbearable. 'Are you having another contraction?' asks Ruth. There's no answer but Judy is breathing heavily, her eyes on the ceiling. What did Sally say? Time it. Ruth looks at the clock on the wall.

Chaz and Sally are back before the contraction is over. How long was it? Four minutes? Five? Ruth doesn't know.

Chaz, like his mother, is wonderfully calm. 'Ready for the hospital shuttle? I'll go and fetch the car. Don't worry, my jeep'll get through anything. It does smell a bit of pig though.'

Chaz hurries out of the door and Sally comes over with a glass of water. 'Try to drink something,' she says to Judy. 'You should eat too, keep your strength up. Shall I make you a sandwich? Someone ought to eat some of the food.'

'No thanks,' says Judy. Ruth is relieved to see that her breathing is almost back to normal. It's odd but having gone through labour and childbirth herself doesn't make it any easier to witness in someone else.

Judy is obviously transferring her affections to the competent Sally. 'Will you come with me?' she asks.

Sally looks nervously around the room. 'I'd like to but I can't really leave . . . Ruth will come with you.'

'Please!' Judy grabs her arm. 'You're a nurse.'

Sally looks at Ruth, who is torn between wanting Sally to take over and not wanting to abandon Judy. The silence lasts until a car is heard outside.

'Come on, Judy,' Sally helps her to her feet. 'Let's get you to hospital.'

'Will you come with me?'

Sally looks at Ruth again. 'OK, I will. Ruth, can you look after Dad? Old George? He might be a bit upset with the floods and everything.'

'Yes,' says Ruth. If she'd had to choose between being Judy's birth partner and babysitting Old George, she's pretty sure that she would have chosen Judy. But Judy seems to want Sally and there's no time to argue about any of it.

Chaz's jeep is at the door. Sally helps Judy into the back seat and gets in beside her. Chaz drives off as soon as the door is shut, leaving Ruth staring after them with a feeling of dread that is slowly turning her body to ice.

She has recognised the jeep. It's the car that followed her home across the marshes.

Nelson looks around his room with distaste. The course is being held at York University, and if this is being a student, thinks Nelson, you can keep it. Single bed, Blu-tack on the walls where posters have been taken down, cracked sink, carpet with stains that look suspiciously like blood. So this is what Whitcliffe described as 'luxury accommodation'. The campus itself, sixties concrete blocks interspersed with ornamental ponds, is a far cry from Nelson's idea of a university (*Brideshead* crossed with *National Lampoon's Animal House*). It has been raining all day and the whole place has a sad, watery feel to it.

Nelson gets out the course programme. '18.00,' he reads, 'Meet and greet. 19.00: Supper in the student union.' It gets worse. '21.00: Police Force Bingo.' Jesus wept. What the hell is Police Force Bingo? Four drunk and disorderlies in a row and you get a cash prize? After pacing the room for a few minutes he decides to ring Michelle. She'd seemed a bit odd when he left, alternately distracted and rather weepy. Women's troubles, he thinks vaguely. As the sole male in a household of women, he tends to attribute everything to this cause.

Michelle's phone goes straight to answerphone but there are four missed calls from Clough. Christ, what trouble is Cloughie in now?

'Hi, boss.' Clough sounds cheerful at any rate. 'Crazy

weather here. Floods everywhere, the coast road's underwater. Cassie and I are stranded at Spalding.'

'Aren't you meant to be going to the do at Blackstock Hall?'

'No one's going anywhere. Half of Norfolk's under water.'

Good riddance, thinks Nelson. But this thought is instantly replaced by worry about Michelle, Ruth and Kate. Where are they all? Are they OK? He can feel his sheepdog instincts taking over, wanting to herd them all to safety.

'Anyway,' Clough is saying, 'thought you'd like to know. We've had the DNA analysis on my mask.'

My mask. Clough is ridiculously possessive about his assault case.

'Go on. Surprise me.'

'Well, it's not really a surprise at all. Guess who the red devil is related to?'

But Nelson doesn't have to guess. Amongst other tests, he asked the lab to compare the DNA profile recovered from the mask against the sample provided by George Blackstock junior.

'He's a Blackstock.'

'Got it in one. Direct sibling or offspring.' Nelson ends the call feeling twitchier than ever. Could Clough's attacker really be a direct relation of Young George's? Offspring must mean Chaz, surely? Young George is an only child so that rules out siblings. He rings Clough back.

'Have Ruth and Johnson left for Blackstock Hall?'

'They won't have gone, boss. Like I say, everywhere's underwater.'

But a flood won't put Judy off if she's feeling determined,

thinks Nelson. He tries her number. No answer. That's worrying for a start. Judy always answers her phone. Then he calls Ruth. It goes to answerphone but that's not so unusual. Ruth has a maddening habit of putting her phone on silent and then not being able to find it. He leaves her a curt message: 'Ruth. Ring me.' Then he rings Tim (maybe he could get to Blackstock Hall to protect the girls), but he too is unobtainable. Michelle is still not answering. He sends her a text message and tries Ruth again. Now her phone seems to be switched off. By now Nelson is seething with frustration. He picks up the course programme and stares at it unseeingly.

19.00: Supper in the student union.
21.00: Police Force Bingo.

Bingo. He thinks of the pets' burial ground, the sound of an old man's grief. Then he picks up his bag and strides off down the corridor, ignoring the course leader, who is hovering by the coffee machine.

Nelson is going home.

Ruth is outside, trying to get a signal. It is a few minutes before she notices that she is soaking wet. Her hood has come down and the rain is trickling down her back. The driveway is now an inch deep in water and her shoes are sodden. She doesn't think she has ever felt more helpless in her life. She has let Judy be driven away by a man who follows women home in the dark, by a man who may well have killed a close relative and fed him to his pigs. What can she say to

Cathbad? Cathbad. She should ring him. Now, while she's got a signal.

Out here, she does have a signal but she notes with horror that her battery is very low. Bloody iPhone. And her charger is sitting smugly by her bed at home. There's a missed call and a text message from Nelson. **Ruth. Ring me.** Typical Nelson – it doesn't take that many characters to say please. Well, she hasn't got enough battery to ring him. Cathbad has to take priority now.

He answers on the first ring. 'Is everything all right?'

'Look, Cathbad, don't panic. Judy's gone into labour but she's fine. Chaz is taking her to the hospital and Sally's with her. Sally's a trained nurse.' Well, she was thirty years ago but Ruth doesn't think it's worth saying this.

'Oh my God. I've got to go to her.'

'No!' Ruth almost shouts. 'You've got to look after Kate and Michael. You can't take them into a maternity ward. Besides, the roads are a nightmare. Flooding everywhere.'

'Yes, it's pretty bad here,' admits Cathbad. 'But I can't just sit at home while Judy's having our baby.'

'Send positive thoughts,' says Ruth. 'That's what I'm doing.'

'You're right,' says Cathbad. 'But positive thoughts aren't as good as being there, are they?'

'No,' says Ruth. 'They're not. But I'm sure she'll be OK. Chaz has this great big car, a jeep. It'll get through the floods.'

'Hazel says that Chaz is a good man,' says Cathbad. 'Do you think so?'

'Yes,' lies Ruth. 'He'll take care of her. I'll ring when I have news.'

'OK,' says Cathbad, sounding sad and a long way away. 'Take care, Ruth.'

Take care. If only he knew. Ruth takes a deep breath and goes back into the house.

CHAPTER 33

Michelle and Tim stare into each other's eyes.

'I've waited for this moment for so long,' says Tim.

'Me too,' says Michelle. She is no longer subdued but now looks almost possessed, her hair wild, her pupils huge.

'Are you sure you want to do this?' says Tim. He wants it to be her choice, irrevocably so.

Michelle just nods and leans in towards him. She is wearing only her silk underwear and Tim reaches round to unhook her bra with one hand. He hopes the gesture doesn't look too practised. He hopes he'll be able to last longer than a few seconds.

The bleep of a text message makes them both jump. Leave it, Tim urges her silently. Just leave it. But Michelle turns and looks at the phone.

'Leave it,' he mutters into her hair. But she pulls away from him and reads the message. When she turns back, her pupils are back to their normal size. Even her hair looks subdued again.

'I've got to go,' she says.

'Why?' asks Tim. 'Is it bad news? One of the girls?'

'It was Harry.'

'Jesus, he hasn't found out about us, has he?'

Michelle shakes her head. Her eyes fill with tears.

'I've got to go home. I can't do this to him.'

'For Christ's sake.' Tim turns away and sits on the edge of the bed, his head in his hands. Michelle touches his naked back timidly.

'I'm sorry, Tim.'

He can hear the tears in her voice and suddenly he's sorry too. He should never have done this, should never have let things get this far.

'It's OK,' he says. He goes to the window. Where, earlier in the afternoon, there had been a sunken Italian garden there is now a swimming pool.

'We might have some trouble getting back,' he says.

Old and Young George are sitting side by side on the sofa. They both look up when Ruth comes in. In their dinner jackets, they look like a couple of old-school entertainers waiting to go on stage. They also look strikingly alike.

'Chaz has taken Judy to hospital,' she says. 'Sally's gone with them.'

Young George says kindly, 'Sally used to be a nurse. She'll know what to do.'

'They'll drown,' says Old George. 'The seas are rising.'

God, thinks Ruth, he's really lost it now. She wishes that she was a thousand miles away, with Kate on a sunlit beach somewhere. She wishes that she had never met the

Blackstocks. But she has promised Sally that she will look after her father-in-law. It doesn't look as if Young George is going to be much help.

'I'm sure they'll be fine,' she says, trying to make her voice soothing. 'Sally will ring when she has news.'

'The phone lines are down,' says Old George. 'Civilisation is collapsing.'

Young George walks over to the desk and tries the phone. He looks apologetically at Ruth. 'I'm afraid the lines are down.'

'But surely Sally's got a mobile?'

'She's got one but we can't get a signal here so she's always losing it.'

Judy's got a phone, thinks Ruth. She never goes anywhere without it. But she imagines that Judy will be rather too busy to be making calls. And Ruth's phone has hardly any battery life left. There's a silence.

'I might as well start clearing things away,' says Young George. 'I don't think anyone's going to come to the party, do you?'

Old George looks towards the window, where the sky is completely black now. 'Is it time for dinner?' he says. 'Who's going to cook my dinner?'

'The house is full of food,' says Young George. 'Sally's been preparing it for days.'

'Buffet food,' says his father scornfully. '*Canapés*. I want a real supper.'

Both men look at Ruth.

*

It all goes fine until the exit for the A17. Nelson flew along the A1, passing everything in a haze of spray, windscreen wipers on overdrive. But now there's a flashing sign saying 'Road closed due to flooding'. Jesus Christ, he thinks, what's happened to the weather? First storms and then floods. What's next? Earthquakes? A line from a hymn that they sung at Fred's funeral comes back to him: 'Speak through the earthquake, wind, and fire, O still, small voice of calm.' He forces himself to stay calm. It won't help anyone if he drives into a ditch. He edges forward, trying to remember an inland route to King's Lynn.

Ruth isn't much of a cook at the best of times but having to prepare a meal for two men – both of them strangers and one of them dotty – in an unfamiliar kitchen is testing her to the limit. Not to mention that they are completely cut off from the rest of the world and Ruth's friend is about to give birth accompanied by an ex-nurse and a possible murderer. It's not the most restful of scenarios.

Ruth looks in the fridge and the larder and decides on shepherd's pie. At least it can be made in one pan and she even finds a packet of Smash, which will save her mashing potatoes. Both Georges come into the kitchen to watch her cook, which is rather disconcerting. But at least Young George pours her a large glass of red wine. 'You're not going to be driving tonight,' he says, which seems a pretty good bet. Her car is probably submerged by now. Oh poor Renault, how could I do this to you? Going outside to see if she can get a phone signal, Ruth steps in several inches of water.

The house is now completely surrounded. Ruth remembers a Winnie-the-Pooh story which she used to read to Kate, Something like 'In which Winnie-the-Pooh is Entirely Surrounded by Water'. She seems to remember that he escapes in an empty honey jar. Or is it an upturned umbrella? Either way, she could do with some friendly talking toys coming to her aid.

As she cooks, Young George talks to her about Norfolk and archaeology and other dinner-party subjects. Old George stares gloomily into his whisky (Ruth has her doubts about the wisdom of giving him spirits). Father and son don't seem to have much of a relationship. It occurs to Ruth that every time she has seen Old George in distress it was Sally that he turned to. Sally seems to have appointed herself her father-in-law's carer. Maybe that's because of her nursing background, maybe she is just nicer than the rest of the family.

The shepherd's pie is OK. The reconstituted potato tastes slightly musty but otherwise it is perfectly edible. The Blackstocks eat without comment. Presumably they are used to women putting food in front of them. Young George does at least load the dishwasher afterwards. Old George just pours himself more whisky.

'Would you like a nightcap, Ruth?' Young George asks. 'Brandy? Whisky?'

'No thanks,' says Ruth. 'I'm just going outside to see if I can get a signal.' She has to stop herself from adding, 'I may be some time.'

There are some gumboots by the back door so Ruth puts

them on. This is a wise move – previously there was a step down onto the gravel path but now the water is level with the doorway. George has placed some sandbags against the door but Ruth wonders how long it will be before the kitchen is flooded. It is still raining. Ruth steps over the sandbags and teeters on the back step holding her phone up to the sky. No signal and only a thin red line of battery. About a metre away, a boulder is sticking up out of the water. It's quite smooth and flat; maybe it was a mounting block or something once. Ruth jumps onto it, almost missing her footing and ending up in the murky depths. On her perch she gets a faint signal. She also has another missed call from Nelson. Well, she only has enough battery for one call. She clicks onto the name Cathbad. He answers immediately.

'Any news?'

'Not yet.' How will she get news anyway? The landline is useless and Ruth can only get a signal standing on a boulder outside the back door. She doesn't say this to Cathbad.

'How's Kate?' she says.

'Fine. She and Michael are fast asleep. I said they could sleep in their den tonight.'

Typical Cathbad. Ruth would have insisted on a proper bed but she's sure that sleeping on the floor for one night won't hurt Kate.

'How are the floods round your way?'

'Pretty bad. It's an unusually high tide, that's what's done it. You could swim down the coast road.'

'Blackstock Hall is completely cut off. It feels very strange.'

'Are you OK?' Ruth is touched to hear the concern in

Cathbad's voice. Even with his worry over Judy and the baby, he still has some left over for her.

'I'm fine. I'm here with George Blackstock and his dad. Old George. I've just had to cook supper for them.'

'Be careful, Ruth.'

'Why do you say that?'

'It's just . . . Hazel says that Old George can be a bit strange. Are you staying at the Hall tonight?'

'Yes.'

'Well, make sure you lock your door.'

The landlord thinks that they're mad.

'You'll never get home in this,' he says. 'Why don't you stay here? After all, you've got a room booked. Non-refundable,' he adds, just to make this clear.

'I've got to get back,' says Michelle. 'Family emergency.'

She looks calm now. She has even tied her hair back. Tim thinks that she looks like a different woman from the maenad in the bedroom. They have hardly spoken since Michelle announced her intention of going home. But there is something compelling about Michelle's determination. Tim watches the landlord quailing under the force of her stare.

'Yes, of course . . .' he mutters. 'I'll get the bill.'

While Tim pays the bill (Michelle offered to pay half but he rejected this angrily), Michelle goes to the loo. She leaves her phone on the reception desk. Tim picks it up and is suddenly seized by an uncontrollable desire to know what Nelson said in his text, the text that caused their romantic night away to collapse into tears, recriminations and a long, dangerous drive home. Keeping one eye on the door, he clicks on her messages.

But even after reading it he is none the wiser. The text reads simply: **R u ok luv?**

'Sleep wherever you like,' says Young George, waving a hand airily at the corridor of closed doors. 'All the beds are made up. My room's over there and Dad's next door.'

Then I'll be as far away from you as possible, thinks Ruth. She remembers Sally talking about the strain of making all the beds. She's pretty sure that she didn't get any help from her husband or father-in-law.

Ruth tries a couple of doors. The rooms all look similar, neat and tidy but with evidence of recent occupation. She wonders which room Frank slept in. But in the third room she sees something which puts all other thoughts out of her head. An iPhone charger. She plugs in her phone and, as it buzzes, she feels as if she too is connected to life again. It's terrible really, being so dependent on a phone. She's sure that Nelson would have something to say about it. She wonders why he was calling earlier. Well, when her phone has charged up sufficiently, she'll creep downstairs and try to get a signal. The thought of tiptoeing through the dark house doesn't exactly fill her with joy. It's very cold in the room. She takes off her shoes and gets into the bed fully clothed.

Tim's car is sturdy and reassuring. They manage the first few miles without much trouble. The roads are wet and sometimes Tim has to drive through deep puddles but he takes it slowly and the car keeps its grip on the road. Once they see a truck full of sheep that have probably been rescued from the flooded fields but otherwise they are on their own. Neither of them speaks and the windscreen wipers beat a slow, steady pulse. But, as they get nearer to the coast, they start to see signs saying 'Road closed'. Michelle has left her car at Blakeney but it becomes clear that they can't get near to the town. They stop by a roadblock, hazard lights flashing.

'I'll drive you home,' says Tim. 'I'm sure we can get there across country. You can pick up your car tomorrow.'

'But I need my car,' says Michelle. 'What will Harry say?'

'You said that he'd be away on the course for two days.' You said a lot of things, he can't help thinking.

Michelle is silent, chewing a strand of her hair. It reminds Tim of his sister when she was young.

'Come on,' he says. 'It'll be all right. I'll get you home.'

Nelson finally gets home at midnight. He is so tired that he has parked his car and let himself into the house before he realises that Michelle's car is not outside. He goes to the window. The street is quiet and rainwater is running merrily along the gutters but Michelle's little car is nowhere to be seen. He climbs the stairs two at a time.

'Michelle? Where are you, love?'

Their bed is neatly made and the room smells, as always, of Michelle's scent. But of Michelle herself there's no sign. He checks the girls' rooms (he still calls them that) and the spare. It is fully five minutes before he admits to himself that he is alone in the house.

Ruth must have fallen asleep. She is dreaming of floods, of airplanes falling through the sky, of Kate and Michael asleep in their den like little bear cubs. She wakes with start because someone is speaking to her. Has the radio come on? Is it morning? She sits up, rubbing her eyes.

Old George is sitting by her bed.

CHAPTER 34

She realises that the old man is speaking, that he has probably been speaking for some time.

'I killed Fred because I thought Lewis was dead,' he is saying. 'We thought he'd been killed in Japan. I thought the whole place was mine and then Fred came back to ruin everything.'

Ruth stays very still. Moonlight is coming through the open curtains and it glitters on Old George's cloudy eyes. He is wearing pyjamas and a dressing gown, like a sweet old grandfather. But if one thing is becoming clear, it's that George Blackstock senior is not sweet at all.

'I was eighteen,' he says. 'I'd finished school and was waiting for my call-up. I was in the orchard cleaning Lewis's gun. I thought, if he'd died, it belonged to me. Everything belonged to me. Then Fred just appeared, walking up the hill from the sea. I thought he was a ghost at first. We were told that he was dead, that he'd drowned when his plane went down. But there he was, standing in front of me. He looked terrible, his uniform all muddy and torn, a gash over one eye.

He told me that he'd survived the crash, that he'd swam to shore but had been too weak to go further. He'd slept rough for a few nights, in ditches and so forth, and then walked all the way to the Hall. "I couldn't think where else to go," he said. "I hate this place but it's home." So I shot him.'

'Why?' whispers Ruth.

'I told you,' says George calmly, 'I wanted the place to myself. Lewis was dead, Fred had abandoned the family, going to live in America like that. It broke my mother's heart. I deserved to inherit the Hall. I was the only one who really loved it. So I shot Fred with Lewis's gun. I think he died immediately. I hope so. I wouldn't have wanted him to suffer,' he adds piously.

'What did you do then?'

'I buried him in the pets' burial ground. The soil was still loose because we'd just buried Trumpeter, Dad's old fox terrier. I dug a fresh hole, wrapped Fred's body in an old tarpaulin and put him in. It was hard work but I was strong then.'

He smiles to himself. Ruth wonders whether she should get out of bed and run for it. But where would she go? George starts speaking again. 'That was the problem. Lewis wasn't dead, he came back. He was a bit mad though. Mother said we had to treat him gently. I was just biding my time. Then his dog died. Poor old Bingo. Lewis buried him in the pets' burial ground and he found Fred's body. Sent him right off the rails. He just disappeared, made a run for it. Annoying for me because I had to wait years before he was declared dead. Mind you, if he'd stayed, I would have killed him too. So it was all for the best.'

'But he wasn't dead,' Ruth can't help reminding him.

'No,' says George. 'That was a bit of a shock, his son turning up like that. But we got rid of him, didn't we?'

Who is 'we'? wonders Ruth. She's pretty sure that George can't have killed Patrick on his own, much less attacked Clough. He must have an accomplice. Who is it?

'I wanted to tell you,' says George, 'because you deserve to know how your dad died. It's been on my conscience a bit, to tell you the truth. I suppose I'm getting old, thinking about meeting my maker and all that stuff. I wanted to confess. Sally said not to bother you, but she's away so I thought we should have a chat.'

He thinks I'm Nell, Ruth realises. This must be her room. If Sally told her father-in-law not to bother Nell, does that mean that she knows the truth about his murderous past? Is she his accomplice as well as his carer? She is just wondering how she can ask George without alerting him to the fact that she's not Nell when the old man gets to his feet.

'I'll be off then,' he says. 'I'm glad we had this little chat. I'll sleep well now.'

He gets up and Ruth hears him shuffling off down the corridor. She waits for a moment and then snatches up her phone. Thank God, the battery is fully charged. She slips her feet into her shoes and opens the door. She needs to get outside so she can make a few phone calls.

Nelson's sits on his bed – their bed – and rings Michelle. To his utter relief she answers immediately.

'Michelle! Where are you?'

'I'm just outside Lynn,' she says. 'I went out with the girls and my car's stuck at Blakeney.'

Something's wrong but Nelson doesn't know quite what it is. Why did she go out with the girls when bad weather was forecast? Why did she leave her car at Blakeney? Who is she with now? He struggles to frame the right question.

'Are you OK? Who are you with?'

'Debbie. She's got a four-by-four.'

'OK,' says Nelson. 'I'll see you soon. Call if you're in any trouble. Tell Debbie to drive safely.'

Michelle rings off but Nelson stays sitting on the bed staring at the phone.

The house is every bit as spooky at night as Ruth feared. The stairs creak and the grandfather clock in the hall ticks ponderously. She edges her way along the corridor until she reaches the kitchen. Here at least it's a bit warmer because of the Aga. Ruth puts on the gumboots and a Barbour that's hanging by the door. Then, very carefully, she opens the stable door and steps outside.

The rain has stopped but the moon shines on miles and miles of silver water. Leonie Blackstock's prediction has some true. The sea really has reclaimed the Blackstock land. Did Leonie know, or suspect, that her youngest son was a murderer? Is that why she killed herself? Ruth doesn't suppose that they'll ever know. She splashes through the water, which is nearly knee-deep now, and climbs onto the mounting-block boulder. Instantly a signal flashes and several messages appear.

The first says: **Ruth. Ring me.**

The second: **Sally here calling on Judy's phone. Judy had a baby girl at 11.45. 8lb, 2 ounces. Mother and baby doing well.**

The third: **Have u heard? I've got a new daughter! Peace + blessings.**

The fourth: **R u home? r u OK? Fx**

The fifth: **R u OK? Call me. Fxx**

The sixth: **Ruth. Ring me!! N**

Despite everything, Ruth smiles in relief. Judy and Cathbad have a daughter – a bouncing baby by the sounds of it. Something good has come out of the horrors of the night. She sends a congratulatory text to Cathbad and one to Frank saying, **I'm OK. Still at B Hall. Will call tomoz.** She also texts Bob asking him to feed Flint in the morning. Then she rings Nelson.

'Ruth? What is it? Where are you?'

'Blackstock Hall. Listen . . .'

'You're at Blackstock Hall. What the hell are you doing there?'

'I came for the party, remember, and . . .'

'You came for the party! Is Johnson with you? Who's looking after Katie?'

'Judy's had her baby. Cathbad's looking after Kate. Nelson . . .'

'Ruth. Stay away from the old man. Old George. He's dangerous. I think he killed his brother.'

Once again she has underestimated Nelson. 'How did you know?'

'It was the word Bingo. He seemed so upset about the dog. I thought, what if he'd seen his brother's body again when he buried the dog.'

'It was Lewis who did that. The older brother. He saw Fred's body and realised George had killed him. That's why he ran away.'

'How do you know all this?'

'George has just told me the whole thing. He thought I was Nell and wanted to get it off his chest.'

'Jesus. Ruth, you can't stay in the house with him.'

'I haven't got any choice. I'm completely cut off here. Just me and Old and Young George.'

'What about Sally?'

'She went to the hospital with Judy.'

'And Chaz?'

'He drove them to the hospital.'

'Well, steer clear of him too. We think he might be the man who attacked Clough.'

Ruth keeps quiet about her own suspicions of Chaz. There's nothing Nelson can do about that now. She wishes he was there with her. She wishes it so much that she feels quite sick with longing.

'Ruth,' Nelson is saying, 'lock yourself in a room and stay there till morning. I'll be there as soon as I can.'

'I thought you were in York.'

'I came home. I'll get a squad car over there in the morning.'

'I told you, the house is completely cut off.'

'I'll get a chopper if necessary. Have you got your phone?'

'Yes, but I can't get a signal in the house.' I'm sounding

pathetic, thinks Ruth. 'It's OK,' she says. 'I'll lock myself in. I'll be fine.'

'I'll come for you in the morning.'

Please God, prays Ruth, the confirmed atheist, as she creeps back through the silent house. Please make morning come quickly.

CHAPTER 35

Ruth finds another room, a smaller one with a single bed and – crucially – a key in the lock. She has no intention of going back to Nell's room so that Old George can pay her another visit. She locks herself in and gets into bed with the key and her phone under the pillow. It's one o'clock. How the hell is she going to survive until dawn? If only she had something to read, something to take her mind off this house, Old George's confession and the image of Fred Blackstock walking up the hill towards his ancestral home. *I couldn't think where else to go. I hate this place but it's home.*

In the bedside table she finds a travel guide to Norfolk and Suffolk. That will have to do. She pulls the covers over her shoulders – she is freezing – and starts to read.

'Norfolk offers a breathtaking variety of countryside from open heath to wild marshland and miles of magnificent coastline . . .'

Michelle gets home at two. Nelson hears the car but Debbie has obviously dropped her at the entrance to the cul-de-sac because he then hears Michelle's heels tapping along the pavement. Only Michelle would wear high heels to negotiate a flood.

He opens the door before she has time to put her key in the lock. She flings herself into his arms.

'Steady on, love. What's the matter?'

'Nothing.' Michelle is half laughing, half crying. 'I'm just tired, that's all.'

'Did you have a nightmare drive? Is the coast road flooded? Debbie did well to get through it. What car has she got?'

'Something Japanese. I don't know. I'm just so glad to be home.'

She looks at him, her eyes shining with tears. She's dressed up to go out – Nelson recognises that – but there's also something different about her. Her hair is tied back and she doesn't seem to have any make-up on.

'I'll make you a cup of tea,' says Nelson. That usually works with the women in his life.

'No,' says Michelle. 'Let's go to bed.'

Ruth wakes with her head on the wonders of Norfolk and Suffolk. Light is streaming in through the curtains and she isn't dead yet. She goes to the window. Water stretches as far as the eye can see. Occasionally trees and hedge-tops mark the boundaries of fields but otherwise everything is uniformly blue and sparkling. It's very beautiful but it's also disconcerting, as if she has woken up to find herself in another world, a watery Narnia. This room faces east, towards the coast. She can see the top of Admiral Blackstock's cross but otherwise land and sea have merged, the liminal zone has vanished and the sea sprites have reclaimed their own. Ruth imagines that this will finally send Old George completely round the bend.

It's seven o'clock. Nelson said that he'd come in the morning but she's sure that it will take him some time to get here, even if he does manage to commandeer a helicopter. She doesn't want to stay skulking in her room. Old George seems much less terrifying in the daylight. And besides, she's starving.

In the kitchen, Ruth makes herself a cup of tea and puts some bread in the giant toaster, presumably bought with the B & B in mind. There's no sound from upstairs. She hopes that both Georges will sleep late. For ever would be nice. She thinks about Judy, enjoying her first morning with her daughter, whose first morning it is. She remembers holding Kate in her arms five years ago. She loved Kate from the first moment that their eyes met but she had missed having Nelson with her, to share in the miracle of their child. It was the only time that she has really felt the lack of a proper partner. Judy might be on her own now but at least she has Cathbad waiting for her at home.

Ruth eats her toast and then goes out to ring Judy. The mounting block feels quite homelike now. To her surprise, Judy answers on the third ring.

'Hallo,' says Ruth. 'Congratulations.'

'Thank you. She's beautiful.'

'Did you think she'd be a girl?'

'Yes. Cathbad always said she would be.'

But he was wrong about the baby being late, thinks Ruth. Aloud she says, 'Have you thought of a name?'

'We haven't decided. Cathbad likes Astarte. I prefer Miranda.'

'Insist on your name. You'll never be in a better position to get your own way.'

Judy laughs. She sounds dreamy and contented. Ruth, standing on her own in the middle of a flood, feels jealous.

'You got there in time then?' she says.

'Yes. Sally was wonderful. Perhaps I should name the baby after her.'

'Is she still with you?'

'No, she and Chaz have left. They spent the night at the hospital but I think Sally was worried about her father-in-law. Is he all right?'

'Yes,' says Ruth. 'Fighting fit.'

She rings off, promising to come and see the baby when she can. Then she rings Cathbad to ask about her own baby. Cathbad, like Judy, is in wonderful spirits.

'Another girl! Maddie wanted a sister. I've just rung her.'

Maddie is Cathbad's daughter by a woman called Delilah.

'How's Kate?'

'She's fine. I'm just making a special celebration breakfast for us all.'

'I'm hoping to able to get out of here today. Nelson said that he would come to get me.'

'If Nelson says he'll come, he'll come.'

'Yes. I know.'

Ruth rings off feeling frightened and depressed. Judy and Cathbad sound so happy. She should be happy for them but all she can think is that she is dependent on someone else's husband coming to rescue her. She stays on her vantage point, looking towards the horizon. As she looks, a dark shape comes into view. At first she thinks that it's a long-necked bird gliding on the water but then she sees that it is a small boat being propelled by someone standing up like a gondolier. The boatman has long hair flying out behind him and for a moment she thinks that it's Cathbad, even though this is clearly impossible. Could it be Chaz finding a novel way home? Or maybe it's a woman? For some reason, Ruth suddenly feels scared. She climbs down from the stone and splashes back towards the kitchen door. She thinks that she'll feel safer inside.

She takes off her coat and boots. Her cup of tea is still on the table. Perhaps she should make some more toast. Eating always makes her feel better.

Then she realises that Old George is pointing a gun at her.

Nelson is trying to locate a helicopter. Unfortunately the police helicopter and the two belonging to the coastguard are both in use.

'It's urgent,' says Nelson. 'I need to apprehend a homicide suspect.'

'I can't help it,' says the controller. 'The chopper's out

rescuing old people from a home in Wells-next-the-Sea.'

'I'll have to try to get there by car,' says Nelson. 'I need someone with a four-by-four. What does Tim drive?'

'How should I know?' says Michelle.

Nelson looks at her in surprise. He had been talking half to himself and had forgotten that he was still in the bedroom and that his wife, prettily dishevelled, is watching him from the marital bed.

'Sorry, love,' he says. 'I was thinking aloud.' He drops a kiss on her head and rings Tim, who answers with admirable promptness.

'You've got a four-by-four, haven't you?' says Nelson. 'My car's useless in these conditions. Clough's is even worse. I need to get to Blackstock Hall this morning.'

'It's a Toyota Rav4,' says Tim. 'Off-road. It's pretty tough. Have you heard about Judy?'

He did hear something about Judy. What was it?

'She's had her baby. A girl. She's just rung from the hospital. Apparently she went into labour at Blackstock Hall last night.'

No wonder she wasn't answering her phone, thinks Nelson. He remembers now that Ruth gave him this news last night but that it has been lost in the general worry about Chaz, Old George and Michelle's strangely protracted journey home. He feels slightly ashamed and this makes him sound uncharacteristically hearty. 'That's fantastic news. Good old Judy.'

'Mother and baby both doing well, apparently. Shall I come and pick you up in half an hour?'

'Tim's a good lad,' says Nelson as he heads towards the shower.

Michelle doesn't answer.

'I've been thinking it over,' says Old George genially, 'and I realised that it was you I was talking to last night not Nell. Stupid mistake. You're younger. And bigger. I don't see so well at night these days. Damn cataracts.'

He could be any old-age pensioner at the doctor's surgery complaining about his symptoms. Except that he's holding a gun in a hand that seems remarkably steady.

'It's loaded,' says Old George. 'I always keep it loaded, just in case. Sally doesn't know. She'd think it was dangerous.'

It is dangerous, Ruth wants to scream. She glances towards the back door, only a few metres away. If she can just distract George for a minute . . .

'Stay still,' barks the old man. 'It's Lewis's gun, by the way.' He switches back to his former pleasant tone. 'An antique really. I thought it would be fitting. It still works though.'

'You don't want to kill me,' says Ruth. 'The police know I'm here. They'd catch you and put you in prison. You'd hate that. Think how it would upset Sally,' she adds desperately.

Old George considers, head on one side. 'No, I'd better kill you,' he says. 'We can always make it look like an accident. My son will help me with that. After all, we got rid of the other one, Lewis's son. We can get rid of you too.'

Oh God, Young George is in on it too. The ineffectual son, who always seems to hover in his wife's shadow, is actually a cold-blooded murderer. It was probably Young George who killed Patrick.

Old George raises the gun. Then he stops and tilts his head again, like a gun dog. He's heard something. Ruth hears it too. Footsteps. They both look dumbly towards the door.

'Morning, all.' Hazel stands in the doorway, wearing waders and a fisherman's jumper. He still has his druid's cloak on though and his long hair flops around his face. It must have been Hazel whom Ruth saw punting across the marshes. Of course, he knows the land well. He would know where to find a boat. Ruth is so pleased to see him that she wants to cry. Hazel is as good as Cathbad at turning up just when he's needed. It must be a druid thing.

'I was just explaining to Ruth why I have to kill her,' says Old George, rather plaintively. 'I'm afraid I told her the whole story last night so of course we've got to get rid of her.'

The old fool is talking as if he actually expects Hazel to help him. Ruth turns towards Hazel – maybe together they can overpower Old George – and sees that he too is holding a gun.

'It's OK, Dad,' he says. 'I've got this.'

Dad? Can Hazel really be Old George's son? It would mean that George fathered him in his fifties but, quite frankly, Ruth would put nothing past him. She stares at Hazel. She had trusted him implicitly because he was Cathbad's friend. It turns out that this was something else that Cathbad was wrong about. For the first time, though, she sees the Blackstock resemblance. Hazel has dark hair and eyes and a strong nose. He looks, she realises, very like Chaz.

Amazingly, Old George seems to think that introductions are in order. 'My son George,' he says. 'His mother was a village girl called Susan.'

'Suzanne,' says Hazel

Old George dismisses Suzanne with a wave of the hand. 'She insisted on calling him George after me, which was a bit confusing because I already had a son called George. But no matter. He calls himself Hazel for some reason. He's illegitimate, which is a shame because it means he can't inherit this place and he loves it so. But he's got some sort of plan about that.'

Presumably his plan involves killing all the legitimate Blackstocks. Hazel must have attacked Cassandra on the spur of the moment when he found out that she was the heir. He was on the spot – Ruth had spent a lot of the evening talking to him – he could easily have sneaked out in the darkness and ambushed Cassandra while she stood amongst the family tombs. They were his family tombs as well, of course. It was probably Hazel too who killed Patrick. God, it was Ruth who actually pointed out the Ancient Mariner to him. Somehow Hazel must have discovered Patrick's identity. He probably just asked him, chatting away with his easy druid's charm before bludgeoning him to death.

Hazel is still pointing his gun at Ruth. 'Sorry, Ruth, but you really do know too much,' he says.

'I don't know anything,' says Ruth. 'Please let me go. I've got a young daughter. I'm all she's got.' She realises that she is crying.

'We've got to make it look like an accident,' Old George is saying.

'Maybe we can drown her,' says Hazel. Old George comes closer to his son, presumably to discuss this interesting matter further. Ruth takes her chance and shoots through the door, out into the hall.

Despite the car's toughness and Tim's skill as a driver, they come to a standstill a few miles outside Hunstanton. They turn a corner and the road has simply disappeared. It's as if they are standing on the seashore except that this sea is interspersed with the odd tree and hedgerow and, several nautical miles away, a grey house sits entirely surrounded by water.

'Can we swim?' asks Nelson. He's only half joking. Both men are wearing waders, but when Tim takes an experimental step off the road, he sinks almost to his waist.

'Bloody hell. It's deep. We can't wade there, that's for sure.'

'We need to get to that house,' says Nelson. 'Ruth could be in danger.'

'The chopper's on its way.'

'The chopper could be hours. She's stuck in the house with a self-confessed murderer.'

'I can't believe the old guy killed his own brother.'

'Can't you?' says Nelson. 'I can.'

Tim is about to answer when his face takes on an expression of almost comical amazement. Nelson turns to see what Tim is looking at. Coming towards them across the flooded fields is a gigantic duck.

'Tell me I'm dreaming,' says Tim.

The duck is bright yellow with a vivid orange beak. It chugs steadily across the water, occasionally emitting a shrill blast of birdsong. As it gets closer, they see that it is actually an amphibious vehicle with 'Norfolk Birds' printed on the side. It is being driven by a man with shoulder-length dark hair.

'Fancy meeting you here,' says Chaz.

'What are you doing on that thing?' asks Nelson.

'It belongs to a mate of mine who does bird tours,' says Chaz. 'I thought it was the only way of getting to the Hall. Want to come along?'

But Nelson and Tim are already splashing towards him. As they climb aboard, they see that Sally is sitting in the bows, incongruously dressed in a black dress, pearls, gumboots and a yellow raincoat.

'Hallo DCI Nelson, DS Heathfield,' she says. She looks tired and worried but still manages to make it sound as if she's welcoming them to a garden party at Buckingham Palace. 'How nice to see you.'

'We need to get to the Hall as soon as possible,' Nelson says to Chaz. 'I think that Ruth might be in serious danger.'

'Oh dear.' Sally wrings her hands. 'I did worry about leaving her but Judy needed me.'

'It's not your fault,' says Tim kindly. 'Judy said you were wonderful.'

'It is your fault,' says Nelson. 'You left Ruth alone with a madman.'

Chaz and his mother look at each other. Neither of them rushes to Old George's defence.

Chaz starts up the engine and the giant bird begins its slow journey across the marshes.

CHAPTER 36

It's like some horrific game of hide-and-seek. Ruth had intended to run to her room and lock herself in but she realised that Hazel would catch her before she got to the stairs. So she dives through the first door she sees and finds herself in a stone passageway. She hears Hazel and Old George in the hallway.

'Where'd she go?' asks George.

'She can't have gone far. I'll find her.'

There are several doors opening off the passageway. Ruth opens the nearest and looks around desperately. It's a utility room with two massive chest freezers and a washing machine. There's also another door. She opens this and finds herself in a scullery, its shelves stacked with giant packets of cornflakes, pasta and rice. There's also an array of jars labelled in neat writing. 'Apple Jelly, Christmas 2008.' Ruth squats down behind a beer barrel. It's not the best hiding place in the world but it will have to do. Slowly, trying not to make a sound, she pulls her phone from her pocket.

Amazingly there's a faint signal. Frantically she presses the green phone icon.

'Nelson,' she whispers.

'It's Ruth.' Nelson is standing next to Chaz in the prow of the boat, willing it to go faster. Peering around the domed head of the duck he can see the Hall approaching but they're not moving quickly enough.

'It's just not built for speed,' Chaz had said apologetically. 'It's built for giving old dears a nice trip along the coast looking at bar-tailed godwits.'

'Ruth?' Nelson presses the answer button.

Her voice is very faint. She says something about Old George and hiding. 'Please come,' she says. 'He's going to kill me.'

'We're on our way,' says Nelson. 'We're not far away now. It'll be OK, love. Just stay put. Where are you?'

But the phone has cut out.

At first she thinks she might be safe. She hears the footsteps receding and Hazel shouting something about upstairs. She moves her legs which are in agony and looks again at her phone. 'No signal' it says helpfully. Could she creep out while Hazel and his father are upstairs? She sees the route through the kitchen as clearly as if she's actually there. The Aga, the dresser, her cup of tea still on the table. She sees herself opening the back door and then . . . What? The house is surrounded by water. Even if she tries to wade or swim, they would spot her in a second. The flood has removed every hiding place for miles around. She would be a sitting duck for Hazel, who, she is sure, was probably taught to shoot ducks by his mad old father. They would kill her and she'd sink under the water, to be discovered days later when the flood finally recedes. What about Kate? Cathbad and Judy might bring her up with their two but she'd always remember Ruth and miss her . . . Ruth sets her jaw. It's not going to happen. She's not going to leave Kate. She has to escape.

Then she hears a door open and footsteps running along the stone corridor.

'Where is the silly girl?' Old George sounds peevish and, she's pleased to hear, distinctly out of breath.

'She can't have gone far.' Unfortunately Hazel sounds perfectly calm and in control.

Ruth looks around her. There's a little window high above her. Can she get through it? It would be too embarrassing – not to mention dangerous – to get stuck halfway through. Didn't that happen to Winnie-the-Pooh too? And Pooh didn't have a man with a gun on his tail. Run, rabbit, run. She hears Hazel opening doors. She climbs onto the beer barrel and pushes at the window.

The house looks peaceful in the morning light. Chaz steers the boat right up to the front door. What's happened to the sheep? thinks Nelson. The water is actually lapping against the walls.

Chaz leaps out and Nelson follows, leaving Tim to help Sally. The water comes up to his knees. Chaz pushes at the front door and it opens, bringing a tidal wave of brown water gushing in behind it.

Nelson steps into the hall. 'Ruth!' he shouts.

He can hear faint banging sounds coming from upstairs. Chaz runs past him and climbs the stairs two at a time. 'Dad?' he calls.

Nelson stands in the hallway, listening. Tim appears behind him. 'Shall we search the house, boss?'

Nelson turns to Sally. 'Where would your father-in-law be?'

'I don't know,' she says. 'He likes to prowl around the house in the mornings.'

I bet he does, thinks Nelson. 'Ruth said she was hiding. Any ideas where she could be?'

'I don't know.' Sally sounds helpless and near to tears. 'It's a big house.'

'Let's go,' says Nelson. He strides off towards the kitchen when a figure blocks his way. It's Old George dressed in pyjamas and a dressing gown and carrying an old Second World War pistol.

'You didn't tell me we were expecting visitors, Sally,' he says.

Ruth manages to haul herself onto the window ledge. Maybe those trips to the gym are doing some good after all. With her head and shoulders out of the window she can see the side of the house and, bizarrely, a giant yellow duck, like a child's bath toy, floating towards her. Somehow Ruth scrabbles herself through the window and falls headfirst into the water.

It tastes horrible. She struggles to her feet, choking. 'Nelson!' she shouts, as loudly as she can. 'Nelson!'

But of course the shouting and the splash has brought

Hazel to the window. He climbs onto the sill, as agile as a cat burglar. Ruth is half wading, half swimming towards the duck. She doesn't know why, perhaps because it's the only spot of colour in the grey-green landscape. The duck will save her.

'Hallo, Dad,' says Sally. 'You know DCI Nelson and DS Heathfield.'

'I remember their faces.' Old George lowers the gun slightly.

Nelson has had enough of this. 'Where's Ruth?' he says. 'What have you done to her?'

'Ruth?' Old George looks around doubtfully.

Then Nelson hears it. Ruth calling his name. It's coming from outside. Regardless of the old man with the gun he runs back towards the door. Tim takes advantage of the moment to grab Old George's arm and force him to drop the gun.

'I'll take that,' he says.

'Come on, Dad,' says Sally. 'Let's go into the drawing room and have a nice sit down. You're freezing.'

Nelson splashes through the water. The duck boat has drifted off towards the left and he heads towards it. 'Nelson!' Ruth's voice again.

'I'm coming!'

Rounding the side of the house, he sees Ruth wading towards him. As he watches, a man drops from a window and, maintaining his balance, levels a gun.

'Stop!' shouts Nelson. 'Police!'

In answer a bullet shoots past his ear.

'Ruth!' yells Nelson. 'Get behind the duck.'

Ruth obeys him, moving towards the floating amphibious boat, but the trouble is the water makes it impossible to move quickly. Everything happens in ghastly slow motion. The man shoots again but he's aiming at Nelson and misses. Ruth has almost reached the boat.

'Police! Drop your weapon!' Another voice behind Nelson. He turns and sees Tim, also holding a gun.

The man laughs wildly and raises his arm again.

'Watch out, boss!' shouts Tim and shoots.

The man screams and falls face-forward in the water.

The duck boat lets out a triumphant blast of birdsong.

In the drawing room, Sally settles her father-in-law by the fire. There are still some embers from last night and it's marginally warmer than the rest of the house.

'I had to do it,' he says. 'The Hall is mine.'

'Of course it is.'

'I want to leave it to George after me.'

'Don't worry about George,' says Sally. 'He would be happy living anywhere.'

'Not your George,' says the old man contemptuously. 'My other son George.'

Sally looks at the man she has spent half her life caring for. She knows that he's an old monster but some subconscious nurse's instinct makes her want to look after him. He doesn't look at all well this morning; he's shivering and his lips have a bluish tinge.

'I'll get you a blanket,' she says.

Old George is about to answer when the door opens. He looks up and sees a man silhouetted against the morning sun. A dark man, dressed in mud-stained clothing with a gash over his eye.

'Fred?' he says.

'No,' says Sally. 'It's Chaz. What have you done to your eye, Chaz?'

But, with a strangled gasp, Old George lurches forward and falls onto the hearthrug.

CHAPTER 37

Nelson turns the man over in the water. He's still alive although a pink pool of blood is spreading around him.

'Who is he?' he shouts to Ruth, who is still holding onto the duck boat.

'He's called Hazel,' Ruth shouts back. 'He's Old George's illegitimate son. I'm pretty sure he killed Patrick.'

'Help me get him into the house, Tim.'

Tim wades over and takes Hazel's feet. Tim looks shaken, thinks Nelson, but otherwise perfectly in control. As they struggle with the weight of the injured man, Nelson runs through events in his head. There will have to be an enquiry. Tim shot a civilian with a weapon that wasn't police issue. But the civilian was armed and it was clearly in self-defence. Nelson and Ruth can both be witness to that. All in all, Nelson thinks Tim displayed great courage and presence of mind. There's also a distinct possibility that he saved Nelson's life.

The journey to the house seems endless. Ruth leaves the boat and comes to join them. It takes all three of them to carry Hazel through the deepest stretches of water. His head falls back and he groans but at least he's still alive. Seeing the tattered druid's cloak, Nelson says, 'I know who he is. He's Cathbad's friend, isn't he?'

'Yes,' pants Ruth.

'And he killed Patrick?'

'He was definitely in it with Old George. He's been trying to kill me all morning.'

Nelson looks down at the wounded man. 'Bastard,' he says.

As they reach the front of the house, a great beating sound fills the air. The water around them is churned up and a shadow hovers overhead.

The chopper has come at last.

Hazel is winched onto the police helicopter and taken to hospital. Old George, who is lying dead on the sofa, is going nowhere.

'Can't take a dead body, I'm afraid,' said the pilot over the intercom to Nelson. 'Let's concentrate on the living.'

Good advice, thinks Nelson as he goes back into the house. No one wants to go into the drawing room where Old George is lying with a blanket over him, so they congregate in the kitchen. Chaz is holding a handkerchief to the wound on his face.

'How did you do that?' asks Sally, who is, of course, making tea. Alone amongst the Blackstocks she had wept when she realised that her father-in-law was dead.

'Grandpa had locked Dad in his room. I broke the door down. Slipped and banged my head on the dressing table.'

'I was no help at all, I'm afraid,' says Young George. Nelson wonders how often he has said those words.

'So let's get this straight,' he says, sitting at the table next to Ruth. 'None of you knew that Granddad had killed his brother all those years ago.'

The Blackstocks look at each other. It is Sally who speaks. 'We knew there was some secret. George got so upset whenever Fred or Lewis was mentioned. And this business about finding the body really unhinged him. But I don't think any of us thought that George . . . I mean, he was only eighteen . . .' Her voice trails off.

'He told me that he killed Fred because he wanted Blackstock Hall for himself,' says Ruth. 'He thought I was Nell so he told me the whole thing. He thought Lewis had died in Japan and Fred had been killed in the plane crash. He was alone in the orchard when Fred just turned up. He'd survived the crash and had been sleeping rough. Fred was exhausted, bleeding from a wound in the head. George shot him with Lewis's pistol.'

'And when he saw me in the doorway he thought I was Fred,' says Chaz. 'That's what gave him the heart attack.'

'You do look like Fred,' says Ruth. 'And you were bleeding from the head. He must have thought that Fred had come back.'

Nelson would have given a lot to hear Old George's tone when he thought he saw his brother. Was there contrition in his voice? Anger? Fear?

'George said that Lewis found Fred's body when he went to bury his dog,' says Ruth. 'He left home – probably couldn't cope with what he'd seen after all he'd been through in the war – and everyone assumed he was dead. But, of course, he wasn't.'

Nelson thinks of Lewis saying that where he was from the land was red with blood. He must have been thinking of this. One brother killing another for their birthright. Jacob and Esau, if he remembers his Bible right. The sight had sent Lewis mad, but he had escaped and been able to build a life for himself in Ireland. The only problem was that, somehow, his son found out about the Blackstocks and had been unable to resist the temptation to visit his ancestral home.

'Lewis wasn't dead,' says Nelson. 'Not till years later anyway. But his son, Patrick, came to find his family and, within a day, he was dead. Did Old George say anything about that?'

'He said that he and his son had got rid of him,' says Ruth. 'At first I thought he meant you.' She looks at Young George. 'Sorry.'

'It's OK,' says George.

'But he meant Hazel. I only realised when Hazel called Old George "Dad". And, of course, Hazel's real name was George too.'

That's why the DNA analysis showed that the Red Devil attacker was a direct relation of Young George's. Except that Hazel was a sibling and not offspring. Turns out Young George wasn't an only child after all. Nelson remembers Judy's interview with Cassandra and the texts from 'Georgie'. Was this Hazel, distracting Cassie so that he could be sure of creeping up on her unawares? And did the text messaging imply that Hazel had distinctly non-avuncular designs on his niece? Nelson decides not to pursue this just yet. He needs to get some other things straight first.

'So none of you knew that this Hazel was actually Old George's son?' he says.

'I suspected,' admits Young George. 'I knew that Dad was never faithful to Mum and Hazel did look an awful lot like Chaz. That's why we always let him stay at the Hall, have his yurt in the grounds and all that.'

'I never suspected.' Chaz sounds affronted. 'Why didn't anyone tell me? I had Hazel to stay at the farm and everything. I never thought that he'd turn out to be my uncle.'

'Do you think that Hazel killed Patrick?' Young George asks Nelson.

'We'll certainly be putting it to him,' says Nelson grimly. 'Hazel seemed obsessed with his Blackstock heritage. He probably attacked Cassie when he heard that she was the heir. He attacked my sergeant when he heard that he could be related to the family. Knowing Clough, he was probably going on about being the long-lost heir, and Hazel lost his head and went for him. Patrick *was* the long-lost heir and that's why Hazel killed him. He probably knocked him over the head and dumped his body in with the pigs. You say he knew the farm well, Chaz. Would he have known which pigs were likely to be . . . er . . . hungriest?'

'Yes.' Chaz looks slightly sick.

'You were probably next on his list,' says Nelson. 'You've had a lucky escape.'

'Old George must have told Hazel about Fred being buried

in the pets' burial ground,' says Ruth. 'When Devil's Hollow was sold to Edward Spens, Hazel moved the body there to try to stop the development.'

'He was always obsessed with stopping the building work,' says Chaz. 'I thought it was some weird druid thing, sacred land and all that.'

'It probably was that too,' says Ruth. 'Hazel was involved with the henge dig, all those years ago. I think he did feel strongly about the land. I do remember, though, at the Bronze Age dig, Hazel refused to have his DNA tested. He said he didn't believe in participating in scientific studies.'

'Obviously scared that his Blackstock DNA would show up,' says Nelson. 'Like it did with Cloughie.'

'There's a lot of it about,' says Young George. It's impossible to tell whether he thinks that this is a good thing or not.

'It was me who told Hazel about the plane in Devil's Hollow,' says Chaz. 'Cassie and I used to play there as children and we found all these engine parts.'

Nelson remembers Chaz's conversation with Barry West, the digger driver. He obviously knew, or guessed, that a Second World War plane was buried in the field. Did he really have nothing to do with moving Fred's body into the cockpit? Was that all Hazel's work? Is Chaz really as innocent – or stupid – as he seems? On balance, Nelson thinks he probably is. Chaz and his father like the quiet life. Cassie is the one who enjoys being centre stage, heaven help Clough.

Ruth, who has also been looking at Chaz, says suddenly, 'You followed me. You followed me home to the Saltmarsh one night.'

'You never told me about that,' says Nelson.

'It wasn't a big deal,' says Ruth. 'But I recognised Chaz's car when he drove Judy to the hospital yesterday.'

Chaz looks uncomfortable. 'That was Hazel's idea. He thought that we should keep an eye on you. He said that you were the key to stopping the building work because you had all the archaeological knowledge. But now I realise that he must have been terrified when he heard that you were digging in the pet's graveyard. Grandpa told him that you lived on the edge of the Saltmarsh. Hazel wanted to see the place for himself.'

'He wanted to know where you lived so he could come and kill you later,' says Nelson. 'He attacked Cassie. He would have attacked you without a thought. You should have told me, Ruth.' Sometimes he thinks that worrying over two families will be the death of him. Why can't he protect them both all the time?

Ruth says nothing. Nelson can't tell if she's annoyed or not.

'We'll have to take statements from all of you,' he says. 'It seems that a lot of trouble could have been avoided if only you'd all been straight with each other.'

But, deep down, he knows that this isn't the way families work. Secrets are passed down through the generations, in the same way that DNA is shared by different people in different variations over hundreds and thousands of years.

'We'd better get back to the station,' says Nelson. 'There's a lot of work still to do. Ruth, you need to get back to Katie.'

'How are you going to get there?' asks Young George. 'The flooding's as bad as ever.'

Tim speaks for the first time. He has been very quiet ever since the shooting.

'All aboard the giant duck,' he says now with a smile.

CHAPTER 38

'Do you think he'll enjoy it?' says Kate.

'I'm sure he will,' says Ruth.

They both look at Blue Bear, who is sitting at the kitchen table with them. Kate has been given the honour of entertaining Blue Bear for the Christmas holidays. She is delighted but rather overwhelmed by the responsibility. Ruth, too, feels rather daunted by the pressure to show Blue Bear a good time. So far Nelson has taken him and Kate to see Father Christmas in Castle Mall and Frank has taken them to the pantomime in King's Lynn. Kate has written up these adventures in large wavering crayon and has drawn accompanying pictures. 'We saw Snoo Wit and her doors. It was Fun.' It has all taken far more time than Ruth's holiday marking.

Today, they are going to a nativity play at the pig farm. Kate is worried whether Blue Bear will find it entertaining enough and Ruth has her own reasons for feeling apprehensive about the outing. But Cassie, who has gone into partnership with Chaz, in charge of 'marketing and publicity', is keen to use the farm for community events. There was, of course, some rather unwelcome publicity surrounding Hazel's arrest for murder and Cassie wants to counterbalance this by linking the Blackstock name to something rather more wholesome. Old George's death from a heart attack passed almost unnoticed in the papers. Nelson didn't feel that it was worth publicising the old man's confession, so the man who killed his brother, aged eighteen, and assumed his inheritance is remembered in the obituaries as 'a loving father and grandfather who enjoyed nothing better than spending time on his country estate'. Well, he was a loving father to Hazel, even if he was distinctly lukewarm about his legitimate son. And he certainly enjoyed his country estate, having gone to the trouble of killing to secure it for himself.

But both Ruth and Sally felt that Nell deserved to know the truth about her father's death. So, about a week after Hazel's arrest, when the flood waters had dwindled to solitary lakes in the middle of fields, they took Nell for a walk in the grounds of Blackstock Hall. In Devil's Hollow, building work was beginning again. Edward Spens's half-finished houses had been completely submerged by the floods. However, this did not seem to have changed his mind about the wisdom of building on flood plains. The workmen were busy putting up scaffolding and draining away water.

Sally led the way past the hollow and through the trees. The high tides had pushed the beach stones up into the adjoining fields. Ruth, Sally and Nell sat on a newly created shingle bar and Ruth told Nell the story related to her in the middle of the night by Old George.

Nell's eyes had filled with tears. 'Poor Daddy. To be killed like that when he'd survived the crash. But I suppose he wouldn't have known anything about it.'

'No,' says Ruth. 'George said that it happened very quickly.' Fred had hardly finished his opening sentence when his brother had shot him in the head. The only thing you can say about such a death is that it was quick.

'And he'd be pleased that you came to Blackstock Hall,' says Sally, 'and got to know us all.'

Would Fred have been pleased? He had moved halfway round the world to get away from his mother's cursed landscape; would he be pleased that Nell and Blake are now planning to spend part of every year in Norfolk? Who knows, but families have a funny way of repeating themselves. Sally and Young George have even bought themselves a Jack Russell puppy and called it Bingo.

'I'm certainly pleased I've met you, Sally,' says Nell, putting out her hand to the other woman. Ruth thinks of Frank saying, 'The women in that family are worth ten of the men.' He had a point, she thinks.

Two days after this conversation, Ruth visited Blackstock Hall to watch the episode of *The History Men* entitled 'The Ghost Fields'. She had once sworn that she would never enter the house again, but it looked very different from the moated grange where she'd had to flee for her life and been saved by two men and a duck. The fields were still boggy and wet but the house itself looked better than she had ever seen it. Maybe it was the removal of Old George's baleful influence, maybe it was just because Sally had decorated the place for Christmas. But sitting in the drawing room, with a vast Christmas tree twinkling away in the corner, it was hard to think that this was the room where a villainous old murderer had breathed his last. Nell and Blake were there, as well as Cassie and Clough. Frank came too – he was the only representative of the production company now that Paul and Earl had gone back to the States. The whole event had quite a party atmosphere.

The first shot of the airfield made Ruth catch her breath. Steve, the director of photography, really knew his stuff. The vast empty fields, the sky above, the geese making their way out to sea, it was all so stark and beautiful that it barely needed words. But there was Frank, smiling into the camera, talking about 444th Bomb Group and – oh God – there was Ruth in her best jacket describing the discovery of the plane. Ruth shut her eyes and only opened them again when Nell, in her long grey coat, was walking through the orchard at Blackstock Hall.

'I never really knew my dad,' she was saying, 'but here I can feel him all around me. These are the fields where he walked as a boy, where he played cricket with his brothers, where he taught his dog to hunt rabbits. In the local church he carved his initials on the pew, and it's where, a few days ago, we laid him to rest in the graveyard. Dad belonged to New England but he belonged here too. To Old England, if you like.'

And the orchard is the place where he died, thought Ruth. Shot by one of the brothers with whom he'd played cricket. But she was glad that they had made the programme, glad that Fred had this memorial as well as the one in the graveyard. And she was very glad that, apart from a brief sighting in his purple robe at the funeral, Hazel did not appear in the film.

Hazel admitted to the murder of Patrick Blackstock and the attempted murders of Cassandra Blackstock and David Clough. He was charged under his real name of George Buggins. Cathbad, on a high after the birth of his daughter, had the grace to be rather embarrassed about the fact that his peaceful druid friend turned out to be a murderer. 'I could sense an angry energy in him,' he said, 'but I thought that was to do with the land, with the development and everything.' 'Trust Cathbad,' said Nelson. 'He always has to have the last word.' As for Ruth, she feels that her faith in Cathbad has been rather shaken by his inability to predict both his daughter's birth date and his friend's homicidal tendencies. She's rather relieved about this, to be honest. It's not safe to endow another mortal with too many powers.

Now Ruth straps Kate and Blue Bear into their car seats. She has a new car because her old Renault did not survive its immersion in the flood waters. This is a Renault too, but cars have changed over the last fifteen years. They are rounded and sleek, whereas her old car was friendly and square. The dashboard is a bewildering array of retro dials. She has air conditioning and a CD player. Nelson is delighted that she is driving something with proper airbags and Kate loves the car, which she calls Pascal, after a French boy in her class. Ruth tries not to miss her old car too much.

Ruth puts Pascal into gear and they move away smoothly. They are meeting Frank at the farm. He's due to fly back to Seattle tomorrow, where he is spending Christmas with his children. Nothing more has been said about the prospect of him coming back to England and living in Cambridge. Ruth and Kate are going to her parents in Eltham for Christmas. Ruth hopes that Blue Bear will approve. She has a feeling that there will be rather too much churchgoing for his taste. She has him down as a rather free-thinking bear.

They sing Christmas songs all the way. Kate's primary school, being determinedly secular, did not put on a nativity play but they did present a Christmas entertainment of such all-embracing sweetness that Ruth cried all the way through. The story was rather confused, featuring, as it did, a range of animals and fairy-tale characters, Father Christmas, Old King Cole and Babushka. Kate, in a green sleeping bag, was a caterpillar. Her big number was 'Caterpillars Only Crawl' and they sing it now, bowling along through the frosty fields. The flood has left its mark on the countryside and you can still see fence posts and trees sticking up out of what appear to be lakes. But it's a beautiful winter day with a pale gold sun shining on the sparkly expanses of water. It's hard to see the landscape as doomed on a day like this.

The pig farm too is looking its best. There are Christmas lights draped across the control tower and an inflatable Santa wobbles madly in the field where the planes landed and took off. They follow the old runway to the barn where the entertainment is to take place. There are so many cars parked there already that they have to walk quite a bit of the way.

'Blue Bear doesn't like walking,' says Kate.

'We're nearly there,' says Ruth.

As Ruth and Kate approach the barn, they see a several men with tea towels on their heads and – to Kate's delight – an actual donkey. Cassie is obviously going for realism in a big way. They also see Clough, his arms full of holly.

'Pity it's not mistletoe,' he says, kissing Ruth. 'Hallo, sweetheart,' he says to Kate. 'Looking forward to Christmas?'

'What's the donkey called?' says Kate.

'He's called Carrots,' says Clough. 'Want to say hallo?'

He takes Kate by the hand and leads her over to pay homage to Carrots. It's odd seeing Clough so at home on Blackstock territory. But then, according to his DNA, he is a Blackstock, somewhere in the distant past. There's no doubt though that he has become one of the family. Sally and George are even talking about moving to a smaller house and leaving the Hall to Cassie and Clough. Clough as lord of the manor. Ruth wonders what Nelson would say. Well, she's going to see him today. He said that he was coming. She can't help scanning the field for his car.

'Ruth!' It's not Nelson but Frank who comes striding towards her.

'Hi.' Looking at Frank, Ruth thinks how much she'll miss him, his height and breadth, his blue eyes, his air of expecting to have a good time wherever he goes. But she doesn't have to miss him. All Ruth has to do is ask him to stay. That's all. Why does it seem so much?

Kate comes skipping over and they go into the barn like a proper family. This space too has been transformed. Where, only a few weeks ago, pigs grunted and chomped, now fairy lights criss-cross the beams and the walls have been painted white, the dark-blue ceiling studded with stars. Cassie is ladling out mulled wine at the entrance.

'Hallo, Frank. Hallo, Ruth. Hallo, Katie. Are you looking forward to the nativity?'

'You bet,' says Frank. 'A fine old English tradition.'

'There are real Brownies in the choir,' says Cassie, as if people are in the habit of substituting fake Brownies for the real thing.

'Great,' says Ruth. In a few years Kate can join the Brownies, if Ruth can get over their militaristic habits of saluting and wearing uniforms.

'Hallo, babe,' says Clough, coming up behind Cassie and kissing her neck.

'Darling.' Cassie nestles against him. Ruth moves away. She's very happy for Clough but there's only so much romance she can take.

They find seats near the front, then the whole row is disrupted because Judy arrives with Michael and baby Miranda. Cathbad parks the buggy near the door and waves to show that he's happy to stay where he is. Michael sits next to Kate. Blue Bear sits between them, obviously enjoying himself. Ruth peers into the blankets to look at the baby.

'She looks so like you.'

Where Michael has always resembled Cathbad to a rather embarrassing extent, Miranda has her mother's sweet round face and pink-and-white skin. But is there something Cathbad-like about Miranda's blue eyes and long dark eyelashes? Cathbad says that she looks like his mother, that long-dead Irish wise woman, and there is undoubtedly something farsighted about Miranda's gaze. Will she grow up to be a druid or a policewoman? Time will tell.

'She's gorgeous,' says Frank, leaning over Ruth to stroke the baby's cheek. 'She's lucky to have a cool big brother.' He ruffles Michael's hair. It's nice of Frank not to forget Michael, thinks Ruth. But then he is nice. She looks round and sees Nelson and Michelle standing near Cathbad. The two men are deep in conversation but Michelle smiles and waves. Ruth waves back.

A blast of recorded music and the Brownies launch into 'A Long Time Ago in Bethlehem'. The play is about to start.

After Jesus has been born and the shepherds have visited, complete with a real sheep, and the Brownies have sung their way through *The Children's Book of Carols*, they are free to escape into the weak sunshine. Cathbad takes Michael and Kate to visit the pigs and Judy stays in the barn to feed Miranda.

'Fancy a walk?' says Frank.

Ruth looks round and sees Nelson and Michelle talking to Chaz. She hasn't seen Michelle since the sighting at the gym. She wonders if she's still seeing Tim, who, she knows, is on leave, visiting his family in Essex. After he helped save her life, she can't help feeling slightly warmer towards Tim but she still feels uneasy whenever she hears Nelson praise Tim, which he does quite often these days. She studies Michelle and Nelson for signs of marital unease but they seem to be quite happy. In fact Ruth has observed a particular closeness in their body language today. Michelle has her arm through Nelson's and occasionally she rests her head against his shoulder. Ruth wishes that she could stop noticing this sort of thing.

'Yes,' she says to Frank. 'Let's go for a walk.'

They walk to the perimeter of the farm where the operations building once stood. The pigs are still snuffling around the ruins of the barracks and the cafeteria and the squash court, their breath smoky in the cold air.

'What's happening with your Bronze Age dig?' asks Frank. 'The one with the body that might have been a Blackstock?'

Ruth smiles, though she's now not so quick to claim that her body (she still feels possessive about it) is related to the Blackstocks.

'I've got funding for another dig in the spring,' she says. 'I'm still hoping to find more bodies. I'm sure there's a burial site near here. That's the only thing Hazel and I agree on.'

'The burial site might be underneath those new houses in Devil's Hollow,' says Frank. 'That's an uncomfortable thought.'

'If there's something buried there, it'll come to the surface one day,' says Ruth. 'That's one thing I've learnt in my job. Nothing stays buried for ever.'

They have reached the barn with the mural on the wall. 'I've got something to show you,' says Frank. 'It's in here.'

He lifts the latch and pulls open the heavy door. Once again the planes come flying towards them, yellow triangles on a bright-blue sky. Once again Ruth feels that dizzying time-slip feeling, as if the years are revolving before her eyes.

Frank points up to the corner, where the small dog sits in the clouds.

'I looked up the pilot who was really in the plane,' he says, 'the pilot whose body was found near Devil's Hollow. His name was Douglas Rovington. I looked in the platoon's log books and I saw that his nickname was Rover. I think he might have been the one who painted this.'

Ruth looks at the blue sky and the yellow planes, at the little dog floating above it all. The scene blurs with her sudden tears.

'D for Dog,' says Frank.

Outside, it is starting to get dark. They walk back to the barn where an ever-enterprising Cassandra is selling hot chestnuts and mince pies.

'I'll miss you,' says Frank.

'I'll miss you too,' says Ruth.

Frank takes her arm and they come to halt. 'Have you thought about it,' he says. 'Me coming back to England? Is that what you'd like?'

Ruth looks towards the old airfield, where Nelson is now swinging Kate round in his arms. Michael is clamouring for his turn and Judy watches, the baby swaddled against her. Cathbad is holding Blue Bear. There's no sign of Michelle.

Ruth looks up and sees a small plane tracking slowly across

the dark-blue sky. It could be Fred or any of his companions from 444th Bomb Group. She doesn't know why but it makes her feel very sad.

'I'm sorry, Frank,' she says. 'But there's someone else. I think there always will be.'

ACKNOWLEDGEMENTS

During the Second World War, there were thirty-seven airfields in Norfolk, plus the decoy 'shadow fields' mentioned by Frank. The deserted bases are known as 'ghost fields' and a lot has been written about them. For me, the most helpful book was Roderick McKenzie's *Ghost Fields of Norfolk*, which includes histories, plans and photographs of all the sites. The base at Lockwell Heath is fictional but it owes a lot to abandoned airfields like Docking and Seething (the names are wonderful). The mural is also imaginary but there are many real ones, for example at Shipham, Flixton and Wendling. This artwork, painted on buildings not meant to last, has suffered a lot over the years and there is now a race to record these pictures for posterity. Thanks to Gloria Stephens for the trip to a real-life air base.

In general, my books contain a mix of real and imaginary places. Blackstock Hall is fictional but Hunstanton and the Le Strange Arms are real. The beautiful Blickling Hall is real and does house the RAF Oulton Museum. Dr Raymond Alder, on the other hand, is fictional. The apocalyptic weather in this book is also based on reality. In October 2013 there was a savage storm known as St Jude's Storm and December 2013 saw Norfolk devastated by terrible floods. I need hardly say that the Blackstock family and the events described in this book are all entirely fictional.

For archaeological information, I am indebted to Andrew Maxted, my favourite archaeologist. Many thanks to Mike Silverman for his help on forensics and DNA. For a better description of police forensic work than I could ever manage, I would thoroughly recommend *Written in Blood* by Mike Silverman and Tony Thompson. Thanks also to Dr Simon Trew for his guidance on military research. I should stress that I have only followed the experts' advice as far as it suits the plot and any resulting mistakes are mine alone.

Thanks as ever to my editor, the wonderful Jane Wood, and to my agent, Rebecca Carter. Thanks to everyone at Quercus and Janklow & Nesbit for working so hard on my behalf. I'd also like to thank all the other publishers around the world who publish the Ruth books. Special thanks to Katrina Kruse of HMH for taking me on a fantastic road trip and showing me Walden Pond and the Green Mountains. Thanks to Lesley Thomson for her friendship and support – and for the advice on cars. Love and thanks always to Andy and to our children, Alex and Juliet.

This book is for my sister Sheila and brother-in-law Ian, with love from Eli.

Keep reading for a sneak peek at

THE
WOMAN
IN BLUE

the next thrilling book in the Ruth Galloway series.

Coming in hardback and ebook Easter 2016

Weep, weep, O Walsingham,
Whose dayes are nights,
Blessings turned to blasphemies,
Holy deeds to despites
Sinne is where our Ladye sate,
Heaven turned is to helle;
Satan sitthe where our Lord did swaye,
Walsingham O farewell!

'Ballad of Walsingham', 16th Century, Anon

PROLOGUE

19 March 2014

Cathbad and the cat look at each other. They have been drawing up the battle lines all day and this is their Waterloo. The cat has the advantage, this is his home and he knows the terrain. But Cathbad has his druidical powers and what he believes is a modest gift with animals – a legacy from his Irish mother who used to talk to seagulls (and receive messages back). He has a companion animal himself, a bull terrier called Thing, and has always enjoyed a psychic rapport with Ruth's cat, Flint.

This cat, whose name is Merlin, is a different proposition altogether. Whereas Flint is a large and lazy ginger tom whose main ambition is to convince Ruth that he is starving at all times, Merlin is a lithe and sinuous black creature, given to perching on top of cupboards and staring at Cathbad out of disconcertingly round, yellow eyes. This is Cathbad's third day of house – and cat – sitting and so far Merlin has ignored all blandishments. He has even ignored the food that

Cathbad carefully weighed out according to Justin's instructions. He might be living on mice but Merlin does not look like an animal who is governed by his appetites. He's an ascetic, if Cathbad ever saw one.

But Justin's sternest admonition, written in capitals and underlined in red, was: DO NOT LET MERLIN OUT AT NIGHT. And now, here they are, at nine o'clock on a February evening, with Merlin staring at the door and Cathbad barring the way with his flaming sword. The biblical reference comes to hand because the house is part of an ancient pilgrimage site and is decorated by etchings from the Old Testament. Justin, the custodian of the site, is on a fact-finding trip to Knock, something Cathbad finds extremely funny. He has left the fifteenth-century cottage – and the accompanying cat – under Cathbad's protection.

Merlin meows once, commandingly.

'I'm sorry,' says Cathbad. 'I can't.'

Merlin gives him a pitying look, jumps onto a cupboard and manages to slide out through a partially opened window. So that's why he has been on hunger strike.

'Merlin!' Cathbad lifts the heavy latch and opens the door. Cold air rushes in. 'Merlin! Come back!'

The cottage is attached to the church, with a passageway through it forming a kind of lich-gate. Worshippers have to pass underneath the main bedroom in order to get to St Simeon's. There's even a handy recess in the wall so that pall-bearers can rest their coffins. The back door opens directly onto the churchyard. 'But you won't mind that,' said Justin, 'it's right up your street.' And it's true that Cathbad does like burial grounds and all places of communal worship but, even so, there's something about St Simeon's Cottage, Walsingham, that he doesn't quite like. It's not the presence of the cat, or the creaks and groans of the old house at night; it's more a sort of sadness about the place, a feeling so oppressive that, during his first evening, Cathbad was compelled to call upon a circle of protection and to ring his partner Judy several times.

He's not scared now, just worried about the cat. He walks along the church path, the frost crunching under his feet, calling the animal's name.

And then he sees it. A tombstone near the far wall, glowing white in the moonlight, and a woman standing beside it. A woman in white robes and a flowing blue cloak. As Cathbad approaches, she looks at him and her face, illuminated by something stronger than natural light, seems at once so beautiful and so sad that Cathbad crosses himself.

'Can I help you?' he calls. His voice echoes against stone and darkness. The woman smiles – such a sad, sweet smile – shakes her head and starts to walk away, moving very fast through the gravestones towards the far gate.

Cathbad goes to follow her but is floored, neatly and completely, by Merlin who has been lurking behind a yew tree for this very purpose.

CHAPTER 1

DCI Harry Nelson hears the news as he is driving to work. 'Woman's body found in a ditch outside Walsingham. SCU request attend.' As he does a handbrake turn in the road he is conscious of a range of conflicting emotions. He's sorry that someone's dead, of course he is, but he can't help feeling something else, a slight frisson of excitement, a relief that he's spared that morning's meeting with Superintendent Gerald Whitcliffe and their discussion of the previous month's targets. Nelson is in charge of the SCU, the Serious Crimes Unit, but the truth is that serious crime is often thin on the ground in King's Lynn and surrounding areas. That's a good thing – Nelson acknowledges this as he puts on his siren and speeds through the morning traffic – but it does make for rather dull work. Not that Nelson hasn't had his share of serious crime in his career – only a few months ago he was shot at and might have died if his sergeant hadn't shot back – but there's also a fair amount of petty theft, minor drugs stuff and people complaining because their stolen bicycle wasn't featured on *Crimewatch*.

He calls his sergeants, Dave Clough and Tim Heathfield, and tells them to meet him at the scene. Though they both just say 'Yes, boss', he can hear the excitement in their voices too. If Sergeant Judy Johnson were there, she would remind them that they were dealing with a human tragedy, but Judy is on maternity leave and so the atmosphere in the station is rather testosterone heavy.

He sees the flashing lights as he turns the corner. The body was found on the Fakenham Road, about a mile outside Walsingham. It's a narrow road with high hedges on both sides, made narrower by the two squad cars and the coroner's van. As soon as Nelson steps out of his car he feels claustrophobic, something that often happens when he's in the countryside. The high green walls of foliage make him feel as if he's in the bottom of a well and the grey sky seems to be pushing down on top of him. Give him pavements and street lighting any day.

The local policemen stand aside for him. Chris Stephenson, the police pathologist, is in the ditch with the body. He looks up and grins at Nelson as if it's the most charming meeting place in the world.

'Well, if it isn't Admiral Nelson himself.'

'Hello, Chris. What's the situation?'

'Woman, probably in her early- to mid-twenties, looks like she's been strangled. Rigor mortis has set in but then it was a cold night. I'd say she's been here about eight to ten hours.'

'What's she wearing?' From Nelson's vantage point it looks like fancy dress, a long white robe and some sort of blue cloak. For a moment he thinks of Cathbad, whose favourite attire is a druid's cloak. 'It's both spiritual and practical,' he'd once told Nelson.

'Nightdress and dressing gown,' says Stephenson. 'Not exactly the thing for a February night, eh?'

'Has she got slippers on?' Nelson can see a glimpse of bare leg, ending in something white.

'Yes, the kind you get free in spas and the like,' says Stephenson, who probably knows a lot about such places. 'Again, not exactly the thing for tramping over the fields.'

'If her slippers are still on, she must have been placed in the ditch and not thrown.'

'You're right, chief. I'd say the body was placed here with some care. This was on her chest.' Stephenson holds out an object in a plastic bag.

'What is it? A necklace?'

Stephenson laughs. 'I thought you were a left-footer, Admiral. It's a rosary.'

A rosary. Nelson's mother has a wooden rosary from Lourdes and she prays a decade every night. Nelson's sisters, Grainne and Maeve, were given rosaries for their First Holy Communions. Nelson didn't get one because he was a boy.

'Bag it,' he says, although the rosary is already sealed in a plastic evidence bag. 'It's important evidence.'

'If you say so, chief.'

Nelson straightens up. He has heard a car approaching and guesses that it's Clough and Tim. Besides, he's had enough of Chris Stephenson and his breezy good humour.

His sergeants come towards him. Both are tall and dark and have been described (though not by Nelson) as handsome but there the resemblance ends. Clough is white and Tim is black but there's much more to it than that. Clough is heavily built, wearing jeans and skiing jacket. He's looking around with something like excitement and there's a half-eaten bagel in his hand. Tim is taller and slimmer, he's wearing a long dark coat and knotted scarf and could be a politician visiting a factory. His face gives nothing away.

Nelson briefs them quickly. He calls over the local officer who explains that the body was found by an early morning dog-walker. 'Her little dog actually got into the ditch and was … well … shaking the deceased.'

'If she's in nightclothes,' says Tim, 'she could be a patient at The Sanctuary.'

The same thought has occurred to Nelson. It was the waffle-patterned slippers that first gave him the idea. The Sanctuary is a private hospital specialising in drug rehabilitation. Because a lot of the patients are famous, though not to Nelson, the place exists in an atmosphere of high walls, secrecy and rumours of drug-fuelled orgies. It is quite near here, about a mile across the fields.

'Good thinking,' he says. 'You and Cloughie can go over there in a minute and ask if any patients are missing.'

'Foxy O'Hara's meant to be there at the moment,' says Clough, swallowing the last of his bagel.

'Who?'

'You must have heard of her. She was on *I'm a Celebrity* before Christmas.'

'You're jabbering, Cloughie.' Nelson turns to Chris Stephenson, who has emerged from the ditch and is taking off his coveralls. 'Anything else for us, Chris? No handy name tapes on the dressing gown?'

'No, but it's a good one. Pricy. From John Lewis.'

'Costs a bit to stay in The Sanctuary,' says Nelson. 'I think that's our best bet.'

'Excuse me, sir.' It's one of the local policemen, nervous and respectful. 'But there's a man asking to see you. Looks a bit of a nutter but he says he knows you.'

'Cathbad,' says Clough, without looking round.

Clough is right. Nelson sees Cathbad standing beyond the police tape, wearing his trademark cloak. How strange, and slightly unsettling, that Nelson was thinking about him only a few moments before. He strides over.

'Cathbad. What are you doing here?'

'I'm house-sitting in Walsingham.'

'What about Judy? Have you left her alone with a newborn baby?'

'Miranda's ten weeks old and she's an old soul. No, Judy's taken the children to visit her parents.'

'That's doesn't explain why you're here, at a crime scene.'

'The woman you've found,' says Cathbad. 'Was she wearing a blue cloak?'

Nelson takes a step back. 'Who says we've found a woman?'

He half expects Cathbad to say something about spiritual energies and cosmic vibrations but instead he says, 'I heard the milkman talking about it. Useful people, milkmen. They're up and about early, they notice things.'

'And what did you mean about a cloak? I'm sure the bloody milkman didn't see that.'

Cathbad exhales. 'So it is her.'

'What are you talking about?'

'The cottage where I'm staying, it overlooks the graveyard.' That figures, thinks Nelson. 'Well, last night I saw a woman standing there, a woman wearing a white robe and a blue cloak.'

'What time was that?'

'About nine.'

Nelson lifts the tape. 'You'd better come through.'

The Scene of Crime team have arrived. In their paper suits and masks they look like aliens taking over a sleepy Norfolk village. As Nelson and Cathbad watch, the dead woman's body is slowly winched out of the ditch. The corpse is covered by a sheet but as the stretcher passes them they both see a length of muddy blue material hanging down. Cathbad crosses himself and Nelson has to stop himself following suit.

'Any idea who she was?' asks Cathbad.

'She was in nightclothes,' said Nelson. 'Your cloak was a dressing gown. I'm sending Clough and Heathfield to The Sanctuary.'

'Do you think she was a patient there?'

'It's a line of inquiry.'

The aliens have now erected a tent-like structure over the ditch. The atmosphere has somehow stopped being that of an emergency and has become calm and purposeful.

'Look, Cathbad,' says Nelson. 'I'm going to brief the boys and finish up here. Then I'll come and talk to you about what you saw last night. Where's this place you're staying?'

'St Simeon's Cottage. Next to the church.'

'I won't be long.'

'Time,' says Cathbad grandly, 'is of no consequence.' But he is talking to empty air.

[section break]

Ruth Galloway doesn't hear about the body in the ditch until she's at work. She did listen to the radio in the car but what with the hassle of getting her five-year-old daughter Katem to school in time it all became rather a blur. 'Have you got your book bag … *here's Gary with the sports news* … Can you see a parking space … *Thought for the Day with the Rev…* Quick, there's Mrs Mannion waiting for you. Love you. See you later … *icy winds, particularly on the east coast.*' If the dead woman did make it onto the *Today* programme Ruth missed it altogether. It wasn't until she was at her desk trying to catch up on emails before her first tutorial that her head of department, Phil Trent, wandered – uninvited – into her office and asked if she's heard 'the latest drama'.

'No. What?'

'A woman found dead in a ditch out Walsingham way. It was on *Look East.*'

'I must have missed it.'

'I thought you had a hotline to the boys in blue.'

Phil is jealous of Ruth's role as a special advisor to the police and sometimes she likes to tease him, dropping hints of high-level meetings and top-secret memos, but this morning she doesn't have the energy.

'I doubt it will have anything to do with me. Not unless there's an Iron Age skeleton in the ditch as well.'

'I suppose not.'

Ruth turns back to her screen and though Phil hovers in the doorway for a few minutes eventually he drifts away leaving her to concentrate on her emails. They are the usual collection of advertisements from academic publishers, departmental memos and requests from her students for extra time to finish their essays. Ruth deletes the first and the second and is settling down to answer the third when she sees a new category of email. The subject is *Long time no see*. This is either intriguing or worrying depending on your mood. Ruth is probably fifty-fifty on that. She clicks it open.

Hi Ruth. Do you remember me, Hilary Smithson from South-ampton? Where have the years gone? I understand that you're in Norfolk, doing very well for yourself. I'm coming to Norfolk next week, for a conference in Walsingham, and I wondered if we could meet up. I'd like to ask your advice on a rather tricky matter. And I'd love to see you of course. Looking forward to hearing from you. All best Hilary.

Ruth stares at the screen. It's the second time that Walsingham has been mentioned that morning and, as Nelson always says, there's no such thing as coincidence.